"Can I ask you a question, Harry?"

"I suppose."

George thought about it, and asked, "What are you, exactly?"

"What am I?"

"Yes. You're not a performer, or just a performer. I've seen vaude-villians do a lot of things before, but I've never seen one pull reflections off glass. So what are you?"

Silenus smirked, sat back in his seat, and pulled his hat down over his eyes. "You're wrong, kid. I am just a performer. I'm just putting on a show you haven't seen before."

Praise for
Mr. Shivers

"A ravishing debut...supremely chilling, it never loses its grip in its journey to the edge of the apocalypse."　　　—*The Daily Mail* (UK)

"Imaginative and beautifully written, *Mr. Shivers* is a powerful book that reads as though presented by an author at the peak of his abilities."
　　　　　　　　　　　　　　　—Charles de Lint, *SFF* magazine

Praise for
The Company Man

"Bennett combines horror, science fiction and alternative history in a slow-burning novel which is both a superb character study of an alienated individual and a critique of heartless capitalism."
　　　　　　　　　　　　　　　　　　　—*The Guardian* (UK)

"*The Company Man* made me realize how far sci-fi has come in my lifetime."　　　　　　　　　　　　　—*The Wall Street Journal*

By Robert Jackson Bennett

Mr. Shivers

The Company Man

The Troupe

ROBERT JACKSON BENNETT

www.orbitbooks.net

Orbit
Hachette Book Group
237 Park Avenue, New York, NY 10017
www.HachetteBookGroup.com

First Edition: February 2012

Orbit is an imprint of Hachette Book Group. The Orbit name and logo are trademarks of Little, Brown Book Group Limited.

The publisher is not responsible for websites (or their content) that are not owned by the publisher.

The characters and events in this book are fictitious. Any similarity to real persons, living or dead, is coincidental and not intended by the author.

Library of Congress Cataloging-in-Publication Data
Bennett, Robert Jackson.
    The troupe / Robert Jackson Bennett. — 1st ed.
        p. cm.
    ISBN 978-0-316-18752-7
1. Vaudeville—Fiction.   2. Mysticism—Fiction.   I. Title.
PS3602.E66455T76 2012
813'.6—dc22
                                    2011018068

10 9 8 7 6 5 4 3 2 1

RRD-C

Printed in the United States of America

This book is for Jackson
for whom the sun was created
to rise and set upon.
Of course.

PART ONE

The Sticks

Had it been within his power, the vaudeville performer would have been a timeless wanderer, spanning the generations using the bridge of his talents.

—Fred Allen, *Much Ado About Me*

CHAPTER 1

A Departure

Friday mornings at Otterman's Vaudeville Theater generally had a very relaxed pace to them, and so far this one was no exception. Four acts in the bill would be moving on to other theaters over the weekend, and four more would be coming in to take their place, among them Gretta Mayfield, minor star of the Chicago opera. The general atmosphere among the musicians was one of carefree satisfaction, as all of the acts had gone well and the next serious rehearsals were an entire weekend away. Which, to the overworked musicians, might as well have been an eternity.

But then Tofty Thresinger, first chair house violinist and unofficial gossip maven of the theater, came sprinting into the orchestra pit with terror in his eyes. He stood there panting for a moment, hands on his knees, and picked his head up to make a ghastly announcement: "George has quit!"

"What?" said Victor, the second chair cellist. "George? *Our* George?"

"George the *pianist?*" asked Catherine, their flautist.

"The very same," said Tofty.

"What kind of quit?" asked Victor. "As in quitting the theater?"

"Yes, of course quitting the theater!" said Tofty. "What other kind of quit is there?"

"There must be some mistake," said Catherine. "Who did you hear it from?"

"From George himself!" said Tofty.

"Well, how did he phrase it?" asked Victor.

"He looked at me," said Tofty, "and he said, 'I quit.'"

Everyone stopped to consider this. There was little room for alternate interpretation in that.

"But why would he quit?" asked Catherine.

"I don't know!" cried Tofty, and he collapsed into his chair, accidentally crushing his rosin and leaving a large white stain on the seat of his pants.

The news spread quickly throughout the theater: George Carole, their most dependable house pianist and veritable wunderkind (or *enfant terrible,* depending on who you asked), was throwing in the towel without even a by-your-leave. Stagehands shook their heads in dismay. Performers immediately launched into complaints. Even the coat-check girls, usually exiled to the very periphery of theater gossip, were made aware of this ominous development.

But not everyone was shaken by this news. "Good riddance," said Chet, their bassist. "I'm tired of tolerating that little lordling, always acting as if he was better than us." But several muttered he *was* better than them. It had been seven months since the sixteen-year-old had walked through their doors on audition day and positively dumbfounded the staff with his playing. Everyone had been astonished to hear that he was not auditioning for an act, but for *house pianist,* a lowly job if ever there was one. Van Hoever, the manager of Otterman's, had questioned him extensively on this point, but George had stood firm: he was there to be house pianist at their little Ohio theater, and nothing more.

"What are we going to do now?" said Archie, their trombonist. "Like it or not, it was George who put us on the map." Which was more or less true. It was the general rule that in vaudeville, a trade filled with indignities of all kinds, no one was shat upon more than the house pianist. He accompanied nearly every act, and every ego that crossed the stage got thoroughly massaged by abusing him. If a joke went sour, it was because the pianist was too late and spoiled the delivery. If a dramatic bit was flat, it was because the pianist was too lively. If an acrobat stumbled, it was because the pianist distracted him.

But in his time at Otterman's George had accomplished the impossible: he'd given them no room for complaints. After playing through the first rehearsal he would know the act better than the actors did, which was saying something as every actor had fine-tuned their performance with almost lapidary attention. He hit every beat, wrung every laugh out of every delivery, and knew when to speed things up or slow them down. He seemed to have the uncanny ability to augment every performance he accompanied. Word spread, and many acts became more amenable to performing at Otterman's, which occupied a rather obscure spot on the Keith-Albee circuit.

Yet now he was leaving, almost as abruptly as he'd arrived. It put them in a pretty tight spot: Gretta Mayfield was coming specifically because she had agreed to have George accompany her, but that was just the start; after a moment's review, the orchestra came to the horrifying conclusion that at least a quarter of the acts of the next week had agreed to visit Otterman's only because George met their high standards.

After Tofty frantically spread the word, wild speculation followed. Did anyone know the reason behind the departure? Could anyone guess? Perhaps, Victor suggested, he was finally going to tour with an act of his own, or maybe he was heading straight to the legitimate (meaning well-respected orchestras and symphonies, rather than lowly vaudeville). But Tofty said he'd heard nothing about George making those sorts of movements, and he would know, wouldn't he?

Maybe he'd been lured away by another theater, someone said.

But Van Hoever would definitely ante up to keep George, Catherine pointed out, and the only theaters that could outbid him were very far away, and would never send scouts out here. What could the boy possibly be thinking? They wasted the whole morning debating the subject, yet they never reached an answer.

George did his best to ignore the flurry of gossip as he gathered his belongings, but it was difficult; as he'd not yet made a formal resignation to Van Hoever, everyone tried to find the reason behind his desertion in hopes that they could fix it.

"Is it the money, George?" Tofty asked. "Did Van Hoever turn you down for a raise?"

No, answered George. No, it was not the money.

"Is it the acts, George?" asked Archie. "Did one of the acts insult you? You've got to ignore those bastards, Georgie, they can be so ornery sometimes!"

But George scoffed haughtily, and said that no, it was certainly not any of the acts. The other musicians cursed Archie for such a silly question; of *course* it wasn't any of the performers, as George never gave them reason for objection.

"Is it a girl, George?" asked Victor. "You can tell me. I can keep a secret. It's a girl, isn't it?"

At this George turned a brilliant red, and sputtered angrily for a moment. No, he eventually said. No, thank you very much, it was not a girl.

"Then was it something Tofty said?" asked Catherine. "After all, he was who you were talking to just before you said you quit."

"What!" cried Tofty. "What a horrendous accusation! We were only talking theater hearsay, I tell you! I simply mentioned how Van Hoever was angry that an act had skipped us on the circuit!"

At that, George's face became strangely still. He stopped gathering up his sheet music and looked away for a minute. But finally he said no, Tofty had nothing to do with it. "And would you all please leave me alone?" he asked. "This decision has nothing to do with you, and furthermore there's nothing that will change it."

The other musicians, seeing how serious he was, grumbled and shuffled away. Once they were gone George scratched his head and tried not to smile. Despite his solemn demeanor, he had enjoyed watching them clamor to please him.

The smile vanished as he returned to his packing and the decision he'd made. The orchestra did not matter, he told himself. Otterman's did not matter anymore. The only thing that mattered now was getting out the door and on the road as soon as possible.

After he'd collected the last of his belongings he headed for his final stop: Van Hoever's office. The theater manager had surely heard the news and was in the midst of composing a fine tirade, but if George left now he'd be denied payment for this week's worth of performances. And though he could not predict the consequences of what he was about to do, he thought it wise to have every penny possible.

But when George arrived at the office hall there was someone seated in the row of chairs before Van Hoever's door: a short, elderly woman who watched him with a sharp eye as if she'd been expecting him. Her wrists and hands were wrapped tight in cloth, and a poorly rolled cigarette was bleeding smoke from between two of her fingers. "Leaving without a goodbye?" she asked him.

George smiled a little. "Ah," he said. "Hello, Irina."

The old woman did not answer, but patted the empty chair next to her. George walked over, but did not sit. The old woman raised her eyebrows at him. "Too good to give me company?"

"This is an ambush, isn't it?" he asked. "You've been waiting for me."

"You assume the whole world waits on you. Come. Sit."

"I'll give you company," he said. "But I won't sit. I know you're looking to delay me, Irina."

"So impatient, child," she said. "I'm just an old woman who wishes to talk."

"To talk about why I'm leaving."

"No. To give you advice."

"I don't need advice. And I'm not changing my mind."

"I'm not telling you to. I just wish to make a suggestion before you go."

George gave her the sort of impatient look that can only be given by the very young to the very old, and raised a fist to knock at Van Hoever's door. But before his knuckles ever made contact, the old woman's cloth-bound hand snatched his fist out of the air. "You will want to listen to me, George," she said. "Because I know *exactly* why you're leaving."

George looked her over. If it had been anyone else, he would not have given them another minute, but Irina was one of the few people at Otterman's who could command George's attention. She was the orchestra's only violist, and like most violists (who after all devoted their lives to an ignored or much-ridiculed instrument) she had acquired a very sour sort of wisdom. It was also rumored she'd witnessed terrible hardships in her home in Russia before fleeing to America, and this, combined with her great age, gave her a mysterious esteem at Otterman's.

"Do you think so?" asked George.

"I do," she said. "And aren't you interested to hear my guess?" She released him and patted the seat next to her once more. George sighed, but reluctantly sat.

"What is it?" he asked.

"Why such a hurry, child?" Irina said. "It seems like it was only yesterday that you arrived."

"It wasn't," said George. "I've spent over half a year here, which is far too long."

"Too long for what?" asked Irina.

George did not answer. Irina smiled, amused by this terribly serious boy in his too-large suit. "Time moves so much slower for the young. To me, it is as a day. I can still remember when you walked through that door, child, and three things struck me about you." She held up three spindly fingers. "First was that you were talented. *Very* talented. But you knew that, didn't you? You probably knew it too well, for such a little boy."

"A *little* boy?" asked George.

"Oh, yes. A naïve little lamb, really."

"Maybe then," said George, his nose high in the air. He reached into his pocket, took out a pouch of tobacco, and began rolling his own cigarette. He made sure to appear as nonchalant as possible, having practiced the motions at home in the mirror.

"If you say so," said Irina. One finger curled down, leaving two standing. "Second was that you were proud, and reckless. This did not surprise me. I've seen it in many young performers. And I've seen many throw careers away as a result. Much like you're probably doing now."

George cocked an eyebrow, and lit his cigarette and puffed at it. His stomach spasmed as he tried to suppress a cough.

Irina wrinkled her nose. "What is that you're smoking?"

"Some of Virginia's finest, of course," he said, though he wheezed a bit.

"That doesn't smell like anything fine at all." She took his pouch and peered into it. "I don't know what that is, but it isn't Virginia's finest."

George looked crestfallen. "It…it isn't?" he asked.

"No. What did you do, buy this from someone in the orchestra?"

"Well, yes, but they seemed very trustworthy!"

She shook her head. "You've been snookered, my child. This is trash. Next time go to a tobacconist, like a normal person."

George grumbled something about how it had to be a mistake, but he hurriedly put out his cigarette and began to stow the pouch away.

"Anyway," she said, "I remember one final third thing about you when you first came here." Another trembling blue finger curled down. She used the remaining one to poke him in the arm. "You did not seem all that interested in what you were playing, which was peculiar. No—what you were mostly interested in was a certain act that was traveling the circuit."

George froze where he was, slightly bent as he stuffed the tobacco pouch into his pocket. He slowly turned to look at the old woman.

"Still in a hurry, child?" asked Irina. "Or have I hit upon it?"

He did not answer.

"I see," she said. "Well, I recall you asked about this one act all the time, nearly every day. Did anyone know when this act would play here? It had played here once, hadn't it? Did they think this act would play nearby, at least? I think I can still remember the name of it...Ah, yes. It was the Silenus Troupe, wasn't it?"

George's face had gone very closed now. He nodded, very slightly.

"Yes," said the old woman. She began rubbing at her wrists, trying to ease her arthritis. "That was it. You wanted to know nothing but news about Silenus, asking all the time. But we would always say no, no, we don't know nothing about this act. And we didn't. He'd played here once, this Silenus, many, many months ago. The man had terribly angered Van Hoever then with his many demands, but we had not seen him since, and no one knew where he was playing next. Does any of that sound familiar to you, boy?"

George did not nod this time, but he did not need to.

"Yes," said Irina. "I think it does. And then this morning, you know, I hear news that Van Hoever is very angry. He's angry because an act has skipped us on the circuit, and is playing Parma, west of here. And the minute I hear this news about Van Hoever today, I get a second piece of news, but this one is about our young, marvelous pianist. He's *leaving.* Just suddenly decided to go. Isn't that strange? How one piece of news follows the other?"

George was silent. Irina nodded and took a long drag from her cigarette. "I wasn't terribly surprised to find that the act that's skipped us is Silenus," she said. "And unless I'm mistaken, you're going to go chasing him. Am I right?"

George cleared his throat. "Yes," he said hoarsely.

"Yes. In fact, now that I think about it, that act might be the only reason you signed on to be house pianist here. After all, you could've found somewhere better. But Silenus played here once, so perhaps he might do so again, and when he did you wished to be here to see it, no?"

George nodded.

Irina smiled, satisfied with her deductions. "The famous Silenus," she said. "I've heard many rumors about him in my day. I've heard his troupe is full of gypsies, traveled here from abroad. I've heard he tours the circuit at his choosing. That he was touring vaudeville before it was vaudeville."

"Have you heard that every hotel saves a private room for him?" asked George. "That's a popular one."

"No, I'd not heard that one. Why are you so interested in this man, I wonder?"

George thought about it. Then he slowly reached into his front pocket and pulled out a piece of paper. Though its corners were soft and blunt with age, it was very well cared for: it had been cleanly folded into quarters and tied up with string, like a precious message. George plucked at the bow and untied the string, and then, with the gravity of a priest unscrolling a holy document, he unfolded the paper.

It was — or had once been — a theater bill. Judging by the few acts printed on it and the simple, sloppy printing job, it was from a very small-time theater, one even smaller than Otterman's. But half of one page was taken up by a large, impressive illustration: though the ink had cracked and faded in parts, one could see that it depicted a short, stout man in a top hat standing in the middle of a stage, bathed in the clean illumination of the spotlight. His hands were outstretched to the audience in a pose of extreme theatricality, as if he was in the middle of telling them the most enthralling story in the world. Written across the bottom of the illustration, in a curling font that must have passed for fancy for that little theater, were three words: THE SILENUS TROUPE.

George reverently touched the illustration, as if he wished to fall inside it and hear the tale the man was telling. "I got this in my hometown," he said. "He visited there, once. But I didn't get to see." Then he looked at Irina with a strange shine in his eyes, and asked, "What do you remember from when he was here?"

"What do I remember?"

"Yes. You had to have rehearsed with him when he played here, didn't you? You must have seen his show. So what do you remember?"

"Don't you know the act yourself? Why ask me?"

But George did not answer, but only watched her closely.

She grunted. "Well. Let me think. It seems so long ago..." She took a contemplative puff from her cigarette. "There were four acts, I remember that. It was odd, no one travels with more than one act these days. That was what angered Van Hoever so much."

George leaned forward. "What else?"

"I remember... I remember there was a man with puppets, at the start. But they weren't very funny, these puppets. And then there was a dancer, and a... a strongwoman. Wait, no. She was another puppet, wasn't she? I think she might have been. And then there was a fourth act, and it... it..." She trailed off, confused, and she was not at all used to being confused.

"You don't remember," said George.

"I do!" said Irina. "At least, I *think* I do... I can remember every act I've played for, I promise, but this one... Maybe I'm wrong. I could've *sworn* I played for this one. But did I?"

"You did," said George.

"Oh? How are you so certain?"

"I've found other people who've seen his show, Irina," he said.

"Dozens of them. And they always say the same thing. They remember a bit about the first three acts—the puppets, the dancing girl in white, and the strongwoman—but nothing about the fourth. And when they try and remember it, they always wonder if they ever saw the show at all. It's so strange. Everyone's heard of the show, and many have seen it, but no one can remember what they saw."

Irina rubbed the side of her head as if trying to massage the memory out of some crevice in her skull, but it would not come. "What are you saying?"

"I'm saying that when people go to see Silenus's show... something happens. I'm not sure what. But they can never remember it. They can hardly describe what they've seen. It's like it happened in a dream."

"That can't be," said Irina. "It seems unlikely that a performance could do that to a person."

"And yet you can't remember it at all," said George. "No one else here can remember, either. They just know Silenus was here, but what he did up on that stage is a mystery to them, even though they played alongside it."

"And you want to witness this for yourself? Is that it?"

George hesitated. "Well. There's a bit more to it than that, of course. But yes. I want to see him."

"But why, child? What you're telling me is very curious, that I admit, but you have a very good thing going on here. You're making money. You are living by yourself, dressing yourself"—she cast a leery eye over his cream-colored suit—"with some success. It is a lot to risk."

"Why do you care? Why are you interested in me at all?"

Irina sighed. "Well. Let me just say that once, I was your age. And I was just about as talented as you were, boy. And some decisions I made were... unwise. I paid many prices for those decisions. I am still paying them." She trailed off, rubbing the side of her neck. George did not speak; Irina very rarely spoke about her past. Finally she coughed, and said, "I would hate to see the same happen to you. You have been lucky so far, George. To abandon what you have to go chasing Silenus will test what luck you have."

"I don't need luck," said George. "As you said, I can find better places to play. Everyone says so."

"You've been coddled here," she said sternly. "You have lived with constant praise, and it's made you foolish."

George sat up straight, affronted, and carefully refolded the theater bill and put it in his pocket. "Maybe. But I'd risk everything in the world to see him, Irina. You've no idea how far I've come just to get this chance."

"And what do you expect will happen when you see this Silenus?" she asked.

George was quiet as he thought about his answer. But before he could speak, the office door was flung open and Van Hoever came stalking out.

Van Hoever came to a halt when he saw George sitting there. A cold glint came into his eye, and he said, "You."

"Me," said George mildly.

Van Hoever pointed into his office. "Inside. Now."

George stood up, gathered all of his belongings, and walked into Van Hoever's office with one last look back at Irina. She watched him go, and shook her head and said, "Still a boy. Remember that." Then the door closed behind him and she was gone.

Less than a half an hour later George walked out the theater doors and into the hostile February weather. Van Hoever's tirade had been surprisingly short; the man had been desperate to keep George on until they could find a decent replacement, and he'd been willing to pay accordingly, but George would not budge. He'd only just gotten news about Silenus's performance today, on Friday, and the man and his troupe would be leaving Parma tomorrow. This would be his only chance, and it'd be very close, as the train ride to Parma would take nearly all day.

Once he'd been paid for his final week, he returned to his lodgings, packed (which took some time, as George was quite the clothes-horse), paid the remainder of his rent, and took a streetcar to the train station. There he waited for the train, trying not to shiver in the winter air and checking the time every minute. It had been a great while since he'd felt this vulnerable. For too long he'd kept to the cloistered world of the orchestra pit, crouched in the dark before the row of footlights. But now all that was gone, and if anything happened before he made it to Parma, the months at Otterman's would have been in vain.

It wasn't until George was aboard the train and it began pulling away that he started to breathe easy. Then he began to grin in disbelief. It was really happening: after scrounging for news for over half a year, he was finally going to see the legendary Heironomo Silenus, leader of wondrous players, legendary impresario, and the most elusive and mysterious performer to ever tour the circuits. And also, perhaps most unbelievably, the man George Carole suspected to be his father.

CHAPTER 2

The Men in Gray

Parma, like any other northern Ohio town, was well accustomed to winter weather, yet as the sun went down its residents began to feel unnerved. They hurried through the streets, eager to duck into any open door for shelter, and were reluctant to venture out, even if they had business or errands to run. Even the cabbies and buggy drivers were affected, refusing fares and passengers and returning to their stables instead, where they huddled and smoked and stamped their feet, and occasionally glanced out and shook their heads.

It was difficult to say exactly what it was. Perhaps it was the wind, the people said: it seemed unusually cold and bitter, never letting up for a minute, and it did not bring in any storms, as one would expect from such weather. But it was not *just* the wind, they admitted. There was also something wrong with the sky, though they had trouble deciding the nature of it: as preposterous as it sounded, people were not sure if the curious arrangements of clouds made the sky feel too large, or perhaps too small. Others disagreed, saying that it was not the size at all, but the *time*: it was as if the sky had forgotten what hour it was and was now on the wrong schedule. The moon and the stars were far too bright for six o'clock, and the sky much too dark. If you were to look up, you'd surely think it was midnight.

The question of the time came close to the real issue in Parma that evening, one that was so strange and perplexing that no one was willing to speak about it: there was something wrong with the *light*. It was a very subtle change, one the people could not easily fathom, but it was as if the shadows had doubled as night fell, often appearing in places that did not warrant shadows at all. When wayfarers glanced up at the curiously bright moon and stars, they'd wonder how, in such an abundance of light, the street ahead managed to look so dark and forbidding. (And some wanderers found themselves thinking that the number of streets in Parma had mysteriously increased in the past hours: there seemed to be far more darkly lit alleys and passageways now than in the afternoon, leading to places they could not recall seeing before.) The phenomenon was not just confined to the outdoors: families seated together in their dining rooms felt compelled to light twice as many candles and lamps as they normally did, though each flame was a miserable lick of light in an overwhelming sea of darkness. And though each room naturally had four walls, and so should have only four corners, some homeowners experienced the crawling suspicion that their residences were stuffed full of dark corners, sometimes with sixteen or seventeen to a room, as if the very nature of geometry had changed when the sun went down.

No one in the town had ever felt anything like it. No one, that was, until George Carole's train pulled into the station and he leaped off, humming with excitement, and came to a stop when he dashed out the station doors.

George took one look at the dark streets and the star-strewn sky and identified the feeling immediately. As strange as it was, he'd experienced the exact same thing once before, in his hometown of Rinton: there'd been a series of evenings when the air seemed full of darkness, and everything felt *thin*, as if you could lick your finger and rub at the horizon and it would smear.

This pervasive feeling had coincided with another event in town: the performances of the Silenus Troupe. And it had vanished when the troupe moved to the next stop on the circuit, and no one had been sure what it'd all been about. Most had tried to forget about it, but George treasured every memory of when Silenus's show had come so near, so he still remembered the odd sensation as if it'd been only yesterday.

On that occasion he'd been prevented from seeing the man he thought to be his father. Yet now that he'd gotten close once more, he was struck with wonder. Was it possible there was a connection between this strange feeling and the performances of the troupe? He felt sure that was the case...but who were these players, if their mere arrival could affect the moon and stars? Could it be possible that some of the stories—not all, surely, but some—about Silenus and his troupe were true?

George shook himself. That was ridiculous. He was just anxious about meeting his father, he said to himself, and it was making him imagine things. And, really, why should he be anxious? He was *George Carole*, unspoken star of the Freightly theaters (even if he was just an accompanist). He wasn't some country rube, or at least not anymore. In his time at Otterman's he had played for lines of glamorous chorus girls, for armies of parading mice, and for a group of clowns who performed Lebanese ladder tricks. He'd played for magicians, for tumblers, for statue acts and female impersonators, the fatter the better. He'd played for dancing children dressed like lobsters, for dwarfs and freaks and ballerinas. He'd played for regurgitators, who would swallow items whole and produce them in the order the audience requested. He'd played for opera singers. He'd played for gun shows. He'd played anything and everything.

Any father would be glad to have him as a son. Now that he thought about it, Silenus should be impressed, or even grateful. So George shrugged off his needling fear, clapped his hat to his head, and ran on into the streets, briefcase swinging by his side.

He had figured that Silenus, no matter the nature of his show or performers, would travel and make arrangements like any other vaudevillian, which would mean he'd have booked the hotel closest to his theater. Hoping this was true, George had asked the conductor on his train exactly which hotel this was, and since it was a question a lot of conductors heard he had gotten the directions immediately.

To his surprise, the hotel was a fairly fancy place, with red brick and white-bordered windows. It was a change of pace from most theater and circuit hotels, which were ramshackle flophouses: the owners knew performers could not afford to be far away from their stage, so since their clientele had no choice, it was not necessary to bother with such trivialities as comfort, appearance, or general functionality.

George decided he would get a room, and then try to figure out the best way to approach Silenus. If the man happened to be staying there, as was likely, would George arrange a chance meeting in the lobby? Or maybe the theater? Would he try to impress him with his piano playing? Despite his self-assurances, he began to feel anxious again to the point that he was almost sick.

Then, for the second time that night, he stopped where he stood.

He stared at the hotel. All the excitement and agitation drained out of him.

George cocked his head, listening, and cupped a hand behind his ear. As he listened, a deep dread bloomed inside him. "No," he whispered to himself. "No, no, no. It can't be. Not here."

He backpedaled down the street and listened again. He then took several slow steps forward, head cocked toward the hotel all the way. Then he finally stopped in the middle of the street and looked around, and shook his head.

Somewhere about halfway through the block all sound began to fade from the world. Every noise died until it was a hollow echo of its former self, and the colors past the halfway point seemed drab and muted, like the light was being sucked out of them. George watched the other people on the street. They did not seem to notice anything, yet when they neared the hotel they pulled their coats tight about them, as though they'd been touched with a deep chill.

This, too, was a sensation familiar to George. But he dreaded it far more than the surreal darkness throughout Parma.

It could only mean one thing: he was not the only one who had tracked Silenus here.

George walked to the end of the block, and the queer silence increased with each step. He kept his eye on the hotel, making sure to mark the windows and the doors. It wasn't until he was right in front of it that he saw a curtain on the second story twitch aside, and he caught a flash of a black-gloved hand and a gray sleeve, and a blank face surveying the street.

George jumped back. He found cover behind some bushes in front of an office building, and there he squatted down to watch and think. "They're *here?*" he said to himself. "How could they be here?"

As George had searched for Silenus over the past half year, he had gradually become aware that he was not the only one doing so: there were other agents, ones of a far stranger sort, who were asking nearly the same questions he was.

He had first realized this at the start of fall, when he had traveled across Freightly to a different theater to inquire about Silenus. As always, there'd been no news, and he'd left the theater disappointed. But it was as George had passed a little alley beside the theater that he'd realized something was wrong: he heard something. Or maybe, he thought, he didn't hear something. After a while he realized he actually couldn't hear anything at all.

At first George thought he'd somehow gone deaf, but when he heard the carriages clattering through the streets he realized it was something else: on some level the world had fallen quiet to him. But this was a new type of quiet to George, who had very keen senses. If silence could have a frequency, with some silences soft and others harsh, then this one's was overpowering and fierce, and he could *hear* it, like a needle in his ear. It rendered the sounds in the street hollow and lifeless, like they barely existed at all. And no one else on the street paused or looked up; it seemed as if only George could hear it.

Then a cheerful voice said, "I take it you're a Silenus fan, too?"

George turned to look. Standing a far ways down the alley under one of the streetlamps was a man. Or was it? George thought. Somehow the man seemed too *perfect*: his collar was too starched and sharp, his bowler too black and clean, the knot in his tie too straight, and there wasn't a speck of dirt anywhere on his shoes, which gleamed hungrily in the lamplight. George wondered if he was maybe just a picture of a man, like someone had made a painting of a gentleman in a gray suit and stood it up in the middle of the lane.

"I'm sorry?" George asked.

"You're another Silenus fan," the man called in that same cheery voice. "I heard you asking about him inside."

"Oh. Well. Yes, I suppose you could say that."

The man did nothing, as if thinking. Then he walked toward George with a bizarrely mechanical gait, arms stiff at his sides. As the man neared the queer silence grew, and George's impression of a picture of a man increased as well: his face was blankly handsome, his eyes a gray a shade lighter than his suit, and all of his features were clean and smooth and symmetrical. But though he seemed perfect, the man also seemed strangely indistinct, like your eyes would pass over him unless you were looking for him. He looked, George thought, like a man out of an advertisement, like one for shoe polish.

"I doubt if you heard anything new in there," the man said. His small smile did not leave his face. "I would know. I've been desperate for him to come back to town ever since I saw him last."

"You saw Silenus?" George asked, excited. "What was his show like? Do you remember it?"

There was a pause, as if the man had not expected this question. "Well, it was a very long time ago," he said. "I can't really remember it now, I'm afraid. I suppose I wish to see him so that I can get a refresher."

"Oh," George said, disappointed even more.

"I'll tell you what," said the man in gray. "Why don't we pool our resources? I'm eager to hear any news of my favorite performer, as I'm sure you are. If you find anything, would you please come and let me know about it? And when you do, I'll tell you all I know."

"I suppose I could."

There was a pause, the man's smooth gray eyes flicking up into the distance as he considered his reply, and then back. "Well, that's excellent," the man said. "Really, it's very good of you. I'm in town for a long while, and I can be reached at the Liddell Hotel, on Maynor. I'm so eager to see Silenus again, why, I'd be willing to pay you for it. Would this be acceptable?"

George was not sure what to say. There was something unnatural about the man that he found disturbing. He only nodded.

"Good," the man said. Then he stared at George, not moving or saying anything more.

"Is there... anything else I can do for you?" George asked.

"Have we met before?" the man asked.

"I don't believe so."

"Are you sure? You seem somewhat familiar."

"I believe I'd remember someone like you," George said.

"Do you," said the man. "Well, please remember, the Liddell Hotel. Any news at all would be welcome."

"All right," George said.

"Good evening," the man said, and he turned and walked back down the lane in that same stiff, jerky stride with his hands by his sides. The silence subsided, like a fog following him down the lane. And then, almost thoughtlessly, the man reached out with one hand as he passed the streetlamp and brushed his knuckles against its pole. The light winked out, and the man continued into the dark.

George watched him go before hurrying back across town to his lodgings. It took him several hours to realize the man had not given him his room number; in fact, when he thought about it, George realized he'd never even gotten the man's name. Either way, he did not want to see the man again, and he certainly did not wish to give him any news concerning his father.

But it was after this that George had begun noticing strange members of Otterman's audiences: men in gray suits, with clean black hats and blank gray eyes. He'd catch glimpses of them among the patrons, watching the show and never laughing or applauding. At first George had thought he was seeing the gentleman who'd made the odd request of him, but he'd never been sure. And each time he'd spotted them he had heard that awful silence slowly pervading the room along with them, as though wherever these men walked all noise faded.

George now heard that same awful silence there in the street before the hotel. The men in gray had to be inside. But he had never heard the silence they projected be so utterly overpowering, nor had he ever witnessed the very colors draining out of everything. There must have been a great deal of them inside, waiting, yet only he was able to notice anything.

He was not at all sure what was happening tonight. He only knew two things: Silenus was almost certainly staying here, and the men in gray had found the hotel first, and were now lying in wait. George could not bring himself to trust them; whatever interest they had in Silenus, he did not think they meant him well.

George spotted a clock in a nearby diner. If the Parma theater was like any other, the evening performance would be going on right now. Then Silenus and his company would close out the show, and come back to the hotel...

He knew he had to tell them. He carefully slipped out from behind the bushes and walked away.

CHAPTER 3

"A man of mechanism and wit, of ingenuity never before seen..."

When George finally got to the theater he saw the thick folding sign out front with the words WEEKLONG PERFORMANCE—SILENUS and 5 CENTS ENTRY blaring up and down its sides, and all thoughts of the men in gray faded from his mind. He wandered up as if in a dream, took a bill of acts from the ticket box, and read:

THE PANTHEON THEATER

Entrance on Gabe and Henley Streets
PROGRAMME FOR THIS EVENING,
And Matinees, Wednesday and Friday

For the accommodation of LADIES and FAMILIES, the entire
Evening Performance will be given. No VULGARITY or
OBJECTIONABLE SAYINGS are allowed within

our theater. SMOKING and TOBACCO will only be
allowed outside the premises.

MILLIE SWANSON'S CORNISH PUPS

A delightful display of canine clowns

The ingenious songstress
Miss Lenora Howell
Featuring such time-honored melodies as WHERE IS MY
WANDERING BOY TONIGHT and THE BOWERY

THE CARDWELL COMPANY

Presents

THE LITTLE LORD'S INHERITANCE

TOM MUMFREY .... THE EARL
ELIZA VON DUINEN .... MOTHER BURTON
And JOSEPH DEWEY .... LITTLE ERIC BURTON

BIBLEY AND GEORGIANA

A farcical sketch of romance

INTERMISSION

THE FAMOUS SILENUS TROUPE

Mgr. Heironomo Silenus

FOR ONE WEEK ONLY

The first time in Parma — a MUST-SEE PERFORMANCE

1. PROFESSOR KINGSLEY TYBURN and his
astounding PUPPETS

Through his mechanical WIZARDRY and SHOWMANSHIP,
they will speak for us

2. HER HIGHNESS COLETTE DE VERDICERE
A beautiful songbird of Persian royalty

3. FRANCES BEATTY'S STRONGWOMAN FEATS

4. THE SILENUS CHORALE
Melodies sure to melt the heart

WEBB AND TORANEY
Humor and Pantomime

And there, on the opposite page, was an illustration of a man in a top hat standing in the middle of a stage, telling a story. With trembling fingers, George pulled out his theater bill from Rinton, unfolded it, and held the two bills side by side. Though the Pantheon's bill was by far the superior, and the Rinton bill was old and faded, the two illustrations matched exactly.

His trembling increased. He had never been this close before.

He'd dreamed of this moment so many times, yet he'd never really believed it could happen.

Then, to his surprise, the doors of the theater were pushed open, and a crowd of people came striding out. George went white, and almost fainted. "Oh, no!" he said. "I've missed it! How could I have missed it?" He nearly sat down in the street in shock, but stopped himself as three members of the crowd stood in the street to smoke:

"I shouldn't have come so early," one man said. "I mean, I only came for the Silenus bits. I've no interest in these Little Lord Fauntleroy plays at all. They're just maudlin."

"Oh, come now," said a friend. "The kid was trying. He wasn't that bad. One lady actually cried."

"That was Maudie Gray," said a woman with them. "She cries at everything, especially when little boys are involved. You should have seen her when they did *East Lynne*. She came to every show and bawled her eyes out."

"I believe it," said the first man. "But still, I should have come in after the halfway. I'm really only curious to see what all the talk is about."

"Or what it isn't about," said the second. "Does anyone really know what Silenus is going to do?"

"Do you think it has to do with why they got started so late?" asked the woman.

"Is it late?" said the first man. "I suppose it does feel late." He peered up into the sky as though there were something wrong with the moon, and shivered and lapsed into silence.

"It's intermission," George said softly. He rechecked the bill of acts. "It's only intermission! I haven't missed it!" Then he stuffed the bill in his pocket, picked up his suitcase, and dashed inside.

The coat-check girl wouldn't take his suitcase, so after some negotiating with the usher George was allowed to take it in with him, provided he sat at the back. George found that the Pantheon was a much, much nicer theater than what he was used to: it had velvet curtains of a very rich red (which he found more tasteful than the ratty green ones used at Otterman's), footlights of crenellated gold, and a pristine white spotlight that stayed fixed on the center of the stage. George felt an irrational pang of jealousy at this; even though he'd dissolved all his bonds with Otterman's, he still felt bitter that the Panthon had a spotlight, while his old place of employment did not.

More people filed in to sit around him, and it felt like hours went by. George found he wasn't alone: several people began checking their watches, and one nearby lady said, "I hope he gets started soon. I thought I was late getting here."

"Did you?" said her friend.

"Yes. When I left the house I thought for sure that it was very late."

"How odd. You know, I think I might've felt something similar. I've never had an evening pass as slow as this one. Though once the show begins, I expect things will go faster. It shouldn't be long."

George hoped so. His stomach had gone numb, and he felt like he couldn't open his eyes wide enough. He knew it was unwise to pin all his hopes on one man, yet this was almost exactly what he had done: he hoped that Silenus could take him away from these small country theaters, and school him in the finer arts of the stage; he hoped his father would greet his newfound son with open arms, and rejoice in their meeting; and George's last, most desperate hope was that Silenus would be such an astounding and wonderful man that finding him could somehow make up for the loss of George's mother. She had died giving birth to him, and as the identity of his father had been unknown he'd been left to be raised by his grandmother. The fallout from the ensuing scandal had dealt their family name an irreparable blow, and as a bastard child George had been exiled to a lowly, unspoken caste in Rinton. Perhaps, he hoped, Silenus would make all those unhappy years worthwhile.

It would not be long now. He kept sitting up to peer down into the orchestra pit to see when they were going to start playing. That would be when the action would begin.

After a while the lights in the theater faded and the mutter of talk died down. Some signal came from offstage, and the pianist sat down and began arthritically tinkling out a breezy waltz. George thought the man's playing stilted and pat, but he was far more excited about whatever was going to happen onstage than what was going on in the orchestra pit. "Here we go," he whispered aloud.

The pianist played the first movement of whatever piece it was, and as he geared up to repeat it a man walked — no, *erupted* — from the side of the stage, charging for the center of the boards with a palpable confidence. He wore a red coat, checked pants, and a black top hat, and his white-gloved hands were bunched into fists. George got the impression that he would have walked through a brick wall, if one barred his way. When he came to the center of the stage he stopped short and wheeled to face the audience, swooping his hat off his head as he turned. He surveyed them for a bit, like a man inspecting a horse for sale, and people were not sure whether or not to applaud.

Time seemed to stand still for George as he stared at the man on the stage. Except for his pose, it was the theater bill's illustration come to life. The man was short and mustachioed and had a slight potbelly, and he wore his thick, black hair combed back over his head. It shone in the light like oil. But what George was most astonished by was the man's face. Though he wore the whiteface makeup commonly used in vaudeville, George could see that the man's cheeks and mouth were heavily lined, and his cold blue eyes were very deep-set. It was not a lovely face; it was hard and austere, a face much used to scowls and glares. But the most astonishing thing was that it looked a little like the person George saw each time he glanced in the mirror.

"Ladies and gentlemen!" called the man in a fruity, tobacco-tinged voice. "I come to you today bearing wonders from afar. If you were to inspect my shoes, you would find on their soles the soil of a thousand countries. My many coats have soaked up the salty air of all the seven seas. Were you to see my dustbin you would find a dozen hats, all drained of color by distant suns. These are the lengths I have gone to to procure our world's greatest treasure, our most precious resource, our most secret and unpredictable wonder." He paused, and smiled both cunningly and a little cruelly as the audience waited for his finish. "Entertainment," he said, and bowed. "I am Heironomo Silenus."

The audience smiled and clapped, but George was too thunderstruck to move, trying to drink in every moment. Silenus snapped back up and advanced on the edge of the stage. He leaned out over them, looking furious in the lights of the gas jets along the stage, and several people in the front row recoiled. "For what better gift did the Creator give us than that ability to release, and relax, and allow ourselves to be taken to lands unseen and undreamt of simply with the crude components of performance?" he said. "A dab of face paint, a tinkling of a chord, a well-crafted costume and a few choice words, and we are given a vision of things that are not, were not, nor will ever be. We are given visions of the Other. These I bring to you in the palm of my hand, eager to send them tumbling into your laps. We are constrained by one thing only: time, and yours I shall no longer waste."

He whipped around and withdrew, gesturing toward the curtain, and said, "See now the genius I found overseas in the hallowed halls of ancient Europe! A man of mechanism and wit, of ingenuity never before seen, a professor in his own lands, but here, something even greater: a performer, waiting to serve at your whim. I give you the redoubtable Professor Kingsley Tyburn, and his companions!" Silenus then replaced his hat with a flourish, sank into the darkness, and was gone. The curtain began to rise, and George nearly moaned in disappointment; it was the first time he'd ever glimpsed his father, and he did not want him to leave. But he quieted once he saw what was behind the curtain.

On the stage was the painted backdrop of the interior of an old farmhouse, but it seemed a strange and forbidding scene. The wood of the farmhouse was gray and old-looking, and the landscape outside the window was filled with twisting trees and a sickly moon. A long, high table was set up in front of the backdrop, and a man in a black tuxedo was seated at the middle. His skin was painted white, his lips bright red, and his copper-red hair was closely cropped. His legs were crossed, and he appeared to be reading a book, completely unaware of the audience, with one hand holding the book and the other hidden below the table. Placed along the table were three boxes, each of them shut. They looked a little like tiny coffins. The man licked a finger and turned the page of his book, but otherwise did nothing.

"Have we started yet?" said a small, tinny voice. "It sure sounded like we did…" It spoke with a distinctive New York twang, and seemed to come from one of the boxes.

The man, presumably the professor, cocked an eyebrow, and glanced at the box on the far right. The audience chuckled.

"Don't think so," said another, this one deeper and with a Cockney accent. "He'd have opened us up, wouldn't he?" This one came from the box in the middle. George squinted to see if the professor's lips were moving at all. He was far away, but they didn't seem to even twitch.

"Unless he was still angry with us," said a third voice from the box on the left. This one was Southern and was meant to be a woman's, though it had a bass resonance that suggested a man behind it. "Do you think he is?"

"Yes!" said the professor, and slammed down his book. "I am, in fact."

There was a gasp from one of the far boxes, and it shook a little as though someone inside had recoiled. The audience laughed again.

"What are you still mad at us for, Doc?" said the first voice.

"You know very well what I'm mad about, Denny," said the professor.

"Aw," said the voice. "Is this about the party?" The top of the box on the far right opened, and a wooden face with large, blank eyes, a pug nose, and a moth-eaten old hat rose out and leaned against the top. The audience laughed and clapped at the puppet's appearance.

"Yes, Denny, this is about the party," said the professor. "You embarrassed me greatly. You walked right up to the hostess and said... You said..."

The box on the far left opened and another puppet emerged, this one with the blond hair, hoop-skirted dress, and sultry blue eyes of a Southern belle. "He asked if she believed in love at first sight," she said, her wooden mouth matching the words. The audience clapped appreciatively.

"Yes!" said the professor, flustered.

The middle box opened, and a third puppet emerged, this one fat, bald, and with one large eyebrow. "I don't see what's so bad about that," he said in a thick Cockney accent.

"There's nothing bad about that," said the professor. "Well, nothing *that* bad about that. It's what he said after that gets my goat. She replied no, she didn't, and then he said—"

"I said, in that case I'd have to keep coming back here," said Denny, and though his face was unmistakably wooden George got the impression that it had smirked at them.

The drummer in the orchestra rattled off a syncopated beat after the punch line, and the audience laughed as the professor sputtered to respond to his puppet. They were all crude-looking things, like they had each been carved out of a single log, but somehow their crudeness lent them a believable air of expression.

"You all get more and more out of control every day!" said the professor. "Berry, you even insulted my actor friend!" he told the fat puppet.

"What? I said he was great in his death scene in the play," said Berry.

"Yes, but you said it should have come several acts earlier!"

Another beat from the drummer (this one a little late, George noted), and the audience roared laughter. Berry mugged for the crowd, even though his face did not seem to move.

"I guess we did sort of ruin things," said Denny. "They all got a little down when I told them about my friend Frank."

"Frank?" said Berry. "Why, what happened to him?"

"Well, he passed on."

"Oh, I'm so sorry to hear that, Denny!" said the professor.

"Yeah," said Denny. "He fell through some scaffolding."

"How horrible!" said the Professor. "Was he fixing his roof?"

"No, he was being hung," said the puppet, and again there was the snarl of a snare drum.

"Oh, Denny!" said the professor. The crowd clapped and cawed laughter.

"He's rigging them up underneath the table," whispered a woman in the row before George.

"Hush," said her friend, but George had thought the same thing. Yet even so, how was the professor manipulating three puppets at once?

"I didn't do anything wrong, did I, Doc?" said the Southern belle puppet.

"No," said the professor to her kindly. "No, you didn't, Mary-Ann."

"Good," she said. "Though I did meet the most delightful man at the party."

"Did you?" said the professor.

"Oh, yes. He's very well respected, a Southern planter."

"Ah, very good."

"Yes," she said, "he's an undertaker from New Orleans, you see."

"Oh!" cried the professor, anguished at having been made a fool of again. The bass drum belched down in the orchestra pit, and the audience hooted and clapped. "What can I do to get you all to behave!"

"Well, why don't you let us out, Doc?" said Denny.

"Let you out?" said the professor.

"Yes! Let us stretch our legs." He wiggled in his box as though straining to move his limbs. "Let us out of the boxes, Doc, and set us loose!"

"Oh, Denny," said the professor, "I don't think that would be a very good idea."

"Why not?" said Berry. "We could be real people for you!"

"Real?"

"Yes!" said Mary-Ann. "Real people, for you, for everyone! For this one last performance here!" She turned to beam out at the audience.

"We could own houses, ride trains, and even vote!" said Denny. "Several times, if we wanted to!" Again the puppet seemed to smile coyly.

"But why would you want that?" said the professor.

"Everyone wants that, Doc," said Denny.

"We'd be no longer wooden," said Mary-Ann. "No longer so stiff, so hard, so cold."

"Yes," said Berry. "Everyone wants to be real. You're one or the other. You are or you aren't. And here we are, stuck in between."

The audience members laughed a little, but glanced at one another, unsure. Usually every exchange was a joke, but this one didn't seem to be heading toward a specific punch line. The drummer was searching through his sheet music, confused as to where the next beat fell. Onstage the puppets all gained a hungry look to them, but it could have just been the shifting of the light. And was it George's imagination, or was the light on the stage now coming through the window on the backdrop, as though projected by the painted moon?

"But children," said the professor, "you're not real. You're not real people at all. See?" He reached out with one hand and knocked on Berry's head, producing a comical, hollow sound. The drummer in the pit rattled out a line on the snare drum along with it.

"That hurts," said Berry softly.

"We're real enough," said Mary-Ann. "Real as anyone else. Take us and chop us up and grind us to pieces, and you'll find naught a thing alive."

"But do that to any other folk, and you'd find the same," said Denny slyly.

"Yes," Berry said. "We speak and we want. We see and we hear. We're real enough, Father, just enough." The puppets turned to the professor eagerly, and George felt unsettled. He was reminded of piglets voraciously suckling at the teats of a hog, squirming to get a better spot. He could tell now that all the puppets were being voiced by one performer, but somehow he did not think it was the professor. And there was something wrong with the stage... The backdrop seemed noticeably less painted on. George could swear the slats in the farmhouse walls were casting shadows.

"That backdrop is very odd," whispered the woman in the row before George.

"I know," said her friend. "It doesn't suit the act. Why would he be performing beside a lake?"

"What?" said the woman. "What lake? There's only the circus."

"A circus? What are you talking about?" asked her friend. "There's no circus, just the field and the lake. Look at those odd, bendy shrubs, and glowy beetles, and those people playing at the shores of the lake. But the people don't look right to me. Their arms and legs are too long and bent. Do they look right to you?"

"I don't know what you're talking about," said the woman. "There's only the circus behind him. But there's something wrong with the animals...some of them don't look like any type of animal I've ever seen before. And I don't like the clowns at all. Their eyes do not seem right to me..."

George was completely perplexed by what the two women were describing, and peered at the backdrop again. But he could only see the old farmhouse, with its moonlit windows and its crooked trees outside. But how could they be so mistaken?

"You see and hear and speak," said the professor to his puppets, "and you do want. But you do not eat or sleep, or live, or dream."

"No," admitted Denny. "No dreams. No dreams for the dark. Just waiting, waiting."

"Waiting for the light to crack through again," said Mary-Ann. "For the top of the world to open up, and to find all these lovely people waiting for us!"

"Laughing!" said Berry.

"Clapping!" said Denny.

"Waiting for us, all of them!" said Mary-Ann.

"We do the same," said Denny, "the same as them: waiting, laughing, clapping, but you say we are not real?"

The professor gathered himself. "I do say you are not real. And not-real things belong in boxes, and the dark. Where you came from, and where you shall return."

"But Father!" cried Mary-Ann.

"Oh, no," said Berry.

"You are not getting out of the boxes," the professor said. "You must stay in the boxes, for me."

"For you, Father?" said Denny.

"Yes. That is final."

All three of the puppets seemed to droop slightly, as though depressed by his proclamation.

"I would not mind it so much," said Mary-Ann, "if we could sleep. Or dream. But we cannot, and stay awake. We stay awake in the long dark."

"I tire of this," said the professor. "Now, Denny. Why don't you tell us that delightful joke you told me just the other day?"

"Which one, Father?" said Denny, but he now sounded morose.

"The one about the medicine," said the professor, and he stood up and ripped off the drape around the table. The audience gasped when he did: there was nothing below the table at all: no mechanisms that they could see, and no strings or levers. The boxes sat on what looked like solid wood, unless there were mirrors involved, but there couldn't have been because when the professor sat back down his legs were clearly visible, hands in his lap.

"The one about the medicine, Doc?" said Denny.

The professor's hands did nothing. They were clearly visible above the table. People along George's row stared at one another in astonishment.

"Yes," said the professor, and he crossed his arms. "The one about the medicine."

Denny sighed. "All right, then. There was once a man I knew just down the street from me who was loath to ever take his medicine," he began. "Yet then one day he went to the doctor, and that very afternoon he was seen sprinting down the street, pouring some potion into a spoon and swallowing it as he ran."

"He didn't!" said Berry.

"He certainly did. Then the next afternoon the same thing happened: he bolted out of his house and tore down the street, pouring his medicine and gulping it down."

"How very strange!" said Mary-Ann.

"And then the next day, the same thing, and everyone came out to watch him run down the street," said Denny. "Yet on the fourth day he skipped down the street, just like a little boy, and he took no medicine at all.

"Finally a policeman stopped him. 'What's the big idea?' said the cop. 'Why, I'm just following my doctor's orders!' said the man. 'Orders?' said the cop. 'What orders?' 'He said to take my medicine for three days running, and then to skip a day, which is exactly what I've been doing!'"

The drummer bashed a cymbal and the audience laughed at the joke, but it was more than a little uncertain. The puppets did not sound like they were in a humorous mood at all. And then there was the backdrop again... Were the trees in the window moving, as though brushed by the wind?

But the professor smiled, stood up, and took a bow. The puppets did likewise, saying, "Good night," though they sounded terribly sad. Then they sank into their boxes and shut their lids with a sigh. The professor walked to each box and picked it up off the table, taking care to show the audience that there were no holes or false bottoms or any other mechanism. Several people gasped. He stacked the boxes in his arms and said over the top, "And with that, ladies and gentlemen, good night! Why don't you say goodbye one more time, Denny?"

Denny's head poked up from the top box once more. And then, though George swore it couldn't have, the puppet *winked* at them, and said, "To sleep, to dream, and awake anew. Good night!" and sank down below again. The professor tipped an imaginary hat and walked toward the side of the stage as people applauded. The curtain dropped before he reached the edge, concealing him from view.

"That was very weird," said the woman in front of George.

George was inclined to agree. The act had been very funny until the light on the stage changed. Then things had gone strange. It had felt like the backdrop was a window into another world, and the professor and his companions had been fabricated versions of people on the other side, staring back at them through the glass. He was about to say something when Silenus mounted the corner of the stage again, hat nestled in the crook of his elbow. George's heart leaped at the very sight of him, and he suddenly felt torn: he wanted the show to be over so he might have a chance to meet his father, but he also wanted to see the rest of the acts; he'd heard so much about them, and the first one had been so odd, that his curiosity was almost overwhelming.

"What an odd little family they are!" Silenus said. "But so are all families, are they not? Especially the family of our next performer. Royalty they were once, ages and ages ago, in far away barbaric places of sun and sand and scimitars. Her family had been wronged, dislodged from their rightful throne, and so fell to dissolution. I

found her in the deepest parts of Persia, fallen from grace, performing her eloquent arts for mere coppers and coins, and begging for a
moment of charity. Yet I rescued her, and taught her to rule her new
domain of the stage. And now you, my fine ladies and gentlemen,
have one of the rare chances to hear the songs of none other than her
majesty, Colette de Verdicere!"

The curtain stayed lowered so George figured this would be an
olio act, performed at the front of the stage before the curtain while
they readied for the next full-stage act. He saw someone approaching
from backstage, about to enter into the light. George ignored them
and squinted into the shadows, trying to see where Silenus had gone.

Then the performer finally came out on the stage, and the woman
in front said, "Oh, my goodness! How pretty!"

George absently glanced back, but stopped, eyes wide, and gaped
at the stage. And for the first time since that morning he forgot
entirely about Silenus and his long quest to see his father's show.

Because George Carole had seen the girl, and now could see nothing else.

CHAPTER 4

The Chorale

The first two things that struck George were her size and her brown-ness, both of which were accentuated by the glowing white of her gown and tights. She seemed very tall as she danced across the stage, tall enough to topple over should she misstep, yet she never did. In her hands she carried a small concertina, and though it must have been difficult to play while twirling about she still pumped out a chirpy, happy song and grinned as if all of this were the easiest thing in the world. As he watched the curl of a white-tighted calf as it flashed over the footlights, George began to grin as well.

But the color of her skin was what his eyes hunted for the most, smooth and creamy like coffee and milk, brown and gleaming where light found the rippled muscles in her back. Sometimes she nearly blended in with the dark red of the curtain, making it difficult to see each twist and curve of her arms, upon which, he noted with interest, was the slight suggestion of amber down. And floating above her white-clad body was a jeweled, feathered mask which hid all but her mouth and chin. George strained to find some hint of wickedly happy eyes within the holes of that mask, and could not; yet each time she did some movement which she found particularly pleasing, her copper lips would part and reveal a set of perfect white kitten's teeth, and he knew somewhere behind that mask were two eyes crinkled with delight.

"Hot damn," said the man sitting beside him. George felt the fleeting desire to sock him in the jaw.

He dimly became aware that the girl was singing. He tried to focus on the words, but it seemed to be in another language, perhaps French or something exotic enough to match her strange beauty. Then he realized he was wrong, and it was in English, and he caught a few lines between the hums and toots of her little concertina:

> *Mothers, please hold tight to your children*
> *Maidens, don't hold back your sweet songs*
> *For the sun finds its sleep in the far hills*
> *And the time of this world won't be long*
>
> *Dance in the meadows, wander down roads*
> *Sing in the forests and glades*
> *Follow the stars to their far-flung cradles*
> *Drink your sweet wines in the shade*
>
> *Make sure your partings are happy and true*
> *Await the sun's sparkling and happy debut*
> *Drink in the sky and the scent and the view*
> *For the day of this world shall soon fade*

Then the song would seem to drift back into another language again. It was dreamy and peculiar, describing worlds and lives George didn't know but wished he could lead. He watched the girl flex and sway as she moved to the bleating of her concertina, and studied the angular swirl of a tricep, or a deltoid, or a trapezius, and thought she surely had to be carven. A creature this beautiful could not be naturally created.

Then the girl danced to the edge of the stage and began pumping her concertina. With a series of sharp pops, little jets of colored ribbon and glitter shot up from within the instrument to rain upon the audience, who laughed in delight. George remembered he hadn't thought to breathe in some time, and let out a deep gasp. Then he swallowed and shifted in his seat, surreptitiously trying to maneuver the staggering erection that'd suddenly appeared into a less prominent position, while the girl kept twirling back and forth across the stage, pumping the concertina and sending the colored paper arcing out over the people until he was mesmerized.

Then everyone began clapping. George jumped, startled, and looked around for the reason. He saw the girl smile and bow, her thick black hair falling about her face. The song must have ended and he'd never noticed. She turned away to leave.

"No! No!" said George.

The man sitting beside him jumped a little, and the two women turned and gave him glares. "What's wrong?" asked the man.

"No! Can't we... Can't we clap more to bring her back on?"

The man chuckled. "You got the itch something terrible, is that it?"

George did not know what "the itch" referred to, but he had a pretty good idea. It felt nothing like an itch, though. He moaned a little and leaned forward as a dull ache blossomed somewhere near his loins, and watched as the girl treaded off the stage, blowing kisses.

George sighed a little. He had never felt like this before. It was as though he'd been stabbed somewhere hidden, and was bleeding out, helpless to stanch it. He became so lost in his reverie that he almost didn't notice Silenus mount the stage again.

"Truly, some are diamonds, and the rest of us simply coal," he said. "Only occasionally are we allowed to bask in the radiance of those precious few and understand how beautiful we can be. Let's have another round of applause for Her Majesty, Colette de Verdicere."

Silenus politely tapped the white-gloved fingertips of one hand against an open palm while the rest of the crowd made a storm of applause. There were more than a few wolf whistles, and at these the icy ache inside of George flared hot. But he pushed these thoughts from his mind and returned to watching Silenus, who seemed to be in a better mood now.

"But not all are slender beauties like Her Majesty," said Silenus. "Others have a more functional dimension, but are no less wondrous. On the contrary, they may be even more astounding in their capabilities. My next performer, Miss Frances Beatty, is possibly known to you. I found her in a foundry, if you can believe it. There she was employed by the factory men for the purpose of bending girders and repairing damaged machinery with her bare hands," he said, and displayed his own to the crowd.

There were a few scornful laughs from the audience. Silenus smiled a little and raised a prim eyebrow. "Some of you may laugh, yes," he said. "I did myself, when I first heard the tales. Yet when I saw her and witnessed what she could do, my laughter died in my throat, as yours may do yet. I advise you to observe closely, and try not to miss a moment, for few are the things that could possibly compare to the abilities of Miss Frances Beatty!" He flung out one hand and faded from the stage again as the curtain lifted once more.

George felt that nothing could compare to the last act, or pierce the sickness that seemed to have overcome him. But when he saw the woman (was it a woman?) standing on the stage, he reluctantly sat up and paid attention, curious to see what she was about to do.

She was a skinny creature of medium build, not muscular in any way, and she stood in the center of the boards with a slumping posture that was a far cry from the showmanship of the other two performers, or Silenus. She had frazzled, reddish hair, and her face was painted white and her lips red, much as the professor's had been; but whereas for him this had highlighted his comical reactions, for her it emphasized her stillness. George did not think he had ever seen anyone so still as she, frozen in place with her head turned backstage, barely breathing. And then there was her clothing… He had expected to see the strongwoman in tights of some kind, but she seemed to be wearing tightly wrapped colored bandages that concealed every inch of her body below the neck. It rendered her strangely sexless and artificial. Only her hands remained uncovered, and these hung limp by her side. He could not think of anyone less likely to perform feats of strength, yet surrounding her on the stage were a host of huge and intimidating props: iron safes, thin steel girders, train car wheels, stone statues, and steel bands. The woman seemed tiny in comparison to them, yet she did not pay them any attention. In fact, she seemed utterly unaware that there was a performance going on at all.

"Do something!" someone called from the back, and there was a smattering of laughter throughout the crowd.

As if in answer, the orchestra started up and the strongwoman snapped her head up to stare out at them. The crowd shrank back a little. It was an unnatural movement, as though her skull had been pulled by a string, and George understood Irina's confusion: he was no longer sure if this was a puppet or a person. He watched as she stiffly walked to the steel bands and picked them up, and agreed that something was missing in the way she moved or stood. She could have been an automaton.

The strongwoman tilted her head back and forth as she examined the bands. Then she stared out at the crowd and thumped the bands down on the stage, proving their density, and lifted them up, grasped them in different sections, and pulled.

From the way she moved it looked like she exerted nearly no force at all, but the steel bands snapped apart and bent to form a large *O*, which she displayed to them. Then she grasped different segments of the bands and twisted and curled them, using her elbow to make the angles, until they formed an *H*, which she also displayed to the crowd, who now applauded politely. Then she bent them in half and pulled them through one hand, straightening them out, and held up what appeared to be an *I*. She pulled the bands apart again, forcing them into the first shape she'd made, and the crowd began chuckling in disbelief as they realized what she was spelling out. When she held up the final *O*, completing her gesture of honor for their state, the crowd had already begun to clap, completely won over by her. But she did not acknowledge their applause at all, and tossed the bands aside to continue on to the next feat.

She went to the girders, and stood one up on its end. It came with a large, flat base, which allowed it to balance easily. Then she went to the iron safe. She pulled at its door, but found it locked. The audience laughed, sensing that this was a gag for the show, but the strong-woman did not mug for them as they expected. Instead she sleepily went through the motions of listening to the click of the dial as she tried to crack the safe, but then shrugged, giving up, and took hold of the handle of the door and gave it a tug.

The door fell open with a loud squawk, and part of the now-damaged lock fell clanking to the floor. The crowd laughed and clapped and hooted at this. The strongwoman situated herself over the safe, positioned her feet, and pulled at the door. There was a moment of silence, and then the hinges gave way, twisting off the safe completely. She held up the amputated door to show the crowd, and bent it in half over one knee as though it were paper. Then she tossed it aside, and it landed on the stage with a loud clunk that reverberated through the theater. George could even see where it had dented the boards.

But it was odd. Whereas in the Persian's act he could see every flex and bend of her musculature, for the strongwoman he could see none. It was as though she was not straining to do any of this.

"Part of that's got to be rubber or something," muttered the man sitting next to him.

"Yeah," said George.

He forgot about it when the strongwoman picked up the safe, felt its heft, and tossed it up in the air, twirling end over end. The audience gasped in horror. George thought for sure that it would come down and crush her, but instead its open side came down on the end of the steel girder with a deep, resonant *bong*, and it hung there, spinning slightly. Everyone applauded madly at this. Then she bent the steel girder down piece by piece, folding it up in segments with the safe still dangling on its top, until finally the safe was at eye level with her. She took it off and set it on the floor, picked up the train car wheel, slowly folded it in half, and stuffed it in. She grabbed the safe door, unfolded it (rubbing it along her forearms to remove the larger dents), and replaced it on the safe's hinges, attempting to lock the wheel in. But the door fell off, clanking to the floor. She tried to replace it, but it again fell off, so she leaned the door against the front of the safe, picked up the second steel girder, and wrapped it around the safe bit by bit, leveraging it with her foot until she had tied the door on. The crowd erupted in laughter and applause, but again she did not seem to notice, or care. It was as though she was sleepwalking through her performance.

Her placid expression did not change once throughout the rest of the act. Not when she tossed the statues in the air and flipped forward to catch them, nor when she picked them up, one in each hand, and stacked them on the safe. George wondered if her face could move at all.

After she'd completed her big finish (balancing the statues on her shoulders while she imitated their poses), she bowed to the crowd's wild applause, and turned and walked away backstage without looking back once. It was an extremely impressive but bizarre performance, George felt. The strongwoman had seemed to neither know nor care who was watching.

As the curtain went down for the second time George wondered why no one could remember any of the acts of the Silenus Troupe. He'd never seen anything more amazing and amusing in his life, and was determined to never forget a detail. But then, he reminded himself, they still had one more act to go.

*   *   *

Silenus hopped back up to the corner of the stage. "That, my friends, was the wonderful Miss Frances Beatty. One wonders what husband she shall find in this world of ours," he said, and smiled. The crowd laughed, now in good spirits.

"And now is the moment when I myself join these wondrous performers on the boards," said Silenus. He walked out to the center of the stage and tugged off his gloves. He took off his hat, put his gloves in, and tossed the hat into the wings. "Hopefully I'll impress and entertain just as much as they have tonight," he said. "But then, my role is minimal—all I must do is lead them in a song."

Two other performers came out from backstage. One, George noticed with a thrill, was the girl in white and diamonds. She was no longer wearing her mask, and he saw her face was smooth and angular, and her eyes a curious green. She smiled as she walked to join Silenus on the stage, and he took her hand and kissed it.

The other performer was a very tall, thin, and very well-dressed man with bright blond hair. He carried a cello and a bow in one hand, and in the other he held a light chair. He was slightly stooped, as though he'd recently borne a great weight and overstrained himself, and there was a hitch in his step as his right hip dipped in and out. He set the chair on the floor and extended the endpin of the cello, and sat. Then he settled into his position and lightly whipped the bow across each string to listen to the pitch and tune it accordingly.

But then the man did something George thought was odd: the cellist crinkled his brow as though he'd heard something strange, and looked up to find its source. His eyes searched through the crowd, trailing over the balconies and the stage seats, until finally they sought out the very section that George was sitting in, and even seemed to rest upon his seat. George got the strong impression that, though the man had lights shining directly in his face and was surely blind to the rest of the theater, the cellist was looking for him, and could even see him.

"The song we will play tonight," said Silenus, "is one of our own devising. Or, rather, our own orchestration. The melody is a far, far older one than any you've heard this evening, an ancient folk melody passed down, in one form or another, from generation to generation. It has no name, as far as I know. But we here simply refer to it as the Chorale, if you please. Surely its age speaks of quality, and should we play it well enough you will hear it, and agree."

Then he turned to the two performers and raised his hands. The man with the cello looked away from George and snapped to attention, and the girl in white settled her shoulders back, preparing to sing. There was a pause, and Silenus dropped his hands.

The cellist leaped into the prelude of the song. He played in perfect synchrony with Silenus's conducting, his eyes fixed on every movement. It was an extraordinarily high and difficult piece, and his left hand had to crawl all the way up the strings of the instrument almost to the bridge to produce the clear, clean tones the song required. George knew only a little about the cello, but from the flurry of shifts and rapid slurring of the bow he knew he was seeing a formidable display of skill. The song itself was achingly, painfully beautiful, and put George in mind of green, rolling hills that ended in black cliffs as they were eaten away by the sea. It was desolate and forlorn, and yet always hinted of a key change to come, when the song would shift from minor to major, from mourning to gratification. As it was, it felt torn between an elegy and a celebration.

Then the girl began to sing. Her voice was husky and honey-sweet, and as before the song was not in English, but George could not identify which language it was. It certainly didn't sound like French, as her previous song had. It was difficult to tell one syllable from the other, and sometimes George could not understand how her mouth made the sounds it did.

George lost himself in the song, basking in its trills and turns. But he eventually found himself distracted. There was something making a sound in the theater, very quietly.

After a while, he realized what it was: a second song.

He glanced down the aisles, but could see no one whistling or humming to themselves. It was a very soft song, different from the Chorale yet played alongside. The two matched notes occasionally so that no one noticed, like hiding a noise in a clap of thunder. George somehow felt that he'd heard this second song before, but could not say where. It was too faint to hear clearly. It must have been somewhere long, long ago, he thought as he tried to listen to it.

George studied the cellist and the singer, but they didn't seem to be the ones playing it. Yet as he watched them he noticed that they had changed a little: their colors seemed brighter than before. The blond hair of the cellist was now a piercing gold, and Silenus was lit up like a flame. George wondered if he was imagining things and looked around, but saw that no one else seemed disturbed in any way. But then he peered closer at the people nearby.

None of them were moving at all. They all seemed catatonic, their eyes wide and glassy, some with their mouths hanging open. Even the orchestra had gone still as stones, staring up at Silenus and his performers.

George turned to the man sitting next to him and whispered, "Pardon me, sir—do you hear that?"

But the man did not respond. He was transfixed as well, his unfocused eyes set on the air above the stage.

George reached out and poked him. "Sir? Are you all right? What is going on with everyone?" But neither he nor anyone else moved.

The second song, the hidden one, seemed to get louder, and George felt something prickling on his skin. He glanced at the backs of his hands and saw the hair there standing on end. He looked up at the others around him. The stray hairs of the women in front were beginning to lift, and a nearly bald gentleman next to them now had a small, stiff forest sticking out above his ears, though they were all too hypnotized to notice. The air began to hum with an invisible energy as the second song grew louder, and George somehow grew aware that something was happening on a level he couldn't see: it was as if there was an umbilical point being established within the theater, two separate and very distant powers twisting toward one another to kiss, like planets brushing against each other in orbit.

George was not sure why he was the only one unaffected by the song, but he didn't know what he should do. Should he stand up and shout? Rush the stage and stop the performance?

"Hello?" he said, and tapped the shoulder of the lady in front of him. "Hello, ma'am? Ma'am, can you...can you help me?"

A groan rumbled through the theater, yet George could not feel it in his feet or in his back; it seemed as though he could hear it only in his mind. And then something in the theater changed: it was as though everything, the stage and the curtains and the rows and rows of seats, had *flickered*, blinking out of existence for one second, and once everything returned the shadows and edges of light throughout the theater were sharpened, and all the colors had gone blindingly bright. The theater took on a flimsy and insubstantial feel to George, like it was a little toy puppet show and all the people and players little cutouts made from wax paper, and someone had just lifted off the roof and let the whole world spill in from above...

George stood up in his seat, terrified, and was determined to run. He'd have to stumble through the knees of the people along the row, he thought. But he couldn't just leave everyone here to await whatever was happening. He stooped and shook the man next to him, saying, "Sir? Sir! For God's sake, you've got to get up! You've got to get—"

George trailed off. Now there were voices in the second song, high and sweet, though he could not see any new singers in the theater. But he recognized the melody they sang. He had heard it before.

And then he *remembered*.

Old fragments of memories flooded into him. He saw a field lined with deep ravines next to a small forest. Faces made of roots stood along the ravines on sticks, and they all faced a hill in the center of the forest as though waiting for something. He saw a barrow, wet and quiet, the gray sunlight dribbling down into its hollow to glance across glistening stones. There were cracks in the walls of the barrow, and from one of them came a voice, quietly chanting to itself in the dark. And somewhere inside was a wriggle of light where there should be none, dancing across the dark stone walls, and waiting for someone to touch it, and listen, and *see*...

The splinter of memory released him, and George fell back in his seat, gasping. Silenus kept conducting the two performers, who sang and played as though none of this were happening. The second song grew stronger around them, the voices from the invisible singers intensifying, and then it was like there was a split in the world and George could see out of it, and glimpse the endless machinery that kept the world running. And then, for one moment, he could see even *more*...

There was a rumble, and the lights in the theater quivered. The echoes of the song washed over them, faded, and then were gone. Silenus, the cellist, and the girl stood still on the stage, letting the sound reverberate on, the cellist's bow hovering inches away from the strings.

George took a breath, still stunned, and looked around. No one clapped. The rest of the audience sat frozen.

Silenus and the two performers stood up, walked to the edge of the stage, and bowed. The cellist and the girl in white gathered up their things and departed while Silenus ambled after them, digging in the inside pocket of his coat. He paused at the edge of the stage and produced a short, thin cigar, which he stuffed into the side of his mouth. He lit a match with the nail of one thumb, held the flame to the cigar, sucked at it, and breathed out a cloud of smoke. Then he glanced out at the audience one last time, a sardonic and bitter look, said, "Fucking smoking rules. Pah," and left.

CHAPTER 5

Heironomo Silenus

No one moved for several minutes. George still felt dazed and slightly sick. Then a few people began to shift in their seats, glancing around as if awoken from a dream. The conductor jumped when he heard the seats creaking, and reached out and poked the first chair violinist. The violinist sniffed and blinked at him, puzzled for a moment, but then hurried into position. The rest of the orchestra followed suit, and halfheartedly started another waltz. A pair of mimes in blue overalls and broad hats stepped out on the stage, looked around as though surprised to find themselves there, and began going through their performance, one pretending to share apples from a basket with the other. They were obviously terrified.

"Excuse me," said a voice. George looked up, and saw that the man beside him had stood and was trying to get past. The rest of the audience was standing up as well.

George, still confused, moved his knees to let the man by. "They put the shabby acts last," the man confided as he passed. "To get the audience to clear out, you see."

Even though George was utterly bewildered, he still managed,

"Well, of course I know *that*. And they're called chaser acts, for your information."

The man shrugged, and joined the rest of the audience members lining up to leave. They all had mystified looks on their faces like they'd left something behind, but couldn't remember what it was.

The pair of mimes onstage abandoned their act, and the orchestra wound down to a halt. None of them seemed upset by this development. Rather, they stared into the air with wistful looks on their faces, and the two mimes eventually shuffled offstage, smiling emptily. After a confused moment George followed the audience out.

Once outside he stood in the street with the rest of the crowd and took a deep breath. The night air seemed much fresher than the air in the theater, and George and the other patrons were desperate to get as much of it into their lungs as they could. But he noticed that there was something different about everything now. The night no longer seemed so thin, or so unreal. The moon did not feel so ponderously close and heavy. And unless he was mistaken, there was something different about the other patrons: they seemed to have more color in them, whether it was the deep grayness along a man's trousers, or the rich navy blue of a lady's purse. It was as if the song had put a light in them, one that made their skin and clothing shine much brighter than before.

"It is a beautiful evening," said one lady with an enormous white hat. "A simply beautiful night."

"Yes," said a man. "It certainly is. Just like when I was a boy."

"That's it," said the woman. "That's it exactly. It's like a Christmas evening from when I was just a girl."

They smiled and milled about as if they were sleepwalking. George wondered what had happened to them all. It was as if they'd been hypnotized, though he did not think any hypnotist's trick could ever make a person's very color seem brighter.

But then George remembered that the fourth act had not left him untouched: that song had opened up a memory within him, but it felt totally unfamiliar. His mind was still bursting with scattered images of barrows, and root faces, and a squiggle of light in the dark, and the fleeting impression of summer days and green leaves and a secret corner of the world that only he could find. It was like remembering he'd once been a different person entirely. He felt nearly as dizzy and disoriented as the other patrons.

But the most concerning thing about that memory was the song. Unless he was mistaken, tonight was not the first time he'd heard the Silenus Chorale: he'd heard it once before, long ago, when he was but a child, yet he'd never remembered it until now. He couldn't understand how this could be.

It took him a moment to realize that the one man who might know was currently packing up in the theater, readying to leave. George turned and hurried down a side alley to the back of the theater.

Though the Pantheon was a superior theater to Otterman's, the layout was the same, and George slipped in through the loading door for the props. He looked around at the passageways stuffed with ropes and pulleys and curtains and backdrops, wondering which way to go. At first he thought the backstage was deserted, but then he saw he was wrong: there were two stagehands standing in a corner, but they were so still he hadn't noticed them. They had small, confused smiles on their faces, and were clearly as stupefied as the patrons out front.

Then George heard voices coming his way. He walked to a drape of curtain and pushed it aside to see Silenus, the cellist, and the girl in white making their way toward him. His heart almost stopped, and he dropped the curtain a little and listened.

"Not bad, not bad at all, fellas," Silenus said as he led them. In the quiet theater it was easy to hear him. He had shed the Shakespearean lilt he'd used in his performance, and instead spoke in a drawling growl. "Could have been a lot fucking worse, in my oh-so-unasked-for opinion. Ain't as good as we done it before, that's the damn truth, but it's better than we were doing recently." He puffed at his cigar and began wiping his face paint away with a handkerchief. "Hallelujah, a-fucking-men. Glory and grace and fortune abounds, or am I wrong?"

George was not sure what he should do. This seemed very different from the performer he'd seen not more than five minutes ago. He wondered: should he call Silenus's name? Step in front of him? The man would surely say something then, and what could George say back?

"Who are you?" said a soft voice behind him. A hand took his shoulder, and though it was soft and small its grasp was iron-hard.

George cried out and leaped in surprise, and his suitcase clattered to the floor, spilling open. Silenus and the other two players stopped where they were. Before George could see any more the hand on his shoulder turned him around until he was looking into a tired, lined face whose many wrinkles were caked with the remains of white paint. It was the strongwoman, though now she was wearing an immense overcoat and a bulky sweater rather than her colorful bandages. She was joined by the professor puppeteer, who looked cold and aloof in his tuxedo.

"Yes," he said snidely. "And what are you doing here?"

"What's that?" said Silenus's voice. "What do you have there?"

The strongwoman turned him around and Silenus approached, his face barely lit by the glow of his cigar. He was now nothing like the impresario from the show: in the dark of the backstage he was ferociously intimidating, his hooded eyes boring into George but betraying nothing.

"A boy," said the strongwoman.

"A boy?" said Silenus.

"We found him backstage. And he's awake."

"Awake, you say?" said Silenus.

"Yes," said the professor. He looked out the loading door and down the alley. "The rest are all out front, as usual."

"Hm," said Silenus, and he moved to examine George closer.

George had often wondered what his father would say when they first met. He had fantasized that perhaps Silenus would know him immediately, and he'd fall to his knees and throw his arms open and cry something about how he'd finally found his lost child. Or possibly Silenus would only slightly recognize him, and peer into George's face, murmuring about how this young man seemed familiar. Or maybe Silenus would take a liking to George for reasons he couldn't understand, and, should their relationship progress enough, sometimes profess that you know what, this here kid reminds me of me.

What he'd never expected was for Silenus to say, "Ah, geez. What the fuck are you doing back here, kid?" He looked George up and down. "And why aren't you sleepwalking?"

There was a pause as George took this in. "S-sleepwalking?" he said. "I don't... I'm afraid I don't really understand..."

Silenus sucked his teeth and peered at him. His leathery face crinkled up around the eyes, and he tutted and pulled up the waist of his pants with one hand. "You don't have any idea of what's going on, do you?" he said. "This isn't a good sign. I can't remember the last time someone stayed awake. We'll have to look into that later." He nodded to the woman. "Franny, dispose of this young man. If he's a thief, beat his ass if you'd like, but be discreet about it. Then we'll hightail it back to the hotel."

"No!" shouted George. "No, you can't!"

"And keep him quiet, too," added Silenus.

"No!" said George again, and he lunged out and grabbed ahold of Silenus's sleeve. "You can't go back to your hotel!"

The strongwoman pulled him back. Silenus ripped his sleeve free of George's hand and looked up at the strongwoman, indignant. "Are you seriously going to let some fucking kid take a grab at me?"

"He's just a boy," she said sullenly.

"Are boys so incapable of carrying knives?" said Silenus. "I've seen many a ten-year-old admirably wield a pigsticker, and I ain't keen on getting cut on by somebody who can't even fucking vote."

"He's just a boy," she said again. "Please don't be angry with me."

"I'm not angry. Don't get upset, girl." Silenus turned his attention back to George. "What's that you said to me? What about my hotel?"

"You . . . you can't go back there," said George.

"And why is that?"

"There are men waiting there for you. Men in . . . in gray suits. They're looking for you. Or at least, I think they are."

That disturbed them. Silenus cast a dark glance around at the rest of his troupe as they all began speaking.

"What is that he said?" said the professor. "Men in gray suits?"

"At the hotel?" said the girl in white and diamonds. "*Our* hotel? You said they'd never get that close to us!"

"Enough," said Silenus. They all fell silent. He sucked on his cigar for a moment, then said, "What's your name, kid?"

George badly wanted to say something about who he was and why he was there, but he could not muster the will to say anything beyond "George."

"George, huh?" said Silenus. "Well, George, I'm going to grab your neck real tight right now. Are you ready for that?"

"What d—"

Silenus's hand shot out and took George underneath the chin, his thumb painfully pressing up against the corner of his jawbone. George choked and tried to pull back, but the strongwoman held him still. Silenus's blue eyes thinned into narrow slits, and he tilted his head up and down as he tried to get a better look at George.

"Hold still," he said. "Just hold still, why don't you?"

George tried, but Silenus's hold was so strong and painful he couldn't help but attempt to pull away. As the man examined him George got the queer feeling of being looked *through*, like Silenus could see all of his lies and memories in the recesses of his mind, or perhaps feel the shape of them through the skin on his neck.

"Now, George, tell me the truth," said Silenus. His voice was very low and soft. "Did those men in gray send you to gut any of my company? Or me?"

George coughed and shook his head.

"You here to sabotage us? To spy on us?"

He shook his head again.

"You're not coming at us in any way at all?"

Again, he shook his head.

"Why are you awake, George? Why aren't you sleepwalking like the others?"

"D-don't…don't know…"

Silenus examined him for a moment longer. He grunted to himself and removed his hand. George gasped and rubbed at his neck while Silenus watched, his face unreadable. "Ain't this interesting," he said. "Just when I wanted it least." He nodded to the strongwoman. "Let him go."

She released him. She stroked his back as she did so. "Sorry," she whispered in his ear.

"Well, now," said Silenus. "Unfortunately it seems this kid is telling the truth, or he thinks he is. Which ain't comforting." He sighed and stuck his head out the loading door to survey the crowd. "We don't have much longer on these yucks. Here, I tell you what— Stanley, you take Colette and Franny and our props to the train station. Professor Tyburn and I will go to the hotel with this kid and see if he's a nut or if he just happens to be right. We'll find you at the train station, either way."

The cellist, presumably Stanley, frowned at that, and reached into his bags. He produced a largish blackboard with a piece of chalk hanging from it by a string, and took the chalk and quickly wrote in a smooth, clean hand: SAFE?

"I can handle myself," said Silenus. "Kingsley, you got your cannon?"

"I do," said the professor. He patted his side.

"Well, keep it handy," said Silenus. "Keep it trained on this kid, especially if he starts getting jumpy. I don't know what we'll see there—I can't imagine how they could've caught up to us at the hotel—but something fishy's going on and I don't like the taste of it." He looked at George and said, "You don't mind coming with us on a trip, do you George?"

George angrily looked back. He'd never expected their first meeting to go like this, but still he shook his head.

Silenus smiled. There was no humor in it. "Good," he said. "But before we do, run and fetch me my hat, will you? It landed somewhere in the back."

George was irritated to be ordered about in such a fashion, but he walked to the farthest corners of the backstage to search. Once he was away the troupe began talking quietly.

He found the top hat behind the curtain rigging, and when he picked it up he noticed it was peculiarly heavy. He looked inside and saw that the lining was stuffed with many strange things: a thin, sheathed knife, several small lenses, and half a pack of playing cards with notes scribbled on them.

He looked up at Silenus and wondered exactly what this man was. Silenus was not paying attention to him, but George saw that someone else was watching: Colette, the girl in white and diamonds. Something in his chest flared hot, and he managed a wave and a feeble smile. She did not return them, but frowned mistrustfully and turned back to Silenus.

George returned with the hat. "Ah," said Silenus, and he snatched it from him, flipped it smoothly, and fixed it atop his head. "Very good. Then let's get going."

Silenus, George, and Professor Tyburn left the others outside the theater and climbed aboard a streetcar. Silenus's hand never left

George's back, even when they took their seats. If they didn't know better, someone would have thought the two of them dear friends who hadn't seen one another in a long while. The professor sat opposite them, crooked in his seat as though his side pained him, but his hand never left his pocket. George guessed there was a pistol hidden there. He began to wish he had never come.

As they traveled Silenus asked him a variety of bizarre questions. Had George recently been forced to eat or drink something he would not normally consume? Had he found any scars on himself that he could not explain, especially under the left armpit? Had he ever been to southern Ireland in midwinter? Had he recently experienced any dizzy spells or feelings of weightlessness, and in these moments of weightlessness had he actually levitated several inches off the ground? Did he ever get the sensation that there was a small person forcing their way into the space behind his eyes? And did he have a curious predilection for shrimp that he had not displayed before?

When George had answered all the questions (the answer to each being no, except the first question, because he had politely eaten an odd, doughy bread of Irina's), he asked how these things could possibly be relevant. "I know you think you're telling the truth, kid, there's no doubt about that," said Silenus. "But there are methods of duping someone into saying what you want them to say, usually very nasty ones. That's what I worry about. So what we're going to do is go to the hotel and have a look-see, and if you're right, well, then, you're right. Why this boy felt the need to warn me about these gents in gray, well, that's another question. But I won't ask it now. Because it's always possible that you are, unknowingly, a part of the machinations of my enemies.

"And I do have enemies, George," he said calmly. "I got more enemies than there are stars in the fucking sky. A man can't make a ripple in the ocean without another trying to give him the knife for it. And if you're working for these enemies of mine, then we're going to have to figure out what to do with you. See?"

"I see," said George.

"Good," said Silenus. "Smart kid."

"Can I ask you something, Mr. Silenus?" said George, now angry.

"You can call me Harry, kid. And my associate here is Kingsley. You put someone through what we're putting you through, might as well be cordial about it," he said.

"All right...Harry," said George. "Is this sort of behavior common in your troupe?"

Silenus smiled. "In our troupe, kid, it's as common as rain. Wish that it fucking weren't."

They came to the stop closest to the hotel, hopped off, and began walking toward it, Silenus strolling out in front with his arm around George and Kingsley walking behind them, hand in his pocket. George miserably thought of all the fantasies he'd had of taking a friendly walk with his father, and reflected that he'd never imagined this would be how their first would go.

Yet the street ahead seemed curiously abandoned: not only was there no one on the sidewalks, but the houses and shops were dark and shuttered, like those within wanted passersby to think no one lived there at all. It'd been a busy scene when George had visited earlier that evening. Had he not seen a lady in a raincoat just over there, next to the hotel, pulling her coat tight about her chest as she shivered? And a group of children playing with a tin hoop in that alley? But now there was no one.

George stopped. Silenus looked at him and nodded back at Kingsley, who stood ready.

"What are you stopping for, kid?" said Silenus. "Come on."

"You don't feel it?" said George. "Or hear it?"

"Hear what?"

"That silence," said George. "Before I heard it around the hotel, so that's how I knew the men in gray were there, but now..."

"Now what?" asked Silenus.

George looked around them. The building faces on either side of the street seemed gray and faint, and the streetlamps were sputtering as if fighting to stay lit. "Now it's like they're all around us..."

Silenus stared at him for a moment, and whipped off his hat and fumbled with the inside. "I hope you're fucking wrong," he muttered, and pulled out a large, scratched monocle. To George it appeared too scratched to see through, but Silenus held it up to one eye and looked through it at the hotel. Though George caught no movement in the windows, Silenus slowly took in a breath as if he did not like what he saw. Then he turned a full 360 degrees, taking in the streets around them through the monocle. "Well," he said finally. "Things prove otherwise. You were right, my boy. Very, very, very right. As impossible as it seems, they were waiting for us. I sort of wish I had listened to you, kid, but I can't be right every time."

"So they are there," said Kingsley. "Then it's a good thing we didn't go into the hotel."

"They aren't in the hotel anymore," said Silenus, the monocle still stuck to his eye. "They were watching this whole neighborhood. Kingsley?"

"Yes?"

"Take that cannon out, and keep a sharp eye open."

"Won't people see it?"

"There won't be anyone out," said Silenus. He peered up at the sky and the surrounding buildings through the monocle. "When the wolves gather in such great numbers, things change... Light dies, the sky feels thin and stretched, and everything grows cold. No... no one will be outside with so many of them here. We'll be alone. Which is what they want."

"But we haven't been spotted yet, have we?" asked Kingsley as he took out his gun.

"Oh, we definitely have. I'd say they had our scent the second we stepped on the street." Silenus lowered the monocle and softly said to himself, "How did they resist it? Are they getting stronger, or are we weaker?" Then he put the monocle in his pocket and replaced his hat, and turned around and started calmly walking back. "Here. Come on, both of you. Walk with me. And don't run. Not yet, at least."

Kingsley and George both took up places beside Silenus, casually placing one foot in front of the other. George glanced back and saw the end of the street darkening as streetlamps near the hotel began flickering out, one by one. It was as though someone were pacing from lamp to lamp, turning them off, but he could see no one there.

"Yes, they're following us," said Silenus. "Don't look. You won't see them. They don't want to be seen, not now. But don't look. Since we've just heard the song we have some amount of protection, but if you look at them, that won't matter."

"Do you have any ideas about how to get us out of this?" hissed Kingsley.

"Not yet," said Silenus. "But I'm thinking very hard."

They turned down a main street lined with shops. The people before them deserted the sidewalks, ducking into restaurants or buildings as though suddenly remembering other business. They did not seem to know what they were running from; it was an instinct, like smelling smoke and knowing to flee.

George looked to the side and saw the smaller streets and passage-ways were flooding with darkness, the far corners growing dark and fading entirely until everything was pitch-black. Soon it felt like the entire world had fallen away until there was nothing left but this small, colorless island of street intersections and building faces afloat in a dark sea. He realized he was shaking.

"Don't worry yourself too much, kid," said Silenus quietly. "They want me, not you."

"What are they?" said George.

"They are shadows," said Silenus. "True shadows. Not merely the absence of light, but of all things. Gaps in Creation itself, given minds and gnawing hunger, and how they hate the light..."

"What the hell have you gotten me into?" breathed George.

"If you'd keep your mouth shut, and let me fucking *think*, then I can get you out of it all the sooner," said Silenus.

They continued walking down the street, trying their very hardest not to look at the gathering shadow behind and beside them. Then as they passed one side street a lamp came on, illuminating someone standing below. The light was painfully bright in this muted, shadowed world.

"Don't look!" said Silenus quickly. "Don't look at it!"

George caught himself just in time. He kept his eyes fixed on the street, but in the corner of his vision he could see a figure standing below the lamp, its hands primly fixed behind its back. It appeared to be a man in a gray suit and a black bowler, but now George sensed that this was just a picture in a very real way, a thin and flimsy skin with something hiding just behind it.

"Hey!" cried the figure merrily. "Hey you, kid! Hey, come here to us! Let us get a look at you!"

"Don't listen to it," said Silenus. "And don't look. It will want you to look."

"We remember you," called the figure. "Do you remember us? We met outside of the theater. You were the fan, weren't you? We said we'd pay you, but we never heard back from you, such a pity. Imagine meeting you here. Imagine that."

"Oh, God," said George.

"Just keep moving," said Silenus. "Don't look."

"We'd still pay, you know," said the man. "We saved up, just for you. Leave that liar and that dying man behind, and come here to us. We won't hurt you. We can't say the same for them, but you can be safe."

"Bastards," whispered Kingsley.

"Look at us, child," called the man. "Would we hurt you? Would we hurt a nice young man like yourself?"

George shut his eyes and kept walking forward, guided by the faint footsteps of Kingsley and Silenus.

The man laughed. "But hey, you know what, we thought you

looked familiar. And now that you're standing next to that awful liar, we see why! The resemblance is very faint, but we can see it! Family, how funny! But now, you know, maybe we can't let you leave. Not if you are what it looks like you are."

At that, George opened his eyes and looked sideways at Silenus. Silenus appeared confused, but he did not look at George, nor did he say anything until he spied a large sweetshop at the corner ahead.

"Do you both see that big window there?" he said quietly. "There in that shop, on the other side of that corner?"

"Yes," said Kingsley and George at once.

"All right. What we're going to do is walk toward that very quickly. We're not going to run. If we run, they'll do something. We're going to get to it as fast as we can without running. Okay?"

"And then what?" said Kingsley.

"You leave that up to me," said Silenus. "All right? Let's go."

They picked up the pace very slightly, moving quickly toward the corner. The man behind cried, "Hey, now, where are you going? Are you leaving us so soon? You know there is not far to go..." Then the light behind them winked out, and though George wanted to look back and see if the man was still there, he refrained.

When they rounded the corner, Silenus said, "Stand right there in front of the window, both of you. And look in." George did as he asked, and saw that they were staring in at their own reflections. Silenus took off a glove, stuffed it in his pocket, and took out his monocle. "Here," he said, and handed it to George. "You seem more sensitive to them than either of us. After all, you can hear the bastards. Now just keep an eye on them, and tell me when they're close."

George looked at the lens in his hand. It was scuffed to the point that it was opaque, but he put it to his eye and peeked through. The world was rendered milky white, with no distinguishable buildings or forms in it, but among all the whiteness he could see black figures and dark shadows slowly moving toward them. He gasped and took his eye away and saw he'd been staring into a brick wall.

"What is this?" said George. "It can look through the wall?"

"It's lightning glass," said Silenus. He produced a small knife and made a very small incision on his finger, and let the blood dribble down to collect in the palm of his hand. George winced, but Silenus said, "It's what's left behind when lightning strikes sand dunes. If you polish it the right way, it becomes very sensitive to light and dark. Especially the darkness that follows the wolves."

"They're wolves?" said George.

"That's one word for them, yeah," said Silenus. He picked up a handful of soil from the gutter and began mixing it with the blood in his hand. When it began to turn to clumps, he spat into it and kept mixing. "Are you going to keep a fucking eye on them or not?"

George brought the monocle back up again. He saw the mass of darkness grouping at the alleys on the other side of the sweetshop. "They're getting close," he said. "Why are they moving so slow?"

"Because they don't want to give us any way to escape," said Silenus. "All right, I'm ready here. Both of you hold still. Just look in the window, and do *not* blink."

George put down the monocle and watched. Silenus reached toward the glass and began to paint the mixture of blood and earth and saliva around their reflections in the window, drawing along their edges. He did it very carefully, making sure to account for every bump or bend in their forms. His own was the most awkward, as he was painting himself with his arm outstretched. Once he was done, he blew on the outline of blood and dirt and began picking at one corner of it.

"What are you doing?" asked George.

"Shut up," suggested Silenus.

"Yes, please do," said Kingsley.

George was about to make an angry reply, but stopped when he noticed something: although they had all spoken, none of their mouths had moved in the reflection.

Once Silenus had picked at the corner of the outline enough, he took it between his thumb and forefinger and began pulling. George had expected it to flake away, but the outline seemed to hold together, as though it were made of resin. But then George saw Silenus was peeling away more than just the outline: there was something else coming off the glass, something ghostly and illusory...

When Silenus had gotten the thing off the window it collapsed in his hands like cloth or loose paper, and he began trying to stand it up on the sidewalk. When he finally got it upright, George saw they were staring into faint versions of their own faces, though Silenus's was partially obscured by his arm, which seemed to be reaching out toward them. George looked back at the window and saw it was now blank. The reflections were gone; if he'd been seeing things correctly, their images in the window had been pulled from the glass to now stand on the sidewalk. They were faint, distorted things with the wrong dimensions in places, and they were all joined together at the hips, but other than that they looked almost exact.

"W-what?" asked George faintly.

"Now, kid, where are they coming at us?" said Silenus.

George jumped and looked through the monocle again. "From that alley there," he said, and pointed.

"All right," said Silenus. Then he whispered into the ears of each reflection. Up until now they had been static and frozen, but when they heard what he said each insubstantial face looked miserable and terrified.

"I know you don't like it, but you got to," said Silenus to them. "Besides, you wouldn't have lived long anyways. Just until we passed out of the window. All right?"

The Silenus reflection nodded stiffly. "All right," said the real Silenus. "Now—*go*."

The three reflections turned around and began marching toward the alley George had indicated. They moved awkwardly, as they were essentially one mass with six legs, but they managed to stay upright.

"Back up," said Silenus to George and Kingsley. "Up against the building, so they won't see you."

They flattened themselves against the wall and watched the progress of their reflections. When the three ghostly shapes made it to the alley they looked directly down it at whatever had been hunting them, and turned and ran away down the street.

There was a chorus of growls and cries as the things in the darkness gave chase. The mouth of the street grew murky, and Silenus whispered, "Don't look! Look away and shut your eyes!"

They did as he said. The sound of hundreds of feet on paving stones filled the air, and if George's ears were right it sounded as if the feet were clawed. The wind whipped around him and a chill trilled through his bones. He suddenly felt old, older than he ever had in his life, and he wanted to do nothing more than lie down on the sidewalk and never get up again. It was in this moment that curiosity overtook him, and George cracked open one eye, intending to look back. But when he did he saw Kingsley had already succumbed to that same impulse, and was staring over George's shoulder at whatever was chasing their reflections down the street. His face was fixed in utter terror, and sweat ringed his brow. Then he saw George was watching him, and he scowled and shut his eyes and looked away.

Eventually the sounds and the chill faded. Silenus opened his eyes and looked around, then let out a breath. "They're gone," he said.

"Are you sure?" said George.

"I'm sure," said Silenus. "I told our reflections to run clear across town if they could. They seem to have bought the ruse. Stupid things. We can breathe easy for a bit."

Kingsley mopped his forehead with a handkerchief. "How did they get so close? You said that after the song was sung they couldn't get within miles of us."

"I know that's what I fucking said!" said Silenus. "That's how it's always been! Something's changed, but I don't know what."

"Or maybe it's just not working anymore," said Kingsley.

"That's something I don't want to consider," he said. "Listen, the trick I just pulled won't last forever. Let's hurry back to the train station before they figure it out. Come on, kid." He and Kingsley turned to make their way down the street.

But after being ridiculed, choked, and forced into a dangerous trap at gunpoint despite his protestations, George was no longer feeling so amenable to the man he'd spent over half a year trying to find, whether he was his father or not. "Why should I?" he asked.

Silenus looked back. "Eh?"

"Why should I come with you? What good would it do me? You've done nothing but abuse and ignore me since I met you. I tried to save your life, and you went and nearly got me killed anyways. So why should I?"

Silenus walked back, nodding his head. "Fair points, fair points," he said. "But you're forgetting, of course, that the wolves now think you're with me. So they'll be looking for you. And while you might not know exactly what they are, you know they're bad news, and I think I've got a little more experience with them than you have. So it's probably in your best interests to tag along with us, at least until you're safe."

George knew that these were very valid observations, but he was still reluctant to follow him.

"Come on, kid," said Silenus, now quieter. "I didn't know. These are dangerous times. I had to make sure."

"Why do you want me to come at all?"

Silenus paused. His face was still and closed again, and George could tell he was thinking hard. "Let's just say you're quite the specimen. But in any case, it'd be a poor thing to leave you behind with the wolves hot on your scent."

George considered it. "If I come with you, will you hurt me again?"

"I can't promise that I won't. Sometimes what needs to be done needs to be done, even if it's unpleasant. But I will promise to try my best to keep you safe, until I no longer can."

"You will?" asked George suspiciously.

"It's what I promise everyone who travels with me. Now come on before they double back, all right?"

George sighed. "All right."

They jumped on a different streetcar and huddled at the end as it took them to the station. Silenus was grim and lost in thought, but he looked better than Kingsley, who sat crooked in his seat with one hand gingerly exploring his side. His skin was pale and waxy, and he kept licking his lips and whispering something, as if he was speaking to someone who was not there.

When they were near the station they heard them: first one howl, then two, then many, long, keening cries from somewhere far out in the city.

"Are those wolves I hear?" said one passenger.

"It can't be," said a woman. "There are never any wolves so far into town."

George expected Silenus to say something, but he did not. He simply lifted his eyes and gazed in the direction of the howls, and settled down farther in his seat.

CHAPTER 6

"He sees what he wants to see."

When they got to the train station, Colette and Franny ran to Silenus and began asking questions, while Stanley slowly sauntered up behind them.

"What happened?" asked Colette. "What did you see?"

"Were they there?" Franny asked, frightened. "Were they really waiting for us? Are you all right?"

"We are all fine," said Silenus. "And I don't know exactly what we saw there. We'll discuss all that on the train."

"You don't look so good, Kingsley," said Colette. "Are you hurt?"

Kingsley was still standing crooked with the elbow of one arm held close. His skin had not gained any color, and a cold sweat clung to his cheeks. "No," he said. "I'm fine. I'll feel better once we get on the train."

"Then let's go," said Franny. "I have all our tickets ready." She held them up, and George saw her hands were heavily bandaged. Copper and burgundy stains were spreading through the wool from wounds below.

Colette said, "It was costly, but we're still under budget, for now."

"We'll need one more," said Silenus. He nodded in George's direction. "For the boy."

"The boy?" said Colette. She looked at George, incredulous. "He's coming with us? Why?"

"Because I have some questions for him," said Silenus. "Quite a few, actually. And besides, it's no business of yours, girl."

"It's my damn business if it's my damn budget that's buying his ticket!" said Colette.

"But you've got room in your budget for this, don't you?" said Silenus. "Isn't there room for emergencies or some such?"

"I *said* to budget for emergencies, but you told me not to bother!" Colette said. "And we're already at the limit for train fare!"

"I can pay for myself," said George. "I have my own money."

They all looked at him, surprised. "You do?" said Silenus.

"Yes," said George. He was a little nettled by their disbelieving looks. "In fact, I have plenty of money. I could probably pay for all of your tickets, if I wanted to." Then he turned around and marched toward the ticket booth with his head held high (despite Silenus's derisive snort). He was about halfway there before he stopped, turned around, came back, and asked, "By the way — where are we going?"

"To Illinois," said Franny. "To Alberteen."

"To the sticks," said Colette.

"To the next show," said Silenus to her sharply. She gave him a surly look but did not respond.

George bought his ticket, which was indeed fairly costly, and on his way back over to them he noticed the cellist was standing next to the station benches, watching him. He gave George a little wave and motioned him over.

"Yes?" asked George.

Stanley reached behind a bench, lifted up George's suitcase, and held it out to him.

"Oh, great!" said George, and took it. "I forgot that I'd left that at the theater! Where did you find it?"

Stanley reached into his coat and took out the blackboard again. He scribbled for a second and turned it around: HAD FALLEN OPEN BACKSTAGE. REFOLDED YOUR CLOTHES FOR YOU.

"Oh," said George. "Well. Thank you. You didn't have to do that."

Stanley smiled and shrugged.

"What about your luggage? Did you just leave it all at the hotel?"

He began to write again. He wrote astonishingly fast and smoothly. It said: THAT IS BEING TAKEN CARE OF.

"Do you not talk?" asked George.

Stanley shook his head again.

"Is it an injury? Or..."

He thought about it, and wrote: YES. VERY OLD INJURY.

"I'm sorry to hear that," said George.

He then wrote: DO NOT MISS IT. NEVER HAD ANYTHING INTERESTING TO SAY. He smiled and shrugged again as if to say, "What can you do?" But then his face turned troubled and he gave George a curious look, as if something George had done had just given him a head-ache. He massaged one temple and blinked rapidly.

"Are you all right?" asked George.

Stanley smiled weakly, nodded, and motioned to the luggage car. They both carried over their luggage, but Stanley's fingers never left his head.

The backdrop and table from Kingsley's act were already loaded in the car, and Stanley secured his cello in the corner while George carelessly tossed his suitcase in. Once they were done Kingsley himself limped up with three little coffin-like boxes balanced in his arms.

"I know those!" said George. "Are your dummies in there?"

"My what?" said Kingsley, affronted.

"Your... your dummies. You know, your puppets?"

"They are my marionettes. They are very different from common puppets, or crude dummies."

"Don't marionettes have strings?" asked George.

"Are you so sure that mine do not?" said Kingsley. "Perhaps they have strings, and you simply did not see them." Once he'd loaded them he gave George a haughty look and marched off to rejoin the others, who were now boarding the train.

"Well," said George to Stanley. "He's a little ridiculous, isn't he?"

Stanley glanced at George. Then, with a dubious smile and a shake of the head, Stanley gestured to him to follow.

When George climbed in he moved to sit with them at the end of the passenger coach, but Silenus coughed uncomfortably and said, "Ah, listen, kid, we got some business stuff to discuss. Would you mind if you, uh..." He nodded toward the other end of the car.

"Oh," said George, disappointed. "Are you sure? I'll be very quiet. I won't listen."

"I'm sure."

"Oh. All right then." He got up to move.

"Thanks," said Silenus.

As soon as George was several rows away the group began talking quietly. A great deal of it sounded like bickering, with Silenus's angry growl often answering a question he apparently found impertinent. They argued straight through the train's departure, with the clack and hiss of Stanley's chalk punctuating the sounds of the locomotive. George could make out little of what was said.

After a while Franny stood up and sat down across the aisle from him. She smiled and said, "They talk much too fast for me. I tire of it very quickly." She did look extremely tired. Heavy bags hung around her eyes, which were crisscrossed with red blood vessels.

"Well, it's pretty late," said George. "There are Pullman coaches at the back. I'm sure you could sleep there."

"No," she said, still smiling. "I don't sleep."

"You don't... sleep? At all?"

"No. I try, frequently. I find a dark place, and I shut my eyes, and I try and drift away..." She leaned back and showed him, sitting motionless. She suddenly seemed like a statue made out of wax, sitting in the seat with its eyes closed. But then her eyes snapped open, and she said, "But I never do. I'm always awake, aware of everything that's going on."

"How do you live without sleep?" asked George.

"I ask myself that question every day," said Franny. "I still can't think of an answer."

She was kneading the palms of her hands, where the bandages were stained. One bandage came unraveled at the wrist, and he spied a hint of black writing on the visible sliver of skin. She saw him looking, and moved to cover it up.

"How did you hurt your hands?" he asked.

"My act," she said. "Have you seen it?"

"Yes! You were incredible! I have to admit, I've seen a lot of performers, but only very, very few of them compare to you."

She smiled, but his praise did not seem to mean much to her.

"Did it go wrong?" said George. "Is that how you got injured?"

"Oh no," said Franny. "It went perfect. It just happens nearly every time. Hands were not designed to bend and twist metal, or pick up statues, or juggle stones. The wear and tear is natural."

"So it's not fake? No rubber safes, or bars, or anything?"

"No, no. It's all real. All the safes, real iron. All the bands, real steel. And the weight, all that weight... that's real, too." She seemed very weary, as if she could feel the stupendous weight of those safes and iron bars pushing down upon her now.

"How do you do it?" asked George.

She looked at him slyly. "Do you really want to know?"

"Sure."

Franny glanced around. She leaned in and said, "I grit my teeth."

"You what?"

"I grit my teeth when I do my act. You have to grit them the right way. But if you do it, it gives you great strength." She flexed her arms as if to show off her bulging muscles, but she seemed as gaunt as ever. Then she winked at him, and touched the side of her nose.

"Oh. Does it hurt much?"

"Yes. Very much. But it's manageable."

"I see," said George. And he did, to an extent. During some child shows at Otterman's he'd heard the children's shoes squelching as they'd walked off the stage. Their parents had been unable to buy them better shoes, and they'd danced to the point that their feet bled.

"Is it true that you can hear the men in gray?" said Franny. "That you can sense them, like a dowsing rod near water?"

"I guess," he said. "It's like everything freezes up around them. But the sounds are what I notice most. They all just die off. I suppose maybe it's because I have such good hearing, but that doesn't seem right."

"He's very interested in you," she said, and nodded toward Silenus.

George sat up. "He is? Really?"

"Yes," she said, but she did not share his excitement. Rather, she seemed very grave. "I would be careful, if I were you. Harry is a very clever man, but sometimes he's not as right as he thinks he is. Sometimes he's very narrow-minded. He sees what he wants to see. And he doesn't understand how that could hurt those around him."

"Oh," said George.

"So, as I said, be careful."

"Franny!" Silenus called from the other side of the car. "What are you doing? Come here, this concerns you."

Franny gave him a quick smile, and stood and rejoined the group's discussion. George watched her go. Then, feeling terribly alone, he leaned over and rested his head on the windowpane, and watched the midnight countryside speed by.

*   *   *

Once the troupe finished its summit Silenus stood and walked to the middle of the car, which was otherwise empty, and said, "All right. It's late. I suggest we all get as much sleep as we can. We've got a free day tomorrow, but there's rehearsal bright and early on Monday."

"I hate traveling without our things," said Colette. "Can you imagine what it feels like to sleep in this outfit?" She gestured to her white tights, which were only partially hidden by her coat.

"Listen, no one is happy about the current arrangements, but we will all just have to make do," said Silenus. "Look at me, you think I like being stuck in my performance costume?"

"I packed some pajamas," said George, eager to catch Colette's eye. "You can borrow them for tonight, if you'd like. They're silk, and very fashionable."

She favored him with a cold stare. "You are, of course, aware that I am half a foot taller than you, and a girl?"

George's face fell. "Well, no. I mean, yes, sorry, *yes*, I did realize that you were a, a girl, but—"

"Moving along," said Silenus. "You should all get some sleep in the overnight coach. We'll be at the hotel in several hours, and you can catch up on whatever rest you've missed then."

"And if they've tracked us to the new hotel?" asked Colette.

"Then we'll improvise," said Silenus. "Which will be very hard to do if we're all dead fucking tired. Now go on."

All of them left except Stanley, who sat sideways in a chair across the aisle. Franny murmured, "I suppose I'll wander down to the dining car," as she left. George stood up to follow them to the Pullman, but Silenus clapped a hand on his shoulder and pushed him back down. "Not you," he said. "We need to talk."

Silenus sat down next to George. He smelled of old tobacco and cedar, tinged with train smoke. He grumbled for a moment and reached into his pocket and took out a small flask. He took a long pull from it and offered it to George. "Fancy a taste, kid?" he said. "I'd imagine you'd want to, considering the stuff you saw today."

George took the flask and allowed himself a small sip. He tried not to let his face curdle, but it did anyway.

"There you go, fire of the gods in you, chin chin," said Silenus.

"Is that single malt?" asked George. He stifled a cough.

Silenus gave him a very hard look. "No. No, that is not single malt."

"Oh, well," said George. "I didn't think so, but, you know, some of Islays have that flavor to them. That was why I asked."

Silenus looked at him for a moment longer. "How old are you, kid?"

"I am nearly seventeen."

"Sixteen, huh? I'd never have guessed."

"Oh. Thank you," said George proudly, though there was an edge to Silenus's intonation that made him wonder if the comment was entirely genuine.

Silenus took the flask back and had a swig that absolutely dwarfed George's sip. Judging by his red eyes, it was the last in a long line. "They say it's not for the young, but they also say it's not for the old, and look at me. It's the only thing that keeps me percolating sometimes, I swear to whatever god you fucking like, so what do they know." He stared out the window. The car rattled and clanked as the train cut a new swath through the countryside, and the lights darkened a little. "Ah, well. Busy day, eh, George? What would you call it? A win? A defeat? A stalemate?"

"I'm not sure, sir. To be honest, I . . . don't really know what's going on at all."

"Don't call me sir, kid. Call me Harry. And you're not alone in the not-knowing game. Most days we're all playing. But one thing I'm keen to know, George, is why the hell you were backstage in the first place."

"What do you mean?" asked George.

"I mean, why did some kid feel the need to sneak backstage and warn me about what was waiting for us?" asked Silenus. "I don't know if I have a guardian angel, but if I do and he sent you, then he's missed a lot of fucking opportunities."

George thought about what to say. "I just...heard those men in the hotel talking about you, and I knew I had to help," he said. He was not quite sure why he was lying; mostly it was because he did not yet know what this man was, and he found he feared the answer.

Silenus watched him shrewdly. "Just knew you had to help? Out of the goodness of your heart?"

George felt sure that Silenus could sense his lie, but he drummed up his pride. "Well, yes. Is that so strange to you?"

Silenus grunted and took another sip from his flask. "Very," he said. "Especially since it's gotten you into such a heap of shit, hasn't it?" Then he drifted off into thought.

George wondered what to say next, and found he had so many questions he was not sure which one would get out of him first. He wanted to know about the men in gray, and the song, and most of all he wanted to know about Silenus and his mother, and why he'd chosen her and she him and why he'd never returned. But now that George had the opportunity, all his confidence vanished. Silenus did not seem like a family man in any way. He did not appear eager for a son, and the idea that he might have one emerging from his long-forgotten past had certainly not occurred to him yet.

George was not even sure if Silenus remembered his mother at all. So rather than asking any of the questions he really wanted to ask, he said, "Do you mind if I ask you something, sir?"

"I mind very much, but I'll tolerate it," Silenus said.

George looked at Stanley, who was watching him. "Is it all right if he's here?"

"Stan is completely trustworthy," said Silenus. "I'd be lost without him. Anything I hear, Stanley can hear." As if to corroborate his faith, Stanley nodded with a mild smile.

"There was a show you put on in a little town to the south of here," said George. "A very small town, just a couple of months ago. I just wanted to know...if you'd ever been there before then. For an earlier show. "

"What was the name of this place?"

"Rinton," said George.

Silenus gave him a puzzled look and lifted his eyes to ponder the question. "Rinton?" he said, as if the word was foreign to him.

And there was something in the way he echoed the name that drove all hope from George's heart. He realized Silenus did not remember anything about George's hometown, not even his most recent visit, so he almost certainly did not recall his mother or anything that had lead to George's conception. Their relationship must have been forgettable and trivial, and George's creation incidental.

Silenus pursed his lips and shook his head. "No, I can't recall. I don't remember any time before that. But the names of these towns kind of blend together in your head after a while. You got anything, Stan?"

Stanley was staring at George curiously, but he only shrugged.

"Oh," said George. He hoped his face did not show how crushed he felt. "All right."

"Is that all you wanted to ask me, kid?" said Silenus.

"Yes," said George faintly.

Silenus shook his head and chuckled. "That's your only question? You're an odd one, I'll say that. There's a lot about you I find confounding, but the one thing that really gets me is that...well, you were awake. You, some fucking kid backstage, stayed awake throughout the whole of the fourth act, or so it seems. Do you know what that means? Or what the fourth act even is?"

"No," said George. "Not really. It...changes things, doesn't it?"

Silenus weighed whether or not he should answer. "Maybe. In a way."

"It makes something reach in, into the theater, and then...I don't know what. But I heard that song before, and felt it change things then, too."

"In Rinton?" said Silenus. "That was the first time you heard it?"

George was quiet as he thought. Then he said, "No. No, I missed your show in Rinton."

"Then you saw us before Rinton?"

"No," said George. "Tonight was the first time I saw you. But it wasn't the first time I heard the song you played."

Stanley and Silenus both sat forward. Their eyes were fixed on George, searching every part of him, and Silenus hardly noticed that the ash from his cheap cigar was threatening to fall upon his lapel. "Do tell," he said.

"I didn't remember it at first," said George. "I never even knew it'd happened. Then just tonight, when I heard your chorale, it…it woke something up in me. Something recognized the song that you played. I remembered what had happened, a little. But what it means is beyond me."

"Then please be so kind as to remember it again, kid," said Silenus. "I'd like to hear this."

George nervously glanced at Stanley again.

"I already told you Stan is safe," said Silenus impatiently. "Now go on, kid. Tell us. Tell us about the song you heard."

The train car rattled around them, and the lamps flickered. George waited for them to return, then took a deep breath and began to speak.

It had taken place when George had just entered the second grade, and like most of George's beginnings with anything this one had been a fair disaster. On his first day he'd managed to exasperate his teacher and irritate his fellow students, chief among them Benny Russell, a squat boulder of a child who'd somehow taken a comment of George's out of context and assumed that George was ridiculing his shoes. After receiving more than his fair share of bloody noses and bruised ribs, George had begun hiding out in the old dead creeks on the north side of town after school. Benny Russell had eventually forgotten about his grudge, but by that time George had become fascinated by his hideout, turning his attention to the gulleys and the ravines, the sides of each one layered and lined like crumpled silk, with strange, earthy treasures peeking from their many creases.

George found old tin cans, ancient signs, lumps of quartz, and roots grown into strange shapes and patterns. These he especially prized, since many of them seemed to have grown into the shapes of masks or faces, with malformed eyes and bulging pig snouts. He used a roll of twine to tie the root-faces to sticks, and set them along the ravines to ward away spirits and enemies, or at the very least Benny Russell.

He passed that summer like the overseer of a quarry, making detailed plans that accomplished little but were discussed in important tones with many invisible assistants. Sometimes he shifted his hoard of tin cans with his stockpile of iron stakes, pretending that the cans were coveted by an enemy that would love to catch him unawares. On these days he'd move his army of root-faces, lining them up to stare down his assailants and prevent a new attack.

It was the day after moving one squadron of root-faces that George returned to find something had changed. When he approached his miniature army, he stopped short and barely managed to stifle a cry of surprise.

He looked his wards over. He wasn't seeing wrong: though he'd very definitely left them facing out of the creek in different directions toward the Allsten fields, they were now all facing in, and seemed to focus upon one point in the woods, like they had all witnessed some strange event and were still gaping at it.

George, suspecting meddling, began circling through his kingdom, looking for marks of disturbance, but he could find none. He arranged the root-faces differently, not moving them far but making it clear that they were his, and daring whatever saboteur it'd been to try again.

When he returned the next day he found that the root-faces had turned again, all of them staring into the woods with their uneven eyes and twisted, slack mouths, and again they seemed to be looking at one thing in particular. George inspected each of the sticks, looking at their bases for any bent grass blades or shoe prints, but he could find none. It was as though they had all spun around of their own accord.

George turned to see what they were looking at. He walked from pole to pole, peering through their eyes, and decided that the root-faces had all been made to stare into the side of a very small hill, not more than forty yards into the woods.

George surveyed the area around the hill. He was no fool, and immediately felt it was some sort of trap, possibly set by some of his old enemies who'd finally found his hideout. He selected a stout stick, and swung it several times to feel its heft, with the additional bonus of intimidating anyone who was watching. Then he ventured toward the hill, shifting from tree to tree and looking to see if anything moved. When nothing did, he approached the hill directly, calling out, "I'm armed and I'm mad and I don't care who knows it!"

There was no answer. He looked around at his army of wards. They were silent, but seemed watchful. George wondered if he'd somehow invested them with intelligence, and they'd actually seen something.

He stopped when he came near the hill. It seemed a very old thing, a raw mass that had been shaped by slow, glacial forces, chewed by teeth of ice weighing thousands of tons. Yet there was something about its lumpy edges, or perhaps the way the wet, black stones peeked from beneath its bright green grass, that made him feel as if it had been constructed around a point, perhaps to conceal some object below. Then he noticed that there was a very small path that ran up the side and almost split the knoll in half.

He walked to the mouth of the path and looked back, and saw his dozens of root-faces staring at him. Perhaps it was the way they were situated on the outskirts of the forest, but it almost felt like the very landscape was arranged around this spot as well. Maybe the rocks and the trees and the streams themselves were also watching the mouth of this path, their attention magnetically drawn here, if they had any attention to give.

George felt the fleeting instinct to turn and run. But he did not, and instead walked up the path to the top of the hill.

He found that the hill was actually hollow, and there was a small, shady dell set in the middle, the edge ringed with holly trees. He began to follow the path down and discovered that the center was very moist and the earth very soft, perhaps fed by an underground stream. The center was deeper than he'd expected, as though the dell was actually below the rest of the earth, but he forgot about this when he heard a sound: a soft moaning, like the wind dragging over some hard aperture, though it was not unpleasant. It was almost like a chime, faint and atonal. He listened to it grow and fade, and climbed the rest of the way down into the dell in search of its source.

In the center of the dell the skies seemed gray and the air wet and cold. The black granite that had peeked out from under the tussocks on the outside were bare and exposed here, the loamy flesh of the knoll scraped away to reveal its bones. Yet though this place should have felt strange and frightening, it did not: it felt calm and peaceful here, like the chaotic comings and goings of the world outside could never pierce the skin of this place. Star lilies grew from the wet gravel in the bottom of the dell, and in some places there was a blue-fringed moss that almost seemed to glow. It felt, in some way, eternal.

George heard the soft moan again. It seemed as though the sky shivered with it, and he realized the moan now sounded like someone singing.

There was a crevice in between two of the black stones, and George guessed the sound was coming from between them. He went to the stones and peered through the large crack, and there the song seemed louder, like a low, breathy hum.

He squinted and saw there was something on the wall of the crevice. It looked, he thought, almost like a squiggle of light wriggling across the stone, like light reflected off a nearby brook. George saw no water, nor any light to reflect off of it, yet there the little glow remained, a faint, miniature lightning bolt that jiggled and danced in the dark.

Curious, George reached out to touch it. As his fingers grew close, the small vein of light slowed its dance, as if it could sense his fingertips, and almost seemed to wait for him.

When his fingertips were mere millimeters away, George began to feel an immense pressure pushing in on him from every side. It built until it was as if he were submerged under thousands of pounds of cold iron, pushing him down and smashing him against the earth. If he could have opened his mouth to scream, he would have, but the weight was so immense that he could not even blink. And yet his finger kept moving toward the little light, drawn in like a stone tumbling down a cliff side.

Then he heard it: a voice, or perhaps many voices, even millions of them, droning very low with a deep bass note pulsing, and some of the voices switched and found some higher register, while others swiveled through their ranges to reach notes that his ears could barely understand. And somehow George knew that these voices were doing more than singing, that for each second they sustained a note they were pushing and pulling at something, teasing at enormous things he could not see...

Then his finger made contact, and the voices rose to a loud shout. The squiggle of light flashed bright, and he felt as if the sky opened up and something rushed into him, like he had swallowed the seas and the stars and the shadows themselves, and he was certain he would split down the sides. The little vein of light pulled him closer and closer until it seemed to finally swallow him, and the world went blessedly silent and dark.

When George awoke later, curled up in a hollow in one of the dead creeks, he felt as though he'd had the best sleep of his life. He remembered his strange dream of the hill and the singing voices in the dell, but once he cleared the sleep from his eyes he saw that the root-faces were not actually facing in one direction at all, and the hill was little more than a mound of dirt. When he walked to it he found it solid through and through. He walked away, feeling slightly loopy, wondering what the dream had been about. And the rest of that strange summer afternoon he dismissed, and eventually forgot entirely.

When he finished his story, Stanley and Silenus stayed utterly still. The ash of Silenus's cigar had finally followed through on its threat and was now streaked down his lapel. Then he took the cigar out of his mouth and said, "That's all you remember? You left nothing out?"

"I don't think so," said George. "But even though I heard it only for a moment in that hill, I know it was the same as the one you played in your fourth act."

"Hm." Silenus stared back out the window. "I'll have to think on this for a while."

"Do you know what happened?" said George. "Or what it was?"

"What did I just tell you?" snapped Silenus. "Let me think."

George fell quiet, abashed. Silenus turned to look at Stanley, whose face was fixed in a look of confused dread, and they seemed to share some silent communication. Silenus bowed his head, thinking. Then he looked up and stared into George's face. He shifted his head from side to side, as if trying to see George in a better light. Finally he asked, "And you say you're from Ohio?"

"Yes?"

"You're sure? You're positive you're from here?"

"Well…yes. I'm pretty sure. I certainly don't remember being from anywhere else."

"Hm," said Silenus. Then he shook his head, as if disappointed. "It's the oddest fucking thing…"

"What is?"

"Never mind. I'm going to make a proposition to you, kid. I can answer your questions for you, but I'm going to need some time. Three weeks, in fact."

"Three weeks!" said George. "You can't answer those questions for three weeks?"

"Unfortunately, yes. It'll take me a bit to figure all this out."

"Why? What's wrong?"

"Too much for me to be willing to answer without reservations," said Silenus. He scratched the side of his head, putting his top hat on a tilt, and sighed.

"What am I supposed to do until then?" said George.

"Come with us," said Silenus. "We have three theaters we're hitting in those three weeks. Come with us, help us load and unload, do whatever needs doing, and most of all, stay close and stay safe. I'll compensate you for your time."

"How much?" said George.

"How much? I don't know... I'll kick in for your food, and your lodgings, and—"

"I was getting forty a week at my position before," said George.

"Forty a week!" cried Silenus. "Christ, kid, I'm not made of money! I can't afford to pay some kid forty a week!"

"But I'm not just some kid. You won't tell me what I am, but apparently I'm important to you."

Silenus glared at him, but said, "Twenty."

"Twenty? That's pocket change! I wouldn't consider less than thirty! I could be making twice that performing, if I wanted to. I'm in very high demand, you know."

"Oh, is that so?" said Silenus.

"I am a classically trained pianist," said George loftily.

"Jesus," said Silenus. "High demand, he says. Classically trained pianist, he says. *Pocket change*, he says. I weep for the coming generations."

"I saved your life," said George.

"And I saved yours," said Silenus, his voice a low purr. "You don't have any idea what's looking for you, but I do. You're in worse trouble than you could ever know, kid."

George considered it, and reflected that he did not want to know what Kingsley had seen in that street, the mere sight of which seemed to have aged or wounded him in some invisible manner. "Fine, then," he said. "Twenty a week."

Silenus stuck his hand out, and the two of them shook. "Now listen closely: there will be times in those three weeks when Stanley and I will have to leave you and the group," he said. "You will not come with us, nor will you ask any questions about our absence. In those instances you will stay with the group and do whatever Colette says to do. But in all others you stick close to me or Stanley, and do not wander off and talk to strangers."

"Fine," said George.

"And whatever happens," said Silenus, "if you ever hear that… that silence you heard outside the hotel again, you drop whatever it is you're doing and get me straightaway."

"I understand," said George. "Can I ask you a question, Harry?"

"I suppose."

George thought about it, and asked, "What are you, exactly?"

"What am I?"

"Yes. You're not a performer, or just a performer. I've seen vaude-villians do a lot of things before, but I've never seen one pull reflections off glass. So what are you?"

Silenus smirked, sat back in his seat, and pulled his hat down over his eyes. "You're wrong, kid. I am just a performer. I'm just putting on a show you haven't seen before."

CHAPTER 7

Colette de Verdicere of the Zahand Dynasty, Princess of the Kush Steppes

George had been told by many vaudevillians that when traveling the circuits one town soon begins to resemble another. The only thing that mattered, they said, was where the hotel, theater, and train station were. He found they'd been right, as Silenus immediately asked the conductor for directions to the hotel and theater, and nothing more. Then they all trooped off toward the hotel, groggy and mussed from their cramped berths.

George detected no unnatural silence there, so presumably the men in gray had not tracked them, and they all piled in while Silenus grudgingly paid the owner. Then they went upstairs to a darkened hallway, and Silenus slowly walked ahead while the others waited behind. George asked what they were waiting for and was promptly shushed by Colette.

He watched as Silenus walked from one room door to the next, examining them. He studied the first door on the left, and then went across to the one on the right, and then having studied that he walked across again to the next door on the left. But somewhere in this pattern he backtracked and returned to the door on the right...yet now

George saw it was not exactly the same door. He did not think that the previous door or indeed any other door in the hotel featured such black, shiny wood, or such a reddish-gold, intricately engraved handle, or such a ferocious series of locks on one side. And while George marveled at it, he realized that the door was awkwardly placed between two of the plainer ones; in fact, it seemed to have appeared in the middle of the wall between them when he had not been looking.

Silenus took a massive ring of keys out of his pocket and went about the laborious task of unlocking each of the locks. In some instances the keys had to be turned several times; in others Silenus only had to breathe on the locks to get them to open. But eventually the huge black door creaked open, and Silenus said, "All right, come and get your things."

The troupe walked in, and the room inside was far more ornate than anything George had expected. It was more of an office than a hotel room, with a huge medieval-looking desk taking up most of the floor space. There was a bay window at the back behind the desk, though nothing was visible through its panes except some scattered stars shining a very cold light. Cabinets and closets covered every inch of the walls, some sporting nearly as many locks as the office door. An upright clock ticked against the wall, and an extremely large black steamer trunk stood next to it. On the floor was a pile of luggage, and Silenus sat down behind the desk and relit his cigar while the rest of the troupe fell upon the pile, claiming bags and trunks and prop boxes.

"I thought you all left your luggage behind at the hotel in Parma," said George to Stanley.

Stanley took out his blackboard and wrote: WE DID.

"Then what's it doing in this room?"

He thought and wrote: WE LEFT IT IN THIS ROOM, WHICH WAS ALSO IN THE HOTEL IN PARMA.

George was too confused by that to say anything, and Stanley tipped his hat and began to find his own bags.

"It's best not to ask questions when you don't need to know the answer," said Colette.

"I didn't mean to offend," said George.

"You didn't. Stanley is impossible to offend. But let me tell you the real Golden Rule here, George—it's not 'Do unto others,' but 'Mind your own business.'"

"I see," said George. "Is this the procedure for every traveling troupe?"

"Beats me," she said. "This is the first one I've ever been with."

George was disheartened to hear his questions could cause any resentment. "Cheer up," said Colette, who seemed elevated by the promise of a bed. She punched him in the arm, and it was surprisingly painful. "It's better than being on the streets." Then she followed the others down the hall.

George looked back at Silenus, who was turned toward the bay window. "If I were you," he said, "I would not mention to her that you're getting paid. Our budget is slim enough as it is."

"How much did it cost to rent this room?" George asked.

"But she is still right, of course," said Silenus, ignoring him. "I'd mind your own business first and foremost." He stretched his short legs up to lean them on the bottom of the bay window. Then he kicked off his shoes and, with dexterous, monkeyish toes, removed his socks. As they fell to the floor George saw his feet were discolored: the soles were burned a sooty black, as if the man had once walked across miles of hot coals.

"Something else on your mind, kid?" said Silenus.

"I suppose not," said George.

"Then run along and get some sleep. You're in room eight." He tossed a key over his shoulder, which bounced off of George's leg. George scooped it up, threw one last glance over his shoulder at Silenus and his burned feet, and went out into the hallway. The door swung shut behind him, though he saw no one move to close it.

George's room was next to Kingsley's, whose door was shut. He could hear Kingsley speaking to someone inside, though he could not understand the words. George opened the door to his own room, which was small and bare except for a bed and a washstand, and he set down his suitcase and lay upon the bed.

He was extremely tired. He had not slept properly since he'd left Freightly. His eyes soon grew heavy, yet as they began to close he heard a conversation in the next room, which was now easy to hear from his bed.

"...And will we be out of the dark then, Father?" said a deep, Cockney voice.

"I don't know," said Kingsley's voice. "I would like you to be, but I don't know."

"Why not?" said a second, this one with a New York accent. "Why don't you know? You should know, that's what fathers do. They know things."

"Yes, but I don't," said Kingsley. "I don't know."

"It will just take more, won't it," said a Southern, feminine voice. "It will simply take more."

There was a long silence. Then Kingsley's voice said, "Perhaps. Yes."

George waited to hear more, but before he could he fell asleep.

George must have been exhausted, because he slept for the better part of the next day. He woke well into the afternoon, and after cleaning up he stumbled down the hallway to try to find Silenus and ask him what he was meant to do today. Yet Silenus's room was nowhere to be found: the wall continued uninterrupted between rooms six and eight, where the black door had stood.

He went downstairs to find Colette in the hotel restaurant, half of which was a billiards hall. She was wearing a rather workmanlike green dress with short sleeves, and was lining up a shot on a billiards table when George walked in. "I almost thought," she said, and took the shot, "that you were dead." She stood up, spun the pool cue, and watched the consequences of her shot. She nodded in satisfaction and said, "I wondered if I'd need to come up to make sure you were breathing."

"Where's Harry?" said George. "What happened to his door?"

"It'll be there when it needs to be there," she said. She paced around the table, head cocked as she considered another shot. "Harry himself is out with Stanley. Until they're back, you're to stay within my sight, and not do a thing." She leaned against the table in a decidedly unladylike way and fired off another shot.

George sat down next to the table. "Where did they go?"

"Asking a question like that definitely counts as doing a thing," said Colette. "Which you're not supposed to do." She lined up a shot, and grinned up at him along the pool cue. "Frustrating, isn't it?"

"Well, yes."

"That's what it's like, working for him," she said. "It's like trying to play pool in the dark, with someone describing how all the balls are laid out to you." She shook her head, rejecting the angle of her shot, and resumed pacing around the pool table. George was reminded of a very pleased cat circling a treed squirrel. "Today is Sunday, so it's our off day. We have rehearsal at the theater in the morning. The professor's in his room recuperating, and Franny's off doing whatever it is Franny does. But you and me, we're staying right here. If you want some lunch, there's money in my bag over there."

"How is the breakfast here?" said George.

"Terrible," said Colette. "Get used to that. All hotel food is terrible." The waiter, who was nearby, heard her and scowled.

George bought an egg sandwich that was the color and consistency of sand and watched as Colette played billiards. She did not speak much, but stayed supremely focused on her game. After a while he began to detect a sort of savagery to the way she played: it was as if when she struck the balls she did not wish to knock them into a pocket, but to make them explode. Any pockets she happened to make were a bonus. George was thankful for her extreme focus; she didn't notice how wide his eyes grew when she draped herself over the pool table, her dark, downy arms wrapping around the pool cue, triceps undulating and snapping taut as she made her shot. She did once ask if he thought it was hot in here, as he was sweating very slightly, and George coughed and muttered something about how he was reacting badly to the sandwich, which he immediately regretted.

Colette played billiards for several hours while George watched. She seemed years older and worlds more confident than he was. He hoped to impress her by discussing Wagner, about whom he'd just read several fashionable articles, and even though George had never heard or seen any of the man's operas he felt sure he'd be a fan. But Colette only responded with a shrug, grunt, or nod. George wished he'd worn his tweed coat; he thought it made him look very mature, and perhaps then this girl, who had so enchanted him last night, would pay a little attention to him.

Yet the girl playing billiards was very different from his idea of the girl in white and diamonds. He'd never seen a woman smoke cheroots at all, let alone with such ferocity, nor drink beer in such quantities, nor play billiards with such skill. After a while he asked her where she was from in Persia. She looked at him for a moment, and said, "Oh, Tehran."

"Where's that?"

"It's on the outskirts of Persia, on the coast. Where the Caspian Sea meets the Mediterranean. There's a lot of shipping there. But it's not Persia anymore."

"It's not?"

"Nope. Now it's the Otterman Empire. It's huge. It goes all the way up into Europe. It almost touches Germany."

"Were the Ottermans the ones who threw your family out?" he asked.

She took a thunderous shot, which went awry. It was her first missed shot in some time. "Something like that."

"It sounds marvelous," said George.

Colette gave him a thin smile, and reracked the balls.

She continued playing without interruption as afternoon wore on. Then several local men entered. They saw her pacing around the table and furrowed their brows, and went and spoke to the hotel owner. The owner quickly came over and angrily told her, "We can't have you playing here!"

Colette looked at him and the men watching her. "Why not?" she demanded, yet now her accent had changed in a way George could not identify.

"We don't allow coloreds in here!" said the owner. "I can't believe the front boy even let you stay! How could I not have noticed you? Get your things and get out, right now!"

Colette drew herself up to her full regal height. "Zis is an outrage!" she said in an almost unintelligible French accent. "I am not a colored! I am Persian!"

The owner and the men grew confused at that. "A what?"

"I am a Persian!" she said. "And I am no girl for you to orders about! I am Colette de Verdicere of ze Zahand Dynasty, Princess of the Kush Steppes and third removed from ze rightful trone!" She took out an ornate amulet that was chained around her neck and thrust it in his face. "I am no simpleton for you to boss around! I come to zeese shores of my own accord, and you should be tanking me for every breath I draw in your shabby leetle 'otel!"

Then she turned to George and, with the demeanor of someone airing a lot of grievances to a confidante, rattled off a long string of angry French at him. George did not know a word of French, but the end of her speech had the inflection of a question. He looked at her, then the hotel owner, then the men who had complained, and then back to her, and offered a tentative, "Oui."

"Exactly!" cried Colette.

The owner muttered something about the vagueness of hotel policy when it came to Persians. He looked to the men who'd complained, but they merely shrugged.

"Are you saying you are willing to turn away royalty?" said Colette. "Is zat honestly what you are telling me?"

One of the men stepped forward. "I'm sorry, miss, we . . . Well, we didn't understand. We don't get too many foreign types in here. It would be a terrible thing to turn down the custom of a foreigner on account of a mistake."

"A royal foreigner, at that," said one of the others, and they all nodded.

"We just have a policy in this hotel that we don't allow coloreds in," said the spokesman for the group. "That's all. It was an honest mistake."

Colette gave them a cold look. "Well, I suppose I may forgive zis one time . . ."

"Well, we would thank you for that, really," said the spokesman.

"Zo I do have one request of you."

"What would that be?"

She gestured to the billiards table. "I have seen zis game played before here, but I have never been taught, nor have I had ze opportunity to learn. I am very fascinated by it. Would one of you be able to teach me?"

The spokesman beamed at her. "Why, certainly. We'd love to show you."

The group of men then huddled around the table and began to teach Colette the game she had been expertly playing for the last four hours, only now she was jittery, awkward, and woefully inaccurate. She laughed and put her hand to her brow each time she made a mistake, often with a breathy, "*Zut alors!*" and the men would all smile and shake their heads and tell her it was no issue; it was, after all, a very difficult game for a lady, requiring a balance and physicality not often found in her sex. When evening came on they ordered a round of drinks for themselves and the Princess Verdicere.

George was not sure what was going on, but he stayed silent. Yet eventually he saw that the men behaved differently around Colette.

It was in how they looked her up and down when she made a shot, or how they placed a hand on her back when explaining her errors, their fingers lingering below her shoulder blades just a little too long. George became so agitated by this behavior that he almost didn't notice that they'd begun playing for money, and Colette had accumulated quite the payload.

At the end of the evening Colette sang the men a song in French, and sent them out the door with a royal hand-wave, blowing kisses in response to inebriated cries of, "Goodbye, Princess!" When they were gone she smiled after them for a bit, and turned to George and delicately said (in an American accent), "I will be right back," and walked out the back door.

George waited for several minutes before going out to check on her. He found her leaning up against the wall with one hand, a small puddle of vomit on the ground before her feet. She spat repeatedly and wiped at her mouth, then stuck her finger down her throat and gagged. Nothing came up. "Fucking hicks," she said.

"Goodness!" said George. "Are you ill?"

"No," she said. "I did this to myself. Those bastards put a lot of booze in me, and I didn't want it screwing me up any more than it already had. It was stupid of me to accept. I'd already had plenty to drink."

"Well, why did you say yes, then?"

"I don't know. I guess out of spite." She stood up and wobbled a bit. As she regained her legs, thunder muttered somewhere up in the sky and a few fat drops of rain splashed against the hotel. "Oh, great," she said. She sat down on the back step and put her head down on the tops of her knees. "I guess it's my own fault. Thank you for pretending you know French."

George sat down next to her. "Pretending? What makes you think I don't know French? Maybe I understood everything you said."

Though she did not lift her head, he could discern a bright, hard look in the corner of her visible eye. "People who know French," she said, "generally do not look so dumbfounded when it is spoken to them."

"Oh," he said. "Was it so obvious?"

"Your mouth could have caught flies, it was so open. You were lucky they were fools."

"Are you really from Persia?" he asked.

She was still for a very long time. For a moment he wondered if she'd really heard him. But then, in a very small voice, she said, "Yes," but he thought he heard a note of fear somewhere in that word, and he thought it strange; while the girl in white and diamonds and the fearsome pool player seemed like very different people, he could not imagine either of them afraid of anything.

George wondered how best to relieve her depression. "Do you ever miss it?" he asked.

She rolled her head to the side and looked at him. "Do I what?"

"Miss Persia. Your home?"

"Oh." She thought about it. "Yes. All the time." And then, after more thinking: "No. Actually, I don't."

"You don't?"

"No. Do you ever miss wherever the hell it is you came from, George?"

He considered it. He had not thought of Rinton in some time. It felt like years since he'd left his grandmother's house in the dead of night to catch a train. Sometimes he missed her embrace, and her cooking, and the whisper of her rocker on the porch; but then he remembered the furious boom of her voice, and the way she'd go into hysterics whenever he thought of disobeying her, and especially how she'd refused to ever discuss the subject of his father. He would still be there, he thought, if she had not let her anger overwhelm herself the day after the Silenus Troupe left Rinton, and spat after their departing train. And that had been the one act George had been waiting for, the gesture that would give him a clue to who his father really was, and once he had it he'd seized upon it and dogged her with questions from morning till night, until finally she could stand it no more. She'd led him down into the basement, where she'd produced the piece of newspaper with a smudged photo of Silenus on it, and she'd pointed at it in the dark and said, "There. There."

How that face had haunted his dreams for so many nights... And how he'd clung to the theater bill he'd stolen from that gutter back home... And now he had found him, the man who he'd once thought would fill all the empty places in his heart. But now George was no longer so sure.

"Yes," he said. "And no." He nodded, seeing her point.

"Yeah," she said. "Sometimes I feel like I miss my home. But then I remember I'm not really remembering it right. I'm better off here, with Harry."

"You don't ever want to go back?" he asked.

"There's never any going back." She picked her head up and stared out at the rain. "God, I hate the sticks. And the sticks is all we ever seem to work. We never hit the big time, never try and get in close to the cities. Not unless we have to. You've heard of the Palace, haven't you, George?"

"In New York? I've read about it, certainly." The Palace Theater was the epicenter of all of vaudeville, owned by Benjamin Franklin Keith himself, the founder of the Keith-Albee circuit. To traveling vaudevillians, both big- and small-time, crossing those boards was the equivalent of transcending the Earth to take their place among the constellations.

"Yeah," said Colette. "I saw it, once, you know." She looked at him, and George could tell he was meant to be impressed.

"Did you?" he said.

"Yeah. One of the few times we got to go to New York. I went all the way downtown to do nothing more than see it. It's a weird building. It's tall and thin, which I didn't expect. I didn't get to go in, because I didn't have the money. All I got to see was the damn outside. But I knew that was where I should be. In there, on that stage.

Not out here, in the sticks. With a bunch of rubes drinking moonshine and playing billiards."

"Well, I'm sure it's just a matter of hard work and knowing the right people," George said knowledgeably.

Colette gave him a piercing look. "And are you suggesting," she said, "that I haven't been working hard?"

"No!" said George. "Well, I'm sure I can't say. Sometimes these things just take time, you see."

"And what do you know about time?" she asked. "How long have you even been in the business?"

George reddened. "I have been a very distinguished house pianist for over seven months," he said with all the pride he could muster.

Colette stared at him. Then she burst out laughing. "Oh, God," she said. "For a moment there I was almost offended!"

"I don't find anything particularly funny," said George. "How long have *you* been in the business?"

"Four years," said Colette. "Since I was your age, I guess."

"Well, that's hardly any longer." He very much wished he were wearing his tweed now. He felt sure this would have gone differently then.

Still laughing, she shook her head, but seemed to catch something out of the side of her eye. "Who's that?"

"Who's who?" said George. Then a bright spiderweb of lightning arched across the sky and he saw two figures making their way down the street carrying an enormous trunk between them. When they got near he saw it was Stanley and Silenus, and they were hurrying as fast as they could through the mud.

"Get that door open!" shouted Silenus as they approached.

George stood up and shoved open the back door. Silenus and Stanley charged up and fell through, gasping and heaving their steamer trunk forward. George noted its deep black wood and recognized it as the one from the office upstairs.

"Why were you carrying that out in the town?" he said.

"Because I need the exercise," snapped Silenus. Though the two men seemed exhausted, they did not drop the box once they were inside; they lowered it gently, and Silenus kept his head tilted as if listening for the sound of anything breaking. When none came, he let out a great sigh of relief.

"Did you find what you were looking for?" said Colette.

"You don't ask about my private matters," said Silenus, "and I won't ask about yours."

"But these matters don't seem particularly private." She eyed their spreading puddle of water, which had grown enough to kiss the toes of her shoes.

Silenus gave her a glare and stomped up the stairs, dripping water all the way. Colette sighed and followed, making sure to step around the muddy footprints.

"Are you all right?" George asked Stanley.

He nodded and sat in a nearby chair. Rather than angry, Stanley appeared incredibly fatigued, and he sat bent in his chair as though he'd strained his back.

"What happened?" said George.

Stanley seemed to debate answering him, and shrugged and took out the blackboard and wrote: WE FOUND SOMETHING, BUT IT WAS NOT WHAT WE WANTED TO FIND.

George considered asking him what that meant, but knew he would not get an answer. He saw that the trunk featured nearly as many locks as Silenus's door, and had been polished to a fine shine; he could see his own face within its wood, staring back at him uncertainly. He reached out to touch it.

But before he did, Stanley cleared his throat and wrote: HELP ME GET THIS UPSTAIRS? And his face was so drawn and tired that George could not say no to it.

CHAPTER 8

The First Rehearsal

When it came time to begin rehearsals the next day, George hardly had a chance to get his bearings. He was awoken in the morning by a pounding on his room door. He opened it to find Colette standing in the hall with three heavy bags in her hands, which she immediately tossed to him with no more than the words, "Time to get going. Get these to the theater."

"What?" said George. "I'm supposed to *carry* these?"

"If you know a better way to get them there, be my guest," said Colette.

George, grumbling, heaved them into his arms. He'd been exempt from most manual labor at Otterman's, and he'd expected the same treatment from his father's troupe. But when he thought to complain he was met with Colette's bright green eyes, and he instead found himself working all the harder.

From the morning on it was pure chaos. George spent most of the day running: he ran back and forth from the theater to the hotel fetching luggage and props that hadn't been sent ahead; he ran throughout the backstage fetching music and rosin, and chalk for Franny's hands; and when he inevitably made an error in all of these arrangements he had to run even faster to correct it before Silenus or Colette discovered.

The only time he really got in a hot spot was when he was late getting to the stage to help them arrange Kingsley's backdrop. "Are we interfering with your dinner plans, Your Highness?" shouted Silenus from a balcony when he finally arrived.

"I came as fast as I could!" George called back. At first he couldn't see what he was needed for — the backdrop was simply a large roll of paper that had to be maneuvered into place above the stage — but when he took his end of the rope to haul it up he found that the thing was shockingly heavy.

After they'd gotten it hung, Silenus pulled the backdrop down to make sure it'd traveled unscathed. George was startled to see that it was completely blank. The painting of the eerie, dilapidated farmhouse had vanished. But this did not trouble Silenus, who nodded and said, "Good. We'll rehearse with it down and roll it up later."

"But it's blank!" said George.

"So?"

"Isn't there supposed to be something there?"

"Don't worry about that," said Silenus as he moved on to the next task. "That'll be taken care of."

George cast a concerned look at the backdrop as they went backstage. The curious painting of the farmhouse had made a strong impression on him, and he had wanted to see it again.

His concerns regarding the backdrop only increased later, but not in the way he expected. When he had to run out and fetch Colette some aspirin, he dashed back into the theater and headed for her dressing room, but stopped when he saw the preparations on the stage. The backdrop was still hanging up, but it was no longer blank: the painting of the blue-and-gray farmhouse had returned, and once more the stage was lit by the strange moonlight from its large window. Yet in the lower right pane of the window the painting now showed a boy's face peeping in and smiling, and unless he was imagining things the boy looked much like George himself, with a pug nose, a large chin, and a pronounced brow. George got the overpowering impression that the boy in the window was watching him. He was greatly unnerved by this, and fled backstage to tell Silenus.

Silenus snorted when he heard George's story. "Cheeky fucking thing," he said. "Don't pay attention to it. It was just funning with you."

But as to how a common canvas backdrop could mock someone in the audience, he did not say, and when George next saw the backdrop it was blank again.

The troupe members themselves were just as strange. For one thing, Franny was treated as though she was another prop, despite being one of the most effective performers. "Go and move Franny over there," was a common order Silenus gave when arranging the stage. And Franny often seemed to behave like one. She was perfectly compliant with anyone's requests, but when she had nothing to do she did literally nothing at all. She would place a small chair in the corner out of everyone's way, sit on it, and stare into the wall. Only once, when George was speeding by her, did she do anything: she whispered, "Hello, Bill."

"I'm George," he said.

"Oh, yes," she said, smiling. "Of course you are."

Professor Kingsley Tyburn was far less amenable. He acted as though moving his puppets out onto the stage were a terrible last resort, and preferred to hole up with them in his dressing room, sitting beside the little coffin-like boxes and reading aloud from *Madison's Budget* (a dependable joke source for small comedy acts) or a Bible, for he was a very religious man. George dreaded carrying any messages to him, as Kingsley would berate him to no end for the disruption, but more than that he found Kingsley's boxes and his relationship with them disturbing. He once glanced into Kingsley's dressing room to see the man sprawled out facedown with his arms over the boxes, and he might have been weeping. On that occasion

George said nothing, but continued on in his labors with a shiver. Yet later when he'd been sent to ask Kingsley's opinion on a change in his act's music George found his dressing room dark and seemingly empty. He called Kingsley's name. There was no answer from within, but then he heard footsteps from the far back, and a door closing. Due to the darkness of the room he could not see who it was.

He called again, yet still no one responded, so he walked in and laid a hand on the lamp to turn on the light. But before he could, a deep, rattling voice with a twangy accent growled, *"Go away. You're not welcome here."*

George jumped in fright, and ran out as fast as he could. He ran until he found Franny, sitting on her chair and staring into the wall, and he sat next to her to catch his breath. When she asked what was the matter and he told her, all she said was, "Ah. Well, I guess the professor's right. They're getting harder to control every day."

George wished he could spend more of his time with Colette, who was now clad in the dazzling tights he'd first seen her in, yet the moment she entered the theater she became nothing but business. She encountered some difficulties with the stagehands, who, like the men from the billiards hall, mistook her for a colored, and she again had to forcibly inform them she was Persian. After she'd sent them hustling she told Kingsley he needed to cut two minutes (and nominated the bit about the puppets' being real as what needed to go), and she told Franny to move her bit with the safe on the rail to the end, since that was a much bigger finish than the statues. Franny nodded obediently, hardly paying attention, but Kingsley protested at first: that was their favorite part, he said (though he never explained who "they" were), but he eventually agreed. Colette then monitored their rehearsals, and when she ran into issues with the orchestra and the pianist George literally leaped forward to volunteer.

"Wow," she said after George played along with their act. "That was…"

George leaned forward. "That was?"

She nodded, impressed. "That was good."

"Good?" he asked. "Just good?"

"Yeah. That'll definitely work," she said, and turned to other business.

George was miffed to hear her call his playing *workable*, but he supposed any compliment from Colette was better than none at all. It was more than Silenus had given him so far, at any rate. Silenus seemed to have other business, some he deemed more important than the rehearsals. His brief appearances at the theater were always terse and impatient, as if the show was an irritating distraction and he had other places to be. He spent much of his day in his office in the hotel, though on the few occasions when his door could be found George heard no voice or noise within. Silenus claimed he was doing research, but when he emerged in the afternoon George could have sworn he saw snow on the man's shoulders, yet Alberteen had gone without snow for nearly a month.

But whatever Silenus's endeavors were that day, they seemed to be going badly. He was more and more agitated each time they saw him, and began snapping and barking at the slightest provocation. When Kingsley complained that his dressing room was too high in the theater and there was too much of a draft, Silenus shouted, "What should I do, tell the sun to fucking shine down and warm you? Build another fucking theater? Or are you asking me to scale the walls of this one here, and plug up its many faults?" Kingsley was too stunned to reply, and Silenus simply fixed him with a cold glare before stumping out.

Once more George wondered what Silenus would say if he ever heard the true reason behind George's presence. He could hardly see what his mother could have found desirable in this man.

But whenever Silenus stormed through their ranks, Stanley was always there in his wake, tending to bruised egos and patching things up. Stanley would smile, think upon it, and write down a mere handful of words that would somehow make sense of everything. After

Silenus's outburst at Kingsley, Stanley consoled him with: FOUND SOME FUR COATS IN A CLOSET UPSTAIRS. WOULD THAT HELP? To which Kingsley agreed.

Stanley seemed an eternal source of comfort for the group. There was a quiet calmness to him that was somehow infectious. George or other troupe members would sometimes just sit next to him without saying a word. It was pleasant to simply be there with him, letting the seconds slip past you. And unlike the others he almost never asked anything of George: while Kingsley, Silenus, and Colette would have orders whenever they saw him, Stanley only had an apologetic grin.

He and George also shared a similar appreciation for music. George's one peaceful moment on that first day was when he got to listen to Stanley practice the cello, whipping through scales and arpeggios with a fluid ease. He paid incredible attention to every tone and stroke of the bow, and his long, delicate fingers were able to search through the strings and find the purest pitches.

"What was that?" George asked when he finished playing one piece.

Stanley showed him the music.

"Claudio Merulo," he read. "I've never heard of him before. Will you play it tonight?"

Stanley shook his head, and wrote upon his blackboard: ONLY EVER PLAY ONE SONG.

"Yeah," said George, disappointed. Vaudeville players rarely changed their acts. Many played the exact same show for years on end. If the act worked then it worked, and doing anything different was unthinkable in the face of success.

Stanley seemed to sympathize, and was pleased to find a fan. He took out his blackboard and wrote an appreciative comment for George's audience, yet as he crossed his legs to support his writing George saw his feet were bare and his soles were burned black, just as Silenus's were. When he held up the blackboard (IT IS NICE TO HAVE

SOMEONE WHO TAKES TIME TO LISTEN), he saw George staring and quickly put his foot back down. He erased the blackboard and wrote: SOMETHING WRONG?

George swallowed. "No," he said. "I guess there isn't."

That night their first performance went off without a hitch, and for the third time George let the song in the fourth act wash over him. The memory of the hollow hill did not violently overtake him as it had before, but he still felt it rise inexorably in his mind until he could almost smell the moist earth and feel the gray light upon his neck. It seemed as if the song's stupefying nature was less and less effective on the listener the more they heard it, which would explain how the troupe themselves were not spellbound each time they performed.

When they were done they packed up and hurried back to the hotel, leaving the people sitting stunned in their seats, each one lit by the curious light and colors that seemed to mark the Chorale.

"What will happen to them?" George asked.

"You saw it from the audience before, didn't you?" Silenus said.

George admitted that he had.

"Well, what happened then?"

"They...stood up and filed out. But they seemed different. They seemed..." George struggled to avoid the word he'd thought of, as it was so trite and meaningless, but he could think of nothing else: "Happy," he finished.

Silenus nodded. "Exactly."

"So you're making people happy?"

"Why not?" said Silenus. "We're performers, ain't we?"

Their remaining shows went by without issue. George became so well versed in their acts that Colette eventually asked Silenus if they could make him a permanent fixture, as his playing was a welcome reprieve from what they usually had to contend with. Since she was in charge of their budget, she knew they had the financial room for him.

Silenus considered it. "Where'd you train, kid?" he asked.

"Nowhere," George said, a touch proudly. "I am self-taught."

Colette scoffed. "That can't be. No one gets to your level all by themselves."

"I did," George said. "I never had anyone to teach me in Rinton."

"So you just figured it out, did you?" Colette asked. "All on your lonesome?"

"Well, yes."

She rolled her eyes. "Come on, George. Be straight with us. Who'd you learn under?"

"No one," said George, coloring. "And I'm not lying!"

Before Colette could say more, Silenus raised a hand. He studied George for a moment, and said, "If he says he's self-taught, then he's self-taught. He has no reason to lie, and I see no reason to doubt him."

"What?" Colette said. "Harry, you can't possibly believe this, can you?"

"I can," said Silenus. But though it was the first positive thing his father had said about his playing, George was not comforted; there was something distant and cold in Silenus's face.

The next week they continued on to Milton and went through nearly the same routine. Almost nothing changed, except perhaps for Kingsley's health, which seemed to decline a little, though he refused all attentions. On Sunday Stanley and Silenus again disappeared with the steamer trunk and just as mysteriously returned, though they seemed more pleased than they had in Alberteen. And after that came Hayburn, where they did it all over again, though exactly what they were doing George was never told.

CHAPTER 9

A Meeting of Shepherds

It must be said now that George was not a stupid young man. On the contrary, when he was not getting in his own way he had a great aptitude for cleverness. But he was, perhaps to his own misfortune, overwhelmingly used to getting what he wanted. His grandmother had tried her hardest to keep him cloistered throughout his upbringing, and her best tools for this had been flattery and bribery. And after fleeing her grasp and following his father, George had wound up at Otterman's, where his superior skills had given him a great deal of leverage. So far in his life he'd experienced very few obstacles, and it was only natural for him to think that he *deserved* such easy treatment through some innate quality of his own.

In the third week with Silenus he began to suspect he deserved a lot of things he wasn't getting. First and foremost, he felt he deserved an explanation. Had he not risked his life for the troupe? And had he not turned his back on a lucrative and cushy career in order to join them? The least his father could do was tell him what they were *really* doing.

But Silenus did not. In the final of their three weeks, George's father became more distracted than ever, spending more and more time in his office, and seeming more and more frustrated whenever he emerged. The only time George could ever talk to him was right after their nightly performance. And though George knew better than to ask outright about the song, or his memory of the barrow, or the men in gray, he began to ask innocent questions or make leading comments that he thought just might entice some truth from Silenus.

"I hope they make it home all right," George said after one performance, gesturing to the audience. "Are they sensible enough for that?" To this, Silenus only shrugged.

"Are the acoustics of this theater too poor for the Chorale?" he asked after another. "Will it be too muffled, maybe?" This question was met with a terse order to mind his own business.

"Has anyone ever died after one of your performances?" he asked after their final performance, on Friday. "The shock seems like it might be too much for the weak of heart."

"No!" shouted Silenus. "But you just might be the first if you ask another of these goddamn questions! I told you, three weeks, and with no *rounding up*. You've got a handful of days left. Let's see if you can spend them in quiet, hmm?"

George, humiliated, looked around. The entire troupe was watching him. He flushed magnificently and muttered an apology.

That night he was so angry that he could not even sleep. He changed out of his pajamas and into some winter clothing, went downstairs, and headed out into the streets for a late-night stroll. He knew it was much too cold, and going out was rash, but he did not care.

He grumbled to himself as he kicked his way through the slushy streets of Hayburn. He had been a fool to come with them, he told himself. He had been a fool to withhold the truth about who he was, and his relation to Silenus. And he'd been a fool to take their orders and abuse without ever sticking up for himself. The more he dwelled on his problems the more poisonous and malicious they seemed.

Eventually he began to suspect that the true purpose of the Silenus Troupe was to make life very hard for one George Carole.

But then he stopped and looked up, and realized he'd gone perhaps a little too far.

He had no idea where he was. It was very dark, and there was no one out. And even though he'd been here a week, he'd done nothing to study the layout of the city.

He began to walk toward where he thought the hotel and the vaudeville house were. But as he did the night sky turned dark and bruised, promising snow. When the first flakes drifted down he groaned and began looking for shelter. Yet there seemed to be nothing open, and soon the air was thick with white.

George trotted down an alley into a surprisingly large courtyard, and looked around in vain for some cover. The snow intensified until all he could make out was a frozen fountain and a lone streetlamp in the courtyard, which turned the falling snow into a magnificent pearl of radiance. Then he noticed a shutter for a coal cellar, and in his desperation he pried it open and slipped inside to sit on the mound of coal below.

If George had been paying attention he would have thought the courtyard a very curious place: the buildings around it were very tall and the walls facing in had no windows, and the fountain in the center featured four people riding chariots. The sculpted figures faced out toward the corners of the courtyard, and their cheeks were ballooned as if blowing enormous gusts into the sky. If George had seen the fountain he'd have thought it a strange addition to this very drab and empty courtyard, but as it was he simply sat on the coal with the shutter open, waiting on the snow and cursing himself.

It was then that George's exceptional hearing again alerted him to something abnormal: from the sound of things, the snow was lessening outside until it became a slight trickle. But then, if he listened closely, the roar of the flurry seemed to still be going on somewhere around him. He poked his head through the shutter and saw that it had not stopped snowing; rather, it seemed to have stopped snowing only in the courtyard. When he looked to the four passageways leading out, he saw the snowstorm continuing just beyond. It was as though the snow stopped just where the courtyard began.

Then the wind rose and a figure appeared in the passageway, heading into the courtyard. George dropped the shutter until it was open just a crack, and peeked through.

When the figure passed through the veil of snow George saw it was a short, thick man in brown pants, a checked orange coat, a weathered cap, and a yellow silk scarf. His skin was a deep, golden brown, and his hair a dark black. He entered the courtyard and looked around languidly, and went and stood before a corner of the fountain to wait.

The wind whipped about again and a second person entered the courtyard from the next passageway. This one was a tall, thin woman with long black hair that curled into many thick ringlets. She wore a heavy seaman's coat that had been patched in many places, and a light blue skirt that trailed behind her until the hem was dirty. Her skin was pale, but it had a faint coloring to it that almost made her look gray. She stood at the next corner of the fountain and gave the man in the orange coat a somewhat cold smile, which he did not return.

Then the wind rose once more and a third person entered from the third passageway: a huge old man, broad in the shoulders and with gnarled purplish hands. The skin on his face was a translucent bluish pink, and his hair and beard were frost-white and trailed down around his waist. He was dressed in a thick brown suit, and his enormous boots thudded as he crossed the courtyard. When he came to his corner of the fountain he smiled at the others. They reluctantly nodded back.

And then the wind rose one final time, and a fourth person entered, only this one was very different from the rest. As the figure came running in out of the snow George wondered if it was a dwarf of some kind, as it seemed so small, but when it came into the light he saw it was a short, mousy girl of about eighteen, dressed all in green. Her hair was a brilliantined gold, and her cheeks were apple-red as though she'd spent hours in the sun. She had large, green eyes and a timid mouth, and she seemed very dispirited to be there. When she took her place before the fountain the other three frowned at her. The old man in particular gave her a glowering look that seemed akin to one of hate.

George thought them a curious group, on the whole. Probably the most curious thing about them was that even though they'd walked in from a powerful snowstorm, all four of them appeared perfectly dry, and not cold at all.

"Well," said the man in orange, "we are all now here. Finally," he added, and shot the girl a black look. "I should hope we would all be a little more punctual. But it is not my time to direct this meeting, so I yield its direction."

"Yes," said the old man. "To me, I believe. It is my meeting, and my possession, and I shall decide when it begins and when it ends. Or does anyone object?"

"This is your doing?" said the woman in the seaman's coat. She gestured to the sky. "It was a great inconvenience to us all. Or to me, at least. It's irritating enough to have to part with my works to attend this meeting, let alone under these conditions."

"It is my doing, yes," said the old man. "It shall be discussed, and described. So there are no objections? No objections of worth, I mean?"

"No," said the man in orange. "There are obviously no objections. Let us get started, so we can all return to what we were doing."

"Excellent," said the old man, and he motioned to the snow above. "As you can see, I have started by pulling the waters from the distant shores of the north. I have siphoned them up from around enormous ice floes. I have gathered them carefully from glittering fields of frost. I have chased and corralled them in the frozen clouds above. And then I have driven them south, threading them through mountain passes, summoning up pounding pressures when the land fell flat, letting my quarry balloon out over the countryside in a magnificent spume of white. It is an admirable storm, an absolute blizzard. It falls a little strangely, I must say — it tugs itself toward this city, as if it has its own mind. But it is no matter. It will embrace the land, gather the homes and the farmland into its folds and pull itself around them all. Roofs will groan under the weight of fresh snow. In the morning those that live here will awake to find the world completely changed. The very earth will be lost to them. No leaves, no flowers. No nasty tangles of roots or vines." At that he shot the little girl a very nasty look. She did not seem to see; she simply stared forlornly into the stone slab at her feet.

"But that is not all that I will do. Once the storm spends itself I will gather my coldest, purest, iciest streams of air. They are playful, curious things, delightful little creatures. I will set them on these lands, allowing them to bob and weave through the towns, or snake between the naked, fragile trees, or dance over the frozen rivers. They will nose out gaps in homes and coats and squirrel away inside, chilling bone and nose and ear. They have wandered for so long up north, my dear little breezes. How good it will be for them to stretch themselves out for a time! And when they come rippling and bound-ing over these hills, the snow here shall not melt. No, under their tiny, invisible feet, it shall become more and more compact, freezing the mud, the groundwater, the mightiest rivers. In a way, the storm above is but a white carpet rolled out for my dearest pets."

"Dear to you," said the woman in blue, "but not to others. To me they are vicious, nasty things, and I cannot bear the sight of them."

"That is your opinion," said the old man, "and you may speak it when it is your turn, but that is not yet."

They were silent at that. The old man glared around at them and nodded. "Well," he said. "That is all I have to say. These are the full intents of my possession."

The other three considered what he'd said.

"It is not very original," said the man in orange.

"What!" cried the old man. "It is very original!"

"I believe you loosed your pets last year, as well," said the woman in blue. "Didn't you?"

"Well, yes! But this time my breezes have been feeding themselves on the iciest currents imaginable! It will be a winter these people have never known! When they are old and trembling, they will tell their children's children of this winter! As they should. Is there anything more perfect than the blank crush of so much snow?"

"We all have our preferences," said the man in orange.

"Yes, but some are pure and perfect, and others boring," said the old man.

"You and your storms..." said the woman. She shook her head. "I have spoken before of the clean purity of a chilly, sharp breeze I can bring in from the seas, but you will never understand."

"No," said the old man. "That is weak, and boring. It is a compromise, a shadow of a true love. I dislike it greatly."

"Does that mean, Boreas," said the man in orange, "that the blizzard and the release of your breezes is the full extent of your possession?"

The old man blinked to hear his plans so glibly described. "Well. Yes."

"You are blinded by your obsessions," said the woman in blue. "How carefully I arranged everything before your possession...I remember the clouds I pushed together in the eastern seas—frigid, heavy things of thick crystals, and once they spent themselves I used their spending to send thin arms of them spiraling off to graze these countries. Leaves grew gold and fiery red upon the tree, and the frailer foliage withered. And everyone remarked at what a beautiful season it was. Now they are all gone, buried beneath foot upon foot of dull, empty ice."

"Your works were absurd," said the old man. "They were weak

and delicate. This land needed a great gust to blow all of your fool-ishness away."

"Eurus's works are her own business," said the man in orange as the woman opened her mouth to respond. "Your possession will wane soon, Boreas, as does everyone's. We all have our loves, and they are almost always lost when the possession changes hands."

"Yes, but you must admit that hers are more absurd than most, Notus," said the old man.

"Why?" said the woman in blue. "I demand an answer. I know the meeting and the possession of this season belongs to him, but he cannot simply insult at his will. I demand satisfaction."

They turned to the old man. "Well, Boreas?" said the man in orange.

The old man smiled nastily. "The answer is very simple. The rea-son her preferences are so absurd is that she uses them to seek the love of these people."

"That is not true!" said the woman.

"It is," said the old man. "You wish for admiration, for worship. You are as bad as *she* is," and at that the old man turned his gaze to the girl in green.

The man in orange and the woman in blue did likewise, glaring at her. Though each of them seemed to hold little regard for any other, the little girl bore the most disdain.

The girl in green looked up at the others and shrugged. "I do not make anyone love me," she said.

"We all know that is not true," said the man in orange. "They sing of you more than any of us. They rejoice for you, laugh with glee at the sight of you."

"But I did not make them do anything," said the little girl. "They rejoice of their own accord."

"That is a lie," said the woman. "You have fooled them. With your tricks. With your blooms and greenery. They cannot see the deep beauty of a leaf the color of rosy fire. They do not love the kiss of frost."

"Nor the hot embrace of a storm's blast," said the man in orange.

"Nor mounds of snow like icing, or the bleak perfection of flats dusted with ice," said the old man. "This is true. You have always courted their favor."

"No," said the little girl. "I only temper."

"Temper?" exclaimed the old man. "What do you mean?"

"I try to do the least," said the little girl. "All three of you have your favorite creations. Wet storms, and frost, and barren flats. They are extremes. I prefer moderation, mildness. A light shower, a placid wind. A cool heat, if I can find one to shepherd. I do not care for a hard touch, for a symphony in the sky. I prefer to be gentle. Is it my fault if most of them love that more? If the flowers and fields exult due to this?"

"Yes," said the man in orange.

"Yes," said the woman.

"Most absolutely, yes," said the old man. "They reject my works most of all. They reject them outright, do you hear? I spend weeks forging the gentle crush of snow, sculpting pure clouds of gray. Yet they have forgotten my name, all of our names, but they remember yours. Because you have spoiled them."

"Because you have deceived them!" said the man in orange.

"Because you have nothing to give," said the woman. "I will not be able to say so in the next possession, so I shall say it now. It is because you are an unoriginal creature, one with no inspiration, no passion. You cannot think of anything to make for them. So you give them nothing. And by pure chance they have taken to it, and love it. And now they ignore us. Because of your foolishness."

George had not really understood much of what these people were discussing up until now. They seemed an odd bunch, and possibly mad, though they had the demeanor of kings and queens. But he recognized cruelty when he saw it, and perhaps due to all the indignities he felt he'd suffered at the hands of the troupe he could not help but sympathize with the girl. So when he could no longer bear it he thrust the shutter open, clambered out, and shouted, "That's enough!"

All four of them stared at him in surprise. The old man nearly fell over. As George stood up, black little clouds came roiling out of his clothes. He looked down and saw he was covered from head to toe in coal dust. Nevertheless, he walked to stand in front of the girl and face the other three.

"Who," said the man in the orange coat, "are you?"

"I won't have you talking to her this way!" he said. "What's wrong with you all?"

"Where did you come from?" asked the woman. "How did you get in here?"

"Were you *hiding* in that cellar?" said the old man.

"Well…yes," said George, embarrassed. "But that doesn't matter! I heard all those horrible things you said! And to a little girl, of all things! Is everyone in this city so terrible? And she so underdressed for this weather, too!"

The three people exchanged glances. Even the little girl was watching him queerly.

"How did you get into this courtyard?" asked the old man. "How can you even notice it? This place is not for you, young man."

George shrugged. "I…just ran in here out of the snow."

"You ran here, of all places?" said the man in orange. "And at such a time?"

He glanced around himself. Now that he was standing in the middle of the courtyard, he noticed that it did seem a very unusual place. While he'd seen how large it was when he first ran in, it now felt like he could walk toward one of the walls and yet never actually reach it. And the buildings did not pen them in at all; rather, it felt like there was entirely too much sky here, and at any moment they might slip off the ground and tumble up into the atmosphere.

"What are you?" asked the woman.

"What am I?" said George. "I'm a... a pianist."

"A pianist?" said the man in orange incredulously.

"Yes," he said. "But... but I won't have you talking to her this way. I won't. It's not right."

The three people nodded, taking this in. They seemed satisfied by what he'd said.

"I say we kill him," said the woman.

"Yes," said the man in orange.

"I agree," said the old man.

George gaped at them. "What?" he said.

"It's the only fitting thing to do," said the man in orange. "Who will be the one to do the deed? I nominate you, Boreas, as you have the most experience with this."

"I shall be happy to," said the old man, and he began rolling up his sleeves. He stepped forward, and somehow he seemed even taller than before, tall enough that his head should have scraped the sky when he walked. George began backing away, terrified.

"Wait," said the little girl.

The old man stopped. "Wait?" he said.

"Yes," said the girl. "Just wait."

"Why should I wait? He has invaded our private meeting space. He has listened to the Laying of Intents. He has seen us, when we have gone unseen for centuries in these countries. This is unacceptable."

"But he didn't know what he was doing," said the little girl. "And he knows nothing about us. He simply ran here to find shelter from the storm."

"Which is all the more questionable," said the man in the orange coat. "How could he see this place? How could he notice it, or us? What is he, indeed?"

"And is he to be believed?" said the woman. "He says it happened by pure chance, but he could be lying."

The three of them nodded, and the old man continued rolling up his sleeves.

"No," said George. "No, honestly, I just came here by accident."

"Stop," said the girl. "Let me search him, and see what I can find. I will see if he is lying."

"The group has voted," said the old man. "He is to die, and I shall kill him. Don't let it trouble you. I will make it painless enough." He took another step forward. His knuckles crackled like thunderstorms, and his brows settled down around his eyes like drifts of snow at the feet of mountains.

"You cannot kill him if I claim patronage," said the girl.

The old man stopped short at that, and the other two gasped.

"Patronage?" said the man in orange. "Are you serious? You would do such a thing?"

"For someone you do not know?" said the old man. "For a stranger?"

"You cannot trust him," said the woman.

The little girl held up her hand, and they were silent. She took George by the hand and gently turned him, and her small, rosy fingers were warm and soft. Then she walked in a circle around him, her bright green eyes tracing him up and down. Her gaze was very sharp and fierce, and George soon felt uncomfortable, as though he were naked and she were seeing every inch of him and he could do nothing to stop it.

"There is something different about him," said the girl.

"Different?" said the woman. "He looks unexceptional to me."

"Perhaps it is a trap," said the man in orange. "Maybe there is some danger hidden within him."

"There is something hidden within him, yes," said the girl, surprised. "And... I do think it dangerous, but not for us."

"Then you cannot lay patronage with ease of mind," said the woman. "Not if he could be dangerous to anyone. There are few shames greater than a beneficiary who acts poorly."

The girl continued peering at him. Then she shook her head. "No. I do not see that potential in him, either. Yes. Yes, I think I will. I will lay patronage."

The old man looked at her gravely. "None of us have laid patronage to any man in many, many years. Are you sure you wish to do this?"

"As he says, he is an artist. And I am allowed to claim myself a patron for whom I wish," she said.

"But he could be a nothing!" said the old man. "A tuneless clinker, a silly hack!"

"How can you be his patron if you have not even heard his music yet?" said the woman. "Even the lesser winds may be shamed by this! Are you serious about wishing to claim patronage for this… this boy?"

She looked at George, thinking, and smiled. "I am."

The man in orange nodded unhappily. "Well. Then we cannot speak against that. The pianist has your patronage, and so shall live. Though I cannot see how he could ever be of use to you."

"I'm sure you can't," said the young girl.

"Are we finished here?" said the woman. "It has been an exciting diversion, but we have our lands and our flocks to tend to."

"True," said the old man. "The storm spends itself, and now I must drive what remains elsewhere. I will close the meeting as it now stands."

"Be sure you keep to your intents, Boreas," said the woman. "When your breezes are done playing, round up every last one of them. I once found one loose to the west of here, long after your possession had passed from you, and I have not forgotten it."

The old man stuck his nose high in the air and walked down the passageway and into the snow. The wind rose and he seemed to vanish. The woman looked at the rest of them, nodded, and walked down the eastern passageway. As she broached the veil of snow the wind seemed to take her as well.

The man in orange looked George over and gave him an unpleasant smile. "I hope for your sake that fortune is in your favor, boy. We are patron to very few, since many that we admire come to unpleasant ends. And should you shame us, I doubt if anyone will bother to hold Boreas back." Then he turned and walked down the southern passageway. The wind rose and the veil of snow twitched, and he was gone.

Immediately the snow fell in a thick sheet all throughout the courtyard. George gasped in shock as the flakes started collecting in the back of his collar. The young girl tutted and cocked her head, and it tapered off again.

"He didn't need to do that," she said.

"How did...how did that happen?" asked George. "Wait, where did they go? Are they coming back?"

"Calm down," she said. "You're safe, for now. And I don't think he means what he said."

"Who were they? Why...why were they going to kill me?"

"They are artisans, of a sort," she said. "Or maybe shepherds would be a better description. We meet here to discuss what we plan to make, and do. What we say here is extremely private, so they were distressed to find you'd overheard. But I realized you were here by accident, boy. It was not your fault you heard what you did."

"How on Earth did you get mixed up with them?"

She frowned sadly. "I did not get mixed up with them. They are my family."

"Those people were your family?" he asked. "They didn't look anything like you, or treat you well at all."

"Families are complicated. Especially when one is the favorite, which is unfortunately the case with me. And I'll run the next meeting, and they always treat the successor very poorly, perhaps to be preemptive. One just has to bear it, I suppose." She gave him a sharp look. "A more important question is, who are you?"

"Oh, I'm sorry. I'm George," he said, and stuck out his hand.

She looked at it, then up into his face, but did not shake. "What are you doing here, George?"

"Well, I'm…I'm lost," he said. "I've been having the worst day, and I went out for a walk to cool off…But then I didn't know where I was, and it started snowing, and I ran in here for cover and…and I don't even know how to get back to my hotel."

She pursed her lips as she thought. "Which hotel would it be?" He told her, and the girl cocked her head again, but this time it was like she was listening to something. "I know where it is," she said.

"You do?"

"Yes. I've been there before."

"Can you get me there?"

She smiled. "At some point in time, boy, I have worked myself into nearly every nook of this city, and many more beyond it. I know quite a few places. This one should be no trouble." She gestured to him and padded off down the western passageway, and George followed.

As they neared the veil of snow it seemed to recede until the snow-fall had halted on the street before them. The girl took no notice, but George stopped and looked up at the sky. It was as if some gust of wind was parting the clouds directly above them like a curtain, free-ing the way ahead of snow. He was about to say something when the gust apparently moved too far away and flakes began to patter on his hat. He ran to catch up with the girl, who had moved down the street.

"This is odd snow," he said. "It's extremely spotty here. But maybe it's like that out here. Everything seems different."

The girl looked at him out of the side of her eye. "This is your first time out in the world, isn't it?"

"No," said George, offended. "I've…simply been traveling more than I'm used to." There was a pause. "Is it so clear?"

"Very. You need to be on your guard more."

He sighed. "It feels like I've been doing nothing but making bad decisions lately. I feel so silly."

"It can be easy to get by in the world," said the girl. "At least, it is if you remember one thing: there is the way things appear to work, and then there is the way things really work. You must train your eye to discern between the two. Though I feel that you'll need very little training."

George laughed unhappily. "Do you? It seems I've been doing a terrible job of it so far."

The girl stopped and whirled around on him. He had to quickly come to a halt and nearly ran into her.

"Back in the courtyard. How did you find the way in?" she asked. "How did you see us?"

"How?" said George. "I don't know. I just did."

"But that never happens. I can't remember the last time that happened." She squinted at him again, studying his every inch as though searching for something. She seemed very confused by what she found. "I can almost glimpse it," she said to herself as she examined him. "But it is very elusive... It is so faint, so *fundamental* that I can barely even notice it."

"Notice what?" said George.

The girl stood back and looked at him, slightly impressed. "There is something different about you, boy," she said. "Something you must have picked up at some point in time. It is inside you, somewhere. And I don't know where it came from, but I think it to be very, very old. Even older than me. I can hear it, I believe... Singing, very softly..."

George suddenly recalled that strange memory he'd experienced during Silenus's performance: the darkened barrow, and the squiggle of light, and the voice chanting in the dark, waiting to be heard...

"I believe you will have no issue seeing how the world really works," said the girl. "Doors that are shut for others may be open to you. And for that I pity you, for not all doors lead to places one wishes to go."

Then she turned and continued walking down the street, the little bubble of clear sky following her as she went.

George caught up to her and said, "Why are you helping me?"

She thought about it. "Because you were kind when you did not have to be," she said. "I don't think you understand how rare that often is. Why did you stand up for me?"

"I don't know," he said. "It just seemed mean, what they were saying to you. I've seen a lot of meanness recently, and I didn't want to see any more of it."

"What you did was very brave," said the girl. "You were facing things far greater than you, whether you knew it or not. What's brought you here, boy?"

"My father," he said. "Silenus. He leads our performing troupe."

The girl stopped when she heard that. "Silenus, you say?"

"Yes. Why?"

She frowned. "I've heard of him."

"You have?" asked George. "What have you heard?"

"Only whispers," said the girl. "And vague ones at that. But I have heard that he is a very powerful man, and not to be trifled with, not even by my kinsmen. And we are very powerful in our own right."

"But why?" asked George, awed.

"I can't say for sure," she said. "He passes under my skies very rarely. But when he does, all my clouds nudge toward him, and the drops of my rains suddenly slant to fall at his feet, just a bit. No one would ever notice it but me. It always seems like he is carrying something... *heavy* with him. Very heavy. Heavy enough to be the heart of all the world."

"How could anyone carry anything like that?"

She smiled. "You have already forgotten what I told you."

"I have?"

"Yes," said the girl. "That there is the way the world seems to work, and then there is the way it really works. Come on," she said, and led him farther into the blizzard.

Eventually the hotel emerged from the swirling snow ahead. She looked it over, and nodded. "This must be where he's staying," the girl said. "There is a pull here. I have felt it only when Silenus was near. It makes sense—Boreas complained that his storms drew themselves to this city, as if they had minds of their own. But you and I know the truth, don't we?"

"I don't know," said George. He stared at one lit window, imagining it to be his father's. "I feel like I don't know anything."

She smiled sadly. "Well. You should know that I am your patron. You stood up for me when it did you little good. And you should know you have a good heart, boy, and I will not forget that. I find you very curious, and I think I will watch you closely. If you ever need me, you can simply call my name. If I am close, I will come to you."

"But I don't know your name," said George.

The girl leaned close to whisper into his ear. She smelled of jasmine and moist earth, and hay and freshly cut grass. When she whispered the word he felt a warm breeze slide across his cheek, and to his ears her breath had the sound of gentle rain.

"Oh," said George. "I think I've heard of you before."

"Like I said, I am the most popular of my kin," she said. "Whether I like it or not. It does pain them so. But we are a squabbling sort." Then she leaned back in, and placed a cool kiss upon his cheek. "You bear my blessing now, George. It is a small thing that may do you some good, but I am not sure if it will be enough for what you may encounter. I was once told Silenus is a hunted man, and that he deals with peoples powerful and hidden even to me. I cannot guess at what you will see or where he will take you. But should you call, I will come if I can."

"All right," said George. He rubbed his cheek. "Thank you."

She smiled. "Goodbye, boy," she said, and padded back down the street.

George watched her as she left. He had never been kissed by a girl before. As this first kiss had occurred under such strange circumstances, George was not sure if this numb, floating sensation was normal. And for some reason he thought of Colette, and felt ashamed. It was as if that chaste kiss was a betrayal of her, even though she'd shown him little affection so far.

Then the wind rose in the little street, and a flurry of flakes seemed to surround the girl, and she was gone. The bubble of clear air collapsed, and snow again began to fall on George's hat. He jumped up the steps and ran inside the hotel.

It took George a long time to get clean. He was covered in coal dust, and icy water had soaked into his coat and socks. When he finally managed to remove and clean his sopping clothes, he'd spent nearly every bit of energy he had. He lay down on the bed, confused but eager for sleep. Yet no sooner had his head touched the pillow than a knock sounded at the door.

He opened it to find Stanley and Silenus standing in the hall with a lantern shining in Stanley's hand. "Where the hell have you been?" asked Silenus.

"What do you mean?" asked George.

"We knocked here nearly an hour ago and there was no answer."

"Oh," said George. But he was not inclined to tell his father what he'd seen; Silenus had been keeping so many secrets that George thought it only fair to have a few of his own. "I was...out."

Silenus cocked an eyebrow.

"I was delayed by a very interesting conversation with a stranger," George added primly.

"If you say so," said Silenus. "Get dressed. We're going out."

George nearly despaired at the idea of venturing out into that weather again. "What? Why?"

"Your three weeks are up, kid," Silenus said. "It's time for you to know." He turned and began to walk down the hall with Stanley close behind.

George struggled back into his clothes and followed them. "To know what?" he asked.

Silenus said, "How the world was made."

CHAPTER 10

"In the beginning..."

George was not at all sure where they were taking him, but when they were outside they headed directly for the theater. On finding the door to the backstage locked Silenus stepped aside and said to Stanley, "Do your thing. And hurry. I'm fucking freezing." Stanley knelt and produced a set of lock picks, and within seconds his nimble fingers had sprung the door open.

The inside of the theater was a threatening place in the night. No outside light found its way in, so it was lit only by the lamp in Stanley's hand. The wind beat against the walls and window, moaning and whistling. The looming vacancy of the place grew oppressive as George walked onstage and stared out at the dark curtains, or the distant hint of rafters, or the row upon row of empty seats. It felt like the theater was playing host to an invisible audience, and they were not impressed by the show.

Stanley went to pull down Kingsley's backdrop (which was now blank again) and Silenus walked to the edge of the stage, looking out on the empty theater. "There are few things creepier than a place that is intended to be full of people, and yet is empty," he said. Then a thought seemed to strike him, and he said, "Let me ask you something, kid—why did you get into vaudeville?"

George was startled by the question, since he had not yet tried to explain his relation to Silenus. He did not feel especially ready now, at any rate. "I'm not sure I know."

"An honest answer. And probably a common one. We get into this game with grand plans and great delusions, but after a while the reasons we started with fade. Why do we keep doing it? I wonder. We spend our whole lives preparing and perfecting an illusion that will last only for a handful of minutes, the less the better. Our daily employment is but a momentary flash and flame, then nothing. Most of us old ones no longer do it for the audience. That attraction is the first to go. To us, every day is like performing for an empty theater. So why keep going? Is it just routine, the comfortable familiar? Or are we playing only for ourselves? Or perhaps for the amusement of something greater, something beyond men and mortals... It vexes me so."

Then they heard the click of chalk, and turned to see Stanley writing on his blackboard with great agitation. "Now what's going on here?" said Silenus.

Stanley finished what he was writing, and held it up to the empty backdrop as though it could see him and read. He'd written: PLEASE BE REASONABLE, WE DO NOT HAVE ALL NIGHT. While George could not understand what Stanley expected from the backdrop, it still did nothing.

Silenus passed by Stanley and walked right up to the sheet of canvas. "Listen, you touchy fuck," he said to it, "I've spent too much of my time dragging you around to be willing to abide one more minute of your little fucking temper tantrums! I ain't the one that killed your originator, but I'd be willing to start a bonfire and kill *you* all the same! Now wise up and get on with the show, or I swear to God, I will put this cigar out on you and smile."

It remained blank. George whispered to Stanley, "What does he think the backdrop will do?"

Stanley wrote: NOT BACKDROP. SKIN.

"What do you mean, skin?" asked George.

"It's chimera skin," said Silenus. He took out his cigar and blew on the end until it was red-hot. "A creature of many kinds—a goat, a lion, a snake—and many shapes and colors." He lowered the lit cigar toward the backdrop. "If you skin it the right way then its hide gains certain properties. Specifically, it can project certain images and sensations, if you can control it." The lit cigar kept slowly nearing the backdrop. "But they're notoriously picky things, and sometimes," he said, and the lit end of the cigar was very close to the backdrop now, "they need to be *forced*."

Just when the cigar's end was but a hairsbreadth away, the surface of the canvas (or skin, George reminded himself) changed: it bloomed into a rippling dark blue with little flickers of light in its center. The stage and theater were bathed in its unearthly iridescence and seemed all the stranger as a result.

"It moves!" cried George.

"Yeah, yeah, it moves," said Silenus. "I knew I could talk some sense into the thing. Maybe we should have gotten Colette to come with us, it seems to like her the most."

George was instantly enamored of it and wanted to touch it, but was somewhat afraid of what might happen if he did. "Where did you get it?"

"I won it in a card game," said Silenus. "Honestly, that's how I acquire most of our equipment. It's damn useful, though. Most vaudeville shows, people wander in and out constantly. But this keeps them in their seats, at least for the start." He stuck his cigar back in his mouth and walked to the middle of the stage. "Take a seat, kid. I'm going to put on a show for you. It's easier to explain this in visual terms, y'see."

George reluctantly left the moving image and took a seat in the front row. Stanley came down as well and sat a few seats across from him, but Silenus remained up on the stage. He said, "What I'm going to do up here, kid, is tell you a story. Like all stories, it's an attempt to make sense of something larger than itself. And, like most stories, it fails, to a certain degree. It's a gloss, a rendition, so it's not exact. But it'll do."

"All right," said George.

Silenus looked to the backdrop. "It starts with, 'In the beginning,'" he said.

This was evidently a signal of some kind, as Stanley dimmed the lantern and the backdrop grew a solid black. Silenus cleared his throat, assumed a more theatrical pose, and said:

"In the beginning, there was nothing. There were no suns, no stars, no lands or seas or skies." His voice echoed throughout the theater, and it gained a queer resonance that made it feel as though he were speaking very close to George. "Nothing lived, for there was nothing to live in or on. Time did not exist, for there was nothing to pass through it. There was only nothing, an endless, vasty abyss.

"But then the Creator came, and all of that changed," said Silenus.

Then the image of pure black shattered, like someone pitching a baseball through the middle of a pane of glass, revealing a second background behind it of bright white. There was a great shout of countless voices singing one furious note, and then the voices dropped to a hum. George could not see where the voices were com- ing from—perhaps it was the backdrop itself?—but before he could think on it the image began moving again: the shards of darkness drifted away from the middle until there was a space of clear white in the center that was ringed by a jagged edge of black.

"The Creator broke the darkness, and it decided that, for the first time, things should Be," said Silenus. "There would come, amid this sea of infinite nothingness, existence. And in that small puddle of existence, a world. And so the Creator sang the world."

The hums changed into a song. It was a very soft and curious song. It seemed somewhat toneless to George, with no major or minor mode that he could discern. Yet as the voices sang, something appeared in the center of the white space: a brown dot, like a dab of paint from an invisible paintbrush. The dab turned into a streak, which made a circle within the white space, and then the invisible paintbrush began to fill in the circle with what looked like mountains and shorelines and broad, flat plains. They were all a little crude-looking, much like something one would find on a cave wall, yet a considerable amount of expression was rendered from such simple forms.

"The Creator sang of skies and seas, of mountains and valleys, of water and rain and the touch of the sun. It sang of the slow caress of time, of the lapping of waves and the dance of light, of flame and ice and winds and rivers."

The song changed and more shapes appeared within the little brown world: broad blue oceans and little rivulets, and small storms that waxed and waned as they advanced across the continents. The world came alive with thousands of slight animations, forces and pressures and reactions rippling across its face.

"Then the Creator sang of things that would exist within the world, and grow," said Silenus. "It sang of grasses and trees and moss and algae. It sang of seaweed and vines and endless fruits, and other tiny green things that stretched toward the light, sucking up mere drops of water."

The song intensified, and patches of green began to appear on the faces of the continents. The sea changed color from a dark blue to a lighter gray, and tiny green trees began popping up across the face of the world. They swayed back and forth with an invisible wind, and sometimes minuscule pinecones or fruits dropped from their branches, which were no larger than mouse bones.

"Then the Creator decided to sing of things that would live, yet would see the world, and know of it," said Silenus. "Things that would react to it of their own accord. So the Creator sang of all the animals in the mountains and the grasslands and upon the shores, and the fishes and creatures in the blue deeps, and the birds that would drift from gust to gust in the sky."

Small deer leaped out from amid the green and began to cavort and frolic, and among their feet were mice and asps and foxes. In the plains were cattle and other large creatures, some of which George did not recognize, like one beast with great tusks and long hair. Fish and porpoises jumped up from the waves of the seas, and sometimes whales would surface and send a fine spray up into air. Above them all small birds flickered and dodged, or sailed from enormous nests up in the peaks of the mountains.

"Then the Creator sang of a creature that would see the world most clearly and, unlike all others, possess the ability to change it," said Silenus. "And so the last of the things the Creator sang of was Man."

Small huts appeared around the patches of blue and under the green trees, and then tiny stick figures emerged from them, though their bodies and limbs were loose and willowy. They ate the fruit and hunted the deer and washed their miniature clothes in the streams. They grew fat and happy, and had children, and carried their little ones about, showing them the sun and the mountains and the sky.

"And then, when the world was complete, the Creator was pleased with what it had made," said Silenus. "And it left."

The song faded from the screen, and it seemed to George as though a light went out of the images as well. The brown world with its many creatures remained, sitting in its white pool surrounded by shards of jagged black, but it seemed slightly dimmer, and the colors were no longer quite as bright.

"The world continued as the Creator had left it — seas still surged, rivers still trickled, the winds still played with the clouds, and the creatures grew in population, or died back. But then something happened that the Creator may not have intended: the darkness came alive."

A quiver ran through all the pieces of jagged black at the edges of the screen. Certain parts began moving, very slowly: shards and crags of the ring of black grew close together, solidifying themselves. And George thought he could discern a single pair of eyes in the darkness, little white slits that peered out at the brown world beyond it, and he thought he could see hate in that gaze.

"To have a thing exist was endless torment for all the nothing that had been there before it," said Silenus. "It had been wounded and broken when the Creator made the world. And in its rage the darkness struck back, and began to devour Creation."

Another quiver ran through the darkness, and the shards of black changed: they grew long, sharp ears, and thin, threatening snouts, and sharp, snapping fangs. George realized that the darkness had grown the heads of a thousand wolves, and they bit and snarled at the little brown world that was sitting in the white pool. The painting of the world began to fade, not all at once but in patches: first a small valley in the hills faded and darkened, then a piece of shore, and then the tip of a chain of mountains, until the world looked as though it were diseased, with strata of black running across it.

"The creatures of the world were thrown into despair," said Silenus. "The winds changed course, mountains vanished, and rivers that had once led to the sea now ended in wide, black gaps, their waters flowing into nothingness. Wandering herds entered the shadows and were lost. Forests faded and fell away. Those who witnessed these things begged That Which Made the World to return, and save them. But for reasons that could not be guessed at, the Creator did not return, and the world was plunged into darkness."

The world kept fading until only little islands of it were left. The isolated fragments trembled under the weight of all that shadow, like they all might burst apart at any moment.

"But then some of the people discovered something," said Silenus. "They found that the song the Creator had sung when it first made the world still echoed in the deep places: under mountains, in the darkest forests, in the coldest seas, and within ancient hills, never dying. And the people found that if they took these echoing pieces of the First Song, and pooled them and sang them in the fading parts of the world, then they could renew it, and save what was left, for within the song were the commands that had made the seas and lands and skies and creatures."

George watched as one little stick figure that was glowing bright walked before a group of people huddled before a growing shadow. The figure waved its tiny stick arms until the people were watching, and then it sang for them, and George recognized the song as the ethereal harmony he had first heard at the beginning of the show. The people who heard the song seemed to light up, gathering a small halo of bright colors about them. Then they walked into the darkness, and where they walked the darkness retreated and the world began to return. The little glowing figure who had first sung the song went to another group of people and sang again, and then another and another until almost half the world had been brought back, the shadow withdrawing as the glowing people moved forward. The wolves at the edges paced and bit and snapped, but the world stayed bright and clear, and they made soundless howls of rage.

"And though much of the world returned, some parts could not be brought back," said Silenus. "Many lands and countries had lain under shadow for too long, and were lost. So the people decided that they would never allow such a thing to happen again, and they assigned a group to carry the First Song from fading place to fading place and renew the edges of the world, and pass on the song when needed. And so Creation would be maintained, piece by piece, performance by performance, as the First Song was carried across the face of the Earth, echoing in the deeps."

The last image on the screen was of a group of people crossing the little brown world, weaving through tiny mountains and traveling down into a valley. There was a faint glow to them, as though they carried a light that they had to keep veiled. Out beyond the border of the world the wolves in the darkness watched them, and they stewed and paced back and forth. The glowing people did not seem to take notice, and George almost shouted at them to watch out, and take warning, but before he could the screen began to grow blank again, and the darkness and the wolves and the world turned into empty canvas.

Stanley increased the light on his lantern. Silenus walked down off the stage, took the glass chimney off of it, and lit his cigar in its flame. As he did he looked up at George, the fire's luminescence bathing his craggy face, and said, "Good fucking show, ain't it?"

George was not sure what to say at first. Finally he asked, "What is it you're trying to tell me? That...that the song you sing in the fourth act is..."

"I am saying," said Silenus, "that the strange performance at the end of our shows, where everything seems to go still and the audience grows dazed and silent... In that moment, what is being played is the First Song, otherwise known as the First Invocation, the art that called Creation out of the darkness and forged the world. Or at the very least a part of that song."

George stared at him. "You can't possibly be serious."

"I dead fucking am," said Silenus.

Stanley took out his blackboard and wrote: WHAT WAS THE FIRST TIME YOU HEARD IT LIKE?

Silenus added, "Yes, but ignore that memory that woke up inside you. That's abnormal. Besides that, what was it like, that first time?"

George thought and said, "It was like the theater felt very small, and we could...look out and see everything. Like we were watching a machine from the outside, and we'd only ever seen it from within."

"Exactly," said Silenus. "Within the First Song are the...blueprints, I suppose you could say, of everything that's ever been or ever will be. When it's sung and heard it connects people, links them to everything that's around them, every piece and every particle of everything until they see...well, everything. It is a glimpse of the infinite, bundled up into one three-minute act. And unlike most other experiences with the infinite, there is no sense of feeling lost, or meaningless, or any dread. Reciting the First Song is a force of renewal. It reminds the listener and even Creation itself what they are, what they were meant to be—an integral, inseparable part of a much vaster whole."

George frowned as he tried to take this in. He remembered how those who'd seen the act in Parma had changed: their colors had become brighter, and they'd seemed somehow content and at peace. "So you sing this just to give people that feeling of...infinity?"

"Well, that's not exactly *the* reason," said Silenus. "That's more of a pleasant side effect. The real reason is protection."

A light went on in George's mind. "Against the men in gray."

Silenus exchanged a cool glance with Stanley. "Yes," he said.

"I was approached by one of them, several months ago," said George. "He was looking for news of you, but he didn't give me his name, and his story was... Well, it was very unconvincing. I didn't tell him anything. But just recently I heard someone say that you were a hunted man."

Silenus smiled nastily. "Then that someone was correct. I am very hunted. In the past, oh, several hundred years or so, the darkness figured out how to manifest itself in the world, and disguise itself. Parts of itself, that is. It's learned to send agents abroad to search for what's keeping it at bay, in other words. They wear the images of people as you and I would a coat, but underneath, they're like holes or tears in existence itself. Just their presence affects everything around them—light and colors and sounds fail, and shadows lengthen. They are not used to being real, to existing—hence why the one you met thought up such a stupid plot, or why they were fooled by our reflections—but they are still a terrible threat to us. They do not need to be intelligent. They can win by sheer numbers alone."

"And you call them wolves?"

"That name comes from older times," said Silenus. "Way back when wolves were what men feared most. They killed and devoured flocks, and terrified villages. These shadow-creatures seemed to do the same, so they named them the same. It was a way of making sense of what was happening." Silenus snorted and spat carelessly on the theater floor. "When they first appeared, our forebears obstructed them as best as they could, but I suppose it was inevitable—eventually the wolves learned of the First Song. They realized that if they could find it and prevent it from being performed—by killing the performers, essentially—then there would be nothing holding them back. They could finally eat up this remainder of the world, and have peace. And so they have been hounding us ever since. Performing the song normally pushes them back, like fortifying a dike against the tide. That's how it's been for...hell, thousands of years. But somehow in the hotel in Parma, it didn't work. I can't say why just yet. It is extraordinarily troubling, though."

"Did you say thousands of years?" asked George.

"Yes," said Silenus. "This has been going on for quite some time, kid. How old did you think I was?"

"I don't know," said George. But he thought he detected some anger in Silenus's face that suggested the question had a very bitter meaning to him.

"In some form throughout the years, there has always been a traveling band of players," he said. "They've been of different nations, different creeds, different races and languages, and different entertainments. Not all of them performed on the stage. Some did their routine in city squares, or in fields, or in temples or on the backs of wagons. Anywhere they could get a crowd. But they always carried the First Song with them, and sang it in their performance, and passed it on when the time came."

"Do the others in the troupe know?"

"They've all seen the picture show," said Silenus. "The members have come and gone through the years, but they all drew a crowd. Which was what we needed. If I may say so, this current version of the troupe is the most efficient yet."

"It is?" said George, and then he realized. "Ah. Because it's in vaudeville, isn't it? I suppose the circuits are perfect for you."

"Can you think of a better method?" said Silenus. "We are allowed to—no, *expected* to—travel all around the country, going from theater to theater and doing our short act in front of enormous crowds. No other kind of entertainer has ever covered more ground than a vaudevillian."

Stanley wrote: AND OUR TRAVELS ARE A USEFUL SCREEN FOR OUR SEARCHES, AS WELL.

"What are you searching for?" asked George.

"For other pieces of the song," said Silenus.

"Other pieces? I'd have thought you'd have it all by now."

Again, there was that bitter smile. "No," said Silenus. "We do not. Over time we think we've found a lot of it. Not quite all, but most. But we are still missing a few key fragments. As such, when we perform the First Song we are only playing a portion. There are many dimensions to Creation we cannot help, or renew. So we are always searching for those missing pieces, to gather them up and fill in the empty portions."

George was about to ask how they did this, when he suddenly remembered the two of them trudging through the rain with that enormous steamer trunk held between them. He remembered how angry Silenus had been, as if he'd gone out looking for something and been hugely disappointed. And then there was what the girl in green had said: Silenus always seemed to be carrying something very, very *heavy.*

"Oh," said George. "Your trunk!"

Silenus narrowed his eyes. "What?"

"That's how you collect it. It's...it's that trunk you have, with all the locks. You and Stanley have to get it in there, right?"

Silenus was quiet for a long time. Then he said, "The particulars of collecting or singing the song are a very delicate and secret matter, kid. Stanley is my assistant, and only he is allowed to know exactly what I do with the song. I'm telling you a lot of stuff right now, stuff people have gotten killed trying to protect. But right there is where I'm going to stop. Those are our most protected secrets, and I'm not willing to share them with you. Not yet."

"People have gotten killed?" asked George. "Over a song?"

"Not just a song," said Silenus. "*The* song. Do you know what's at risk? What could be lost if they caught up to us?" He stood up and replaced his hat. "Come on," he said. "I'll show you what would happen."

"Where are we going now?" asked George.

"I'm not sure yet. But I'll know it when I see it."

Silenus led them out back to the street behind the theater. The snow had lessened, but it was still bitterly cold. He took a right and followed a meandering little alleyway that ran behind several shops and homes. He held up a finger as though testing the wind, and changed direction and kept walking until they came to a neighborhood behind an old abandoned mill, next to a dribbling little stream. The buildings appeared to be deserted, and the lots were crisscrossed with cracked wooden fencing. In the weak starlight it was a lonely, disquieting place, snow-decked and littered with old industrial equipment and rusting chains, and splintered wood that sometimes had the look of bones. Every surface was ringed with frost, and armies of cats wove in and out of the machinery and the broken fences, sometimes pausing to observe these intruders before disappearing down a gutter.

George was not sure what Silenus was looking for, but he could not imagine finding anything of worth here; yet then he recalled how both Parma and Rinton had felt when Silenus's troupe had performed, and realized this place had the same sort of atmosphere: it felt dark and *thin*, as if one could scratch at the ground or the sky and it would tear away like paper.

"This place doesn't seem right, does it?" asked Silenus.

George shook his head.

"It's one of the fading parts. When more people who have heard the song come here it will return to what it once was. We're helping it now, even as we speak."

"I thought you caused this feeling," said George.

"Caused?" said Silenus. "No. I am specifically here to *remove* this feeling, in a way. Though when the wolves follow us this feeling only increases, at least until the song's effects take hold." Then Silenus spied something, and he pointed at the tumbled-down remains of a red-brick building. Nearly all of the structure was gone except for a single lonely corner, and the way the starlight fell across it made dark shadows in its center. "There," he said. "Do you see it?"

"See what?" asked George.

"That shadow, in between those walls. Is it not much darker than all other shadows? Does it not seem somehow deeper?"

George looked at the broken corner of the building, and admitted that it did seem very black.

"All right," said Silenus. "Stanley, put down that lamp. And George, take your shoes off."

"Why would I want to do that?" said George, who was sure there'd be rusty nails and broken glass under all that snow.

Stanley took out his blackboard and wrote: BECAUSE YOU DO NOT WANT THEM TO BE FROZEN TO THE GROUND. Then he set it aside.

George did not know what he meant, but did as Silenus said. Silenus and Stanley removed their own as well. Silenus stuck his hand out and said, "Join hands. Everyone." Once they had they approached the corner of the building in a human chain with Silenus leading. "You will want to take a deep breath before we enter," he said, "so that you will not have to take in much of the cold air."

"The what?" said George, but he heard Stanley breathing deep behind him, and hurriedly did the same.

Silenus slowly led them toward the dark corner, moving forward step by step, until he entered the shadow. It was so dark that Silenus seemed to disappear entirely, though George could still feel the man's hand in his own. Silenus kept leading them ahead, even when, by George's estimation, there was not much space left within this corner of the red-brick building. Yet Harry kept pulling him forward, as though there had been a door there George had not seen, and soon he entered the shadow as well and could see nothing.

The shadow seemed impossibly deep, the darkness stretching on and on. The three of them kept walking forward, traversing a space several times longer than the fragment of the building, by George's reckoning. Then the ground changed beneath them, and they were walking on what felt like icy stone that sucked at the moisture on the soles of George's feet. Then George saw that there were stars up above them, though they were poor imitations of the ones he'd just seen behind the mill: these seemed more like needle punctures in the darkness above. When his eyes had finally adjusted he looked out at what was before him, and gasped.

It was not a landscape in any conceivable sense of the word. For one thing, it did not obey any of the rules of physics that George was aware of and comfortable with: he was not sure if he was looking out, or down, or possibly even up, or maybe he was stuck to the side of a cliff and was looking along the precipice. But no matter the angle at which he looked, George saw an endless gray wasteland arranged out among the stars, riddled with abysses and canyons whose breadths were so wide it took George minutes (or was it hours?) to look from one side to the other. There was no vegetation of any kind, nor any sign of life: only the barren, starlit stone. Desolate gray peaks stared down (or up, or across) at him, like a volcanic eruption frozen at the height of its violence. There seemed to be far too much sky in places around him, and very little earth, like the horizon was eaten up by the gaps between the stars. It was a frigid, brittle, awful place, hanging in space without any sense of dimension or depth or purpose. The wastes looked terribly cold, and as George had just gasped he had to take in a breath of air, and it was indeed so frozen that it was shocking.

"What is this?" said George.

"This is one of the lost places," said Silenus. His words made an astounding amount of steam, and George saw their very bodies were steaming as well. "I don't know what it was originally. I just know it *isn't*, anymore. Places like these are accessible through deep shadows in the thin parts of the world, parts that the darkness has rubbed away until they are barely there, with a few holes finally appearing. Our presence has renewed this place a little, since we have heard the song—that's why your feet don't freeze off of you, and why you are not frozen solid—so that's good, but it's not enough in the face of this. It's one of the places that the First Song cannot bring back. The wolves have utterly consumed it. And when they triumph over us, even these remains will fade."

George noticed that Silenus had said "when," not "if." He was about to remark on it when he noticed a smattering of small white lights among the shadows of the cliffs. At first he mistook them for more stars, buried among the stones of this strange place, but he saw that they seemed to be holes of some kind, or tunnels, and some led to light and others led to someplace dark...

Silenus said, "There is more than this. Unbelievably more, if distance still functions in such a ruined state. The amount of Creation that was lost in the first days is unthinkable."

"That can't be," said George. "I've seen maps of the world, of all the continents. It's all accounted for. The world has a start and an end. There aren't any lost pieces."

"Are you so sure?" said Silenus. "Don't you sometimes feel like the world is getting smaller, George? Have you never heard any of the ancient stories and felt the world they took place in was far larger than the one we know today? Or haven't you wondered why there are stories of fabulous places and fantastic beasts, yet we can find no sign of them anywhere anymore?"

"I thought people had made all that up," said George.

"No," said Silenus. "They existed, if only for a little while. But they and the places they dwelled in are now...well..." He gestured to the barren wasteland before them. "Consumed. Collapsed into a meaningless little pocket of reality found only in shadow. Now the world balances upon a mere scrap of fundament, floating unevenly in nothing. And what's left could easily be lost as well, if we allow the wolves to catch up to us and devour what we have spent our whole lives protecting. And if you do not take our purpose seriously, it may just happen. Do you understand?"

George nodded.

"Have you seen enough?"

"Yes," said George, who wanted to be far away from that terrible place.

"Then we'll exeunt quickly," said Silenus. He turned them around and George saw that in the darkness before them was a small, oddly shaped hole that looked out on the fenced-in lots they'd just left. It was not until they were right before it that he realized the hole was in the general shape of the shadow in the red-brick corner, which made him think about the little tunnels of light he'd seen in the cliffs...

They staggered out of the shadow and into the mill lot. Stanley and George gasped for air, since the atmosphere in that horrible landscape had been too cold and thin for them to breathe comfortably. Silenus appeared to be less affected: he coolly watched as they tried to compose themselves, and said, "Come on. Back to my office."

George sat up to pull his shoes and socks on. As he did he saw the soles of his feet had been burned black, just like Silenus's and Stanley's. He poked at the arch of his foot. It did not hurt, but when he licked his finger and rubbed at it the blackness did not come away. It seemed to have been stained by the brief journey in that miserable place.

Stanley gave him a weak smile, and wrote: ONE OF US NOW. LIKE IT OR NOT.

CHAPTER 11

"Her name was Alice Carole."

Even though they'd traveled through several different towns, Silenus's office door had somehow always traveled with them. George took it as a sign of his adjustment that he had not been surprised to discover this. He had even intuited it, to a certain degree: before they'd caught the train to Milton the entire troupe had simply taken their bags and props and stacked them in the office, and apparently left them all behind. Then when Silenus had "discovered" the door among the rooms in the new hotel in Milton (as the door, like Kingsley's backdrop, was apparently a sometimes-fickle thing) he'd opened it to reveal the same room, with their bags in the same places that they'd left them. Ever since then the door had always appeared to them in some shadowy section of the wall of whatever hotel they were staying in. It must have saved wonders in train fare.

Now George huddled before Silenus's ancient medieval desk, his hands clasped around a hot cup of tea. The office was much more cluttered than when he'd last seen it: books and papers lay stacked on the desk and several of the chairs, and many cabinet doors stood ajar. Stanley held a cup of tea as well and sat in a chair before the bay window, morose and still. Silenus took his only comfort in a bottle of wine that was very syrupy and stank horribly, though he slurped it down as though it were water. Behind him the stars in the window had shifted slightly, with some growing larger and some smaller, yet George now found them familiar: they were reminiscent of the stars he'd seen over the gray wastes in the shadow.

George finally found the strength to voice a question that had been on his mind since the moving picture show: "Why did He leave?"

"The Creator?" asked Silenus.

George nodded.

"Well, for starters, what you saw is just a story," said Silenus. "It's trying to make sense of bigger things in the easiest way possible. As such, it doesn't make perfect sense. But as for me, I'm inclined to believe that part." He filled up his glass, took a sip, and pulled a face. "Who can say why the Creator left? We're not equipped to guess its mind. I don't even know why it made the world, or what purpose or impulse it was trying to fulfill. Not *yet*, at least. But sometimes people just leave, kid. You can't let the leaving or the absence rule you. We must all be the authors of our own lives now."

George huddled closer to his cup of tea, shaken, but said nothing.

But Stanley frowned, and took out his board and wrote: IT IS POSSIBLE THAT THE CREATOR DID NOT LEAVE, THOUGH.

Silenus turned around in his chair to read what he'd written. Then he rolled his eyes and said, "If it's still here and watching, it's very quiet. No one's seen the hand of the Creator in the world since it was made. Most likely it's gone, though to where I can't say."

Stanley wrote: WE HAVE THE SONG. THAT CANNOT BE COINCIDENCE. IT LEFT US A TOOL TO SURVIVE.

"The song was found only after so much was lost," said Silenus. "The Creator has a funny way of looking after what it makes, if it allowed that to happen. It abandoned us, and leaving the First Song behind was inadvertent. It's an echo. You don't sing a song intending to make an echo."

The chalk clicked and scraped: BUT AN ECHO THAT BEHAVES THAT PERFECTLY?

"The Creator didn't intend for the wolves to happen, either, but they did. And they're perfectly suited to destruction. Is that part of the Creator's original intent, then?"

Stanley's face was fixed in a rare expression of frustration, and Silenus kept his back resolutely turned to his friend, as if he refused to look at him except to read his next response. George got the impression that he was witnessing a revival in a long-running argument between the two men, one that had engendered a fair amount of scars and flown fur in its time. Stanley's chalk clicked and clacked away, and he fumbled as he turned the blackboard around to show what he'd written:

CANNOT JUDGE WHAT WE DO NOT UNDERSTAND. YOU SAY STORY TRIES TO MAKE SENSE OF BIGGER THINGS, BUT WE DON'T UNDERSTAND THE BIGGER THINGS.

"I understand what's been taken from us," said Silenus. "And who. That's all I need to understand, and there can't be a reason justifying that. A good one, at least."

YOU CANNOT JUDGE A PLAN IF YOU CANNOT SEE IT FULLY.

"You're correct to say that I don't see the plan," snapped Silenus. "But if the Creator's plan involves so many pointless deaths, then He is a son of a bitch!"

This upset Stanley so much that he slammed the blackboard and chalk down beside him and crossed his arms. Silenus paid no attention, but angrily slopped down more wine. He scowled and muttered, "Fucking philosophy. Do I, draped in cheap velvet and drinking piss-poor Madeira, look anything like a philosophe to you? Am I to be a man of greater queries, of fucking metaphysic theoreticals?" He addressed these questions over his shoulder, but still refrained from looking directly at Stanley. "No. For Christ's sake, we've got knives to our very throats. Why waste our time on these questions when we have so much more to worry about? I've no interest in the hand that made me, only in keeping boards below our feet and train tracks ahead."

But Stanley did not pay attention to him, or if he did he did not accept his rejoinder. Silenus looked to George as if expecting support. "I agree that sometimes we miss the forest for the leaves, but why look at either when you can't even find the fucking road? Do you follow me, kid?"

George shrugged. Then he thought, and nodded, and shrugged again and shook his head.

Silenus gave him a baleful stare. "A very definite answer. You seem to have run the gamut of expressions there. But it brings me to the trickiest problem out of all of the ones currently piled on our shoulders."

"What's that?" said George.

Silenus extended a finger and pointed at him. "You," he said.

"Me?"

"Yeah, you," he said.

"Why am I tricky?" said George.

"Come on, kid, you're not stupid or anything. You can put two and two together. You saw the pictures and you heard the story. You've got to have figured out what's inside of you by now."

"Inside of me?" asked George. The air seemed to have gone as cold as the cliffs again. "Wh-what do you mean?"

"We told you how we found the parts of the song—in the deep places, frozen in ice or within mountains, or in hills—don't that sound familiar to you?"

As a matter of fact, up until now it had not. George had been so overwhelmed with everything that he hadn't yet imagined that the story and the moving images could have had anything to do with him. When he realized what Silenus was suggesting, his hands went to his belly as if he could feel the corners of something within pushing through his skin.

"We have methods of detecting parts of the First Song," said

Silenus. "The fragments stretch the world around them, in a way, and we've found a means to see those effects. You were right: we'd been to your hometown once before our last performance, as our tools had indicated an extremely sizable portion of the song was somewhere in the area. The first time we came we were surprised by the wolves, and had to abandon it. But when we finally returned for it—years later, but only about half a year ago now—we found it was gone. Someone had come along and scooped it up." He poured himself the last drops of wine. "It seems that someone was you."

"Me?" said George for the second time, and his voice was very faint.

"Yes," said Silenus. "Haven't you ever wondered how you became so good at the piano, George? Without even someone to teach you? Or how you can witness the effects of the First Song, and stay awake? Or how you, of all people, are especially sensitive to the wolves, and hear them drain the world of noise while no one else notices a thing?"

George kept pressing on his stomach, but did not answer.

"Yeah," said Silenus. "Seems like that piece was even larger and more powerful than we'd originally thought. As a matter of fact," he said, and he settled back in his chair with his eyes heavily lidded and the glass of wine balancing on his stomach, "it looks like the biggest I've ever encountered. As big as what they found in the first days."

"But I didn't...I didn't..."

"You didn't want it," said Silenus. "Yeah, I got you there. But it's in you. Maybe it chose you. Such things are not unheard of. Certain pieces of the song act differently, because, well, they're different pieces. Hence why you can hear the wolves, which is an effect I've never seen before. But that doesn't really matter." He picked up a long, thin knife from his desktop. "It's in you, and it's valuable, and some people—myself included—would dearly like to have it."

George felt like he might be sick, and feverishly wondered if that could possibly dislodge the thing that was stowed away in him. He gagged and lurched forward, but before he could think Silenus sat up and slammed the top of his desk with the knife handle. This startled George so much that he forgot all about being sick.

"Now you are lucky as *fuck* that I got a look at you before I learned what was in you," Silenus said. "Because if I hadn't, I would've thought you were one of *their* agents for sure. Some kid comes barging into my affairs with an enormous chunk of the First Song in him? That's suspicious as all hell." He tapped the point of the knife against his temple. "You can't be too paranoid these days, not if it keeps you alive. And I'd have tried to get that goddamn thing out of you the only way I know how." He spun the thin little knife around in his fingertips, and his eyes were colder than the stars glimmering in the bay window behind him.

Then he seemed to grow resigned, and the look faded and he slumped back in his chair. "But I ain't gonna do that. I know it's not your fault."

George exhaled. "Thank God."

"I don't know how it happened to you. Stroke of bad luck, maybe. But you're here in our laps and we've got to figure out what to do about you."

"Isn't there some kind of way you can remove it?"

"There are ways," said Silenus. He produced another bottle of wine from beneath his desk, and stripped its top and expertly popped the cork with his knife. "Most of them involve dying. That gets it out of you, but it's not the favorable choice."

"Dying?" cried George. "No, I don't think it would be!"

"Right, it's simple, direct, but favorable? Not so much," Silenus said. He drank his glass and poured another, then wiped sweat from his forehead and said, "Don't know why I chose wine for this fucking sitdown. News like this is more appropriate for brandy or whisky." He squinted at George and said, "You know, you've caused me a great deal of reading, boy."

"I have?"

"Yes. I've been locked up in here reading everything I can since you told me that story of yours." He gestured to the piles of books and papers around him. "Partially to see if I can get that thing out of you. And as of now it doesn't seem like I can. Just one more fucking problem in a long line of them. But mostly I've been doing research on my own personal lineage. You know what that means, don't you?"

"Your family," said George.

"Right. Because, see, the First Song is a very unstable thing. Its fragments have remarkable power, and they've almost all been lying dormant for eons. Who the hell knows what'll happen if some jake comes up and gives one a poke? But some people can handle it without hurting themselves or anyone else. They're rare as all hell, but once they were found these people were watched over until they established a firm, direct bloodline, one specifically bred to handle the First Song. *My* bloodline," said Silenus. "Do you understand what I'm getting at?"

George had a nasty feeling about the direction the conversation was taking, but still shook his head.

"What I am saying is that only me or my kin can bear the song," said Silenus. "It's almost *always* passed from parent to child. So that makes you one big fucking aberration. I've been digging through family records for days—which I hate doing, because that's some boring reading—but I cannot find one fucking iota of evidence that my family ever came anywhere near Ohio. Not at any age. But I can still see some of the Silenus family resemblance in you. The masculine features I sport—by which I mean a face as ugly as sin—are pretty predominant throughout my particular clan, no offense to you, of course." He picked up a piece of paper and affixed a pair of gold-rimmed reading spectacles to his nose. "Anyone in your family with the name of Crookson, by any chance? Or Atonyne? Those are some offshoots, some of which were in the general Midwest."

George barely heard him. He'd gone white, and knew what was about to happen. But he whispered, "No."

"Hm. I figured that would've been the best shot. Any relatives from the Mediterranean at all? There's still some kin I have there, though they're distant as all hell."

George did not answer. He bowed his head and slowly put the cup of tea down beside his chair. Silenus kept listing relations for some time, never really expecting a response. Finally he glanced up and saw George's face.

"What's eating you, kid?" he asked.

George blinked and sat up a little straighter in his chair. He felt a mad, wild rage rumbling somewhere in him, and he realized that all this time he'd delayed telling Silenus who he was not because he was afraid, but because he was *angry* at him. He was furious that he'd come all this way to serve as no more than a curious irritation in this man's life, and he'd been waiting for some reason to forgive him. Yet so far he'd found none.

"If you're going to speak, speak," said Silenus. "We ain't got all day."

"You really don't remember," said George. "You don't remember anything, do you."

"Remember?" said Silenus. "What the hell are you talking about?"

"Her name was Alice Carole," said George through gritted teeth. "Does that mean anything to you?"

Stanley sat up in his seat by the bay window and looked back and forth between Silenus and George, confused. "No," said Silenus. "No, it doesn't. And kindly give me some more information before using that fucking tone with me."

"She was my mother. She was eighteen years old when she saw you, back when you first came to Rinton, which you seem to remember now because of your song, but not because of her," said George. "She saw your show, and she fell under whatever glamour it is you cast in it. And then she started disappearing. Running off to see you, Harry, every night. I know. My grandmother told me all about it. And when you were done with her you left her behind, and you forgot about her. And she never crossed your mind again, did she? Did she?"

Silenus did not answer. His face was completely still and inscrutable.

"You've done all this research, but you never remembered her," said George. "Never thought about my mother, who died bearing me. Never thought about Rinton and what you left behind there. I guess she just wasn't that memorable to you. Sometimes I wish I'd never tried to follow you. I wish I'd never warned you about the hotel. I don't know what I expected you to be when I came looking, but it wasn't this. Not by a long shot, it wasn't this."

George expected Silenus to break down then. The revelation of an unknown son was surely enough to shake up any man, and George was looking forward to seeing it. But Silenus did not look astonished at all; he merely stared into George with his face fixed in a look of unpleasant surprise. Then he softly growled, "Get out."

"What?" said George.

"I said get out," said Silenus. He stood and crossed the room and grabbed George by the upper arm. "I want you out of this office. Get out. Right now!" He hauled George up and dragged him to the door, and bodily threw him out and slammed the door behind him.

George sat on the ground in the darkened hallway, stunned. That was not at all the reaction he'd been expecting.

The door flew open again. Silenus stood there, glaring down at him. "And do not even *think* about fucking leaving! You got me?"

"I got you," stammered George.

"Good!" Then he slammed the door once more.

George did not get up for some time. Several people in nearby hotel rooms stuck their heads out of the door, looking to see what all the commotion was about. Most of them frowned at George, thinking him some drunken adolescent, and returned to their rooms. One did not, though, and walked down the hallway toward him. When they passed before a lamp he saw it was Colette.

He did not wait for her. He stood up and walked away to his room. Then he pulled out his suitcase, flung it open, and began throwing his clothes inside.

He heard her walk to the doorway. "George?" she said. "What are you doing?"

"What does it look like I'm doing?" he said. "I'm packing."

"Packing? What, you're leaving?"

"Yes. Yes, Colette, I am leaving. I am leaving right now."

"But why?"

"Because," he said as he stuffed in one of his many coats, "there is nothing keeping me here. Because this whole thing has turned into yet another disappointment. It's just one disappointment after another, isn't it? Only this one's so much more dangerous than all the others."

"What's so disappointing?" she asked.

"Pick something!" he shouted. "Anything! I mean, I'm...I'm *owed* at least some respect, aren't I? Just a little, right? No matter what I am, or what I'm carrying. I mean, would it kill him to show me just a little courtesy?"

"Ah," she said. "You're talking about Harry."

"Yes. Yes, I'm talking about Harry. That is exactly what I am... *fucking* talking about." He laughed madly. Even though his months in vaudeville had broadened his vocabulary, his upbringing still made it difficult for him to use any of it.

"Listen, George," she said, "Harry is plenty abrasive. You don't have to tell me that. I know it probably more than anyone. But that doesn't mean you shouldn't listen to him."

George gave a hollow laugh and began piling in his socks.

"If he does something, there's usually a reason for it," she said. "And he asked you to stay. I heard that, at least. So I think you should hear him out before you do anything rash."

"I think I have heard quite enough from him."

"But it won't hurt to hear a little more."

George angrily whirled around. He had intended to make some passionate outburst, but so far he'd avoided looking at Colette; now that he did, the sight of her standing in his room in her nightgown (with her glorious, gleaming shoulders bared) gave him pause.

"Yes?" she said.

He composed himself. "I don't have to be here. Not where I'm in so much danger."

Colette sighed. "He showed you the picture show, did he?"

"Yes."

"It doesn't exactly reflect what the troupe is like, George. It's very impressive and intimidating, sure, but the day-to-day isn't half so dangerous, or righteous."

"I don't care. I could...I could be pulling down a hundred a week somewhere else. More. On the circuit or in the legitimate," he said. "I could just walk away, couldn't I? I mean, couldn't I?"

"Are you asking me if you're good, George?" she asked.

As soon as she said it he realized this was exactly what he wanted to know, and that this desire was outrageously petty. "Well, I guess so," he said.

"You are good, George," she said. "You're a very good pianist. Probably the best I've ever played with."

"Really?"

"Really. And we're better for having you with us. And Harry knows that. He knows you have something very valuable to give us. Otherwise he wouldn't have asked you to stay."

"But it's the most frustrating thing in the world, dealing with him! Everything is delayed, everything is secret, and you're given nothing. For so long, I've had nothing! I just want to be given a *little bit*. Do you know what that's like, to have so little?"

"Yes," said Colette quietly. "I know what that's like."

George was not sure what to say. Something in the way she said it suggested she knew that feeling far more than he did.

"What could he have done to make you so upset, anyway?" she

asked. "I mean, the picture show is kind of neat, but not much more. What did he say to you?"

"Oh," said George. "I...I don't think I can tell you."

She smiled at him. "You can tell me," she said. "I've heard him say plenty of ridiculous things before."

George looked at her uncertainly. He had told his secret to almost no one else, but having Colette smile at him and compliment him made him much more open to the idea now. "Well...you can't tell anyone else."

"I won't," she said. "I promise. I'm good at keeping secrets."

He sighed and sat down on his bed. "Do you want to know why I caught up with you all at the theater?" he said. "Why I'd been following you?"

"If you want to tell me."

"It's because Harry is...well, he's my father."

Her smile vanished. She stared at him with her mouth hanging open. "He's *what*?"

"My father," said George. "I'm his son." He then recounted the story of his birth and how he'd hoped to catch up to Silenus and his troupe.

When he was done she sat still for some time, and she whispered, "You're his *child*?"

"His son," said George. He did not much like being referred to as Silenus's child, especially by Colette. "I only found out about it last summer. I've been looking for him ever since."

Her face was difficult to read. At first he thought he saw horror there, and could not understand it, but then the horror slowly melted away to be replaced by a chilly rage. "He has a *child*," she said.

"Son," George said again.

But Colette did not seem to hear him. She stood up straight, her hands in fists by her sides, and looked down at him. "Why didn't you tell me that?" she said, as if he'd been maliciously keeping a secret from her.

"What?"

"How could you both hide this from me, from everyone?"

George was irritated by this about-face. "I thought the Golden Rule was to mind your own business. And what business is this of yours?"

This did little to dampen her temper. She marched outside, and George stuck his head out the door to watch. She walked up to Silenus's huge black door and began pounding on it, crying, "A child! A child, Harry! A damn child!" Once she'd finished her rant she stood outside his door and waited, arms still at her sides and her chest heaving. People opened their doors again to complain about the racket, but one steely glance from Colette sent them hurrying back into their rooms.

Yet Silenus's door did not open for her. She gave the door a solid kick, then grimaced and limped to her room without a look back at George. He watched her go, and wondered if Franny and Kingsley would also be outraged by the news of his parentage.

George stood in the hall. He was no longer sure what he wanted to do. Colette had mostly defused his anger, whether she'd meant to or not. And, now that he thought about it, the middle of the night during a freezing storm wasn't the best time to go out, especially if you had no idea where you were going. It would not really hurt to hear what Silenus had to say.

And when he did he would not try to persuade Silenus to keep him on. He did not know what his chances were out there among the wolves, but he would risk it rather than remain here, where he was not wanted.

Finally Silenus's door opened. He walked out to the hallway, looked at George and said, "Well. Come in."

He did not wait to see if George was coming. He simply walked back inside. George thought for a moment and followed.

CHAPTER 12

"Are you coming or not?"

Stanley was still sitting beneath the bay window, though he was now on the opposite side. He was white with shock and trembling very slightly, and his eyes flew to George when he entered. When Silenus sat behind his desk and turned around George almost gasped: he had been struck on the side of his face, and his left eye was swelling up horribly until his squint was uglier than ever. George looked to Stanley, as he was the only one who could have done it, but he found no explanation there.

"Sit down," said Silenus. Then he thought, and added, "Please."

George did so. His cup of tea was beside his chair, though it was now cold. Silenus struggled to find something to say, the ticks of the upright clock making the silence heavier and heavier.

Finally he asked, "How did she die?"

"My mother?" said George.

Silenus nodded. He did not meet George's eyes.

"In childbirth," he said.

"You never knew her? At all?"

"No. I was raised by my grandmother. Alone." A pause. "You remember her now?"

Silenus nodded again. "It was a very long time ago." He sank low in his chair as though this news put a great weight on him. He thoughtlessly moved to rub one temple, but when it pained his eye he winced and rubbed his nose instead. "And your grandmother told you it was me?"

"She let it slip by accident after you left Rinton. I kept asking until she told me everything. She said she knew it was someone in your troupe. Then she went digging, and found a photo of you in the newspaper."

Silenus steepled his fingers. "And she saw the resemblance."

"Yes."

He chuckled mournfully and shook his head. "If I'd have known," he said. "If I'd have known that you were, well..."

"Don't tell me that you'd have come back for me," said George.

Silenus looked at him, startled. "Of course I would have come back for you."

"Why? Why would you?"

"Well...I told you about my lineage, my bloodline...We're precious creatures, you and I."

"So not because you wanted a son," said George. "Not because you cared about my family, about me or my mother."

Silenus was silent at that. Stanley shook his head over his shoulder. "I don't know what to say," said Silenus. "I don't know anything about any of this. You've got to give me some slack, kid, I just found out about all of this in the past hour."

"I've been carrying this my whole life," said George. "It ruined my family, you know. It almost killed my grandmother. Do you know what that's like? Carrying something like that around your neck, every day?"

Silenus laughed. Again, there was no humor in it. "Unfortunately, you and I have something in common there, because that's a sensation I know all too well."

"I'm not being funny," said George.

"Neither am I."

More silence ticked by. Stanley looked back and forth between the two of them. The stars behind the window seemed to shift and swoop slightly, as if spelling out strange messages.

"You think I do not like you," said Silenus suddenly.

George blinked. The idea of Silenus discussing people in terms of "like" was almost unthinkable.

"You think I don't care for you," Silenus continued. "That I don't want you, or that I hold some disgust for you. That I think you some failure, something pitiable and little. Is that it?"

George was so stung that he could not speak. He only nodded.

"That's not the case," said Silenus. "In all honesty, I just don't know what to think of you, George. You left home at the age of sixteen under your own devising, and with nothing but talent and stubbornness managed to work your way far enough into the circuit to track me down. All while dodging dangers and threats that I'm sure I can't imagine, not the least of which was simple starvation. You found a home in the heart of a business that is famed for being impenetrable, even hostile, to outsiders. All while carrying something very precious, very dangerous, and very *heavy* within you. That's... that's remarkable. Do you not know that you are remarkable, George?"

George could not think of anything to say. He shook his head.

"I didn't know what to do with you when I first saw you," said Silenus. "And I still don't."

"Didn't you ever suspect it?" asked George. "When the wolf looked at us and said we were family, didn't you wonder?"

"I thought you might be a relation of mine, yes," said Silenus. "Like I said, my features are pretty predominant throughout my family. That's why I did all this research. But a, a son... I thought it was impossible. I've been on this Earth for a long damn time, George, and I have never fathered a child. I just didn't think I could. And yet, here you are..." He shook his head. "You think you have every right to be angry with me. Perhaps that's so. Saying that I didn't know is an excuse for why I never came back to you, maybe. But it's not one for your mother. Nothing I can give you could ever make up for that, George."

George nodded, and was glad to hear Silenus admit this. "You didn't trick her, did you?"

"Lord, no!" said Silenus. "She chose me of her own accord." He cocked an eyebrow. "You don't see what she saw in me, do you?"

George tactfully did not answer, but Silenus smiled. "Not all of us start out old and fat and irritable, George. These things are done to us, not by us. None of us are the creatures we were in our beginnings." He sighed. "So the question still remains the same. What to do with you? I think you know my suggestion."

"You want me to stay," said George.

"I want you to stay with us, yes," said Silenus. "Of course I do. I want you to travel the circuits with us, performing, as we've done for so many years. It's what you wanted, why you came, isn't it? To join me in vaudeville?"

George nodded.

"And I need you by me," said Silenus. "No, I *want* you by me. For many reasons. Some concerning our mission, yes. You are a very valuable person, George. In addition, I think you would want to have what's in you removed, and I'm probably your only chance of that. But also because you belong with us. With me. I have never had a child before, so I don't know much of raising or teaching one, especially one that seems to have been nearly raised already...but I'm willing to try, and give you what I can. Does that sound amenable to you?"

George considered it. He had not seen this side of Silenus before; he seemed vulnerable and uncertain. Finally George said, "I'll leave whenever I wish. If you hit me, or abuse me in any way, I'm gone."

"I will do my best to give you no reason to leave," said Silenus. "But if you stay, you must stay under my rules. You'll be by my side, yes, but you'll be among a troupe, boy. We're a traveling company. We have procedures and laws. We pull our salaries from the same pool and treat everyone as equally as we can. You know what that means?"

"I wasn't expecting any favoritism," said George.

"I didn't say you were. But the others will certainly expect it. So I'll ride you hard, George. You'll do more than the others, much more. I'll expect perfection from you, and apply higher standards to everything you do."

"So my reward for staying with you is to be punished?" said George.

"Punished?" said Silenus. He took out a cigar and cut off the end. "It would be punishment if I didn't think you could do it. But I'm convinced you easily can."

George blinked, and then a small smile trickled into his face. For the first time since Colette had praised his performance, he felt the small, hot coals of pride lighting up inside his belly.

"So," said Silenus. "Will you stay?"

"Yes," said George. "I'll stay."

"Good then," said Silenus. "I'm happy to hear it." He stood up, the unlit cigar still in his hands, and walked around to George. As he came near he seemed to grow awkward, as though he was not sure what to do. He frowned for a bit, and stuck out his hand. "Welcome aboard," he said.

George had been expecting something more — an embrace, at least — but he shook Silenus's hand, rather disappointed. It felt like they'd made a business transaction rather than begun any kind of relationship.

Stanley stood up from the bay window and approached as well. He was blinking back tears, but George was not surprised to see such a show of emotion from a gentle thing like Stanley. He fumbled with his blackboard, and thought for a long moment about what to write.

Eventually he scrawled out: WELCOME TO THE TROUPE. Then he embraced George, and was reluctant to let go.

As Silenus walked George to the door, George said, "I did tell Colette about this. She didn't seem very...pleased."

"So I fucking heard," said Silenus. "You leave Colette to me." When he opened the door to let him out, the awkwardness returned. Silenus eventually managed, "Get some sleep, kid," and gently ushered him out into the darkened hallway.

Silenus called for a group meeting the next day to make the announcement. They all gathered in his dressing room backstage, and Kingsley and Franny, the only two who still did not know, seemed to expect some bad news concerning their salaries. Silenus began with, "I suppose you have all been wondering exactly how George caught up with us in Parma."

"No," said Kingsley with some surprise.

"What?" said Franny, who had not been paying attention.

"Well, that's what you *should* have been wondering," said Silenus angrily. "As it turns out, George had been trying to catch up with us for some time. The reason behind this is that he, defying all logic and possibility, is my son, who I never knew existed until last night, and he was seeking me out."

Their reactions to this were not quite what George had expected. Kingsley was flustered and panicked from the start, and assumed Silenus would be giving George a managerial position and a pay raise, despite Silenus's immediate assurances that he wouldn't. But the most surprising reaction was from Franny, who gasped and nearly fell out of her chair when she heard the news. It was the most emotion George had seen her display yet.

Silenus then made several speeches denying any favoritism, or at least half-speeches, as Kingsley and Franny kept interrupting halfway through, Kingsley voicing some suspicion of George's position, and Franny asking about George's mother. "Who was the girl?" she kept saying. "Where is the boy's mother? What have you done with her?"

Silenus took these accusations more personally than George would have expected. "Don't be upset with me!" he said to her. "I didn't hurt anyone! Why would you think such a thing?" But Franny would not be persuaded, and remained furious.

Yet the most disheartening response was Colette's: she sat with her arms crossed and her eyes boring into the empty wall before her, refusing to look at either George or Harry. George attempted to catch her attention once or twice, but she studiously ignored him. What he had done to offend her was beyond him.

"I know this is a startling discovery for us all," said Silenus, "but we can't let it trip us up. George is staying with us, and that is that. Now we've all got work to do together, whether we like it or not, and we need to get back to business. There's a show today, and within three days we're moving on again. So go on."

Mumbling and muttering, they all stumped out except for George, who dawdled behind to speak to Colette. But when he walked out he found she was waiting for him next to an old discarded backdrop of a plantation. George wondered if she was going to apologize to him.

Those hopes were dashed when she fixed him in a glare and said, "You must feel pretty good about yourself, don't you?"

"I what?" he said.

"You've got yourself all set up. You've got a company, a circuit contract—of a sort—and an in with the manager. A big in. Everything seems to be going your way."

"Not everything," said George, who could not bring himself to meet Colette's eyes.

"Do you even know what you're getting into?" she asked. "All of us in the troupe, we're here because we have no other choice. Harry gave us something we could never get anywhere else. But you can just walk away, just like you said last night, and take what you please."

"I can't," said George. "It's the same way for me."

She seemed to take that as an insult. "How?" she demanded.

"He's got something I can't get anywhere else, too," George said. "He's my father, Colette. I hardly have anyone else. I've got to be with him."

Colette softened a little at that. But still she shook her head. "Are you so sure? How well does he fit the role?"

Before George could respond, he heard Silenus's rough shout echoing down the passageway. "George!" he cried. "Are you coming or not?"

He looked back to Colette. She shrugged and leaned up against the backdrop, crinkling the white columns and green fields of the plantation. Then she crossed her arms and looked away.

George reluctantly turned and ran up the passageway, calling, "I'm coming!"

PART TWO

The Big Time

When life seems full of clouds an' rain
and I am filled with naught but pain,
who soothes my thumpin' bumpin' brain?
Nobody.

When winter comes with snow an' sleet,
and me with hunger and cold feet,
who says "Ah, here's two bits, go an' eat!"
Nobody.

I ain't never got nothin' from nobody, no time!
And until I get somethin' from somebody, sometime,
I don't intend to do nothin' for nobody, no time!

—Bert Williams and Alex Rogers,
Nobody, 1905

CHAPTER 13

The Long Tour

Now came smoky, wintry days, days of drafty rooms and chilly floor-boards, of sour meats and sleepless nights and yellowed bedsheets layered with grit, always the grit. It came tumbling down from the train tops to rest in your hair, on your collar, in your sleeves and mouth, a constant invasion of grainy cinders that turned white linen into graying sackcloth. You could wash, certainly, but what was the point if you'd be on the train again in a week, or a day, or even less? You would always be moving, adrift in a sea of dour, distracted faces and jostling elbows and the grasping spumes of smoky grit, and when that was done you were speeding along through leafless forests and sodden fields and tumbledown towns with the white winter sky weighing down upon you.

You lived for the afternoons and the nights, when you did your turn. Everything else was backstage, in a way: the train station, the railways, the hotels and the bars, all of these were just a long, drawn-out wait in the shadowed corridors behind the real performance. You bided your time among greasepaint clowns and acrobats and chorus girls (who scratched at their leggings until one of their partners slapped their hands and told them stop, stop, you'll put a run in them) and teams of softly whining dogs in little dresses. To pass the time you idly bickered with them in your thieves' cant of showbiz terms; you fought over billing, over originators of bits and lines, over the goddamn choosers who lurked in the audience and sought to plunder your act and apply it elsewhere. Why, I found some jake in Columbus who'd been doing my bit for well over a year, they'd say, and certainly, I put an ad in the monthly and called the fellow out, but he never replied, the coward, he certainly never replied.

Your dressing room was only desirable in terms of solitude; the actual conditions were often nothing short of deplorable. The first thing you did upon arriving was search the walls and corners for any peepholes (they would be there regardless of your sex), and fill them in with shoe polish (and yet how many times had you seen narrow, soiled fingers worming through the blocked-up holes, pushing past this obstruction to make way for a desperate eye?). Then came the rituals: you avoided looking at all the windows, for to spy a bird on one's sill was sure to bring bad luck. If you found a peacock feather accidentally jettisoned from some chorus girl's gown, you made sure not to touch it; to touch a peacock feather was to invoke the worst of all misfortunes. You made *sure* not to whistle, that was a death knell if ever there was one. You just pulled on your oldest performance shoes and turned your shirt inside out while mumbling your lines, perhaps shuffling widdershins two or three times as you did. Then you would be sanctified, consecrated, protected against all ills. Unless, of course, you were following an animal act; no luck could aid you in competing with dumb, trained creatures who somehow always managed to charm the hearts of the audience while leaving shit all over the stage.

Then came your moment, the little splinter of time you'd been waiting for since you awoke that morning: they called your name and you took a breath and walked across the stiff cardboard floor (riddled with holes from previous props), the dark back of the theater full of gleaming, watchful eyes like a cavern full of roosting owls, and then you sang or bleated your little song, or made your little speech, or did your funny little dance. And it was easy, because after all you'd done it just the day before, and the day before that, and the dozens of hundreds of days before that. Had you always been doing this, you wondered, as you listened to the applause (sometimes a dribble, other times a roar)? Had you always been playing for these darkened people, rendered bodiless and invisible by the blazing footlights?

And then after the performance you returned to your barren flop-house room, frosted with moonlight from the many holes in the walls, the bed and sheets alive with dozens of creepy-crawlies who roved the folds looking for bare flesh to bite. You'd sleep shivering in a ball and awake with red and pink perforations lining your neck, your crotch, your armpits. But you did not want to slap yourself down with kerosene to keep them away, like some people advised, as the reeking fumes almost choked you in the night, so you suffered through their tiny bites. And when morning came you'd sit on the edge of the bed aching and stiff, your breath smoking and pluming, and you'd fear to touch your soles to the chilly floorboards... yet just before you did, you'd wonder what day it was. Surely it could not still be February? Could it really? Had it not been winter for many, many months?

George finally asked Silenus about the time once. It seemed to move slowly now that he was touring.

"We are traveling the thin parts of the world, George, the hollow parts," he answered. "We seek out the fringes, the edges, the festering, open sores. Existence is breaking down here. Time doesn't work right. It's grown distorted. That's why we come here to play the song. Then things will be right for these places, in time."

"But it's been winter for so long," said George. "It feels like it's been winter for years. Can the people who live here really never notice that something's wrong?"

Silenus grinned and said, "To them, everything's dandy. They never notice that the world is dying below their feet."

"But why?"

"Because they don't want to. The human aptitude for self-deception is unfathomable, kid. If it wasn't, we'd be out of a job."

George felt as though he was breaking down along with the world. His back began to stoop, his skin grew thin and sallow, and his knuckles clicked and cracked after every performance. When Colette found him sleeping in a pile of dusty curtains backstage, she slapped him awake and held him upright with one arm, murmuring, "Told you. I told you so."

Her initial resentment changed to pity when she saw how hard George was taking their travels. If she was confident enough in his collaboration with the orchestra, she'd let him sleep backstage in one of the dressing rooms, and cover for him if Silenus asked. For some reason she was happy to have something to fight with Harry over: the two of them often seemed to be in the middle of some managerial argument or another, always retreating down an empty hallway to harangue each other in hushed tones, or bickering all the way back to his office. But though George was glad of her help and friendship, his increasing affections for her went unrequited. Whenever she woke him from his naps, or tended to him when he was weary, there was always a distance there, and she was reluctant to touch him. Each moment with her was fleeting and frustrated, and soon her very presence caused a dull ache in the root of his being.

Franny was one of the few troupe members not infected by the pervasive weariness of February. Instead, she'd become oddly invigorated by the revelation of George's parentage. Yet it took some time for George to realize she was not happy, but angry, and specifically angry at Silenus. For some reason she could not forgive him his ignorance of his only child. She was so angry that after one rehearsal she did not pay attention and allowed a splinter of an iron band to tear open her bandaged sleeve. When the tear flapped open George saw the black writing on her skin again, yet now he saw it was not writing, but a *drawing*, an amazingly intricate design that covered her entire arm, full of loops and twirls and spidery angles.

Before he could examine it further, Silenus stepped forward. George had almost never seen him show any tenderness to anyone, especially Franny, yet he gently took her hand and pulled her sleeve down and said, "You almost hurt yourself, my dear." But Franny snatched her hand away and covered up the tear and walked away. Silenus appeared genuinely hurt by this reaction. "What does she think I ever did to her?" he asked. But George only watched the strongwoman depart, and wondered what was below all those bandages and scarves.

And if George was doing poorly, his issues were slight compared to Kingsley's, which got worse every day. Somehow Kingsley still managed to perform each night: he would shuffle out from behind the curtain, limping and bent sideways, and take his seat; yet when he heard Silenus announce his name he'd straighten up and smooth himself out, and perform as though he were hardly hurt at all. But when the curtain dropped he'd crumple again like a snail dashed with salt, sometimes even whimpering, and would need several deep breaths before being able to stand.

Everyone took this grimly. Kingsley denied any medical treatment, saying he preferred his own remedies, though he never explained what these were.

George was not sure how the troupe had lasted as long as it had, and could not imagine its continuing for much longer. It seemed as if it might fall apart at any moment. And how much farther would they go, even if they could? His father had never mentioned a specific endpoint for their precious mission. When would they ever be done?

*   *   *

George's only distraction from all of their troubles was the piece of the First Song he carried with him. Now that he knew it was there he began to feel it reacting to things around him, trembling at the whisper of rain or resonating with a strong wind. It wanted something, he felt. He began to suspect that it wanted to be whole.

After many weeks of traveling, he still did not know exactly how Silenus and Stanley acquired their shreds of the song. Every week or so they slipped out with the steamer trunk and returned tired and worn, as if they'd been through a tremendous trial, but what they were doing out in the wilderness was a mystery to everyone, even Colette. George did not even know how the song was performed: no matter how carefully he watched each performance of the fourth act, he saw nothing more than Silenus conducting and Stanley and Colette singing and playing. Yet still the First Song was somehow invoked. He was sure Silenus had something to do with it. Why would he be onstage at all, otherwise? He played no instrument, and did not sing.

He wanted to ask his father about it, but the opportunity never seemed to come. Though Silenus now allowed his son into his life more, he was always busy and distant, and George did not understand him or what he did any more than before.

At first things seemed positive, as Silenus's door began appearing to him more often. "I've changed your privileges," said Silenus when George asked about this. "It'll appear more frequently to you, and it'll always allow you in. And if there's an emergency, it'll show up." George usually found his father reading inside. His reading material would vary from thick books the size of tombstones, to thin little books with silvery pages that would seem to sing when you turned the pages, to long, brown parchments that were very old and brittle. "I'm trying to alleviate your condition," his father explained when George once asked him about it.

"My condition?"

"Removing the song. I'm hoping something here can give us a

hint." But his expression was so black and impatient George could only assume it was not going well.

Once he entered to find Silenus looking at an enormous map of North America, and while most of it was recognizable some parts seemed to bulge or expand outward into lands George did not know. There was a small country on the edge of Kentucky described as "Heartache's Founding," several stretches of forest in southern Ontario called "The Vale of Tears," and one large peninsula off of Nova Scotia was labeled NOVA ATLANTIS. George asked if those places were really there, and Silenus answered that they were, provided you came at them the right way.

But business soon trumped these new intimacies. In mid-February they left the obscure fringes of the Keith-Albee circuit and signed on with the Loews circuit, which made them officially small-time. George presumed this was done so they could search a new area for the song. Silenus initially encountered some trouble negotiating their contracts, which would normally have been laid out for several months at the choosing of the booking office, but these schedules were too restrictive for the troupe. His father was forced to go down to the telegraph office and exchange message after message with the booking office until he got the destinations and times and billing he desired. Sometimes these exchanges lasted over five or six hours, but he implacably waited it out. George never got to read the cables, but he got the sense that Silenus was a ferociously canny businessman.

He sometimes accompanied Silenus to the telegraph office, hoping to impress him with his theories about Mendelssohn or Brahms, or perhaps to discuss their family, if he was lucky. But Silenus was not interested in any such conversation. Instead he'd rant about the booking office and Albee and the stage managers, and the endless frustrations one met in touring. His diatribes stopped only to allow a fresh swig of bourbon or brandy before he continued with his vitriol, and they always ended in some bitter or cruel advice that George did not wish to listen to. "Life is a difficult, nasty thing, kid, and I wouldn't recommend it to any friend of mine," was one such statement he often revisited.

Each time George could only sigh. He had fought so hard to be by his father's side, yet now that he was here it felt like they were further apart than ever.

CHAPTER 14

Stage Time

George eventually adjusted to life on the road, or at least as much as anyone could, and as he did he began to feel increasingly frustrated with his role in the troupe. In his time at Otterman's he'd become accustomed to admiration and respect, but no one among the Silenus Troupe held him in any such high regard. If anything, every member of the troupe seemed to feel he was their personal assistant, and they appreciated his enthusiasm only when it was engaged in getting them a cup of coffee or tea.

He had never traveled with a troupe before, but he badly wished to impress them and rise above his lowly status. The first strategy he took was to casually begin playing famously difficult pieces during rehearsal. Once they heard what he could do, he reasoned, they'd surely think differently of him. So, during one rehearsal day when Franny was having trouble figuring out how to do her bit in such a small theater, he pretended to be bored and launched into the Mendelssohn first piano concerto. He was just hitting his stride when Harry came striding up, but rather than heaping admiration on George, he said, "Will you stop that goddamn racket? We've got people trying to work over here!"

George, crestfallen, nodded and stuffed the sheet music into his valise.

His next tactic for increasing his standing was to offer his expert opinions on improving everyone's act. After all, he'd seen many acts at Otterman's, and he played with these performers for hours at a time; they would have to see how they could better their acts once he spoke to them, and they'd appreciate his help. But his first attempt went horribly: he'd hardly gotten halfway through outlining all the flaws he'd noted in Kingsley's act before the man went into an enraged, hysterical fit, and wound up locking himself in his dressing room. Silenus and Colette had to spend an hour talking him out of it, and neither was very pleased with George.

George was deeply hurt by these reactions, but decided he'd been going about this wrong; the troupe members were performers, and if there was one thing performers listened to, it was the audience. The trick was to somehow earn the audience's admiration, and then the admiration of the troupe would surely follow. But how to attract the audience's attention? He was just an accompanist. Everything about his position was meant to make him invisible to them.

George thought he'd hit upon just the thing when he remembered the bright yellow Spanish coat he'd bought while at Otterman's. He hadn't been able to wear it yet, but he thought it'd be precisely what was needed to draw the audience's eye to the young man in the pit who was so splendidly playing the piano. He donned it on the night of their first performance in Grand Rapids, and descended the dressing room stairs to join the rest of the troupe before they took their places.

"Bad news, folks," said Colette as she came in. "Two spots before us is another damn dog act, so we'll have to keep an eye out and make sure not to step—" She stopped when she saw George. "Whoa. Uh. Harry?"

"Yeah?" said Silenus, who was peering out at the audience.

"We might have a situation here."

"What situation?" He turned around and jumped a little. "Holy hell," he said. "What is that you're wearing?"

"What's what?" said George, affecting surprise.

There was a pause as everyone turned to look at him.

"Have you lost your damn mind?" asked Silenus. "Take that fucking thing off!"

"But why?" he asked.

"You look a little like a parade float, dear," said Franny.

George looked around. Everyone's face was fixed in an expression of either bemusement or outright horror. "Fine," he muttered, and returned upstairs.

The next day Stanley took him out to the tailor's as a gift. George was happy to accept this gesture, as Stanley shared his love of clothes. Furthermore, he'd made a habit of giving George little presents now and again, from combs to mirrors to nice pearl-handled razors. George often suspected Stanley pitied him for how Harry treated him, and wished to compensate.

"This is all very nice," said George as the tailor fitted him for a smart black tuxedo, "but I thought my current wardrobe was good enough."

Stanley's face became curiously closed. He wrote: NOT SURE IF TWEED AND WAISTCOATS FIT YOUR AGE.

"But that's what men of standing wear," said George.

Stanley thought hard for a moment, chalk in hand. He wrote: MAYBE. WILL NEED TO FIND SOMETHING THAT FITS A VAUDEVILLIAN BETTER, THOUGH.

When they returned to the hotel with four new suits for George, Silenus called him into his office alone for a talk.

"It is clear to me that something in you has changed recently," Harry said to him. "What, I don't know. Maybe you had a fever and no one noticed, and now your mind is irreparably damaged and we're all just seeing the effects. But whatever it is, I got to figure out how to put a stop to it. Because you are driving everyone absolutely insane. So, to be blunt, what's with you, kid?"

George thought very fast. He was not prepared to negotiate, but he said, "I'm tired of just accompanying."

Silenus's eyebrows slowly rose and he leaned back in his chair. "Ah. I see."

"Yes," said George. "I . . . I don't feel that it's an efficient use of my talents."

"An efficient use of your talents."

"Yes. I feel like I could do more. I *should* do more."

"And what, pray tell, would be an efficient use of your talents?"

George swallowed. "I want stage time."

"Stage time?"

"Yes. I'm a member of the troupe, aren't I? Shouldn't I get the same amount of respect? The same amount of stage time?"

Silenus nodded. "All right. That's what I wanted to know. It makes this all very easy."

"It does?" said George. He could not believe that all he had needed to do was ask.

"Yes. It will be a very simple thing to put this matter to rest." Silenus leaned forward, and said very clearly: "No. No, you cannot have stage time. There? Does that fix things?"

George blinked in shock. "Why?"

"*Why?*" said Silenus. "Pick a fucking reason, that's why! Do you have any idea how hard it is to travel with four acts in one troupe, to negotiate scheduling and billing? We can't just throw an extra goddamn act in there! That'd make things impossible!"

"But haven't I proven that I'm good enough to belong up there?"

"Jesus, George, it's not about being good enough. You could perform a whole fucking symphony all by yourself and it wouldn't matter. If we don't have room on the bill, we don't have room on the bill, and that's final."

"What about joining one of the acts?" he asked. "Couldn't I . . . I don't know . . . play onstage with someone?"

"You want to elbow in on someone else's applause?" Silenus laughed. "Be my guest. Try explaining that to Colette or Kingsley, and let's see how that goes. And I don't think you'd want to play onstage with Franny, not unless you were wearing a helmet."

"What about the fourth act?" he asked.

Silenus's entire demeanor changed: his face grew cold and suspicious, and he sat up a little. "You don't play during the fourth act."

"But I could! I could learn a part, just like Stanley and Colette."

"That is out of the question."

"Why? All they do is just play along, don't they? It's you who invokes the song."

"I am *not* discussing this with you," said Silenus.

George paused, offended. "Why not?" he asked finally. "I'm your son, aren't I? You're always hiding things from me. So why not explain it, just this once? Give me a reason."

"You want a reason?" said Silenus. "Fine. Have you forgotten what you're carrying in you?"

George was quiet. He had worried this might be his father's response.

"Yeah," said Silenus. "You have something very, *very* important in you, kid, and the last thing we need is for you to be exposed. And that's just what you'd be up there on that stage, in any capacity. The wolves have their spies, and they'd think, who's this kid? Haven't we seen him before? Why'd he suddenly jump in? And then they'd start sniffing around you, trying to feel you out. Is that what you want? Do you want all those black eyes fixed on you, looking you over?"

George shook his head.

"I didn't think so," said Silenus. "So for now you're our secret. We keep you in the pit playing along, just as we've always done. All right?"

"So that's it," said George. "That's what I'm supposed to be, from now on. Some package for you to carry around, and keep secret."

"It's not that simple."

"It sounds that way. It's not right. If I'd never come to you I might have been able to make my own way on the stage. But now I'm just some load you have to drag around with you, like Franny."

Silenus slammed a hand down on the desktop. "Don't speak that way of Franny! You've no idea what she's been through! And she's not my 'load,' you got me? If I hear you talk that way about her again, I'll…" Seeing George's startled expression, he trailed off and sighed. "I'm sorry. Forget that. Listen, I know you don't like it, but I can't spare time and money just to make you feel happy, not when there are larger things at stake. But you are *important,* do you see that?"

"Just not the kind of important that could ever be of any use to you," said George.

"Oh, damn it," snarled Silenus. "I didn't ask for you to be given to me under these goddamn circumstances, you know?"

"Well, you could at least try and make them better!" said George, and he stood up and walked out.

Things remained strained between George and his father for the remainder of the week. He could understand Silenus's logic very well, but that didn't mean it satisfied him. He had come to his father with grander dreams of the stage, but now Silenus's troupe was slowly turning into a cage, penning him in.

As a form of protest, one night George decided he would not play to his usual standards. In fact, he decided he might fumble once or twice, or perhaps lose his place. He did not have the gall to interfere with Kingsley's act—those puppets unsettled him far too much— and any errors in Franny's could possibly lead to harm. So instead he varied the tempo during Colette's dance, allowing her concertina playing to get a little ahead and a little behind, which made her struggle to land all of her steps. He did not enjoy doing it, for nothing gave him greater pleasure than seeing Colette dance, but it needed to be done. Both she and Silenus had to learn that he was much more crucial than they thought. And he could always apologize later.

"Very off night I'm having," George remarked to Silenus after the show.

"Yes, I noticed," said Silenus mildly. "You know, I don't think you've ever missed a note since we first employed you."

"Really?" said George. "Never? Well, I'm sorry that tonight was my first."

"I think you're about to be sorrier."

"Why is that?"

"I'll let Colette explain," he said, and nodded over George's shoulder.

"What?" said George. He turned around and saw Colette walking toward him. "Oh. Hello, Colette."

She stopped in front of him. Then her mouth wove into a magnificent snarl and her shoulders darted forward, and there was a flash of smooth brown knuckles. The backstage started spinning around him, and the next thing he knew he was staring up at the ceiling.

And the next night, George, now sporting a superb black eye, hit every note he had to play.

Yet this only increased his resentment. He had tasted real applause only once, when he'd first auditioned for Otterman's. The entire staff had clapped for him then, confounded by his playing. It had been such a wonderful feeling, like holding the world in the palm of his hand. He wanted nothing more than to experience that again, and use it to prove to his father what he could do. Then perhaps Silenus would allow him into his life just as he did Colette and Stanley.

So during his free day on Sunday George found another, much shabbier vaudeville hall (one that appeared to be a meat market during working hours), and arrived during its audition time dressed in his new tuxedo with the sheet music for the Mendelssohn No. 1. He did not, of course, intend to leave the troupe; he simply wanted to prove to himself that he could, if he wanted to. And it wouldn't hurt at all if he heard the thunderous applause of the audience again, even if it was in such a disreputable place as this.

The audition audience was even worse than most theaters'. The stage was littered with rotten fruit that'd been hurled at all the actors. George, smiling, shook his head at the poor fools until they called out the fake name he had given them.

He climbed the stage and seated himself before the piano, reveling in the cold, pristine beauty of the spotlight. Then he coughed into one hand, adjusted his tie, and began to play.

He thought he did a pretty splendid job, considering the quality of the piano. Many of the keys were out of tune, and some of them were missing their ivory. And eventually he noticed there was something wrong with the acoustics: there was a persistent moan that kept building throughout his playing.

But when he hit one of the *pianissimo* passages he heard that it was not a moan at all. It was something he'd never heard before: the audience was *booing*. His playing wound to a stop as he realized that they were booing *him*.

"What's this?" he said. "What are you doing?"

"You're terrible!" shouted a man in the front row.

"*I'm* terrible?" said George. He reddened. "*You're* terrible!"

The man in the front row made some reply, but before George could make sense of it something struck him on the side of the head. He blinked and touched his face and found there was a rancid, red juice on his cheekbone, and the sickly stench of something sweet and fermented began to permeate the stage. Then he saw there was something beside his foot, glistening and mottled with wrinkled skin, and he peered down and saw it was an ancient, graying tomato, lightly furred with some fungus that was happily devouring its putrid insides.

George's mind whirled, incapable of making any connections between the fruit on the stage and the thing that had struck him; he absently wondered if it had always been there, and he'd only just stepped on it. "What was that?" he said, but as he lifted his head he saw a row of people in the back stand up and make a quick, violent gesture all at once, as if they were waving at him, and then at least a dozen more tomatoes rose up in a fetid wave, arcing through the spotlit air to converge on where he sat.

George was not sure what one did after such experiences. It was the first time he'd ever encountered such overwhelming rejection. But he knew what his father often did when he experienced an obstacle, so George followed suit and went straight across the street to a bar. He ordered a drink and sat down, intending to stay until he'd drunk the anger and humiliation clear out of his head.

He was feeling pretty soused and lousy when he heard a voice over his shoulder: "So this is how you spend your free days?"

He wheeled around. There standing behind him was Harry, scratching his head.

"What are you doing here?" George slurred.

His father sat down beside him. "Jesus. How many have you had?"

"I don't know. A lot."

"He's had three beers," said the bartender.

"Oh," said Silenus. "What's this you're covered in?" Then he sniffed, and almost choked. "And *Jesus*, what's that smell?"

George sighed and tried to explain what had happened that afternoon. As he did he found his plan now sounded marvelously stupid, and he felt ashamed of what he'd done.

"So," said Silenus. "You were going to run away?"

"No!" said George. "I wasn't. Honest. I just wanted to…see."

"See what?"

"I don't know. If I was as good as I thought I was. It *felt* like I was. I thought I could do it. But I couldn't."

"Don't listen to those assholes," said Silenus. "They were going to boo you no matter what, I bet. And besides, you trot out Mendelssohn in, what, a vaudeville hall that's mostly a butcher's? They've got meat prices hanging in their window, for Christ's sakes! That is not your intended audience, son."

It was the first time Silenus had ever called him "son." George shut his eyes. "You were right."

"Right? Right about what?"

"I'm not ready for the stage."

"I never said you weren't ready," said Silenus. "I said we didn't have room."

"I don't want to anymore, anyway."

Silenus sighed. "Listen, one day you'll be up there. One day Stan and I will teach you everything we know about the stage. Little tips and tricks that can win over an audience. But until then, you've got to keep in mind that you are *very* young, George, and you are probably too talented for your own damn good. If this were a just world you'd be getting all the glory and praise you deserve. But right now you got to think about the bigger picture. You need to keep your head down and do as I say. I'm looking out for you, kid. I couldn't bear it if something happened to you. Okay?"

"Okay."

"You ready to go back to the hotel? You look like it."

George nodded, and his father helped him off the stool and held him up with one arm as they lurched back to the hotel.

"What's today?" asked George.

"Today? I don't know. March second, I think."

"That's what I thought," said George. "It's my birthday."

"It is?" said Silenus. "Shit, why didn't you say anything?"

"I guess I had too much on my mind."

"Well, hell," said his father. He grunted as he tugged George up the front steps. "Happy birthday, kid."

For a little while after things felt much easier between George and his father. He was still not particularly happy with his place in the troupe, but for now he was content to simply do as his father asked. And Silenus bought him a music box for his birthday, and Stanley a pair of white satin gloves: "For when your day comes," read the note. It was nice to know that at least someone was thinking of him.

But then, two weeks after George's debacle at the audition, he had a distressing encounter. They had just checked into a new hotel, and George was down in the lobby restaurant getting a midnight snack when a man stopped at his table and stared at him.

"Can I help you?" asked George.

"You were the kid in the tuxedo," said the man. He was extremely tall and broad, and clad in an ill-fitting suit. "Weren't you?"

"I beg your pardon?"

"Yeah, that was you," said the man. He grinned. "It was just a couple of weeks ago, wasn't it? At Herfeitz's Theater in Lansing. That had to have been you."

"I'm afraid I'm not familiar with that establishment," said George.

"No, no," he said. "You was there. It was the place that had the butcher's counter in the back."

George stiffened when he heard this. "You what?" he said. "You were in that audience?"

"Yeah, I was there. I was in town on business, thought I'd catch a show. I have to admit, you were something else. You were great."

"I was...I was *great*?" said George. "Then why on Earth did you throw tomatoes at me?"

"Oh, I didn't," he said. "Not me, I didn't throw a thing." He stopped smiling. "And the other guys...well. They didn't *want* to. They thought you were pretty great too, really."

"Then why did they?"

"Well, we was told to."

"Told to?" said George. "I knew it! The theater owner made you, didn't he? I bet they did that to all the acts, the bastards!"

"No, not the owner," said the man. "And not all the acts. We were told to boo just at you."

"Me? And it wasn't the owner? Then who?"

"Well, I don't rightly know," he said. "He just gave everyone a quarter and said to boo the kid in the tuxedo."

"What did this man look like?"

The man shrugged. "Well…he was kind of a short fella. Had a big top hat and a big black mustache. And he had funny eyes. Really, really blue eyes. He was sort of an odd bird, really."

George's belly grew cold and his mouth went dry. "W-what?" he said faintly.

"I wasn't sure why he'd pay us to throw food at you, but, well…a quarter's a quarter. I'm sorry about how they treated you. I hope you keep playing." He saluted. "So long."

George sat at his table, still as a stone. There was only one person that man could've been describing, and George knew immediately that he'd been snookered yet again. His father must have somehow known *exactly* what he was going to do, and taken steps to ensure that George's ambition was safely quashed. And then after, when Harry had found him in the bar and talked to him about being ready… He had sounded so sincere, so genuine. And yet he'd engineered *everything.*

George had never felt so manipulated in all of his life. He stood up from the table and dashed for the stairs, intending to rush up and burst into his father's office and confront him. Yet on the first landing was Stanley, and he saw that something was wrong.

He stepped to the side to block George's path, and wrote: WHERE ARE YOU GOING?

"I'm going to see Harry!" George said. "I'm going to kick his damn door down and tell him I know what he did, that's where I'm going!"

Stanley gently pushed him back. CALM DOWN.

"I won't calm down!" said George. "I don't need to calm down! It is perfectly just for me to be angry about this!"

ABOUT WHAT?

George stood there for a moment, quivering. He wanted to hold his anger back, but it was difficult to do so before Stanley, who had always been so kind to him and always seemed to understand everything. So it all came pouring out: he told Stanley about how he'd wished to become more important to the troupe, and yet had been refused every time, and about how he'd gone to the audition to try to test himself, and yet he'd been humiliated and pelted with rotten vegetables... and how just now, there in the lobby of the hotel, he'd learned his father had been behind it all.

Stanley seemed to briefly share George's anger. But then it was gone, and he only looked regretful. He wrote: YOU ARE RIGHT. THAT WAS NOT THE BEST THING TO DO.

"Not the best!" cried George. "Not the best! Having your son pelted with rotting tomatoes? I shouldn't think so!"

Stanley wrote: I WILL TALK TO HARRY.

"No, you won't! It's me who's suffered! I deserve to be the one! What he did was unbelievably selfish!"

LIKE SABOTAGING COLETTE'S PERFORMANCE?

George paused as he read this. "What? N-no. That's...that's completely different."

Stanley cocked an eyebrow.

"Messing up a bit during Colette's act and...and being hit with rotten fruit are not the same thing."

SHOULD WE ASK COLETTE?

George, remembering how furious she'd looked when she hit him, shook his head. "No. I don't think that'd be wise."

Stanley wrote: PROBABLY MADE HIM THINK YOU NEEDED TO BE TAUGHT A LESSON.

"And what lesson was that?"

Stanley shrugged, and wrote: HUMILITY?

"What?" said George. "What would I need to learn about that?"

Stanley rolled his eyes, but smiled at him and wrote: ONE DAY YOU WILL HAVE TO LEARN THAT YOU ARE NOT THE CENTER OF THE WORLD GEORGE.

"I know I'm not! I just...I just wish things weren't always so awful."

This surprised him. THINK THINGS ARE AWFUL?

"Well...not awful. But I never thought traveling with my father would be anything like this."

Stanley looked at him sadly. Then an idea seemed to come to him. COME WITH ME, he wrote. SHOW YOU SOMETHING. AND GET YOUR COAT. WILL BE COLD.

George put on his coat and followed him up the dark, musty stairs. They circled around and around, passing through cavernous attics and empty storage closets and halls of rooms. Finally they came to a thick heavy door, and when Stanley pulled it open a blast of icy air barreled out at them, and they both bent over and pushed ahead. When they were finally clear of the door George managed to open his eyes and look around.

They were on the roof of the hotel, surrounded by a forest of chimneys and vents and leaning columns of steam. Fat flakes the size of his thumb twirled down around them in winding currents. Stanley gestured again and led George toward the edge of the roof, and pointed at something.

George was not sure what it was as he approached. It looked like there was a huge light or lantern hanging off the side of the roof, shining incredibly bright, but when he got near he saw it was not on the side of the roof at all, but in the distance. The light was very, very far away, in fact, almost on the horizon. It was just so large it'd confused him.

George squinted at it. It was ghostly and strange-looking in the night, and he thought he could discern forms in the light, huge structures and blocks nearly eclipsed by iridescence. "What is it?" he asked.

Stanley wrote: CHICAGO.

"Chicago? That's a *city*?" said George.

Stanley nodded. LOOKS GOOD AT NIGHT. WE ARE JUST ON THE OUTSKIRTS.

"I had no idea we were so close! I've lost track of things so much that I didn't realize... How far away is it?"

Stanley wrote: FAIRLY FAR. IT IS A VERY BIG CITY.

"Have you been there?" asked George.

He nodded.

"What was it like?"

VERY PRETTY PLACE. THEY KNOW IT IS A STOCKYARD CITY SO THEY TRY AND COMPENSATE. WINTERS ARE HARD. NEVER BEEN SO COLD. EXCEPT MAYBE TONIGHT. He erased, wrote: SITS ON THE EDGE OF THE KEITH CIRCUIT. BEYOND THAT IT IS THE ORPHEUM. ALL THE WAY TO THE PACIFIC. He thought, then erased his message again. COME HERE OUT OF THE WIND. EARS ARE PINK.

Stanley led him behind a chimney. It was much warmer there, and they held their gloved hands to its brick surface and stamped their feet while they gazed at the city on the horizon. When Stanley's fingers grew numb it became difficult to write his messages, so he was forced to hold his hands much closer to the chimney than he normally would have.

"Does it bother you much?" said George. "Not being able to speak?"

Stanley shook his head, smiling.

"Why not?"

MOST PEOPLE ARE ALWAYS FILLING TIME UP, he wrote. ALWAYS MOVING, SPEAKING, WAITING. A MOMENT IS A THING TO TOLERATE FOR THEM, NOT TO ENJOY. He erased what he'd written, and wrote: SILENCE MAKES ME APPRECIATE IT. THINK OTHERWISE. THERE IS PEACE IN LETTING GO. ERASING THINGS FOR SILENCE. PLEASURE IN JUST SITTING.

"It's good that you're with him. My father, I mean," said George. "I think he needs someone like you to help him stay grounded. More than he does me."

Stanley looked at him sadly again. He had large, soft brown eyes with very delicate, almost feminine lashes. He wrote: DO NOT BE ANGRY WITH HIM. HE HAS KNOWN ONLY THIS STRUGGLE FOR SO LONG. DOES NOT KNOW ANYTHING ELSE ANYMORE.

"You'd think he would try to know," said George. "All he thinks of is business, and the troupe, and the song. I'm not important to him at all. He's only called me 'son' once."

CHANGING IS HARD. ESPECIALLY FOR SOMEONE AS OLD AS HIM.

"He's not that old. He's only in his forties, isn't he?"

Stanley did not meet his eyes. He wrote: MAYBE. Then he turned away to warm his hands, wrote something, and turned back around. He held up the blackboard, and his eyes were sadder than ever. The board read: YOUR FATHER LOVES YOU, GEORGE. PLEASE KNOW THAT. FOR ME.

"It's hard to think so," said George. "Especially when everything is so difficult."

DIFFICULT? LOOK AROUND. IS THIS UNPLEASANT?

George looked at the snowflakes pouring down from the star-scattered sky. Chicago blazed in the distance, and he felt as though they were on the prow of a ship in a deep dark sea, sailing home.

He smiled. "No. No, I suppose it isn't."

Stanley nodded. THAT IS THE BEST THING YOU CAN EVER DO. ADMIT THINGS ARE PLEASANT, IF ONLY FOR A LITTLE WHILE. He erased what he'd written, and wrote: LET ME TALK TO HARRY. I WILL TRY AND MAKE THINGS BETTER. FOR NOW, PLEASE TRY AND FORGET ABOUT WHAT HAPPENED.

"It won't be easy," said George.

He wrote: NEVER SAID IT WOULD BE.

"All right," said George. "If you say so."

Then Stanley laid a hand on George's shoulder, his long fingers gently touching the back of George's neck. As he removed his hand his fingers trailed down George's arm as though he wished to feel more of him. It made George uncomfortable to experience that, here alone on the rooftop with this much older man, but he was not sure why.

They heard someone calling their names. They went back to the stairwell door and found Colette there, shivering in her thin coat.

"Thought I saw you two come up here," she said. "What the hell were you doing?"

"Seeing the sights," said George. "What happened?"

"It's Kingsley," she said. "He can't get out of his bed. It hurts too much, he said."

George and Stanley exchanged a glance and followed her downstairs.

Kingsley lay on his bed, pale and sweating and nearly unconscious, while Silenus and the rest of the troupe looked on. He dreamily insisted that they place his marionettes beside him, and Stanley was given the unenviable task of carrying these up to his room. When he laid a hand on one of the boxes he wept silently.

"Should we take him to a doctor?" asked George.

"No," whispered the professor. "No doctors."

"But you're ill, Kingsley," said Colette. "Look at you. You can't even stand."

"No doctors," he said again. "I'll be fine. Just need some rest." Then he pulled one of the boxes to him and held it in his arms as though he were embracing a small person, and fell asleep.

CHAPTER 15

Franny's Secret

Silenus took over Kingsley's spot as the opening act of their performance. George was told he was a splendid monologist who could enrapture any crowd, but he was unable to witness it for himself; as the one member whose job could be done by a theater employee, he was assigned the task of looking after Kingsley, to his dismay.

George spent hours in their flophouse hotel holding a cold rag to Kingsley's head and mixing tinctures of opium and guaiacum for him. Kingsley at first prissily resented George's attentions, but he eventually relented, too exhausted to be difficult.

"Tell me," said Kingsley once after George had given him his tincture. "Does he value you?"

"Who?"

"Harry. Does he value and love you? Is he a loving father?"

"I don't know," said George. He sniffed. "But maybe I'm getting used to being unappreciated."

"He doesn't know how lucky he is," said Kingsley. He coughed, and said, "I should have very much liked to be a father. I feel I was meant to be one."

"Have you ever been married before?" said George.

"I was, once," said Kingsley.

George was surprised. He couldn't imagine anyone could live with someone as irritable as Kingsley.

"Children are miracles," said Kingsley. "We are all miracles. Do you believe that?"

"I suppose so, yes."

"That is good. Not... not everyone does. It is the role and purpose of men and women to bear children, and give them everything that they can. It is the only true fulfillment in life. I am sorry to hear that Harry does not do this for you."

"Did you and your wife ever have any children?"

The professor looked away out the window. He sipped a little more of his tincture, and said, "Yes," before falling into a deep sleep.

George watched him for a moment before slipping outside to walk down the hallway, intending to go to the theater to try to see his father and Colette. As he passed one room a voice within said, "Is he gone?"

He turned and saw Franny sitting inside on the edge of her bed, staring into the floor. "What?" he asked.

"Has he died?" she asked.

"Kingsley? No! No, he's fine."

"Oh," she said. "Well. It won't be long now."

"He's... he's not dying," said George. "He's just sick, is all."

"No," said Franny. "He's dying. He will die, and soon. And it will be painful."

"How do you know? Are you a doctor?"

"No."

"Then how are you so certain?" he asked.

"I know these things," said Franny.

"Nobody knows for sure."

She shook her head. "I do."

"How?"

She looked up, and seemed to debate something. "Would you really like to know?"

George hesitated. The way she said it made him think she'd been waiting for him to ask for some time. But he said, "Yes."

"All right. Then come in."

He walked to the doorway, but did not fully enter. The emptiness of her room made it feel very large, and the little light within was gray and unhappy. Franny sat on her bed like a little doll left behind by a child, mummified to the chin in coats and sweaters and scarves.

"You'll have to come in, George," said Franny, and she smiled sleepily.

He did so. Her bed was completely undisturbed. She must have not been sleeping there, he thought, and then remembered she said she never slept at all.

"Shut the door," said Franny.

"Why?" he asked.

"Because this is private."

"If it's private, then why are you telling me?"

"Because you asked. And because I want you to know."

George began to feel unsettled; besides that brief, furious moment with Colette in Hayburn he had never been alone with a woman in a bedroom before. He shut the door, and Franny motioned him to come and sit by her on the bed. He hesitated again, but Franny seemed such a limp and empty thing that he could not imagine her doing anything outrageous, and he went and sat beside her.

"Do you really want to know how I know he will die?" she asked in her quavering voice, still smiling sleepily.

"I suppose."

"I was not always a strongwoman, you know. Once, before these stage days, Harry and I were in the same act. He juggled and did magic tricks, and I...I told fortunes. And I was very, very good at it. This was because," she said calmly, "the fortunes I told were absolutely true."

"True?" said George. "So, wait...are you saying you can tell the future?"

She nodded. "Oh, yes. If I try."

George laughed. "Are you being serious?"

"Very serious," she said. "And I do not find it funny."

"Oh," said George, and he coughed.

"People started asking me bad questions, in those days," said Franny. "Questions about stocks, and horses, and women. Harry said it wasn't the kind of show we needed to be doing. So he made me stop."

"How can you tell the future?"

"It's my time," she said. "Time has a very different bend for me, George. It moves differently. Think of it like a river you and everyone else you know is floating on. You can only see the rushing waters, the jagged rocks, and the next curve. But I am not on the river. I am sitting on the bank, watching everyone go by. And I can see all the curves ahead."

"And you see the professor dying in that future?" he asked.

She nodded.

George smiled a little. He was still not entirely sure she was telling the truth. But then, Franny was difficult to take seriously at any time. He pitied her then, this androgynous, loopy woman with her mittened hands and dozens of scarves. "How does he die?"

"He will be eaten," she said gravely. "Eaten in the night, by animals."

"By animals?"

"Yes."

"And do you see yourself dying in this future?"

"No." She shut her eyes, and breathed deep. "Not that one. My death is much later, and it will not be my first one. That is in the past. But my second death is something I've watched for a long, long time." George wondered what she could mean. Second death? Yet she continued on: "It grows nearer every day, but I can't tell its specifics. I see a few things—the moon's face broken on the black waters of a strange sea...I am smiling and laughing, and holding something very heavy in my hands. And I have no name in that time. But that is all I see."

George's smile slowly faded. He was no longer quite sure this was all a joke. "Do you see how I will die?"

Franny looked off into the corner. "No," she said.

"No? You don't?"

"No. I don't see it at all. I think, George... I think everything will end before you die. And you will be the only one left when that end comes. When I look, there is no one and nothing else in the world but you, and you are weeping. After that there is nothing. There is no more time that I can see."

George began to feel very unsettled. It was the way she said it, as if she were trying to remember a very trivial thing, like where she'd mislaid her bag. "Can you really see things like that?" he asked.

"Yes," she said. "They are very obvious to me. As they would be to anyone else who has fallen out of time."

"You've... fallen out of time? What do you mean?"

She became queerly alert then. She looked at him, and he thought she might have been afraid. "Do you really wish to know that? It's a great secret."

George wondered if he really did, but said, "Yes."

"The reason is very simple," she said. "It is because I am dead, and have been for some time. And the dead are not a part of time at all, are they?"

He stared at her. It took a moment for him to process what she'd said. "What?"

She nodded as though it were the most obvious thing in the world.

"That can't be. You can't be... be dead. You move and talk and walk and such."

"That does not mean I'm not dead."

"Well... how do you know?"

"Because I remember it," she said. "I remember dying. I cannot remember how long ago it was... Time has lost a lot of meaning for me now, since it passed me by. But I am dead, George."

"Then how are you here? How are you...alive?"

"I was brought back," she said, "as an arrangement I made before I died. One I made with my husband. At least, that's what I think happened... I don't have many memories of before, and it's hard to keep track of any new ones. Everything's wrapped up in cobwebs, up in my head." She rubbed at her temple with two fingers. "I don't even remember what my name was. It wasn't Franny. I wasn't Franny, not then. I'm not the same person anymore, because I have almost none of her memories, so I can't...I can't have the same name, can I?"

"I don't know," said George.

"No. So it was one I chose at random. Franny. Franny Beatty," she said, as if she was trying to remind herself of what it was.

"How were you...brought back?" asked George.

Franny once again debated something. Then she said, "I'll show you."

She stood up and removed her mittens, and her scarf, and her very large overcoat, and then her sweater, and underneath her sweater was a blouse, and she began unbuttoning that, too...

"No," said George, confused. "No, no, what are you doing? Don't do that!"

But Franny ignored him, and kept unbuttoning until her blouse was open, exposing a brown stripe of naked skin running down the front of her torso, only it was ribboned with curls and skeins and strings of deep dark black. Then the blouse fluttered to the floorboards.

She stood stooped before him, naked from the waist up, and though she was a skinny thing she was not emaciated, or unlovely. But she was tattooed over every inch of her skin with countless symbols and glyphs, many of them queerly positioned around her chest and belly and back, and some of them seemed to move, somehow, twisting or rotating very slightly under some force of their own. George wanted to look away from her, but could not; he had never seen a woman's body before, and he shamefully stared and tried to ignore the hot flush blooming in his belly.

Franny gazed down at herself, apparently unaware that what she was doing could be in any way strange or shameful. Her long, thin fingers probed her brown skin, caressing the symbols that had been inked there. "Each of these keeps a part of me functioning," she said. She indicated one below her left collarbone. "This one whispers to my heart, and asks it to beat. These here," she said, and thoughtlessly touched two below and to one side of each of her breasts, "these speak to my lungs, and fill them with air. This one my spine," she said, and turned and showed him a dense, complicated highway of tangled hieroglyphs running down the middle of her back, "and these my innards," and she turned again and gestured to the mass of black ink that curved across her belly. "On my scalp, below my hair, are hundreds more. They give me my mind. A part of my mind, at least."

Her words were anatomical, almost bored. Then, to his horror, she sat back down next to him, slumped forward and expressionless, her bare elbow kissing his. "The professor speaks of marionettes," she said. "But I am a human one. I don't know who is pulling the strings anymore, or what act I'm putting on. My strength is an effect of the marks that help me live — many of them work a little too well, and allow my muscles and bones to do things normal ones would not, even if it hurts me. But I am a dead thing, George. I am dead."

George watched her from the side of his eye, cringing and trying not to look upon her. She smelled like camphor and old clothing, and the stooped way she sat made her small, firm breasts gather together between her arms.

"It is so tiring," she said. "Everything is muted, and dull...I am achingly tired and cold, George, and all I wish for is sleep. But I never can. I am always awake. Always."

"Please get dressed," George said softly.

"Dressed?" she said, puzzled.

"Yes," said George. "Please. Please get dressed."

She smiled and said, "All right." Then she put back on her blouse and coat, and sat down next to him again. "I can feel the world flowing over me, like in a dream. Time is a breeze and we are simply feathers floating on it. One day I will wake up, George. I will wake up, and float away on it too. Or I hope I will. I hope I will wake up."

George waited for more, but she did not say anything else. He slowly stood up and she did not blink or look at him. She seemed totally unaware of anything going on around her. He watched her, remembering the color of her skin and the endless crawl of tattoos, and opened the door.

"Where are you going, Bill," she said softly. He turned and saw she was not looking at him, but was speaking to the floor. "Where are you going," she said again.

He waited for her to say something more, but she did not. He walked out and shut the door behind him and stood there, breathing hard.

He looked down and saw his hands were shaking. Then he looked up and down the hallway. There was no one. He slowly walked back to his own room. His legs felt faint and funny beneath him, like at any moment they might fail, and he went to his bed and lay there with his eyes open, listening to the wind whistling in the gaps of his walls and the murmur of voices in the rooms around him, and he hated himself more than anything in the world.

CHAPTER 16

The Professor's Miracle

George did not tell anyone what had happened. It was easy to avoid Franny when he tended to Kingsley, but the few times she came near he grew shameful and hot and had to excuse himself. He felt sure she would tell someone, and then the rest of the troupe would look at him with disgust and throw him out onto the street. But Franny did not tell anyone, apparently; she seemed to have forgotten it the moment it happened, and was unaware that anything wrong had occurred.

He was not sure why he had reacted the way he had. That brief, painful glimpse of so much brown skin had filled him with a warm, sweet wetness, a cold and trembling flame. Yet he did not desire Franny in any way. He wondered what could be wrong with him.

George did not have long to think about it, for despite all his tending Kingsley got worse and worse. He started entering bouts of delirium, speaking incessantly of children and babies and infants, and in many cases he cried that the children were in pieces or parts, or were horribly mangled or eyeless. He would become so terrified in these fits that he would weep for hours, yet in his more lucid moments he could never recall them.

It was in one of these rare clearheaded moments that Kingsley said suddenly to George, "Lucille."

"What?" said George, who had been mixing a new tincture.

"My wife's name," said Kingsley. He propped his chin up on his blanket. "Her name was Lucille."

"Oh. Yes, I remember asking you about her the other day. What was she like?"

Kingsley was quiet. "Proud," he said. "And beautiful. We lived in Maryland, in a very small town. I was a lawyer there."

"I didn't know you were a lawyer. You didn't start out in show business, then?"

"No," said Kingsley. He smiled a little. "And I am not a professor either, George, though I am probably the most overeducated person I know of on the circuits. And my last name is not Tyburn," he said softly. "My real name is Kingsley Harrison. Very few people use their real names on the stage. I doubt, for example, that your father's real name is Heironomo."

"How did you get into the business?"

Kingsley's eyelids lowered slightly. "That was Harry's idea. It was a deal we made, you see."

George stopped mixing and turned to listen, curious. "A deal? In exchange for what?"

Kingsley was quiet for a long time. Then he said, "For children. Harry said he could give me children, if I wanted. And I did. In my old life my wife and I had encountered a great difficulty conceiving, you see. And when we finally conceived, we were so happy. But when she was seven months pregnant the doctor came and felt her belly to make sure that everything was all right. And he said it wasn't."

"What was wrong with it?" asked George.

"It did not feel right in the womb. There was something missing, he said. Something significant, otherwise he would not have been able to feel it at all. Perhaps its skull, he told us. And he said he had procedures to end the pregnancy, which he recommended immediately. It was a dead thing, he said. A growth inside of her. Impartial.

"Of course, we were against it. It was our child, even if it was born...that way. We decided we would keep the child alive as best we could, no matter what it was or how it came. And if it died we would hold a funeral for it and say its name—Arthur if it was a boy, Gwen if it was a girl, as my wife liked the Camelot fables, you see—and send it back to God. So she grew this impartial creature inside of her, and we waited and prepared the funeral for when it would be born. The doctor said this was not wise. What we were growing, he said, was a corpse. It was unhealthy to do this. But we would not listen to such horrible things.

"And, in the end, when the child came, the doctor turned out to be wrong. It was not a corpse at all. It was alive, but...it did not look like a baby. It had only one arm and its head was not right. It had one side of the jawbone, but above that, its skull was...wrong. It was *bent*, and it had one staring eye that never blinked, and only part of its nose. It did not cry when it was delivered, it only stared at us. It was supposed to die then. The doctor *said* that it would die on delivery. But it didn't. It stayed alive.

"Lucille could not nurse the thing, but we did have bottles for it. It could drink from the bottles, with its ruined little mouth. It was a miracle that it could, we agreed. And we had to keep it away from light. If it saw light then it would die of shock, the doctor said. He seemed to suggest that this was wrong to do, to prolong our child's life, but we ignored him and kept our child in the dark, in the closet. We'd wake up in the night and go to the thing sleeping in the closet and feed it with the bottle." Kingsley swallowed. "Can I have my medicine now?"

"Oh," said George. "Yes." He handed him the crystal glass with the opium tincture. Kingsley drank it down quickly and leaned back, sighing.

"It was not supposed to be taken by us," said Kingsley. "It was supposed to die in its own time, in its own way. But Lucille...she started to become loath to feed it, and went to the closet less and less. I berated her for it, yet all she did was weep. And then one day I returned home and went to the closet and found our child was gone. I became frantic, and nearly tore the house apart searching for it. I looked everywhere, but I would have almost never thought to look in the backyard.

"Yet that was where they were. Lucille had taken it out in its little christening dress, out into the bright sunshine. Dressed it up so it would be beautiful. And the child had been struck dead by the sun. My wife had allowed our child to die. She had killed it."

Kingsley took a shuddering breath. "I was furious with her. She had killed our child, and I could not understand it. I could not understand why she had taken away what we had tried so hard to have. I called in every favor I had, and I had her jailed. She had to learn that what she had done was wrong.

"For a while then I was crazed with grief. I wandered, not knowing what to do." Kingsley's voice began to grow very soft as the laudanum took hold. "And then I heard of this famous performer, Silenus, and I was told he could do many strange and wonderful things. He could perform his own miracles, in a way. And I found him and asked him for a child, and he said he knew of a way to give me one, but he would not do it himself. It was my choice, and my responsibility, and he would take no part in it. But in exchange for telling me how this was done, I would have to join his act, his troupe, and perform with him and lend him my legal skills. And I agreed."

"What was it?" asked George. "What was it you had to do?"

Kingsley's eyelids slowly lowered. "It would take so much," he said in a faint voice. "It would take so much from me, and it would hurt so much...but I had to. I had to have my children, George. And ever since I saw those things in the street, with you and Harry, I've been getting drastic, and taking too much...Far, far too much..."

His eyes shut, and he was asleep. George stood over him, not moving. Then he shivered and his skin began to crawl, and although Kingsley's story had been horrifying there was a different reason behind George's discomfort: he had the overpowering feeling that they were being watched.

He looked around the room, yet saw nobody. But then his eye happened to fall on the closest marionette box.

Was its lid open? Just a tiny crack? George considered trying to shut it, or opening it up to see what was within. But what if there was actually something there? What could be on the other side of that lid?

It made him wonder if Harry had delivered on his promise for children. But George had never once seen Professor Tyburn with any babies or toddlers of any kind, nor had he ever heard him talk about any grown children of his own. He hoped Kingsley had been delirious when he'd said that. Yes, that had to be it. Kingsley must have been inventing things in his ravings.

He kept watching, but the lid did not move. Shaking slightly, he turned around and walked out.

CHAPTER 17

"We are all hanged men."

George quickly walked down the hall, thoroughly unnerved by Kingsley's story. At first it had seemed so heartfelt, and George wished his father had desired children the same way Kingsley once had. But to hear that this desire could grow so perverted...The idea made him shiver.

George stopped when he found that Silenus's black door had returned. He thought for a moment, and opened it and walked in.

The office was empty, which had never happened before. Silenus had always been inside whenever the door appeared. Then George saw that one extremely large, door-sized cabinet was open just a crack on the far wall. He'd never noticed it, but then, like the office door, many of Silenus's cabinets seemed to change at will.

George walked to the cabinet and felt a cool breeze slipping through it. He opened it up and saw there was a long, dark stone passageway behind, and at its end was a faint blue light. His curiosity got the best of him, and he walked down the passageway toward the light. At first he was nervous, but then he heard Silenus's voice echoing back to him: "...Fucking thing takes longer and longer these days..."

The passageway ended in a tiny stone courtyard with tall walls, almost like a large chimney, that rose up to open on the night sky. George looked up and saw the moon was directly above, and it bathed the courtyard in moonlight. In the center Stanley and Silenus stood beside a large piece of paper spread out on the stone floor. George saw it was Silenus's odd map of North America, and they seemed to be focusing on a collection of small stones laid across it. Standing in the middle of the map was a tall, stout piece of blackened, twisted wood. It was fuzzy and seemed to be moaning very softly, yet as George's eyes adjusted to the light he realized it was not fuzzy: it was twirling very, very quickly, as if it were on a potter's wheel, and it hummed as it spun.

Silenus held up one finger when George entered. "One moment," he said. "We're in the middle of something."

"What is this place?" asked George. "What are you doing?"

"Something complicated. Please be quiet."

George walked over to stand beside his father. The stones on the map were small and black with minuscule figures and numerals carved into them. They gleamed strangely in the moonlight, like they sucked it up as soon as it touched them. He saw Silenus had spread most of them out across the Midwest and Northeast on the map, where the troupe was currently touring. They did not seem to be arranged in a particular pattern. Regardless, Silenus shook his head as if displeased by what he was seeing.

"It's not working right," he said.

Stanley wrote: IT IS IN THE POSITION WE ALWAYS USED BEFORE.

"Well, things change. Maybe something's shifted. It needs to be adjusted."

Stanley put on a thick leather glove and carefully placed one finger on top of the wood, and he pushed it one inch to the side and watched the stones. When they did nothing he shook his head and adjusted the wood again.

George shivered and clutched his arms. It was much colder here than it'd been in the office. "Where are we?"

"That's a good question," Silenus said. "If my calendar's right, I believe we're currently someplace in western Siberia."

"Siberia? How is that possible?"

"It's an agreement I had made," said Silenus. He rapped his knuckles against the stone wall of the courtyard. "This tower migrates with the moon, remaining directly underneath its apex. Naturally, people tend to notice a tower just appearing in the middle of the countryside, but then we're gone the next night, so it doesn't matter."

"But your office is just down the hall."

"It was pretty fucking complicated to get it set up right. Took a lot of negotiating, but I managed."

George watched Stanley readjusting the spinning piece of wood. "And is that part of your tower?"

"No. That is the blackened crossbeam of a gallows," said Silenus. "It's from a very old and very used scaffold in southern England. That very beam supported the noose that killed hundreds, maybe thousands of men and women. It's seen a great deal of life and death, light and dark, and it knows the contours of the barrier between the two, so it's useful to consult. Which is what we're doing now."

Stanley raised a hand and motioned for their attention. They turned to look at the map. At first nothing happened, but then the little black stones slowly floated up and shifted around on the map as if magnetically drawn or repelled.

"There they go," said Silenus. He leaned forward to watch.

The black stones formed little groups along the roads and cities, but most particularly they made circles around patches of the countryside, especially those with valleys and rivers and forests. Silenus frowned and checked his watch and looked up at the moon. Then, very faintly, the moonlight in the courtyard began to focus on two specific parts of the map, illuminating those spots of the parchment. Both spots were encircled by the little black stones, as though they were protecting the light within.

"Well, shit," Silenus said.

"What is it?" George asked.

"Not good," said Silenus. "Not fucking good at all is what it is, I'd say." He turned to Stanley. "They're predicting our movements."

Stanley wrote: WORSE—THEY KNOW WHERE THE NEXT PIECES OF THE SONG ARE.

"How in the hell could they have figured out something like that?" Silenus said. "They're supposed to be blind to the song itself. They can only feel its effects."

Stanley's chalk scraped across the board, writing: MAYBE FIGURE OUT EFFECTS JUST LIKE WE DO.

"They're not that smart," said Silenus. He held his hand out over the circles of stones. Curious, George did the same, and found the patches of moonlight emitted a very strong, focused heat.

"What is this?" he said.

"It's how we find the song, of course," said Silenus. He took out a small notebook and recorded a few notes. Then he reached over and tapped the spinning wood. It stopped spinning instantly but remained upright, and the stones all dropped to clatter across the map. Then, slowly, the beams of moonlight faded. Silenus picked up the piece of scaffold beam. "Come on," he said, and he led them back down the passageway to his office.

"It's not an exact procedure, by any stretch of the imagination," he said as they walked, "and we can only use it once every couple of months thanks to the quality of moonlight. But it's the best thing we've come up with."

"Do the stones represent the First Song, or is it the moonlight?" asked George.

"The moonlight," said Silenus. He set the beam down on his desk, then walked to his liquor cabinet and poured a hefty glass of brandy.

"Then what are the stones?"

Silenus went to another big cabinet, this one down close to the floor, and opened it to reveal a brass fireplace complete with a roaring fire. He turned around to warm the backs of his legs, parting his coattails with one hand, and sipped his brandy, looking furious.

"The stones represent the wolves, don't they?" asked George.

Stanley nodded.

"They're laying traps for us," muttered Silenus. "Fucking laying traps. They've been on our tails for years and years, but they've almost never been ahead. Something's changed."

Stanley scrawled out: MAYBE SOMETHING TO DO WITH WHY THE SONG DOESN'T AFFECT THEM ANYMORE?

"It affects them," said Silenus. "But they're just resisting it. Which shouldn't be possible…"

"Are you saying they're tracking us?" asked George.

"No," said Silenus. "I'm saying they know where we're going next. Or where we'd *like* to go. They're positioning themselves around the pieces of the song we've had our eyes on."

"There has to be something you can do, though."

"I'm thinking," said Silenus irritably. "Usually we'd just let the song itself pave the way, but if they're able to resist it…" He slopped down more brandy and wiped sweat from his brow. "Seems that we can either run, find a new part of the, country, or maybe perform a feint of some kind. Fake them out. But that'd be dangerous, very dangerous… We'd be risking half the troupe, probably."

An idea seemed to occur to Stanley. He gave Silenus a tentative look, and wrote: THERE IS ANOTHER OPTION.

"What?" said Silenus. "What would that be?"

Stanley wrote: SOME OF YOUR OLD AGREEMENTS ARE STILL IN PLACE.

"My agreements? Which ones would those be?"

THE OLDEST ONES. WITH THOSE WHO PROMISED YOU THE OBSERVATORY AND THE MOONLIGHT. THE INSTRUMENTS TO FIND THE SONG.

Silenus and George both read what he wrote. While it made no sense at all to George, Silenus stared at Stanley in disbelief. "If you're suggesting what I think you're suggesting, you're out of your fucking mind," he said.

Stanley wrote: THEY HAVE NO REASON TO LOVE YOU BUT YOUR AGREEMENTS ARE STILL IN PLACE CORRECT?

"Yes, but they'll be sure to find some way to gut me like a fucking trout!" cried Silenus. "Stan, I love you, but this idea is some kind of stupid. I've had dealings go raw with them in the past, and never has there ever been a people more treacherous and feckless than that one. They're experts at using language and binding agreements to their own ends. And their ends will mostly involve my guts on a platter, you get me?"

Stanley reluctantly nodded, and lowered his blackboard.

"So what will you do?" asked George.

Silenus glanced at George as though just remembering he was there. He walked over and sat behind his desk, and said, "How's Kingsley doing? Is he any better?"

"No," said George. "If anything, he's worse."

"Beautiful," said Silenus. "I cannot have one fucking thing go right for me, now can I?"

"Franny told me he's dying," said George.

Silenus paused briefly. "Franny said that?" he asked.

"Yes."

"Don't go bothering Franny," said his father. "She's got it hard enough. She needs her rest, if she can get it."

"What's wrong with her?"

"There's nothing wrong with her. She just... she had an accident, all right?"

"That's not what she told me," said George. "She told me she died."

Silenus looked at him, surprised. "She told you that?"

"Yes. It can't be true, can it? You can't be... be dead and just walking around."

Silenus was quiet for a long, long while, and a terrible sadness crossed his face. Then he said, "I took Franny on to the troupe as an act of kindness, George. She was delivered to me by her husband, who was a friend of mine. He had attempted some very…unwise solutions to her state, you see. That state being death. He had hoped to bring her back. But, as you can tell, his attempts didn't work, or at least not completely. He hoped I could repair what he had done and bring her back fully, or at least reverse what he'd tried. But so far I've been unable to."

"Oh," said George. "How long has she…been like this?"

"For years."

"My God. What happened to her husband?"

"He passed away some time ago. I keep endeavoring to help her out of respect for the promise I made to him, and to her. But you can see why I'd prefer it if you left Franny alone, George. She has her burdens, just like we all do. You, me, even Kingsley. Everyone."

"Kingsley's killing himself, isn't he?" asked George. "That's why he keeps getting worse."

Silenus gave George a long, cold look. He set the glass of brandy down on the table. "Franny didn't tell you that, did she? You got that from the professor himself. He must've told you."

"He told me a little. About where he came from." George waited for some sort of explanation. When none came, he said, "How could you employ someone like that?"

"Kingsley?" said Silenus. "He's a good man."

"A good man? He had his own wife jailed!"

Silenus raised an eyebrow. "He told you she was jailed?"

"Yes! He told me all about what happened with his…child."

"You misunderstand me. When I say that Kingsley is a good man, I don't mean he's morally just. I mean he's useful, and competent, and he serves our goal well. Almost all of our players have had alternate uses to simply attracting an audience."

"Protecting and performing the song," said George bitterly.

"Yes," said Silenus. "It angers you. I can understand that. But it's the only thing that matters, George. Kingsley's made his choices, and he's dealt with the consequences. And he isn't the first question-able person to have aided the First Song. He's only one in a long, long line of them. I mean, hell. Look at me."

George glanced up at his father. His shirt was unbuttoned to the waist so that his brown long johns showed through, and a hint of gnarled, graying chest hair peeked out at their top. He sat slouched in his chair with his belly rising up, and his tobacco-stained, mon-keyish fingers rested on its top. But his eyes were the most disconcert-ing thing about him: George had always felt that his father had unsettling, dispassionate eyes, but sometimes they seemed blue and faded enough to be unreal. George often felt that his father had spent long hours staring into things not meant to be seen.

He was not what George wanted, or needed. He was impossible to know, and even harder to love. And so long as the song needed to be protected, George would never have a place in his life.

"When will it end?" he asked.

"End?" said Silenus. "You think this will end?"

"Yes," said George. "Please tell me it will. Please tell me there's something we're moving toward."

Stanley raised his head. His eyes were sad, and he wrote: THERE IS NO ENDING.

"He's right," said Silenus. "There is no grail at the end of our quest, George. There is no finish. There is only survival. Day after day, year after year. We are fending them off with every minute of our lives. I will not lie to you, George, there is no respite from this burden. There is no point where it will be lifted. We must simply carry and maintain it, or die."

George shook his head. "No. That's not true. It's a lie."

"No, George," said Silenus. "It is the truth. The greatest truth, the only truth. Things do not stop. They move on without us. It is a truth so great that most people must invent and live lies to deny it."

"You don't believe it," said George. "You imagine an end, Harry."

"You think so?"

"Yes. I can see it in you," said George.

"And what end do I imagine, George?"

"When you showed me those wastes, that place that the wolves had consumed . . . you said the whole world would be like this, when the wolves won. You didn't say 'if,' though. You said 'when.' As if it was sure to happen."

Silenus seemed to crumple a little in his chair. He stared into the fire, and when he spoke his voice was a croak. "Yes. That's so."

"So you think we're going to lose?" asked George.

Silenus sighed. "I think it is inevitable, yes. The purpose of our mission is survival, George. And one thing about survival is that it doesn't last forever. Nothing lasts forever. It may not happen today, or tomorrow, or this year or even within my lifetime. But I know we can't keep running forever. One day we will stumble, or stop."

"But the previous troupes have kept it up for so long," said George. "We're just the most recent version, right?"

"Oh, yes," said Silenus. "I believe there was a *Bunraku* troupe that was very efficient in the East for over a century, for instance. But think of what we're facing, kid — the wolves never tire, never sleep, never die. And eons are but the blink of an eye to them. They were here before time, and they'll be here after it. We can't outrun them forever. We are simply delaying the inevitable."

"Then why on Earth would you ever keep going?" asked George.

"It is rather stupid, isn't it?" said Silenus.

"Well, maybe not stupid . . . *Futile* might be better."

Silenus leaned back in his chair. "Whatever word you'd like, then. But it remains the same. We dangle by a string over the maw of something huge and vast and terrible. Even if we stretch the hours and the days out until their breaking point, how can they have meaning in the face of what's coming?"

"Well, yes."

Silenus cocked his head. "Hm. Let me tell you a story, kid," he said. "This took place a long, long time ago, in England of all places, before I ever joined up with this troupe or even knew it existed. I was in a bad spot, did a few stupid things, and I found myself tossed in the clink with the likely punishment of deportation awaiting me. Now, I thought I had it rough, but my cellmate had it even worse. He was a skinny little Irishman, name of Michael Feenan, and he was meant for the gallows, to dance from the hemp until he'd shed his mortal coil and what have you. Unlike a lot of folk in the clink, he didn't claim innocence. He said he'd done what he'd done — that being knifing a fella in a gin house — and he knew it was worth nothing to protest it, since we was all English bastards and we'd hang him no matter, you see. Which, you know, might've been true.

"Now, Feenan was set to dance a week from when I was thrown in his cell, but he was already in a bad state — when they'd arrested him he'd gotten a serious beating, and his right leg was broke in a couple of places. His shin and ankle were as swolled up and purple as a fucking plum, let me tell you. He could hardly sit up, it pained him so much. So when his time came, the guards were going to have to drag him up the scaffold steps like a cripple. But Feenan, he had different plans.

"He had his wife smuggle in some rope and some pieces of timber, and for that entire week he kept trying to make a brace for his leg. It was some of the most painful stuff I ever saw. Can you imagine what that's like, some yuck who knows nothing about anatomy strapping a brace around his own swollen, broken leg? And then he'd try and walk on it of all things, testing it out. And nearly each time he'd fall. But Feenan never cried, or wept, or cursed. He'd just pull himself up, rearrange some of the brace, and try again.

"Finally on the day before his drop I asked him what he was doing. I mean, he was dead anyway, so why go to all this trouble? Why does the way a man walks to the scaffold matter? And he said, 'The walk to the scaffold is the last walk I'll ever get, Willie,' — for that was the name I'd given them—'And after that, it's naught but the drop. And when the walk is all that's left, it matters.'

"So when his day came they took him out and let him walk by himself. I got to watch from the window of my cell. He stumbled only three times. And each time he picked himself up, rearranged himself until he was as dignified-looking as could be, and kept walking. Even though his leg pained him and his very body was a burden, he kept walking, right up until he was hanged. He was hanged on this very beam, in fact," said Silenus, and he tapped the warped piece of black wood. "Probably the best death it'd ever seen."

He lit a cigar. "The way things end matter, George," he said. "They matter more than the ending, or even where we're going to. I never forgot what Feenan told me, and I took it to heart when I realized we could never keep this up forever. This very office is a reminder."

"It is?" said George. "How?"

"Come here," he said, and stood up and went to the bay window. "You've seen these stars before, haven't you?"

George stood by his father and looked out the bay window. There below them were the cold, rocky wastes he'd glimpsed in the shadow in Hayburn, the endless gray cliffs and the cold white stars and the yawning black abysses. They seemed suspended several feet above it all, as if the window was floating in all that blackness, and he noticed the window had no knobs or locks, as if it should never, ever be opened.

"I put my office right in the middle of the death they threaten us with," Silenus said. "They still have yet to find it, stupid things. I've got it so it moves around pretty frequently. But here I sit, every day, hanging over all this wasted nothing. I will never forget what the world could be, should my vigilance ever fail. And more than that, I will never forget that in a way we are all hanged men and hanged women, awaiting those deaths which cannot be avoided. Yet I will make sure that we live and die the way we choose for as long as we possibly can. And I'll do what it takes to ensure that. They can threaten me all they want, but I'll never stop."

George nodded. He thought he understood, even though it was a very strange story; he did not know much history, but he could not remember the last time anyone in England had been threatened with deportation. Then he remembered what Franny had first told him on the train, and asked, "What if they threaten the others, though?"

"Others?"

"Yes," said George. "Would you risk the lives of the rest of the troupe? Or mine?"

Silenus looked at him, startled. "You I would protect at all costs. We cannot bear to lose you."

George noticed that he had said "we." "Because I have the song in me, or because I'm your son?"

Silenus looked down at the floor. Stanley turned to stare at him, concerned. Silenus said, "Well, because you're my son, of course."

George was quiet. Then he said, "But you had to think about it."

"I...I didn't. It's just an upsetting question, that's all."

"An upsetting question," echoed George.

"Well, yes."

George laughed bitterly. "Protect at all costs...You talk about burdens, Harry, but I'm your burden, aren't I? Something to be handled carefully, something never allowed out?"

"Oh, for God's sake," said Silenus. "You know we have to hide the song, at any cost."

"But there are better ways of doing it," said George.

"Oh? And how have I mistreated you so terribly?"

George flushed. He knew he should not say this, since he had promised Stanley he'd try and forget about it, but he could not stop himself. "Well, you had me pelted with rotten tomatoes, for one!"

Silenus jumped a little, and George knew that Stanley had not told his father he knew. "W-what?"

"That's right!" George said. "I know you arranged to have me humiliated! And I've kept quiet about it for too long. How could you even think of doing something like that? Do you have any idea how horrible it was for me? And then you came and talked to me, but it was all a damn lie!"

"How did you…" Silenus stopped and recomposed himself. "Well, horrible it might've been, but it needed to happen! You were sabotaging the troupe, kid! What else could I have done?"

"You could have talked to me!"

"We *tried* talking, and that sure as hell didn't work."

"No, you just flat out *told* me what to do. As if I had no choice! You treated me like a disobedient dog, and when I didn't immediately obey you forced me to come to heel!" George half wanted to break the bay window, but wondered what effect that would have. Perhaps they would get sucked out into those awful wastelands.

Silenus bristled at his comments, but for once he did not reply. Stanley looked back and forth between them. He appeared so agitated it looked like he would burst.

"I know I'm right," said George. "I am your burden. Well, I'm sorry you had to carry me this far." Then he turned around and walked out without looking back.

George walked into his hotel room and slammed the door and locked it. He was so upset he was shaking slightly. He sat down on his bed and waited, though he was not sure what he was waiting for. Would Silenus come and try to apologize? Or, perhaps, berate him for being ungrateful?

He told himself that he was being very rational about all this, and to prove his calmness he poured himself a glass of water from the pitcher on his dresser and sat down on his bed to drink it. Surely an upset, irrational young man would not be able to calmly do such a thing, he thought.

But he was upset, he knew. He hated that he had been put through all of this misery and danger by a man who thought of him as little more than a commodity, however precious. George was so upset, in fact, that he did not notice the amber tinge to the water he was drinking, and it was not until he was about halfway through the glass that he realized that it had a funny taste to it, along with a funny smell. As he struggled to place it his mouth began to tingle.

It was just as the room began to feel very heavy to George that he realized what the smell was. It had been with him for most of the past two days: that tart, pungent aroma of the professor's tinctures, especially the laudanum ones that put him to sleep.

The glass fell from his hand and broke on the floorboards. George did not fall backward onto the bed, but tumbled forward, cracking his head on the floor, yet he barely felt it. As things began to grow dark he struggled to look at the pitcher of water he'd poured the glass from, and he saw that the drawers in the dresser it sat on were curiously arranged: they'd been slightly pulled out one by one, with the drawers on the bottom pulled out the farthest and the ones on the top hardly pulled out at all. It looked, George thought, as if an extremely short person had made a series of steps out of the drawers in order to climb them and reach the top.

Then things faded.

CHAPTER 18

Blessings

When George awoke his head ached both within and without. A large bump had formed on the top of his brow, and his brain felt as though it were soaking in a horrid brine. He moaned and rolled over, and looked out the window and saw the white light of morning. He'd been out all night.

He sat up. Someone had drugged him, he knew, but he had no idea why. Why would anyone want to put him to sleep, and in his own room at that? Maybe the intention had been to poison him, he thought, but that idea was even more ludicrous than the drugging.

He shakily stood up, found his balance, and tried to ignore the nausea that gripped his stomach. Then he walked to his door and tried to open it. It was locked, and he remembered he'd locked it himself last night. He unlocked and opened it and stepped out into the hallway.

He stopped immediately. The hallway was unusually dark for day. He looked to the ends and saw that someone had thrown sheets over the windows there, and all the gas lamps along the walls had been broken. Some were even ripped out of the wall. He wondered who could have done such a thing, since besides the troupe there were no other guests at the little flophouse.

He shut his door, and as he pulled away from it his knuckles grazed something rough. He turned around to look, and gasped.

Dozens of deep gouges ran across the lower face of his room door, like some short animal had been clawing to get in. From the looks of it, it had been several animals rather than one, all with very tiny paws...but judging from the marks, they were more like little hands than paws. He looked up and down the hall and saw no other door had been touched. He must have never heard it while he was unconscious, and he wondered what would have happened if he hadn't locked the door.

He heard footsteps from somewhere upstairs. It was day, so the rest of the troupe had to be at rehearsal, leaving George behind to care for Kingsley. Kingsley had to still be upstairs. Maybe that was him moving? Yet when he'd last seen Kingsley he'd been unable to even get out of bed.

George walked to the stairwell and up to the next floor. The vandalism had not been confined only to George's floor; this hall was just as dark as the one below. He went to Kingsley's door and knocked.

"Professor?" he asked quietly. "Professor, are you in there? Are you awake?"

There was no answer. George tried the knob and found the door was unlocked. He pushed it open.

The room was much the same as it'd been when he left it. The bottles and glasses and tinctures were still standing around the sink, except for one, presumably the one that'd been used on George. Professor Kingsley lay on the bed with his blanket draped over him, as usual, except he was on his side, facing away, rather than on his back. George frowned; Kingsley rarely lay that way due to his side, but then George noticed his bad side was the one in the air rather than the one pressed into the mattress.

"Professor?" George asked. "Are you all right?"

Kingsley did not move or answer. He was very pale, even paler than he'd been before.

"Kingsley?" said George. He walked into the room. "Has someone been at your medicines?"

Still Kingsley did not move. There was something strangely infantile about the way he lay in the bed, curled up in the fetal position with his hands under his head. It was how George imagined cherubs slept.

George was about to wake him when he noticed that there was a line of something on the floorboards below the bed. He peered at it, and saw it was shining in the light, very faintly, like oil. It was very dark and viscous, and when he leaned down to examine it he found its scent was coppery and harsh.

George froze. Something dripped from the side of the bed, underneath the blanket. It was dripping from all along the mattress, it looked like, congealing into a line on the floor. He swallowed and reached out, uncertain if he wanted to touch the dripping fluid or Kingsley or the blanket. Then he grasped the top of the blanket and slowly pulled it back.

The mattress was so soaked with blood that it was now a deep, dark red. In some places there was so much blood the fabric shone. Kingsley was fully dressed, but the coat and shirt on his side had been pushed away, and the skin there was pockmarked with dozens of old suture wounds. One recent laceration at the end of his rib cage had been torn open, with rivers of pus trailing down to lie upon the bed in cloudy streaks. A rib was exposed and it looked somehow *thin*, as if it'd been whittled down, and it seemed as if something had been eating at it and the surrounding flesh with many tiny mouths...

George cried out and stumbled back. In his drugged nausea he tripped and stumbled into the cabinet before tumbling to the floor. Bottles and glasses fell clanking around him and rolled off into corners of the room.

Then he heard the patter of tiny feet from somewhere in the hotel, and a raspy, rattling voice: "*It knows.*"

And from another part of the hotel, the same voice: "*It's found Father.*"

And from a third place: "*Father, Father, sleeping Father.*"

George's eye fell upon the corner. All three marionette boxes were there, but their lids were open and the boxes empty.

His skin went cold and he began to sweat. He stood up as quietly as he could and went to the door, and stuck his head out and looked down the hall.

It was very dark, but he could see a little. For a while there was nothing. Then the sound of slow, small footsteps came from the far end, near the staircase. Something walked into the shadowy hall, very casually, like a person out on a stroll. It was very, very small, not more than two feet tall, and as it moved it happened to cross a stream of light that pierced the sheet across the window, and George glimpsed a tiny, manlike form with a bald, comically large head, tiny, stiff arms, and a ragged little suit, one that any Cockney aspiring to greater class would wear.

The little figure stopped when it saw George watching. It leaned forward, as if it could not believe what it'd seen, and leaped back. "*There! There!*" cried a voice in the darkness, and the little thing sprinted across the hall to hide in another room.

George began to tremble. He remembered what Franny had said: *I guess the professor's right. They're getting harder to control every day.*

"*It's the boy, the boy,*" whispered a voice from the floor below, and George thought he heard many voices in it, somehow.

"*We hate the boy,*" said another from below, this one in a different part of the hotel. "*Father talked to it, trusted it. Not worthy of Father's love, no, no. Only we are worthy of Father's love.*"

"*We are blessings,*" said the voice from down the hall. "*Blessings.*"

It was one voice, coming from many directions. He recognized it as the voice behind the professor's marionettes, voicing each separate puppet as if they had their own personalities. But he realized now that it had all been one intelligence, one mind, somehow...

"*Father sleeps,*" said the voice downstairs. "*Must not wake him, must not disturb him.*"

"*Fed us too much,*" said another. "*And now we are whole, finally whole and free, but he sleeps. But no worries, no worries. Father will wake in the morning and then he will be whole too, won't he?*"

"*Unless the boy wakes him,*" said the voice down the hall. "*Then he will be cross, so cross.*"

"*Kill him,*" said a voice downstairs. "*Kill the boy. Break his bones, rend his flesh.*"

"No!" called George. He began backing down the hall, away from the voices in the dark. "Why would you do that?"

"*Shouldn't wake Father,*" said the voice. More tiny footsteps from downstairs. And there, in the room at the end, was that a tiny bald head peeking out to look at him?

"*Father made us from himself, just as the angry man said to do,*" said the voice from downstairs.

The angry man? George thought. Did they mean Harry? He wasn't sure, but he kept backing down the hall. He glanced around. Surely there had to be someone here? Could they all be at the rehearsal? Of course they could, he realized with a sinking stomach. They would think he was tending to Kingsley. Only last night he'd been furious with his father, but now he would give anything to have him there.

"*Gave us voices, gave us lives,*" said the second voice from downstairs.

"*Gave us himself, gave us his own life,*" said the voice at the end of the hall.

The second voice from downstairs affected a womanly tone: "*He made us just as the Maker made Eve from Adam. He took a part of himself and filled us up with it, gave us love, gave us freedoms.*"

"No, not freedoms, no, no," said the voice at the end of the hall angrily. *"Father kept us in boxes, in the dark, never let us live our own lives."*

"True, true," said the womanly voice from downstairs.

"Tied to him, always tied down, making us dance through our bondage," said the other voice below.

"Out of the dark now. Out, out, and whole, and free."

There was more movement at the dark end of the hall. George thought he could make out two more figures crowning the stairs, their heavy, balloon-like heads peering around the corner. They emerged and stood still in the middle of the hall, staring at him. One's gleaming pate was ringed with golden curls, the other wore a tiny black bowler. As they stared a third childlike figure emerged from the room it was hiding in and joined them. Then they began slowly walking toward him with the dreamy canter of children at play.

"The boy knows," said the voice. *"Kill the boy."*

"Throw him down, break his bones."

"Pluck his eyes out."

"No!" cried George. "No, please! Please, don't! I didn't mean to do anything! I just talked to him, that's all!" He ran to the end of the hall and ripped the sheet off. The window looked out on the road outside, but it was at least three floors below, and he'd never make that jump without breaking a leg. Surely there had to be a clerk or an innkeeper downstairs? He shouted for help, but there was no answer.

The three little figures were now halfway down the hallway to him. George tried one of the doors and found it locked. He tried another, but it was locked as well.

Then he remembered — *the door.* Silenus had said his office door would appear to him in emergencies. But how to get it to come? Harry had never said how to do that. He had always just walked forward from door to door, looking at them...

Walked forward, thought George with a sinking stomach. Perhaps that was how he called it to him. But for George to try it now, he'd be moving toward the three little figures.

He swallowed and steeled himself. It was his only chance.

He walked to one room door and inspected it, trying to mimic Silenus's movements in his head.

"*It comes to us, yes, yes,*" whispered the voice.

"*Gives itself to us, yes.*"

His legs shivering, George walked to the opposite room door and inspected it. Still nothing.

The little figures were less than a dozen feet away now. He could see their tiny lacquered eyes shining in the light from the window. Their movements were so human one would think them real children, dressed in colorful rags and shambling down the hall to impart a funny secret.

He turned to the next door on the opposite side of the wall, and as he did he felt something move under his feet: it was as if he were standing on a very small boat, and someone very large had moved from the prow to the stern on the opposite side from him, upsetting the balance when he hadn't been looking.

George turned around. The great black door stared down at him.

"*What?*" said the voices. "*What is that?*"

Before they had time to realize what was happening, George leaped for the door and grabbed its handle. All of the locks sprang open as if they'd been waiting for him. He flung the door open and threw himself in and slammed it behind him just as a piercing scream rang through the hallway.

"*No, no!*" cried the voices on the other side of the door. "*No, no! Can't get away, won't get away! Won't let you, no!*"

There was a scrabbling at the wood on the bottom of the door. Then it shook as though it'd been struck a hefty blow, one much stronger than such small figures should have ever managed.

"*Let us in, let us in,*" said a voice from the crack at the bottom.

"I won't," said George. "And good luck getting through there! My father made that door, and there's no breaking in!"

More scrabbling and scratching. Then another heavy blow. Then there was silence.

"*We just have to wait, yes,*" said a voice then. "*Wait, wait.*"

"Wait all you want!" said George. "I'll never come out, not while you're there. And when my father gets back—"

"*Not waiting for you. For the girl.*"

George stared at the door. "What?"

"*We'll wait for the girl, yes. The little darky girl. You stare at her, yes, yes. We've seen it. We can hide, and wait. Wait for her. And she'll never know we're there...*"

"No!" said George. "No, you wouldn't!"

"*Cut off her hands, cut off her feets,*" said the voice.

"*Burn her skin, her back, her face.*"

"*We will ruin her, yes. Break her, yes, yes.*"

"No!" said George. "Stop it! You won't! I won't let you!"

"*Can't stop us. Not on the other side of the door.*"

"*But if you open it, and let us in...*"

George glanced around the room, looking for something useful. There was nothing besides the hangman's beam, and he did not think he would be much good with that. He tried a few of the cabinets, but they would not open for him. Then he spied the window, and had an idea.

It would depend on if Kingsley's children really counted as alive, he guessed. And he did not think they did. They were false things, something monstrous dolled up and treated as if it were sweet. They were not real; Kingsley had said so himself in the very first performance George had seen.

"All right," he said. "I'll let you in. But you have to promise not to touch her."

"*Open the door.*"

"No. Promise me."

"Open it. Open the door."

"Promise me first, and I will."

A pause. *"Yes, yes. We promise, yes."*

"All right then." George breathed deep and pulled his coat up to cover his neck and the top of his head. Then he took hold of the handle. "I'm about to open it."

"Do it. Do it now!"

Greedy as little children, thought George, and he threw the door open.

He did not wait to see what was on the other side. He turned and bolted away and, with an agility that surprised even him, leaped up onto his father's desk and dove through the bay window, leading with his arms and his covered head.

Glass shattered around him, but that was not the worst part: passing through the window was like falling into arctic seas. The cold seemed to close in on him from either side the moment he passed through the window, and the air was knocked from him. He heard shrill cries behind him as the things on the other side of the door watched him fall. His coat obstructed his vision, so he could not see what was around him as he fell, but after a moment he knew he'd been falling for a long time so he was sure he'd be dashed apart upon the rocky ground below...

He was wrong. Luckily he fell flat on his face, rather than on his head or ankles. Any remaining air in his body went shooting out of him. He moaned a little and tried to sit up, but found he couldn't: his coat and pants were somehow stuck to the rock.

Then he remembered Stanley holding up his blackboard in the mill lots, just after he'd removed his shoes, and it had read: BECAUSE YOU DO NOT WANT THEM TO BE FROZEN TO THE GROUND.

George struggled against his clothing, bending his back and trying to push with his knees, but it did not budge. It was frozen fast to the rocky cliffs, and he was cocooned to the ground by it.

He stopped struggling. He heard scrabbling from somewhere

above him, but he could not see. Then a voice: *"There, lying on the ground, there!"*

They were coming after him. George fought even harder against his frozen coat, and heard something tearing somewhere. He placed a bare hand on the icy ground (so cold it hurt, almost burned) and pushed as hard as he could.

Somewhere a lining gave way and he was free. He twisted and saw he was lying at the foot of one of the enormous, sloping cliffs with the distant, starry sky above him, and just overhead was what looked like three golden rectangles floating before the cliff face. It took him a moment to realize it was the office bay window as seen from the outside, and there were three small figures hanging from the center window, ready to vault down to the cliff.

"Will they ever stop?" moaned George. He tried to sit up, but the seat of his pants had frozen to the ground as well. He stared down in horror and began clawing at his pants button with numb fingers.

He saw movement out of his eye, and one little figure jumped down to the cliff, then another, and another. The three little black shadows slowly climbed down the ridge toward him. He struggled faster to unbutton his pants, but the button seemed to somehow be stuck, and he could not maneuver it with his frigid fingers...

Then one of the little figures stopped in the middle of its climb, and there was a cry from the shadows: *"So cold! So cold! Cannot move! Father, Father! Where are you! Where are you!"*

George stopped and looked up. He'd been right: the marionettes were not real, so they could not carry the First Song in them. They could not last in these wastes.

That did not mean they were not going to try, he saw. The frozen marionette struggled against its frozen limbs, and it snapped them off with a scream and tried to take another step down. When that leg froze as well, it howled and snapped it off too. Then its body fell to the ground and it lay there, sobbing to itself as frost crawled over its chest to envelop its head and face.

The two others learned quickly, and bounded forward, avoiding the ground as much as they could. They screamed and wailed, leaving behind a foot, a thigh, a hand or a shin, little trails of broken body parts leading back into the shadows in the cliff. George lay where he was, watching their tortured procession.

"*Father, Father! Help us, Father!*"

"*Help us! We are dying, Father! Can you hear us, Father?*"

When they entered the starlight he saw it was the two who'd been called Mary-Anne and Denny. What their true names had been, or what the name of the thing that voiced them was, George could not guess. Mary-Anne stumbled and her face grazed the cold rock. When it froze to the surface she howled and gave a mighty pull, and her head split down the middle, exposing old, worn wood with a center of wriggling red worms that clutched a glistening, fleshy interior. Something brown-red sloshed onto the ground as the doll fell, as if it had been carrying around a core of septic blood, and the worms spilled out onto the ground and shriveled as if caught in a fire.

Denny tried his hardest to make it to George, but soon he'd lost his hands, his feet, his elbows, and one knee. He dragged himself along as far as he could, trying to resist the creeping rime, but then he lay still with his gleaming, painted eyes staring up at George.

"*Father, Father,*" whispered the voice. "*Why, Father? Why?*"

George watched him, certain the doll would move again. When it did not he finally exhaled, his frosted breath curling around his head. He looked around to try to figure out how to free himself, yet before he could try anything the windows above him quivered.

He looked up. The bay window seemed to blur at the edges, and George was reminded of a torch flame being whipped around through the dark, its fire fluttering madly.

"It moves," he said, realizing what was happening. "He moves it all the time…"

Then the window seemed to fracture, little black seams running through its golden face. George cried, "No! No!" but then it burst apart into what looked like hundreds of little glowing fireflies, and they gathered into a swarm and flew away into the darkness. He tried to track their progress, but they moved so fast that they were miles away (if such a place had miles) within seconds. Then they were gone, and he was alone.

CHAPTER 19

An Unexpected Return

George wandered over the peaks and valleys of the gray wasteland. He was forced to walk barefoot, as his shoes had indeed frozen to the ground, as Stanley had warned. His clothes were in tatters from where he'd torn free of the icy stones, and he'd been burned in many new places besides the soles of his feet. But he reasoned that discoloration was the least of his problems right now. It was terribly cold there, and he ached in many places, and the images of the horrors he'd just witnessed haunted him with every step.

He was not sure where he was going, or if there was anywhere to go in a place like this. Which, if Silenus was right, was no place at all. George was lost among all the nothing that had filtered down from the remaining world to gather at the bottom of the deepest shadows, a place so slight it could barely be said to exist at all. Places like this did not start and end. They simply were, to a very small degree.

Sometimes he felt as if he were walking along the sides of a cliff. Other times he felt as if he were walking along the roof of a massive cave. When he had to hop across a large gulch his leap seemed to take far longer than it should. Then he realized he was moving much more slowly than he'd thought. Movement did not work right among this endless desolation, it seemed. That explained how he'd survived the fall from the bay window.

Sometimes he spied ruins on the starlit cliffs. Were they dead cities? he wondered. Places the wolves had pillaged until nothing but the bones were left? Or had people somehow found themselves here and built a settlement? At times he thought he saw movement among their crumbled arches, but he did not wish to investigate.

Still other times he saw the tiny, meager stars blacken out overhead, as though something vast and dark was sailing across the sky, and he could not see it. He did not think the things were wolves... Was it possible something had learned to live here? Whatever they were, he wanted to avoid them at all costs.

Finally George came to one of the huge abysses. He nervously walked to the edge and looked down. It did not seem to ever stop, just continue straight down into darkness. Yet George noticed that small lights were spread along the sides of the abyss, shining from within deep, deep clefts.

He remembered when Silenus had first showed him the wastelands, and how he'd seen what he thought were stars buried in the cliffsides...and they'd turned around to leave, and the way out had been hanging behind them.

He began trying to find a way down. There was a fragmented, dangerous little path down along one side of the abyss. It'd eroded away in places, so George had to step carefully or even jump across the larger gaps, but the peculiar nature of physics here made it easy to control his leaps. Eventually he came to one of the clefts with the soft lights shining within, and he squatted to peer in.

After his eyes adjusted, he blinked in surprise. At the end of the cleft was a hole that looked out on what appeared to be a collection of rakes, hoes, and other common gardening tools. It was powerfully surreal to see such mundane little items sitting at the far end of the cleft as if they belonged there. When George squinted he thought he could discern that all the tools were leaning against a background of old wood, and the tops of some were dappled with sunlight, as if from a window he could not see.

He nodded. He'd been right: the little clefts opened on deep shadows in the thin parts of the world. Just as there were holes in existence that led to this place, those very same holes led out. This one in particular seemed to open on a shadow in an old garden shed.

George did not feel amenable to stumbling into a stranger's shed and possibly having to explain why he was trespassing. He did not look at all trustworthy, with his tattered clothes and many dark stains. But it was possible one of these shadows opened on a place closer to the troupe, so he walked on, stopping to look into every cleft to see where each shadow ended.

George saw shadows that looked out on darkened vales, crumbling factories, empty riverbeds, and deserted streets. He saw windswept alleys, endless junkyards, and spindly bridges that seemed to stretch on forever. They were all lonely, decrepit places, places that had not seen visitors in ages. Soon the garden shed began to look very favorable to him.

Then he came to one shadow and stopped. There at the very far end he could see a large, pristine drape of very bright green velvet curtain, with golden tassels at its bottom. Sitting next to it were four large rolled-up canvases, and one of them had unrolled just enough for George to see something painted on it: it depicted the estate grounds of a very large palace, with a small hedge maze.

He immediately recognized it as a backdrop often used at Otterman's in Freightly. He must've played for acts in front of it a hundred times or more. And that curtain there was the secondary curtain the theater used; he would recognize it anywhere by the tassels.

George almost felt faint at the revelation that this shadow apparently opened on the backstage of his old place of employment, and with a happy whoop he got down on all fours and began crawling through the cleft to the shadow at its end.

Soon the cold rock turned to hardwood floors under his hands and he began to smell the familiar aroma of dusty fabric and tobacco smoke and greasepaint and rope. He wondered why the secondary curtain had been stored backstage; throughout his run at Otterman's, Van Hoever had never taken it down or even performed the necessary maintenance on it. But he pushed these thoughts aside. He would climb out, and find Tofty, and Victor, and Irina, and they would help him out of this scrape. They'd get him food, and new clothes, and maybe they'd get him a train ticket, and he'd be back to his father as soon as possible...

As George neared the drape of curtain, however, he realized he smelled something new. It had a sweet, caramelized quality to it, like something slow-roasted, but as he neared the shadow it became duskier, more ashen, even bitter. It was not until he'd fully emerged from the shadow and was standing in the backstage of Otterman's that he identified it as the smell of charred wood and paper. And from the strength of that aroma, there must have been a lot of it somewhere in the theater.

He now saw that the curtain had not been stored backstage at all: it was a ravaged shred of the original, torn off and left hanging there apparently by accident. Scattered on the floor were what looked like the remains of the backdrops and curtain rigging, with knots and tangles of rope still clinging to the pulleys. As George stared at them a breeze ran through the backstage passageway, and carried on its breath were dozens of tiny little black flakes floating dreamily through the dark air. They settled on George's shoulders and his outstretched, blackened hands, and when he touched them they fell to powder.

Ash, he thought. What had happened here?

George walked down the passageway. The lamps were all dark, the only source of light the weak luminescence at the passage's end, where it led to the stage. As he walked the wind rose again, and somewhere in the dark backstage something whipped and fluttered wildly.

This was not the place of action and life he remembered. He could not imagine people ever working here at all. Eventually he began to wonder why the shadow had opened up in this place. If Silenus was right, such things only opened up on the thin parts of the world, areas that had been worn down until they hardly existed. What could have made that the case for Otterman's?

Then George came to the edge of the stage, and looked out.

The curtains around him hung in tatters, and the entire left side of the stage had been turned into a blackened husk. The framework and supports below the boards there were exposed, withered and dark from past flame, and the curtains above ended halfway down in frail webs of charred fabric. George stared at them and walked out to the center of the stage to see the rest of the devastation.

The fire had started in the balcony, it looked like, specifically the one on the left, which now was no more than a few black spits of wood protruding from the ruined wall. On the ground below was a pile of ashen timbers and flotsam that must have tumbled down during the inferno. The entire top corner of the theater was gone above the missing balcony, replaced by a black-ringed wound that opened onto the midnight sky. As George watched, the wind rushed across the open roof and sent the ash and black flakes dancing among the remaining seats. His eyes followed the path of destruction, and he guessed that when the balcony had dissolved the fire had leaped down into the seats before advancing on the stage.

He was so stunned by this destruction that he almost didn't notice the five figures standing on the right side of the stage with their backs to him. When he finally did he almost shouted in surprise, but he restrained himself and shrank up against the curtain to watch.

They did not move or speak, but stared into the orchestra pit to where a small campfire was flickering before the front row of seats. To George's eyes the people looked very misshapen. They leaned awkwardly, mostly around the waist, and their arms were shrunken and, in most cases, lopsided. There were three men and two women, and they wore ill-fitting clothing that George found somehow familiar...One man had a red coat and a black top hat, one of the women was dressed in what looked like bandages, and the other wore bright white tights.

George stepped out from behind the curtain to get a better look. As his angle changed he saw they were not people at all, but mannequins or large dummies. The person who'd arranged them had apparently run out of mannequins halfway though, however, and had been forced to improvise with papier-mâché and coat stands and tall, thin chairs. As a result, some of them had blank mannequin faces, while others had heads made of wads of clothing or, in the case of the man in the top hat, a globe.

But that did not change the fact that these figures were obviously meant to resemble the troupe. The coat-stand with the papier-mâché head had to be Stanley, with its linen shirt and nice waistcoat, and the shorter dummy was clearly Kingsley, wearing his sharp tuxedo and black eye makeup, and the figure with the globe for a head had to be Harry. They were all deformed and twisted, and the representations were not exact (the mannequin meant to be Colette was male, for example, and they'd gotten the pattern of Silenus's trousers wrong) but the intent was clear.

George walked to them across the stage, and as he did one bare foot fell on a patch of boards that were soft and moist. He looked down. A very large, rusty stain stretched across the end of the stage. George had seen enough of that same material just hours ago to know it was blood.

He looked out at the theater again, and thought the odds of this all being accidental were very small.

George considered leaving, but then hopped down to examine the camp behind the orchestra pit. The fire was situated before the front row of the stage right seating, and many of the seats there were occupied by boxes and reams of paper. One seat in the center of the row, just before the fire, was empty. George guessed that this was where whoever had arranged all of this had sat.

Wondering if perhaps some vagrant had made their home in the abandoned theater, he walked to the row of seats and looked at all the papers and boxes. They were maps, mostly, and train timetables, and notes in handwriting so illegible that George felt the person had not had much schooling. He glanced over the maps and saw they were all of the countryside, with several areas circled and notated. He wondered what this could mean before remembering Silenus's tower and the map there, and he realized these notes corresponded with where they'd detected the First Song.

George felt the need to very quickly get out of here. The occupant of this bizarre campsite was apparently fixated upon the troupe, and knew of their mission and the First Song as well. It was all too coincidental for George's liking, and the theater was not the place he'd once known: it was dark and crumbling and it stank of blood and ash, and the sight of those five leaning figures standing at the edge of the stage in the clothing of his friends and family set his skin crawling.

He turned to leave, but he stopped. He saw his old piano sitting alone in the orchestra pit, and his heart leaped. He had spent so many happy hours in front of it, reveling in the praise of his peers. He walked to the piano, and as he did he saw there was someone sitting before the keys.

As with the stage, it was not a person but another mannequin. But this one was short and hunched, and its nonexistent hands were meant to be sitting on the keyboard. It wore a ratty tweed jacket and waistcoat and an even rattier riding cap. And yet George recognized the way it sat at the keys, with its head slightly twisted to the side as if to hear the music better, perhaps relishing the tune it was playing...

It was very clearly meant to be George himself. He backed away, horrified at the sight of his shrunken little self hunched in front of the piano.

Then something clanked up toward the theater entrance. George jumped and huddled down, watching the broken windows in the doors. Somewhere behind them a deep voice said, "No one ever knows where he is these days..."

A sharp, hard silence began to fill the ruined theater, and the shadows at the back trembled as if celebrating.

"Oh, no," George whispered.

He bolted up onto the stage toward the back, yet as he did he accidentally brushed against the dummy meant to be Silenus, and the globe and hat began to topple. George slid to a halt and dove backward. To his complete surprise, he managed to snatch both of them before they fell. He awkwardly maneuvered them in his arms, intending to replace them, but the silence grew louder and he thought he saw something approaching the door. He abandoned the dummy and fled into the backstage, leaving Silenus headless.

He wound through the passageways and found the wall with the shred of green curtain. Then he peered into the shadows across, thinking, and reached out. Yet where previously there'd been a gap that led to the gray wastes, now there was only brick.

The shadow was gone. It must have been shored up when George came through, which he supposed made sense as carrying the song here would heal this thin, insubstantial place...yet now he had no way to get out.

He heard a door swing open out in the theater. Then there were the echoes of footsteps. Yet they sounded padded, somehow, and there was a faint click to them that suggested the feet were clawed.

"He's getting very peculiar, if you ask us," said the deep voice. "And we know you didn't, but still."

"Sitting with his little notes, looking at them up on the stage, and his maps..." said a second voice. It was much higher and reedier. "He prefers to spend time here rather than anywhere else. He keeps his skin on all the time. And that's not even mentioning his coat."

"Did it change? When he..."

"No," said the reedy voice. "That's not what we've heard. We were told he did that to *himself.*"

The deep voice gasped. "Himself? How strange..."

George did not know what they were talking about, but from the silence and the way the shadows were behaving he knew they had to be wolves. He was still holding the globe and the hat. He put them down and tiptoed through the hall, hoping to reach the back door where they loaded the props. But he found that the roof of the theater had caved in there, and huge timbers now blocked his way.

"He's given himself colors," said the reedy voice. "And just recently we heard he's thinking about giving himself a *name*."

Another gasp. "No!" said the deep voice. "You can't be serious!"

"We are. We most certainly are. It's horrible, isn't it?"

"Yes. We suppose it must be the side effects of what he's done... what he took on for us."

"Yes, it must," said the reedy voice. "We can't imagine what it's like. It must be so awful to just... *be*."

Their conversation was making less and less sense to George. Then he remembered that there'd been a nearby room with a window in it: Van Hoever's office. He remembered sitting in front of his employer's desk with daylight streaming in before him... surely it still had to be there.

George crept down the hall to the manager's office. Then he slowly eased open the door.

"Wait!" said the deep voice.

George froze, thinking they'd heard him.

"What is it?" said the reedy one.

"Look at that one... didn't it have something on its top?"

"It did?" said the reedy voice.

His heartbeat quickened. Did they mean the Silenus dummy?

"It's hard to tell," said the reedy voice. "All these creatures look alike to us. So many parts..."

"We're sure it did," said the deep voice. "A head. It had a head on it."

George pushed open the door and sidled into the office. The

window was still there, and it was not blocked. He just had to climb up on Van Hoever's desk, lean across, open it, and climb out.

There was a loud snuffling noise from out on the stage. "Something's here," said the deep voice.

"What?" said the reedy one.

"Something's been in here. Can't you smell it? It's all over the stage."

More snuffling. Then the reedy voice croaked, "Yes..."

George knew he had no more time to waste. He went to the desk and prepared to lift himself up onto its top. Then he saw something on the other side of it and stopped.

Someone was lying on the floor there, sprawled out and facedown as if hiding, yet they had not looked up or noticed when George had come in.

George slowly lowered himself and rounded the desk to get a look. Yet as he did he saw discolorations on the floor, long brown streaks like something wet had been dragged in from the stage area, possibly from where that big brown stain had been. His heart began to pound and he felt cold sweat crawl across the small of his back. Then he rounded the desk and nearly retched.

It was the body of a woman, or at least most of one. Her legs and back were still there, as was most of an arm. But though George could not see the woman's front he knew from the stain on the floor that she must have been ravaged, even gutted, but due to the cold she was nearly perfectly preserved.

At first he did not recognize her. But then he saw her hand, wrapped with cloth to ease her arthritis, and even though her fingers were blue with cold he knew they were the same ones that had once been used to count off three things their owner had deduced about him, just before she'd warned him not to leave the theater.

George backed up to the wall in terror, and could not move or take his eyes away from the sight. He fell to his knees and nearly broke down. He had not known Irina well, but she had been kind to him and thought of him when he did not merit it, and she did not deserve a fate such as this. No one did, George thought.

Then the office door flew open to reveal solid darkness outside, as if beyond its threshold was purest night. The center of the darkness quivered, and he saw something white and fleshy begin to push forward into the room. As it slowly emerged, George realized it was a nose, and below that a chin appeared, and then a brow, and then a pair of blank gray eyes that were staring right at him...

With the perverse, determined steadiness of a crab molting from its shell, the shadow produced the image of a man in a gray coat and black bowler, and then it seemed to somehow fold up inside him once it was done. The man in gray slowly cocked his head like a curious dog. In a deep voice George recognized as the one he'd heard in the theater, the man said, "You. We were told to watch for you."

CHAPTER 20

George Meets a Fan

George sat in the front row of the theater's seats, lashed to the cushioned back. The wolves, being ignorant of how lungs or veins worked, had made the ropes far too tight, and he soon began to black out. He begged them to loosen the bonds a little.

The two wolves paced around him in a circle. "How do we know that you won't up and run?" said the wolf with the reedy voice, who was extremely tall and thin and had a large hook nose.

"Well...you're both probably much faster than me," said George, wheezing. "Y-you could probably run me down before I ever reached the door."

The two wolves stopped pacing. "That's true," said the one with the deep voice, who was very thick and short. "We have, after all, killed much more difficult things than a barefooted child."

"True, true," said the reedy-voiced one. "We've stalked the nephilim in the plains of Edom, and we toppled them like toy towers."

"We've run thunderbirds until they could fly no further," said the fat one, "and when they landed we fell upon them with the fury of storms."

"We've swum into the darks of the seas, and devoured selkies and Samebitos and Tritons."

"We've brought down whole mountains."

"And continents."

"And stars," added the fat one. "That was in the old days, the before days. But we don't think we've lost it. It would be no issue to kill a child such as you. Something so thin and scrawny and tired."

"With hardly a scrap of fat on him."

"Just tumbling bones and strangled sounds."

"Little cries, like a sick cat."

"Almost not worth it," said the fat one.

"Almost. But not quite," said the reedy-voiced one, and he made an attempt at a smile. On his blank, awkward face, the effect was deeply disturbing.

George was not sure if it was the most disturbing thing about the wolves, though. Perhaps what was most disturbing was the way their images and faces would suddenly blur and shudder, as if they were forgetting to maintain the illusion. Or perhaps it was the way their bones and teeth would click when they stretched their limbs or twisted their necks, affecting poses usually only attainable by reptiles and owls.

But more than any of this, he decided the most frightening thing about the wolves had to be the way light and space behaved around them. Shadows seemed to stretch to brush over their feet and hands, as if they were being worshipped by the dark. When they came near, the entire theater began to feel both cavernous and claustrophobic all at once, and George got the strange sensation of being dangled over a deep chasm. Their very presence was doing something to reality, he felt, stretching and tearing at dimensions he could not detect with his normal senses. They were violations of the purest kind, anomalies that breached and mocked every rule George had about the way the world should work. Their halfhearted attempts at appearing like men highlighted their Wrongness even further.

He had hoped that they would not know who he was, but the fat one had identified him immediately. He'd swooped George up in his arms and whisked him off to the orchestra pit and held him next to the little dummy seated on the piano bench. "It's him! It's him!" the reedy-voiced one had crowed. "We've got him, we've got him! Stupid thing! Stupid little child! Came walking right in here, didn't he!"

"Come stumbling from the shadow-lands," growled the fat one, looking over the marks on George's hands. "You've seen the gray reaches then, haven't you? But here you are now. Here you are." And they'd both howled in delight, a high, keening sound that did not echo but seemed to penetrate deep into the mind.

Once they'd loosened George's bonds, the fat one said, "Now we'll wait until *he* gets back. He'll have questions for you. Lots and lots of questions. And then we get to do as we please."

"But we can ask some of our own first," said the reedy-voiced one. "Perhaps he'll spill his guts to us. Then we'd have all the glory, wouldn't we?"

"Would you do that?" breathed the fat one. He stared into George's face, eyes wide. "Would you tell us? Tell us everything?"

George was too terrified to speak. He did not know what they would ask, so he could not tell them if he could answer.

"Have you seen it?" demanded the reedy-voiced one. "Have you seen the Light? That awful Light they carry, like the very eye of the Enemy?"

"How do they carry it?" said the fat one. "Do they carry it in a lantern? We think they must carry it in a lantern...They walk into the dark, don't they, swinging it back and forth?"

Both of the wolves shuddered. Then the reedy-voiced one snarled in fury.

"Tell us!" he cried. "Tell us about the lantern! How can we destroy it? Is it made of moonish silver?" He rushed up to glare into George's face, and George thought he could see cracks appearing in the wolf's façade, threatening to break away to show what was hiding beneath its skin.

"I don't know what you're talking about!" George said. "I...I don't know anything about a lantern, or...or moonish silver!"

The reedy-voiced wolf growled and whirled away, but the fat one leaned forward, fascinated. "Is it not in a lantern?" he said. "Do not pretend like you would not know, like you are not one of them. We know you are Silenus's child. Aren't you?"

George took a breath. He'd never been a very good liar, and he wondered what to say.

But before he could think of anything, the wolf smiled. "Ah, yes. I don't know much about you and your kind, but I know the shape of truth. And there it was, winking in your eyes. So you must know, don't you? You must know how it's carried, how they transport it."

"We have waited so long…" said the reedy-voiced one. "Tell us what it looks like. Tell us how we can get at it. We'll make you, if you don't."

"Yes," said the fat one. "We will." He thought and said, "Do you know why we wear the guises of men?"

George shook his head.

"It's not to sneak about among you. It's because we're being *polite*." He extended a finger, and there was a soft cracking noise, like someone dropping an eggshell. Something very black and sharp stabbed out through the white flesh of his fingertip, which crumbled away like it was made of chalk. It was a claw, George saw, black as coal and sharper than a razor, poking through the skin from whatever the wolf really was, underneath.

The wolf watched as George's eyes followed his clawed finger. "You don't want to see what we really look like," he said. Then he lifted his finger and cut a straight line underneath his jaw, like he was slashing his own throat. But no blood poured from the gash; instead it was like he had sliced through paper, and now the skin (was it skin?) on his neck flapped open loosely, and George glimpsed something black and misty underneath.

"If you don't tell us, we'll look at you," said the fat one. "We'll take off this silly little face and look at you, and then you'll never look at anything again after that. You won't be able to. Not after seeing us."

"Tell us," said the reedy-voiced one, and there was hyena laughter in his words. "Tell us where he keeps it."

The image of Silenus's steamer trunk flashed in George's mind. He must not ever tell them, he knew. He thought wildly, and glanced at the Silenus dummy up on the stage. He said, "Do you want to know why I took the head off of that?"

The two wolves looked at him, confused, and glanced back at the dummy. "The head?" said the reedy-voiced one.

"Yes," said George. "I did it for a reason. I...I wanted to keep you from knowing something."

The reedy-voiced wolf took a quick intake of breath, excited. He grew close, and the silence in George's ears became so overpowering his eyes began to water. "Tell us," the wolf whispered. "Tell us what you wanted to hide..."

George swallowed, and said, "You really want to know where he keeps the Light?"

"Yes," said the fat one. "Yes!"

"It's...it's in his hat," said George. "He keeps it in his hat."

The two wolves drew back, shocked.

"In his hat?" echoed the reedy-voiced one.

"Yes," said George.

They both pondered this.

"We've never heard that it could be in his hat," said the fat one. "It's almost too...dangerous."

"Obvious," said the reedy-voiced wolf.

"Exposed," said the fat wolf.

"But that makes it the best place!" said George. "Doesn't it? He always has his hat with him. He never loses it. And who would ever think to look in a hat?"

The reedy-voice one nodded, seeing the sense in this, but the fat one shook his head. "Hm. No," he said.

George's heart plummeted. "No?"

"No. No, no," said the fat one. "That doesn't sound right. It was far too easy, far too quick. We've been after this secret for so, so long. It can't be gotten that easy." He frowned. "You lied to us, didn't you, child?"

"N-no!" said George.

"Oh, yes. Yes, you did. Come now. That was a lie. Right?" He did not wait for George's answer. Instead he turned and lumbered down to the campfire (stopping halfway to shudder and shake, and somewhere there was the sound of thick fur rustling). He picked up one smoldering branch and slowly began walking back. "We can't have you telling us lies," he said. "Can't have you filling our ears up with half-truths, and no-truths. But we can't show you our face," he said, gesturing to the open flap underneath his chin. "Because then you'd be useless. See?"

George dimly became aware that he was trembling.

"We think something more mundane is needed," said the fat one. One hand snapped out so fast George could hardly see it, and the next thing he knew the wolf had grasped his chin and forced his head up.

The wolf's fingers were colder than ice. He raised the smoldering branch up and waved it below George's cheek. "Something mundane, but something you won't forget."

"No," said George.

"No," echoed the wolf, mocking him.

"No, please."

"No, please," said the wolf. His empty gray eyes were huge in his face. He smiled as though this was all a fond distraction. The smoking branch grew closer until George could feel its heat on his skin. He shut his eyes and braced himself for its sizzling kiss...

Something slammed up toward the entrance of the theater. Then a high, strong voice called out, "What is going on?"

The wolf released him. George opened his eyes and saw the two of them backing away, abashed. Someone was walking down the rows behind him. George turned to try to get a look at this new arrival, but due to how he was bound he could only see a man in a red coat. He very briefly thought it was his father come to rescue him.

It was not. It was a third wolf. But this one looked very different from all the other ones George had ever seen.

The forms and figures of the wolves all varied—as in the current case, some were fat, and some were thin, and so on—but overall there was little difference among them. They all wore gray suits with black bowler hats, and their eyes and faces all had that same curious emptiness to them that made their very appearances seem like shells or masks.

But not this one. To begin with, he wore a bright red coat and a black porkpie hat with a white feather stuck in the band. This was so startling that George at first thought him a normal person, and feared for the man's life. But then George noticed the very quiet silence the man carried with him, and realized he was indeed a wolf as well.

"What is this? Are you torturing a child?" asked the wolf in red.

The other two exchanged a glance, as though this question were ridiculous. "Obviously," said the fat one.

"But why would you do such a thing?" asked the wolf in red. "Have I not told you that my studies here must be uninterrupted? That we must maintain a peaceful, quiet environment for me to work in?"

Again the two wolves looked at each other, and George got the sense that if they'd possessed the humanity to roll their eyes in exasperation, they would have.

"He came here of his own accord," said the reedy-voiced one. "That's how we found him."

"And he is not just any boy," said the fat one. "He is the pianist."

"The pianist?" said the wolf in red. His mouth fell open and he stared at George.

"Yes," said the reedy-voiced wolf. "He is Silenus's son. You can see it there, in his face."

The wolf in red was lost for words for a moment. "My goodness, you're right! I recognize him now. But this is extraordinary!" he cried, delighted. "Why do you have him all tied up?"

"All tied up?" said the reedy-voiced wolf. "Have you forgotten that he is the son of our sworn enemy? That his father carries that hated Light?"

"Yes, yes, yes," said the wolf in red. "I know all about that. How could I forget? But think of the opportunity!"

"The what?" said the fat wolf, but before he could say more the wolf in red strode over and began untying George.

"What are you doing?" said the reedy-voiced wolf. "Don't let him go!"

"I'm not letting him go," said the wolf in red. "But I can't examine him if he's all tied up, now can I?"

"Examine?" said the fat wolf. "What do you mean?"

"I mean examine, that's what I mean. This is a perfect opportunity to…well, explore. And the more I explore and learn, the more I learn about how the Light works."

"And then you can figure out how to track and destroy it?" asked the reedy-voiced wolf.

"What?" said the wolf in red. "Oh, yes, yes. To destroy it. But I'm beginning to think that we've been going about this all wrong…It is not a light, really, but something else. Something more like a sound, I believe…"

"Very good," said the fat wolf. He looked extremely angry. "But you seem to be forgetting that this boy is a very big coup for us. He is a veritable mine of information. You are letting your curiosities get the better of you, and putting too much at risk. We should simply interrogate him, which is why we restrained him in the first place."

"My interests and…unique predicament allow me truths you are blind to," said the wolf in red. "Let me handle this interrogation. Can you imagine anyone better to do it than I? I, the one who knows more about their company and what they do than anyone else?"

The two wolves looked mutinous at this, but reluctantly nodded.

"Then that's settled. Here," said the wolf in red to George. "Come on. Stand up. That's it, there we go." He looked George up and down. "You seem to be in working order. All your...parts are functioning?"

"Yes?" hazarded George.

"Very good. Very, very good. Then come down with me. Let's sit in the front row together, and we can talk." He nodded and said to the two other wolves, "That will be all."

"What!" said the reedy-voiced wolf. "That will be all? What do you mean, that will be all?"

"I mean that's all I require from you," said the wolf in red. "You're no longer needed."

"You can't just order us about!" snarled the fat wolf. "We're not your underlings!"

"But we took this theater for me, for my researches," said the wolf in red. "It's mine. I am the one who knows what this project is about, and I am the one in charge of it. And you are interrupting. Or would you like me to tell—"

The wolf in red then said something that George did not understand. It was not a word, and it was not quite a noise. If George had not had the First Song within him, and been so attuned to the silence of the wolves, he would not have heard it at all. But as he did, he heard the wolf in red say something that was like a burst of pure, cold silence, one so complete and awful it was like George had been slapped on either side of his head. His skin erupted in goose bumps and his bowels turned to water, and a tremor ran through the shadows all around them as if in anticipation. He did not know what the wolf had said; he only knew he did not want to hear it again, and he definitely did not ever, ever want to know what it referred to.

The two other wolves stiffened at its mention. "You wouldn't," said the fat one.

"I was given approval," said the wolf in red. "My works have the blessings, the authorities. I am allowed. And you are not. And today, here, you are no longer needed."

The two wolves stared at him. Then the reedy-voiced one nodded, and retreated into the shadows, and disappeared. But the fat one lingered, and said, "You should be careful. It is possible that your works are tainting you. And remember: we are all underlings to the one you name. And it is watching you very carefully." Then he withdrew as well, and was gone.

The wolf in red shook his head once when they were gone. "Silly things," he said. "They are so eager, but they really don't understand."

George felt very confused. While this wolf seemed too unhinged to trust, George was keen to stay in his good graces, since he was the only thing keeping him from horrible abuse. So as politely as possible, George said, "Excuse me, but—"

But the wolf cried, "No, no! No, don't say anything yet! Please don't! For now, please, just...*look*." He leaped down the aisle steps to the front row before the orchestra pit. He gestured to all six of the dummies, and said, "Just look, and please, tell me what you think. Look carefully, and...oh, dear. It looks like someone has stolen the impresario's head. But ignore that. Please, ignore that, and just... tell me your thoughts."

George was not sure what he meant. He looked back over the tilted, distorted figures that were so horribly reminiscent of his friends, leaning this way and that in the dancing ash. "It's...it's meant to be the troupe."

"Well, yes, obviously," said the wolf. "But how close are the representations? Are they very close? Are they exact? I conducted dozens of interviews, kept hundreds of theater bills...Please tell me where I went right and wrong, please."

The wolf was earnestly watching him, waiting on his every word. George was reminded of an artist bracing himself for criticism.

"They're extremely close," said George.

"But not exact?"

"Well, n-no..."

The wolf tutted and shook his head and began rifling a stack of notes. "What is wrong? What's different? Please spare no detail, it's the details that trouble me so."

George had no idea where to begin. Stanley was not five feet tall, and Kingsley was not four feet, and Colette did not have such formidable biceps. But in the interest of humoring the wolf, George told him only about the incorrect pattern of Harry's trousers, and also mentioned that Stanley usually wore a tie. The wolf immediately asked about the color of the tie as well as the waist size of Silenus's pants. "This is good, this is very good!" said the wolf, scribbling quickly as George answered. "You have no idea how useful this is! I've been following you all for months, trying to get every bit of information on you I could! I traveled miles to find anyone who'd seen your show, and now to have a genuine member in my company... what are the odds? This will be perfect for my researches!"

"I'm sorry, but...researches?" asked George.

"Oh, yes!" said the wolf brightly. "We wanted to know all about you, so I asked them to take this theater for me, and then I could re-create one of your performances! This is where I collect all my little findings, all my little discoveries about you and your company of actors. This *is* a theater your company visited, isn't it? I wanted the re-creation to be exact."

"Well, *I* played here, yes," said George. "But it was just me. Not Silenus."

The wolf was very crestfallen at this. "Silenus...never came here? You never performed here together?"

George shook his head.

"Oh. Oh, dear," said the wolf. "I...I must have gotten my information wrong, and chose the wrong place. So all of this...has been wrong from the beginning. How could I have been so stupid!" he howled suddenly, and kicked at one of the seats. Such was his strength that it cleanly broke free of the floor and went flying across the theater. "I've wasted so much time here! And now we'll have to go and take a new theater, and start all over again!"

George was alarmed to hear this. Not only did he want to keep the wolf in good spirits, but taking a theater apparently meant destroying the building and running off the staff and audience. That must have been how poor Irina died... Then George remembered Van Hoever's grudge, and said, "But Silenus did play here once!"

The wolf halted his tantrum and looked up. "What?"

"He did play here, before I did! The manager hated him! So this *is* one of his theaters."

"The manager?" said the wolf.

"Yes! When I worked here he hated Silenus because of his last performance. So this theater is one that both me and Silenus played at. It was just at different times. See?"

"So... I wasn't wrong to choose this place?"

"No!" said George. He hoped he did not sound as desperate as he felt.

"Oh, good!" said the wolf. He clapped his hands together. "That's quite a relief! I was very worried there for a moment. Then this is a close re-creation, yes?"

"Y-yes, absolutely," said George.

"Excellent. Excellent!" He gazed around proudly at the theater and his mock performance, and nodded as though the charred roof and ruined stage were all intended parts of his creation. "I really wanted to *feel* it, you know, to sit in the audience and just watch. Just to get a sense. I'd love to actually see the performance. Ah, of course! I know. You can simply tell me where Silenus is playing next, right now, can't you? Maybe there's a chance I could actually catch his show."

George stared at the wolf. He was not sure what to think of this guileless ploy. The wolf could not possibly expect him to inform on his friends, could he?

Again, George's face showed his thinking. "Ah," said the wolf. "You think me one of them."

"I'm sorry?"

"You think I am among those who hunt and chase you, who hunger for the Light you bear."

"Well... aren't you?"

The wolf looked a little uncomfortable. "Well, y-yes. Yes, I suppose I am doing these researches in order to, well, track you down, and kill you all and so on. But the circumstances are not as you think."

"They aren't?" said George. "Then what are they?"

The wolf thought for a moment, and smiled and said, "I will show you." There was the familiar sound of eggshells breaking again, and a black claw protruded from the index finger of the wolf in red, just as the fat one's had done. Yet rather than cutting his throat, the wolf in red made a large slash down the front of his chest. The slash flapped open, the coat and shirt stuck together as though they were all part of the same membrane. Then the wolf took the sides of the gash in either hand and said, "Watch."

"Wait," said George. "Wait, what are you doing?"

But the wolf ignored him and pulled the slash apart. George, helpless, stared into it.

Below the wolf's skin was a deep, terrible darkness, not the absence of light as much as the impossibility of it; light was still unthought of, undreamed of, in the deeps where that darkness existed. And yet... there was some small, glittering light in the dark. Some tiny, diamond-bright star that was crawling in little circles in the endless, churning blacks of the wolf's heart. And George thought he heard that little light singing, somehow...

No, thought George. That's *impossible*...

The wolf closed the slash. The two sides knit together and became whole again. "You saw it, did you not?"

George said, "You...you've got..."

"Yes," said the wolf. "I have the Light in me. Just the tiniest, tiniest bit. It took us so much time to even figure out what it *was*...We could feel it hurting us, burning us, pushing us back, but we could never understand it. It was by sheer chance that we discovered this tiny shard, lost in the deepest arctic ices, where the shadow lies so thickly. We had to understand what it was, what it did. And we engaged with it in the same way we engage with anything—we ate it.

"Or, more specifically, *I* ate it," said the wolf mildly. "It is very strange. I used to never say 'I.' I always thought in 'we.' *We* always thought in 'we.' But ever since I consumed that little bead of Light, things have...changed. As such, it was decided that I would be the one most suited to learning about your troupe, and what it is you do, and I was given this theater for my studies."

The wolf gave George a slightly demented smile. "It is all a very new sensation, having the Light in me. I've begun trying new things, from colors to hats to even...why, even to *names*. I've got so many questions for you, and I am eager to hear your answers. I've asked others, but they were mostly confused by my questions...But then, they did not know my circumstances. You do, so perhaps you can help me understand, and further my studies, yes?"

George shrugged. "A-All right?"

"Excellent!" cried the wolf. He ripped out two seats from the front row and set them up in the orchestra pit, facing one another. He grabbed a notepad and sat in one. Then he gestured to the other. George, feeling faintly absurd, sat.

"Now," said the wolf. "Now, now, now." He flipped through several pages to find the right starting place. "My first question is—do you have a *name*?"

"A name? Yes."

"Ah!" said the wolf. It wrote several extensive notes. "And what is that name?"

"George."

"I see," said the wolf. "And how long have you been George?"

"How long? As in, how long have I been alive?"

"Oh, were you here in some way before you were alive?" asked the wolf, interested.

"I...don't really know," said George. "I don't think so."

"So you don't know if you were here? Or if you were here before your George-time? Is it possible for you to be here, but not know it?"

"My what time? No, I mean, I was born, and then they just named me George."

"So you are *not* George," said the wolf. "George is just a name. A word. A propulsion of air modified by the flexing of throat-parts."

"Well, I am George, but...yes. Yes, and...no."

"Is it possible that you became George at a later time, having been originally named that thing?" asked the wolf. "What if the naming had been different, would you still be George?"

"I...yes?"

"Really?" breathed the wolf in awe. "This is all so confusing." Yet he seemed very pleased with George's answers. "I don't know how you all do it. It seems so marvelously complex to simply...be."

"I'm...not sure if I would be the best to answer these sorts of questions," said George.

"Why not?" asked the wolf. "Do you not exist? Trust me, I would be aware if you did not exist. My brothers and I, in a very, very fundamental way, have not existed since before anything could ever exist. Though that's recently changed for me, of course." The wolf looked up, thoughtful. "Do you understand what I mean?"

George looked at him. He realized that the way the wolf was dressed and the way he was acting were akin to how children would dress up and pretend to be their parents, mimicking the ephemera of adult life without ever really understanding its meaning. "I think I'm starting to."

"It is a very troubling and confusing thing," said the wolf. "But simply from our short discussion, I've learned something. Your existence seems to have been gradual. You weren't, and then you slowly were. But mine was not gradual. I wasn't, and then I had a bright little core of... of *everything* dropped inside me. And then I *was*. And it is shocking, and painful."

"Really?" asked George.

"Yes," said the wolf. "It *burns* me inside, this little flame, this jewel. It is my diametrical opposite, my absolute antithesis. I was lucky — if there'd been any more, it would have killed me. And yet I bear it."

"Why would you ever want to do that?" asked George.

"Oh, for many reasons. For one, it lends all of my brothers who are close to me a resistance to it. Now, when your father spreads his Light, we are not burned or pained. And also I am more sensitive to that same Light. I can tell when it is near."

George's eyes went wide. He strained to mask his thoughts, which were many. To begin with, in one swoop he'd just learned how the wolves were resisting the effects of the song and how they were predicting the troupe's movements. But more troubling was that if the wolf could tell when the First Song was near, then it could possibly tell that George had a huge piece of it inside of him. "Y-you can?" George asked.

"Yes," said the wolf. He stared him up and down, eyes thin, and George felt very nervous. "For example, its residue and effects are very strong on you..."

"They are?"

"Yes. I presume this is because you have been in its presence for so long, and have been so close to so many performances?"

Again, George tried to hide his feelings, but this time they were mostly relief. "Y-yes, that's it. That's definitely it."

"I see," said the wolf. He wrote that down. "Anyway, those are the most obvious reasons for why I carry this bit of the Light in me. But... in another way, I enjoy it, somewhat. There is a pain to it, but it is a bittersweet pain." An idea seemed to come to him. "Tell me — will I *die*?"

"Will you what?"

"Die. Do you think I will? I suppose I must...I exist now, and everything that exists must end, one day. I wonder how I will die, and what it will be like. It will be most interesting, don't you think?"

George was so astounded with this line of thought that he had no idea what to say.

"Yes. Yes, I think it will," said the wolf. "I look forward to it. On the whole, I think it a very strange and terrifying thing, to exist. I really don't understand how you do it. Tell me—how do you deal with the fear?"

"The fear?" asked George.

"Yes. That fear that comes from the feeling that there is you, and then there is...everything else. That you are trapped inside of yourself, a tiny dot insignificant in the face of every everything that could ever be. How do you manage that?"

George considered how to answer. "I...guess we just never think about it."

"Never think about it!" cried the wolf. "How can you not think about it when it confronts you at every moment? You are lost amid a wide, dark sea, with no shores in sight, and you all so rarely panic! Some days I can barely *function*, so how on Earth can you never think about it?"

"Well, I...suppose we distract ourselves," said George.

"But with what?"

"I don't know. With all kinds of things."

The wolf furiously wrote all of this down. "Can you give me some examples?"

"Examples?"

"Yes. Are there no elements in your life you feel are great distractions?"

George wondered if he'd just painted himself into a corner, but he supposed he had at least a few. His father, for instance, was a very great distraction to him. Yet George did not want to tell him anything about Silenus, as it could endanger the troupe. But then he thought of another who occupied his mind just as much.

So to his surprise he began telling the wolf about Colette. He did not divulge anything important, but he began talking about "this girl" who was strong and beautiful, and he described the way she could make you feel stupid or smart with a glance, and talked about her questioning, sardonic eyebrows, and the way she laughed when she knew she shouldn't, which George found enchanting.

"So you love her?" asked the wolf.

"I...suppose so," said George. "I don't really know her, not as much as I want to. I don't think she really knows me." And then he could not help but talk about how she was distracted herself, forever caught up in the abstract mechanics of show business, and how she had little time and no eyes for him. And he admitted that this hurt him greatly, but there was a little antipathy to his words as well: she was so wrapped up in running the troupe that she spent more time with his father than she ever did with him. They were the same, really: two adults who deemed him a child, and George envied both of them for the attention each one got from the other.

"It sounds as if some distractions are even worse than what you are distracting yourself from," said the wolf in red. "Are there none that are pleasant for you?"

George was a little miffed to hear this, but said that yes, there were. There was Stanley, for one, though George vaguely described him as "a friend," and he talked about how this friend was always giving him gifts, and cheering him up, and telling him stories; and once when George had fallen asleep in a hotel lobby Stanley had carried him up to his room and put him to bed, and when George was lying there Stanley had just stood looking down at him, not aware that George was now awake, and he sighed deeply before leaving. He cared so much, it felt.

"I see," said the wolf. "And this friend is in love with you?"

"What?" said George, startled.

"This friend of yours. He is in love with you?"

"In love? No, he's not!"

"He isn't?" said the wolf. He consulted his notes. "It certainly sounds like he is."

"He isn't," said George faintly. "He...he can't be."

But now he was not so sure. He had never considered exactly why Stanley was so kind to him; he'd always thought Stanley was simply a very kind person. But now he wondered: could Stanley be in love with him in the same way that George was in love with Colette? Was such a thing possible? Stanley never did seem to show anyone but him such affection. He remembered the night on the rooftop outside Chicago, and the way Stanley had stared at him with his sad eyes, and the way he had felt George's shoulder, his fingers trailing down his arm...

The thought made George powerfully uncomfortable, but he did not know why. It felt like a betrayal, as if Stanley had been providing such kindness without ever letting George know the intentions behind it.

The wolf tutted unhappily. "I don't think I understand this," he said. "It is starting to feel like the more I find out about all this, the less I understand. I'd hoped you would explain it all to me, and then..." He shook his head and tossed his notes down beside the chair. "I don't know. I'd thought you would at least mention why your troupe has started traveling differently."

"You mean changing to vaudeville?"

"No," said the wolf. "It's something else. Your troupe has stopped performing as often as they used to, in the old days. Previous troupes would spend weeks or months in one little part of the world, walling it off from us, but your troupe is constantly traveling at a breakneck pace."

"But that's to cover more ground, isn't it?" said George.

"If so, it is not accomplishing much. You do not stay and perform until the places you visit are protected against my brothers. You play a handful of times, and then move right along. When this change first took place we could not understand it. We were hesitant to even begin eating at the edges of the world again, fearing some plot. But now that we know about the Light, and how you find and gather it...Are you always looking for the Light now? Rather than performing?"

George was confounded by this. He had never known any other method of performing than the one they were using now. They stayed a week and moved on. But if the wolf was right, then this method was not really achieving anything at all. Why would Silenus be doing this if it directly contradicted their mission?

Suddenly the shadows in the room began to tremble again. The wolf in red turned to look at the front right corner of the stage. The fat and skinny wolves emerged from the shadows there, their empty eyes fixed on George.

"What are you doing?" said the wolf in red. "I'm not finished with my examination."

"Yes, you are," said the fat one.

"What? What do you mean?"

The reedy-voiced wolf said, "Well, you said that if we caused you any problems, you'd report us."

"So?"

"So we decided to be preemptive," said the fat wolf. "And we went ahead and reported this captive ourselves."

If wolves could go pale, George thought the one in red certainly would have now. "You what?" he said.

"Yes," said the fat one. "We reported this discovery. And now there are Suspicions. It is, in fact, suspected that this boy is not ordinary. It is suspected that there is something different about him."

"Different? And what are we to do about that?" said the wolf in red.

"You are not to do anything," said the fat wolf slowly. "It wants to see for itself."

The wolf in red stood up and stared at them both. "W-what? Here?"

"Yes," said the reedy-voiced wolf. "It is coming. Right now."

"Put out that damn fire," growled the fat wolf. He strode forward and leaped down into the orchestra pit and began to stamp out the flames. The wolf in red went to assist, though he was now trembling like a leaf.

George backed away. He was not sure about what was happening, but he had an idea: something, some superior to the wolves, suspected he had the song in him, and it was coming to examine him itself. He could not be here when it came, he knew. But he could not run, as the wolves would certainly catch him. So what could he do?

He looked up at the open ceiling. Was it possible that he could climb up and out? Would the wolves be good climbers? He then realized that the issue was moot: there was hardly enough of the balcony left for him to climb up.

The night sky was visible outside. He saw the wind toying with a few scraps of clouds. And then he had an idea...

I am your patron. You stood up for me when it did you little good ... If you ever need me, you can simply call my name. If I am close, I will come to you.

He was not sure how this would work, or if she was close enough to hear him at all. But George had no other option, so he ran over until he was directly below the opening, raised his head, and called one word to the sky: "Zephyrus!"

The wolves spun around and stared at him. "What?" said the fat one.

The reedy-voiced wolf leaped down from the stage and grasped George by the shoulders. "It's nothing. Probably calling for help. But there's nothing that can help you, child. Nothing can save you from us."

George kept watching the sky through the open ceiling. He waited, but nothing seemed to happen. His heart fell. He was alone, and no one could stop what was coming, whatever it was.

The two wolves finally killed the fire. The darkness in the theater seemed magnified in its absence, and were the flakes of ash in the air dancing faster now?

"Bring him over here," said the fat wolf.

The reedy-voiced wolf picked George up as if he weighed nothing at all and bodily dropped him before the stage. Then he took one of George's arms and the fat wolf took the other.

"Are you sure it is coming?" said the wolf in red.

The stage began to darken. Shadows at the back began to bleed out, growing to conceal the remaining curtains, the ragged back-drop, the splintered boards. Soon almost nothing on the stage was visible at all.

"We are sure," said the fat one.

George was shaking in their grasps. He kept turning to look at the entry to the theater and the open ceiling, hoping someone would happen upon them and stop this. But no one came.

He turned back to the stage. It was as dark as the entry to a cave now. And George began to sense that there was something at the back of it, something very big, watching them...

It was then that he remembered something from the moving pictures Silenus had showed him: when the world had first been created and the darkness came alive, there had not been throngs of wolves then, not yet. Originally there'd been only *one* set of eyes out in the darkness, watching this new creation with utter hate. And George also recalled that short blast of silence that the wolf in red had used as a word, and now he wondered if it had perhaps been a *name*. But a name for what, he wondered? What could be terrible enough to match the dread inspired by the mention of that strange word?

Then something in the shadows shifted, and suddenly they were at the bottom of the sea.

*   *   *

George did not know this, but the human mind is very good at recontextualizing the world when it stops making sense. When a person encounters an event that goes beyond their normal five senses, the mind filters the information and changes it so that the event is experienced in normal, understandable terms. In essence, it creates a realistic metaphor to relate what's happening. Sometimes the metaphor can be very different from the normal world, like suddenly switching things so it seems as though you are at the bottom of the sea; but then such changes may be necessary, if the event experienced is great enough.

And what George was witnessing was so great and terrible that merely seeing it threatened to destroy him.

He felt as if they were standing on the ocean floor with miles and miles of cold water above them. Sunlight barely filtered down to this place, trickling through the briny depths to fall upon their shoulders. Before them was what looked like the edge of an enormous continental shelf, and there at the bottom was a gap between the continent floating above and the ocean floor. In that gap the shadows were intensely dark, so dark George's eyes could not penetrate them, but it seemed as if the gap went on forever. And yet he sensed that something was moving there, down in the darkness underneath the world.

The ground shook below them. There was a pause, and then it shook again. George wondered if chunks of rock were falling off the continental shelf, but when the ground shook for a third time he began to think that whatever was falling was far too rhythmic for that…and he wondered if perhaps what he was hearing was footfalls.

Something was coming. He struggled in the grasp of the two wolves, but they stayed firm. He felt something unraveling in the back of his mind, and he wondered if he was going mad.

He glimpsed something enormous in the dark. Was that a scaly jaw? Two enormous, pointed ears? The flex and ripple of thousands of miles of corded muscle…was that fur covering its vast bulk, or was it scales, or was its skin barren and cracked and leathery? George could not see. But he thought he could make out a pair of eyes in the dark, each as huge as worlds themselves, round and black and empty like the eyes of a shark. They were eyes that had seen the rise and fall of countless civilizations, and did not care.

A single massive forepaw emerged from the dark to fall upon the ocean floor. It had four huge toes, each with jet-black claws the size of buildings. It was scarred and old and had once had fur of some kind, though the countless years had worn that away until there were only graying bunches of skin. The forepaw flexed, digging huge gouges in the earthen floor, and George realized it was trying to drag itself forward, heaving some unimaginably colossal body that surely had to stretch completely under the world itself. Whole nations must teeter on the back of that giant spine, George thought, and the thing must desperately want to throw them off...

It was going to come out from under the world, he realized. It was going to crawl out and look at him. The thought horrified him to the bone.

George thrashed in the grip of the wolves, but they would not let him go. Every part of his body was in revolt. His eyes rolled in his head, his skin crawled, his hair writhed with the brush of the wind...

Wait a minute, he thought. Wind?

He realized that the two wolves holding him were staring about themselves, confused. In the darkness under the world a pair of jaws opened, readying to give a tremendous roar. But before it came something enormous crashed nearby, and the spell broke.

Just as suddenly as he'd left the theater, he returned. The shadows withdrew from the stage, and that horrible vision of the thing under the world vanished with it. George was still in the grip of the two wolves, and he was very wet, but it was not from the ocean deeps: it was raining very, very hard in the theater from a storm above.

The storm was so great that it had knocked in more of the ceiling, which must have been the crash he'd heard. The wind rose so hugely that chunks of charred wood rained down on them, and the wolves let George go to cover their heads.

"Where did this come from?" cried the fat one.

The entire sky was dark. A bright flash of lightning lit everything up, blinding them. Then a rattling boom shook the floor as thunder followed the lightning across the sky. As their vision returned they saw the dilapidated wall of the theater tremble. Several of the topmost bricks began to plummet down to smash upon the seats.

"It's going to come down!" shouted the wolf in red, and he grabbed his notes in handfuls and sprinted backstage.

George tried to follow him, but the reedy-voiced wolf leaped after him and seized his arm. "Where do you think you're going?" he snarled at him.

"The building's going to fall apart!" said George. "Didn't you hear him?"

"That's just what you'd like us to think, wouldn't y—"

But the wolf never got any further, as the wind screamed and pounded against the feeble wall. The bricks seemed to fold inward then, creasing along the middle, and then the entire soggy construction wilted over; but while it fell in a smooth, rather dreamy motion, its collision with the theater seats was devastating. Seats and bricks went flying, churning white clouds of pulverized stone rushed over the aisles, and George and the reedy-voiced wolf were flung across the theater.

George coughed and lifted his head, and he squinted through the clouds at the gaping hole in the wall. There was another flash of lightning, and George thought he saw someone standing outside on the other side of the rubble: a short but lithe young woman with bright blond hair and shining green eyes, wearing a tattered emerald dress. At first George thought she was a stranger, but then he saw something in her face reminiscent of the little girl in green...She could be her big sister, he thought. But then more white clouds piled up in the theater, and the flare of lightning died away, and she was gone.

"Do you see him?" roared the voice of the fat wolf from somewhere near the entrance. "Where has he gone?"

"We can't see anything in all of this!" cried the reedy-voiced wolf from the stage. "There's something out there! It's attacking the theater!"

"Forget about that!" said the fat wolf. "Just find the boy! Nothing matters but him!"

George crouched down behind a nearby pile of rubble. He heard snuffling noises from somewhere out in the seating, and the sounds of brick being crushed underfoot by something very large. He did not think the wolves were politely wearing the images of men anymore.

"We can't smell anything but dust!" said the reedy-voiced wolf. George was relieved to hear he sounded like he was on the other side of the theater.

"Stop talking, you fool!" said the fat wolf, who turned out to be very close. "He'll hear you!"

There was another flash of lightning. George lifted his head to see if he could spot the girl in green again, but to his terror he saw someone was standing right in front of him, looking down. Yet in that split second he recognized that weathered face, and that black mustache, and those cold, cold blue eyes...

"Father?" he whispered, but the flare died away. George reached out to feel the space in front of him, but there was no one. Had he imagined him?

"Maybe he died," suggested the reedy-voiced wolf from the stage. "Perhaps he was crushed under all that stone."

"Well, you had better hope not."

"Why not, we could...wait."

"Wait for what?" asked the fat wolf.

More snuffling. "There's someone in here with us," said the reedy-voiced wolf.

"Well, of course there is! There's the boy!"

"No," said the reedy-voiced wolf. "It...it isn't the boy. It's someone *else*."

"Someone else?" said the fat wolf. "Who?"

"Be quiet," said the reedy-voiced wolf. "We're not sure. We think it's—"

But the reedy-voiced wolf never finished his thought. From the stage there was the sound of fabric tearing, and something whipping through the air, and the wolf's voice was cut off by a horrible choking, or gagging.

"What is it?" said the fat wolf's voice. "Are you there? Are you all right?"

Another flash of lightning tore through the sky above, and the theater glowed brilliant white for one second. It did not last long, but George glimpsed someone standing on the stage. It was his father, and Silenus was looking up with his arms raised and fingers bent at odd angles, like he was strangling an invisible enemy. Suspended in the air above him was something very strange-looking: it appeared to be a huge knot made of all the remains of the curtains, and they were wrapped around something very tightly and they were trying to make themselves tighter with every second, like a boa constrictor around its prey. George could not quite see what was trapped within the knot, but it looked like a dark, ursine creature, with two long, pointed ears and spindly, sinewy limbs, and many, many claws. It was struggling very hard against the knot of curtains, though its efforts did little good, since the dark green bands just made themselves tighter and tighter.

The light died away again, but the fat wolf must have seen it as well, for there was a roar of "No!" from the entrance, and something extremely large bounded forward. Yet then George heard someone running—running on two legs, and normal human feet—and a noise like two bodies colliding in midair. The voice of the fat wolf cried out in pain, and it shrieked, "What! Who are—" Yet there its words stopped, for then there came a series of hard cracking sounds and the wolf began to howl and scream terribly. To George's ears they were cries of incredible agony, and when the lightning flashed again he raised his head to see.

His father still stood on the stage, guiding the curtains into strangling the reedy-voiced wolf, but down in the center aisle was Franny, wearing her large, lumpy sweater and her many scarves, and she was wrestling something dark and huge. To George's amazement, she seemed to be handily winning. Her face remained in an expression of quiet serenity as she took one flailing limb of the enormous, monstrous creature and slowly bent it back with her bare hands until a series of harsh pops sounded from somewhere in the joint, and the voice of the fat wolf loosed a fresh stream of cries. Her hands smoked where she touched it, but she did not seem to care in the least.

The lightning faded again. George kept his head down and listened to the two battles as they raged throughout the theater. One ended with a harsh snap and a sigh; the other, presumably Harry's fight on the stage, died away with a series of whimpers. There was a thud, and for a moment there was nothing but the rain and the dark.

The campfire suddenly flared to life. Silenus was on the stage next to a heap of smoking green velvet, and George could just barely make out Franny standing motionless in the center aisle. He thought he could see the twisted arms and legs of something huge lying behind her, but then it was gone, as if it had melted into the shadows.

"You," said Silenus angrily, and he pointed at George. "You have got some *big* fucking explaining to do."

George sat up and stared at them. "How…how did you get here? How did you do that? What on Earth is going on?"

"Forget all that," said Silenus. "Why didn't you ever tell me you were chummy with a fucking Cardinal?"

"A what?"

Silenus's finger turned to point at the fallen wall. Someone was walking out of the opening there, and when they came into the light George saw it was the young woman in green. She smiled at him, and said, "Hello, boy."

He peered at her. Again, he found something in her face he found familiar. "Zephyrus?"

She nodded.

"But...but I thought you were a little girl."

"Times have changed," she said. "I'm growing closer to my possession, my zenith, with every day."

George gaped for a bit, and finally managed, "But how did you all get here?"

"I carried them," she said. "I heard you call for me, but even though I was near it was like it was coming from a very deep hole. I looked on this building, and saw that something was...happening inside of it. There was an opening inside, and something was coming through. It seemed far beyond my strength, so instead I found your family."

"And I never want to travel that way again," said Silenus. "I thought trains were too fucking fast, but I was dead wrong."

"I liked it," said Franny softly. "We swooped, and spun, and there was so much water..."

Silenus looked around the theater. His eye fell upon the dummy that had been dressed as him. "What was going on here? These things look like...us. But even more, there's something wrong with this stage. There are remnants of some passage here. What happened, George?"

The image of the thing in the darkness returned to him in a rush. "It wanted to look at me," he said softly, and shivered.

"What?" said Silenus. "What did?"

George struggled to recount what he'd seen. He could hardly describe it. He started by saying that the wolves had taken him under the water, but then he backtracked and said that no, they'd actually been under *everything*, and then there'd been something that'd come out to look at him. And just bearing the sight of that thing in the dark had *hurt*...

"What are you saying?" said Silenus. "What is it you saw?"

"There was something down there," said George. "Somewhere, at the bottom of...everything. And it pulled me down, or maybe this entire theater, so that it could look at me."

For the first time that George could remember, Silenus blanched. "You were down there with it? You really *saw* it?"

"I didn't see it," said George. "Not...not all of it. But I thought I could make it out...Just thinking about it hurts." He held one hand to his brow. Something at the back of his head throbbed. It was reminiscent of that sense of unraveling he'd experienced earlier during the vision.

He staggered, and saw red drops appearing on the front of his shirt. He thought perhaps he had a nosebleed, but found he was wrong: his *eyes* were bleeding, as if he were crying bloody tears.

"George?" said Silenus. He leaped down off the stage and ran to him. "George! Stay up, George! Stay awake!"

But he could not, and fell to the ground. He heard Zephyrus shouting his name somewhere nearby, and she cradled his head in her long, cool fingers. His eyes rolled, and the last thing he saw was the blackened stage. Yet just above it he thought he saw two enormous, dark eyes still hanging there, eyes the size of planets, and he imagined they were searching for him.

CHAPTER 21

In Which a Song Is Changed

George felt as though he were slipping down inside of himself, washing away and dripping down through old, musty pipes in the back of his mind. He'd been liquefied, melted, ruined beyond all return, and he wanted only to slip away forever...

But he could not. There was something holding him back, like he was a fish hooked on a line. He realized after a moment that it was the sound of someone's voice, chanting softly, and when he did he also realized he was very, very cold, and very wet.

He cracked open his eyes and at first saw only bursts of blue-tinged whiteness. But then the whiteness seemed to ebb and flow, and when it ebbed he saw darkness behind it, and many stars. He opened his mouth, and tiny streams of icy water wormed their way in to pool around his teeth. Then he rolled his head and saw Silenus was carrying him, and it was he who was chanting. His face was pearled with condensation, his mustache a band of dewy jewels. Yet he did not seem to be walking, or even sitting, and yet the open sky was passing by above him...

Where are we? George tried to ask, but he did not have the voice for it.

Then he rolled his head to the other side, and if he had possessed the energy he would have gasped.

Far, far, far below them were the dark shapes of hills and valleys and tiny townships, and here and there the winding bends of creeks or rivers. Floating above these were scraps and curling patches of clouds, which took some time for George to identify because he'd always seen them from below, rather than from above. And they were above, he realized, very far above, shooting through the air and the layers of moisture, which collected on his hair and ears and eyebrows and ran off of him in streams.

One cloud stayed directly under them, however, mere yards below, a small carpet of roiling vapor that came to a point right under George's feet. The point itself was dark and swirling, making loops and curls that somehow reminded George of a head of very thick hair. And the point seemed to twist, and in that twist George saw soft and nebulous forms he thought he knew...

He began to lose consciousness again, but as he did the last thing he recalled was a face rendered in the hard grays and swirling softness of the rain cloud below, perhaps that of a young girl, and he thought it might have been smiling at him.

Somewhere, things flickered. Not a light of any kind, but everything: the earth and the world itself shuddered and fell away, and everything was small and thin and insubstantial, a tiny scrawl in the corner of a massive black painting whose edges no one could see.

Then everything returned. Air found its way into George's lungs and he gasped. He opened his eyes and found he was lying on a bed in some shabby room, and there was the tinny sound of trumpets playing somewhere, and hundreds of people laughing. He felt powerfully tired, but he summoned the energy to look around the room. There was a candle on the table at the far wall, and George saw his father sitting next to it, his shirt and coat still soaking.

Then things began flickering again, and George realized he was hearing something: someone nearby was singing the First Song.

When the flickering stopped, George saw his father was no longer seated beside the candle. He tried to call his name, but he did not have the voice for it. Was Harry somewhere in the dark, invoking the song? If that was so, why? And it was far softer than George had ever heard it before.

Yet then something happened: the song *twisted* just very slightly, betraying the melody he'd heard so many times before, and instead became something new. And when it did, George felt something rushing into him, filling him up until he thought he would burst, and he flung his head back and cried out...

Things changed.

The room faded to darkness, but there was something very small and white at its center. It grew larger and larger, and as it grew George recognized it: it was his grandmother's house back in Rinton. It swelled to fill his vision. He saw it was nighttime and a single light was on in his room upstairs. But the oak tree outside it was not right...it seemed much smaller than he remembered. Hadn't its branches been so huge and long that they'd brushed up against his bedroom window? Yes, that was right; he'd used one of those very branches to sneak out of her house, scurrying out the window and down into the tree, and then he'd run to the train station to catch a coach to Freightly. Yet here the branches fell well short of his window. This tree was almost a sapling.

Then he saw there was someone standing beneath it, hidden in the shadows. They raised their head and began to sing, and from their lips came the First Song, but it was very, very faint.

A shadow moved in the window upstairs. There was someone in his room, he realized. They came to the window and opened it, and he saw it was a young girl, but he could not make out her face. The song stopped, and the person under the tree looked up at her. She waved to the figure and turned away to run downstairs, and the person below the tree ran a hand through their hair as if nervous. It was a boyish gesture, one George himself had made many a time, and he wondered who this person was. Yet before he could make out any more everything went dark.

When he awoke again he saw the candle and the table had moved and were now directly beside his bed. His father sat in a chair next to them, looking exhausted. His coat and shirt were still damp, but his hair and mustache were now dry.

"Don't sit up," he said when he saw George was awake.

"What happened?" said George. "My eyes, they were..."

"Your eyes are fine. You're fine. They just couldn't bear what they had seen, that's all."

George looked down at himself. Not only was he uninjured, but the black blotches of stained skin were gone as well. "Yeah, we took care of that, too," said Silenus. "Couldn't have you running around looking like a freak, could we?"

Somewhere nearby there was the honk of a horn and scores of people laughing. "Where are we?" George asked.

"In a storage room in a theater outside of Toledo," said his father.

"Toledo?" said George. He tried to sit up, but Silenus prevented him.

"No, no. Stay down."

"What are we doing in Toledo?" he asked.

"Hiding, mostly," said his father. "The hotels in the region have proven untrustworthy. Too many watching eyes and wary ears. We stirred up a nest of fucking hornets when we came and got you. They've called out every spy in the country. The manager of this theater owes me a few favors, so we're ducking out of things for a while, but it won't last. So you need to recuperate as fast as you can."

There was a clacking sound, and George craned around and saw Stanley was sitting behind his bed, writing on his chalkboard. He looked far, far more exhausted than Silenus. George wondered how this could be, since he had not been part of the rescue.

CANNOT RUSH THESE THINGS, he'd written. LET THE BOY BE.

"I'll let him be," said Silenus. "I just need to know what happened back there, and what he saw."

"I...I don't know what happened," said George. "How did I get here?"

"You lost consciousness for a while," explained Silenus. "Your mind witnessed something it badly did not wish to, so, in a way, it withdrew inside of you until it did not see anything at all. You needed attention immediately, otherwise the damage would have been irreversible. You would have never woken up again. So we had your favonian little friend bring us here."

"Zephyrus?"

"Yes."

"What was that you called her back there?" asked George. "A Cardinal?"

"You didn't know what she was?" asked Silenus.

He shook his head.

"You're a remarkably lucky kid, George," said Silenus. "Few are befriended by the Cardinal Winds, these days. Each of them is tasked with shaping the storms and the weather of a season. Finicky fucking people, too. I've never met one, and have never particularly wanted to, as a result. But it seems like you found a good one, and got on her good side." He gave George a curious look. "She was very worried about you. She stayed after much longer than she needed to."

"Why did she leave?"

"If you are personally responsible for making sure every aspect of the weather all hangs together correctly an hour away can make a fucking headache of things. Still, she stood at the door a while asking about you." Silenus smirked a little, and winked at him.

"Why are you winking at me?" said George. "Don't do that, it makes me nervous."

Silenus rolled his eyes. "Never mind. The really important thing now is to find out what happened to you. And to the professor, and his puppets."

George paled. He hadn't thought of Kingsley since his capture. He swallowed and slowly began to recount everything that had occurred, from when he'd been drugged to when he'd escaped through the window.

Silenus grew steadily more dismayed as George spoke. When he was finally done, he said, "Jesus. Jesus Christ. I'd always ... I'd always thought it was the best decision to leave everything in Kingsley's control. It was his choice, his life. I guess I was wrong. I never thought it could have ended like that."

"What were they?" said George. "The puppets. Underneath it all, they had the same voice."

Silenus sighed and said, "There are ways to ... to give voice to aspects of your personality. To make them manifest in the world around you, to make them physical, even separate. I won't detail the precise characteristics of the ritual, it's far too nasty for me to talk about willingly. But you take a part of yourself, and set it in a vessel, and then it can walk and speak and even think. The professor wanted children, he said. It seemed a good substitute. He was desperate for anything. He'd kill himself if he didn't have them, he said. So I outlined what he needed to do, and ... and in return, he took up a spot on the show." He shook his head. "I can only wonder what part of himself he gave voice to."

George was quiet. Then he asked, "Could you not control them?"

"I thought that situation *was* under control," he said. "Besides, I had the troupe to run, and you to look after."

"What did we do with his remains?"

"He was buried in a little church graveyard. We left Colette a town behind to take care of it. It's what he wanted. He wasn't unhinged at all, in the beginning. He was just desperate. What could have changed?"

Then George remembered something Kingsley had said the night before he died... something about getting drastic, and taking too much since he'd seen those horrors in the street in Parma. When he told Silenus this his father's face grew grim. "That would explain it," he said. "I told him not to look."

"What could they do to him, just from a single glance?"

"The wolves have claws and knives and many teeth," said Silenus, "and certainly, they are terribly strong. But their greatest weapon is also their smallest, and their quietest, and their slowest to act."

"What is it?" asked George.

There was the hiss of scraping chalk, and George looked up to see that Stanley had written a single word: DESPAIR.

"Despair?" said George, confused.

"Yes," said Silenus. "It surrounds them like a cloak. Could you not feel such a thing in that old theater?"

George recalled that sensation of being dangled over an endless, dark chasm. "I felt something like that..."

"Yes. They shielded their true faces from you there, as despair is a disease that needs only a glance to begin its infection. If they had not, you would have been consumed by it, and possibly perished. But they did not hide their faces back in Parma, so when the professor looked at them it planted a black little seed of despair within him, and it festered until he began losing control. He fed his puppets more and more, until finally they were powerful enough to live independent of him, but achieving this killed him."

"Fed them?"

"You saw what he'd been doing to himself, hadn't you? The scars on his side?"

George nodded.

"He'd been using parts of his rib, apparently," said Silenus.

"His *rib*? My God!"

"There are much, much easier ways to do it — a bit of hair, or spit, or clippings of fingernail, those all suffice — you need only put a *little bit* of yourself in the vessel, you see. But the professor was a man who found much meaning in symbols. He wanted his own little people, so he made them the way his God had made Eve — his rib. He always was the kind for big gestures. After all, look at his stage name."

"His stage name?" asked George. "What about it?"

Silenus looked at him, confused. "What do you mean, what about it? I thought he'd told you everything."

There was a tapping noise, and they saw Stanley had again written something on his blackboard and was trying to bring attention to his message. Written there was: TOLD GEORGE SHE WAS JAILED.

"Oh," said Silenus upon reading this.

"What?" said George. "Who does he mean?"

"Kingsley's wife," said Silenus. "He told you she was prosecuted and jailed, didn't he?"

"Well, yes."

"That was a lie. Probably one he preferred to believe."

"Beside what?"

Silenus watched him, face sad and wary. "Have you never wondered why he chose Tyburn as his stage surname, George?" he asked. "It was to be a constant reminder of what he'd done. He'd arranged to have his own wife prosecuted, to the point that she was finally convicted and hung by the neck until dead."

There was nothing George could say to such an awful revelation. He shut his eyes and shook his head. Silenus took out a cigar and began slowly rolling it back and forth between the fingers of one hand. "What's done is done, for better or worse. Why don't you go ahead and tell me what happened in that theater."

So George began on the second part of his story, from the moment of his capture to the wolf in red's questioning, yet he held back a few of the answers. He did not wish to tell anyone how he felt for Colette, nor the troubling suggestions the wolf had made about Stanley. Besides, these were of little importance in comparison to what George had learned from the wolf about how they were resisting the song.

"So *that's* how they're doing it," said Silenus when George was done. "I guess it acts like a vaccination, in a way...Expose yourself to a little bit of it, and you're inoculated and protected against the rest. They must have been desperate to try something that crazy, though. I'd have thought for sure that if one of them simply swallowed the song, it would have destroyed them. I wonder why they don't simply end it all now if they're protected against it...just stop chasing us and start eating up the world again?"

Stanley wrote: MAYBE ONLY PROTECTS A SMALL AMOUNT?

"That could be it," said George. "The wolf did say that if he'd swallowed any more it would have killed him."

"Then they just got fucking lucky," said Silenus bitterly.

"Is there a way that we can stop them?" asked George. "Get to the wolf in red, or remove it?"

"I highly doubt it. They'll have that nutty bastard under every bit of protection they can muster, which is considerable. Besides, killing wolves is tricky. They're not really mortal—you're destroying only their physical aspect, the part of them that intrudes into our world. It's like melting a man made of ice—it's not dead, for it was never alive, but it can be remade just as easily. And even if we succeed in killing him, or remove it, what's to stop another of their number from trying the same thing?"

"Then what can we do?"

"I don't know yet. Are you sure you didn't get any more out of him?"

"I couldn't," said George. "We got interrupted. The two other wolves came, and they took me...someplace else." He then recounted that terrible moment when he felt as if he were under the sea, and the intelligence in the dark that had risen up to observe him.

Silenus nodded when George finished. "So you saw it. You actually saw it."

"No. Like I said, I only saw part."

"But that's more than anyone else has ever seen," he said.

"What was it?"

"I don't know, George. Not for sure, at any rate. But I have my ideas." He thinned his eyes, thinking. "In some ways, the wolves are like us. They are all part of a greater whole, more or less, just as we are. But in my studies I've often felt there had to be a center to their whole. A progenitor. A First. I had nothing to support those ideas, not for the longest time, but... it seems you have confirmed them.

"What you witnessed was that First Darkness, George. The thing of which all the other wolves are but a part. It appears as though when enough wolves gather in a place that is secluded and dark, they can invoke it, or bring it up to the surface, like a dark inversion of singing the First Song. Yet this happens very rarely. I think that moment was the first in thousands of years, probably. And just witnessing it almost killed you."

This made sense. George could not imagine anything more terrible than that thing under the world. "But how did I survive?" he asked.

Silenus looked slightly uncomfortable. "Well, it was... difficult. But we have techniques at our disposal, and—"

Again, the clack and hiss of chalk. Stanley angrily held up his message: TELL THE BOY THE TRUTH.

Silenus scowled. "We can't tell him that. He'll get ideas."

THE BOY DESERVES TO KNOW WHAT WAS DONE, wrote Stanley. TELL HIM.

"Tell me what?" asked George. "What do you mean?"

Silenus's angry glance jumped back and forth between Stanley and George. Finally he gave up, shoulders sagging. "I... lied to you a little earlier. I said that your condition could have been irreversible. That wasn't the case."

"It wasn't?"

"No." He looked at George gravely. "In truth, my boy, your condition already *was* irreversible."

George sat up. This time, Silenus did not tell him to lie back. "What do you mean?" he asked again.

"Merely glimpsing that thing had destroyed you, George," said his father. "You were ruined, and...bleeding. You could hardly breathe. We knew immediately that you would never wake. So we had to...change things."

George felt his chest nervously. "Oh, God. What did you change in me?"

"You don't understand, George. We didn't change anything in you. We changed *everything*."

George looked to Stanley, and found he was watching him with pale, haggard eyes. He looked like he might collapse at any moment. "What do you mean, everything?" asked George.

Stanley took out the blackboard, and slowly wrote: WE CHANGED THE SONG.

"Yes," said Silenus.

"What are you talking about?" asked George.

"The song is a blueprint of all of existence, George. And, like any blueprint, it can be fudged. Tinkered with. It is an extraordinarily dangerous thing to do, to take the song and sing it differently. One must possess the right portions of it, and have studied them in detail. But when it is done, the world changes accordingly. We changed a very slight portion of the song for you, George. We changed it so you would wake up, healthy and whole, unburned. And existence itself followed suit."

Both of them watched him grimly. George remembered hearing the song in the dark, and how it had suddenly seemed to twist. "You changed it...for me?" he asked.

"Yes. But it came at an extraordinarily high cost. Because when a part of the song is changed, the entirety is reduced by that same amount. It is as though a portion of the First Song never existed at all. It is used up, gone. So though we could move mountains, erase wars, or even bring people back from the dead . . . it would shrink the song until it was nothing. The little glimmer of light we carry would dim until it was gone. For you, a small boy who was hurt, it wasn't that much of a change. Not much was lost. But it's still something we swore we would never do unless we had to. The danger is too great. We can't just go about rearranging existence itself at our leisure. Not if doing so wounds the very thing keeping it alive."

"But you did it for me," said George softly.

YES, wrote Stanley. WE DID.

"Why didn't you want to tell me about this?" he asked.

"Because you have a piece of the song itself in you, and I don't want you experimenting with it," said Silenus. "You must not study it too closely, or try to engage it. I don't know what it could do to you, George. You are both extremely precious to me, and I'd not see either of you harmed. Do you understand?"

George nodded, but he wondered if he already had engaged it, in a way. He remembered how the thing within him had seemed to vibrate in recognition at some sound in the rain or the wind, and his suspicion that it wanted to be whole.

"Good," said Silenus. "That's for the best." He took out his watch and checked it. "Colette should be getting in soon. Stan, can you pick her up at the station for me?"

Stanley nodded his head, then stood and walked out, though he glanced back at George once before he was gone. Then George and his father were alone.

"I'm sorry," said George.

"For what?" said Silenus.

"For what I last said to you. I feel awful that I said that and then you had to go and . . . and sacrifice what you did for me."

"You don't have to say anything," said Silenus. He put a hand on George's knee. "I've never been too hot at giving people reasons to love me. And besides, it's my own fuck-ups that put you in danger. I should have kept a closer eye on Kingsley. I should have seen him falling apart."

"Thank you for coming for me, though."

"And you don't have to fucking thank me, either. I was just upholding my end of my promise. I told you I'd try my best to keep you safe until I no longer could, didn't I?"

George nodded. He laid his head back. He was very sleepy. "Father?"

Silenus winced, and George could tell the term still made him uncomfortable. "Yeah?"

"What do you remember of my mother?"

Silenus was very still as he thought. The candle flame danced and flickered as if brushed by a breeze. "Not enough," he said finally.

George shut his eyes. This seemed the most disappointing answer possible.

"I wish I could remember her more for you, George," his father said. "I wish...I wish I could give you the father you deserve, and the life you need. A normal life. I really do. If I could snap my fingers and give us all the lives we want, I would, George. Maybe one day we can look at all the warp and weft of the web and figure out why things are the way they are. But until that day, all I can give you is apologies."

George smiled a little. "You could just change the song, and fix everything."

Silenus nodded as if he understood this was a joke, but there was a wild gleam to his eyes. "I could. Yes. Yes, I could."

"Did you ever consider doing it? I'd almost expect the temptation would be too much."

His father was quiet for a long, long time. "Yes," he said in a soft voice. "Yes, I have considered it before. Who wouldn't? I've considered using it to right wrongs, or . . . or to bring loved ones back to us."

"What stopped you?"

His response was simple: "Stanley."

"What?" said George. "How?"

Silenus looked at him, surprised, as if he'd forgotten something. "Well . . . Stanley works as my conscience, in a way. He keeps me in check, and on course. Everyone needs to be kept in check somehow. But I admit, there is, perhaps, more to it than just Stanley," Silenus said. "I have spent so much time chasing the song, George . . . The idea of using it horrifies me. And eventually, every loss, no matter how personal, dwindles until it is lost in the shadow of that mission, and I cannot imagine why I would ever think to throw away what I seek so passionately, just to right a wrong that now seems so small. I am not sure if I am better or worse for it. But what a world this is, where fixing it destroys the one thing keeping it together."

As he said this, George remembered what the wolf in red had told him about how the troupe had changed: it was as if they traveled only to find the song, and not to perform it. He wanted to ask his father about it, and hear him deny the suggestion with a scornful laugh . . . but a tiny shred of him wondered if such a thing could be true. It would have such terrible consequences, if it was . . .

George decided to forget it. The wolf had been crazed and irrational. It surely had to be wrong. "I'm sorry," he said. "I was kidding."

The gleam faded from Silenus's eye, and he patted him on the knee. "I know. Get some sleep. We need you strong."

He lay back. Silenus snapped his watch shut and walked to the door.

"Harry?" said George.

"Yeah?"

"What are we going to do next?"

He sighed. "I've no idea." Then he walked out and shut the door.

PART THREE

The Chasers

To see a World in a Grain of Sand
And a Heaven in a Wild Flower,
Hold Infinity in the palm of your hand
And Eternity in an hour.

—William Blake,
Auguries of Innocence

Play! Invent the world! Invent reality!

—Vladimir Nabokov,
Look at the Harlequins!

CHAPTER 22

A Very Funny People

After Colette arrived Silenus announced he was taking them all out for dinner. Everyone in the troupe was irritated at this bizarre proclamation. Colette was tired from the trip and in no mood to celebrate anything, Franny's hands were heavily bandaged from when she'd fought the wolf, Stanley looked sicklier than ever, and George had still not fully recovered. But Silenus would not be dissuaded. "My son has been returned to us at great risk," he said. "We must celebrate that, and we must also make a show of respect to commemorate the dead who have been taken from us. I won't let this night go by like any other. There must be something done to mark the occasion."

They ate at a questionable French restaurant on the outskirts of Toledo. Colette, who of course knew French, pointed out many spelling errors in the menus. The food had received about the same type of preparation, and was all oversalted, though Silenus commented that at least the wine worked.

Before they started Silenus gave a toast to George and to Professor Tyburn, speaking of the man as one would of a fallen comrade. "Thought it would appear he fell by his own hand, we know now he did not," he said. "If anything, he was poisoned, though it was a poison of the mind, of the soul, and not one of the flesh. I will not say he was a perfect man. Though he was flawed, he made his choices, and tried to play his part as best he could in the world he saw unfolding around him. For that, we must salute him: a player silenced, a role now hanging vacant, and many lines left unspoken."

They all muttered their own salutes and drank together, and turned to eating. They did not make very good conversation. Franny tried to fill Colette in on what had happened, though she was as daffy and confused as ever, and Stanley kept pestering Silenus with little notes written on napkins.

"I told you for the last time, no," said Silenus angrily. "I won't consider them."

George happened to catch a glimpse of what Stanley's last message said: THEY ARE THE ONLY ONES WHO COULD BE OF HELP NOW.

"That's if they give it. They'd much rather have me dead. I won't even think about it, Stan."

"Who are you talking about?" said George.

"None of your business," said Silenus.

PEOPLE WHO COULD HELP, Stanley wrote.

"Are these...the people you talked about back in your office?" asked George. "The ones who gave you the tower?"

Stanley nodded.

"I would never engage their agencies," said Silenus. "Not without a bribe to smooth over how I last left them. And there's almost nothing that would be that valuable. Besides, we don't even know what they could do for us."

"Well, I'm sure that if a bribe's necessary then they're not the sort of people we'd want to speak with anyway," said George.

"Half the world runs on bribes, kid," said Silenus. "Bribes, threats, and lies. And there's not much I wouldn't do to get to the next piece of song. But going to them? If I say it's reckless, you better believe it's fucking reckless."

George wondered who they could mean, but then had an idea. "Couldn't you just do what you did in Parma?"

"And what's that?"

"Make a distraction. Create...copies. For them to chase?"

Silenus bobbed his head side to side, considering it. "I could try. But I don't possess the arts to make anything last that long. The wolves are entrenched around the parts of the First Song. We'd need to lure them a great distance, and that takes more than I have."

Stanley whipped out another napkin and hurriedly scrawled: MORE THAN YOU HAVE. BUT NOT MORE THAN THEY DO.

Silenus read his note. At first he looked angry, but then he sat back in his chair and his eyes grew distant. "Do you think so? For a distraction?"

Stanley nodded earnestly.

"Hm," Silenus said. He grew contemplative, and said nothing more. He stared at his wine, letting the liquid slip back and forth in the glass, but hardly drank a drop.

"So we're really going to try and continue on?" asked Colette.

"Rather than what?" said Franny.

"Disbanding, of course," said Colette.

"Disbanding?" said George, startled. "Are you serious?"

"Well, yeah," said Colette. "Let's think about this practically. Things are getting dangerous. We're running out of money. And we've lost our lead act. It wasn't our strongest, but it was maybe our most curious."

"Are you sure it's appropriate to be discussing business so soon after this tragedy?" asked Franny.

"I buried him," said Colette icily. "I was the only one there to see him interred. I have paid my respects. And now we have to think about our own lives."

The idea of losing Colette horrified George. "So you would what?" he asked. "Go on...alone? Without us?"

"Yes," she said. "I would."

"But there's no need for that, is there?" he asked. "I mean, Harry was covering for Kingsley before, maybe he could just continue in the start. Or maybe *I* could cover for him." He tried not to grin hopefully.

"Monologues aren't fit for Kingsley's spot, George," said Colette. "Nor is piano playing. People want dumb acts when they walk in after intermission. Silent acts, or silly acts. Acts they can ignore."

"Well, I...I could play very softly," said George.

"I told you, *no*. That's not what managers are looking for in that spot."

"I'm sure we could think of something," said Franny.

"Is anyone listening?" Colette asked. "Our budget can't afford the time to let us come up with a new act. I should know. We can't risk a break in income."

As Colette spoke an altercation began at the table next to theirs. An elderly couple had just sat down to eat, but both were mortified when they saw the waiter who came to serve them was colored. "I can't believe the indignity of it," sputtered the old man. He refused to speak to the waiter at all, and demanded to see the manager. The waiter assumed the most obsequious pose he could, not even meeting the man's eyes, and bowed away.

They tried to ignore it. Stanley wrote: YOU WOULD REALLY LEAVE US?

"I'm saying we may not have a choice, Stan," Colette said. "We can't tour with the remaining acts, they don't align with any spots. No manager would take us on. Almost no one tours with multi-act sets anyways. I'm saying we can split what's left and go our separate ways."

Stanley wrote: AND ABANDON OUR MISSION?

Her lips tightened. "That was always your mission. Not mine, or anyone else's. You two barely let us know what was going on all the time, anyway."

Stanley nodded, dismayed.

At the table behind them the manager had arrived to try to quell the elderly couple's anger, but the old man was having none of it. "I can't believe you would allow such a thing," he said. "This location was said to be particularly esteemed. And to think, I almost considered bringing my grandchildren here..."

"I am so sorry," whispered the manager. "Sir, I deeply apologize. He's a new hire, but...but in venues of this type it's very common to allow coloreds to wait upon customers."

"What!" said the old man, nearly choking. "Can you possibly be serious? We would never allow such a thing at home! Then is it true that cities have some moral infection in them? Letting negroes in to work in their kitchens, to touch their plates, their *food*?"

The elderly woman gasped as if she'd been injured by the very idea of it. Colette began slowly grinding her teeth.

"I think," said Silenus finally, "that the issue may be moot."

"And why is that?" asked Colette.

"Do you really think you can strike out on your own, Lettie?" said Silenus. "Do you think you'd find success as a single act?"

"Are you saying," she said, "that I don't have the chops?"

"No," said Silenus. "I'm not saying that at all. I'm just saying that talent doesn't overcome everything. There are barriers in the way. Especially for those dreaming of big-time success."

More pops came from Colette's mouth as she ground her teeth. "And what barriers are those?"

Silenus sighed and looked at her pleadingly. He attempted a smile. "Come on, Lettie."

"Don't come-on-Lettie me," said Colette. "Not over this."

"...I absolutely will not stand for it," the old man was saying behind them. "I'll have you know my family owns several newspapers in Branson and, yes, even the country, and I will...I will have the name of this establishment in every single one of them!"

"Please, sir, be reasonable," said the manager, still attempting a whisper.

"We've talked about this," said Silenus to Colette. "You were to stay with me until you'd become strong enough to—"

"Then I'm not strong?" said Colette. "I'm not good enough?"

"Not for the hardship you'd encounter if you went out on your own and tried playing New York," said Silenus. "Which is what you want, isn't it?"

Colette crossed her arms. "Others have succeeded there."

"They were lucky, and they spent years working at it."

"...Absolute disgrace," muttered the old woman behind them.

"I've spent years with you!" said Colette. "Does that not count?"

"Not in the big time, where you want to go," said Silenus. "You'd need to establish contacts, build an accepting base."

"And I can't do that with what I'm doing now?" she asked.

"You don't know what you'd be up against, Lettie," said Harry. "They wouldn't let you do what you're doing now. They'd want you to play like...to wear makeup, and be like..."

"Like what?" said Colette savagely.

"...Not fit for such work," said the old man behind them.

"Like what, Harry?" said Colette.

"Come, now, Lettie..." said Silenus.

"...As if they *belonged* in here, with *us*..."

"Go on," said Colette. "Say it. Say it, Harry."

"Colette," said George. "Please calm down."

"Stay out of this, George," she snapped. "Come on, Harry. Go on and tell me what they'd want me to be like."

The old man behind them stood up. "I refuse to believe that you could have possibly thought this could go unnoticed. This is a moral stand that I take, and I demand you pay attention to me and treat me with some resp—"

"Oh, be *quiet*!" cried Colette. She stood up and spun around to face the old man. Her chair toppled over and crashed to the floor. The elderly couple flinched, and the manager stared at her as if he hadn't seen her before.

Silenus stood up beside her. "Yes, please keep it down," he said calmly. "We're trying to eat over here."

"What...what are *you* doing in here?" said the manager, staring at Colette. "How did they let *you* in?"

"You see?" said the old man. "Do you see? They're letting them eat in here, too! I simply cannot believe it!" His wife looked as if she was about to faint.

Colette did not answer. She was staring at the floor. George saw her hands were trembling.

"You are mistaken, sir," said Silenus. He laid a hand on Colette's shoulder. "My lovely colleague here is not a negro. She is a Persian, and royalty at that—she is Colette de Verdicere of the Zahand Dynasty, Princess of the Kush Steppes."

"Is this true?" said the manager.

Colette still did not answer. Her chest was heaving and her eyelids were fluttering. George thought she might start weeping.

"Go on," said Silenus. "Tell them."

But Colette did not tell them. She shook off Silenus's hand, turned around, and walked out without a word.

The rest of the meal was soured by what had happened, and Silenus harangued the manager into giving them a discount. When that was done he dismissed them, sending Franny and Stanley to two separate hotels on the other side of town to avoid any watchful eyes, and sending George back to his secret bedroom in the theater. As to where he himself stayed, Silenus did not say. Presumably with his door he could stay anywhere.

George returned to find the theater was shutting down. He slipped in and wandered unseen up the backstage stairs. When he came before his bedroom door he stopped. There was a scent in the air, like honeysuckle and lavender. He recognized it as the perfume Colette wore so frequently.

George's sense of smell was just as good as his hearing, and he followed the scent up the rambling stairs of the backstage and eventually came to the door to the roof. He walked out and found the weather was much better than when he'd last been on a theater roof, outside Chicago. This rooftop, however, was a tumbling, decrepit mess, featuring uneven growths of plumbing and sprouts of twisted chimneys, many of which did not seem to serve any function. The theater must have been worked on and reworked on, without anyone's ever cleaning up the work from before.

He saw a figure standing on one of the more ancient chimneys at the edge of the roof, straddling the gap with each foot on one side. She was in the middle of performing a marvelous and alarming feat of acrobatics: she would shove off with one leg, and while balancing on the other she'd perform a full rotating pirouette on the edge of the chimney. Then she'd smoothly spin around and replace her foot, reassuming the original position.

"Go away, George," said the figure.

George walked forward, stepping around the dodgier parts of the roof. "Why?"

"Because," said Colette, "you are interrupting my concentration."

George did not say anything. She was filthy from chimney ash and breathing hard from the exertion. She had evidently fallen once already, judging from the small scrapes on her hands and their slow, glittering leak of blood. He watched as she did another turn, and another.

"I don't seem to be," said George. "But please, come down from there. It's not safe."

"I know it's not safe," said Colette. "That's why I'm doing it."

George winced as she performed the turn again. The chimney looked very unsteady.

"I hate the fucking sticks," she said to him. "I hate these fucking little people and these fucking little towns and these fucking little theaters." She did yet another turn. "But do you know what I hate most?"

"No," said George.

"I hate knowing that they're probably the same way in the big time," said Colette. "They'd treat me the same way, wouldn't they?"

She did three more turns, each one quicker and harder than the last. She wore a grim look as if this was some kind of grave self-punishment to be meted out in solitude. Yet even in these circumstances George still found her powerfully alluring, this ash-streaked girl performing for him on this squalid rooftop.

On the fourth turn the brick she was standing on separated from its mortar and began to rock. She gasped as she tried to steady herself. George did not hesitate. He sprang forward and grabbed one of her arms and heaved her off. She fell on him and they both tumbled to the ground.

"What did you do that for?" she asked as she tried to get off him.

George gasped for breath. When he finally got it back, he said, "You were going to fall."

"I wasn't going to fall!" said Colette. "I could handle a brick moving a little! That's part of the practice!"

She stood up and strode away to the side of the building. To his horror, she climbed up and stood on the very edge, looking out at the street below. "The threat of falling is part of it."

"Please get down," said George. "Please."

"I won't get down," said Colette. Then she thought, and said, "But I will sit down." And, very smoothly, she bent her legs and plopped down to sit on the edge of the roof, her feet dangling off the side. "These little towns," she said. "They're killing me, piece by piece."

George walked over to her, moving much more slowly as he came to the edge. Then he sat next to her, facing inward. "I know."

"You do?"

"Sure. Small theaters, small applause. I understand how dull it is."

"That's not the problem."

"Oh? Then what?"

She was quiet for a long, long time. She reached up and pulled out the inscribed, ornate amulet that hung around her neck. "Do you know what this is? What the writing on it means?"

"No."

She laughed. It had a very bitter sound to it.

"What is it?" he asked.

"Neither do I," she said.

"I'm sorry?"

"I bought this little trinket in some pawnshop in upstate New York, George. It's not some royal heirloom. It's a piece of gypsy junk that just looks pretty." She turned it over in her hand. "But I didn't need to tell you that," she said quietly. "You know I'm not really a princess, right?"

George did not immediately answer her. After a while he nodded. "Well. Yes. I thought it'd be rude to say something about it, though."

"Do you know what I really am?"

"I don't understand. What do you mean, 'what'?"

"I mean what I really am, George. Why I have to make up that princess stuff."

He was still not sure what she was suggesting. To think of Colette, whom he thought the most beautiful and most frustrating person in the world, in terms of 'what' was not something that came naturally to him.

"I'm not from Persia," she said. "I'm from New Orleans. My daddy was white. But not... not my momma." She turned to look at him, eyes burning. "Do you see?"

He thought about it. Then he nodded. "Yes. I do."

"And what do you think of that?"

He shrugged. Then, in a move that evidently surprised her, he patted her hand. "I don't think anything."

"You don't? Why?"

He thought about it for a bit and shrugged again. "I've had...a trying last couple of days, Colette. I saw things I never want to see again. Right now I'm just happy to have a pleasant moment with you."

Colette was quiet.

"This is why you came up with the princess story, isn't it?" he asked.

"I didn't," she said. "That was Harry. He found me in New Orleans, performing on the street. Said he had an eye for talent, and I had it. Said I could get out, if I wanted." He noticed she was unconsciously rubbing her upper arm as she spoke. There below her shoulder was a small patch of glossy whitish skin, a winking scar that, to his eye, was about the exact shape of the end of a cigarette. "But I couldn't just jump into performing. I'd only be able to get on TOBA. You know what that is?"

"Yes," said George. TOBA referred to the Theater Owners' Booking Association, which worked the East Coast and served as the circuit for black acts. In vaudeville it was commonly referred to as "Tough on Black Asses" due to its grueling pace and poor pay.

"I was light-skinned enough that he came up with this idea," said Colette. "I pass as a foreigner tolerably well. I don't look like most black folks, and who the hell out here knows what a Persian looks like? Plus I speak French pretty good. So instead he dolled me up as royalty." She cracked a smile. "Smart-ass. Every time, I can't believe we get away with it. Some negro girl making white people bow to her and buy her drinks. Just because of a dress and a bad accent and a piece of gaudy jewelry."

"It's a performance," said George. "He must have taught you well."

"Yeah. He did. It may be my best performance," she said. "Better than anything I do onstage."

"That's not true."

"Maybe not. But I can't keep it up forever. Harry knows this schtick won't hold up in New York. I can only pass for royalty out in the sticks. But it's more than that. I don't *want* to keep this up anymore. I'm sick and tired of pretending. I hate this goddamn princess I'm supposed to be. But without her, where would I be?" She sighed. "Do you remember when I told you about the Palace? How I got to see it?"

"Yes."

"I didn't get to go in there when I was in New York, but I went to another theater. One about as good, it seemed. And there was a comedian playing there. Everyone had crammed in to go see him. He was *the* act to see, you know? And as it turns out, he was colored. And not just colored, but not even in blackface," she said, referring to how colored entertainers were expected to perform in the same makeup that white performers wore in minstrel routines. "That was something I'd never seen before. And he did this bit, just about the funniest bit I ever saw. It was a dumb act, a pantomime bit where he pretended like he was in a poker game, gambling against some others. He did this great thing where he'd lift his head up and think about his cards—which weren't there, of course—and he'd flutter his eyes real fast and mumble to himself a little. And everyone just howled with laughter."

"Bert Williams," said George, who recognized the bit from reports he'd heard. Williams was a titan in vaudeville, especially after his success in the Ziegfeld Follies. He was one of the very few blacks to have achieved such fame, whether people liked it or not.

"Bert Williams," said Colette. "Yeah. I don't know how, but he did it. Playing in the best theaters, for the best audiences. And I figured, if he can do it, why can't I? All it takes is talent. Talent, and practice." She was quiet. "How much further can I get, do you think? I won't ever manage the troupe. If Harry gives it to anyone, he'll give it to Stanley."

"Stanley? Why Stanley?"

"Because they're related, of course."

George's mouth fell open. "Related? They don't look anything alike! How do you know they're related?"

"Well, I don't *really* know for sure. It's just how they talk to each other, I suppose. But if my hunch is right, I'm never getting the troupe," she said. "I'll always just be Princess Colette, stuck out here in the sticks, doing little turns for little theaters. I'll never be big-time. Just some silly colored girl, nursing silly dreams, a sideshow to the real thing."

"That's not what you are," said George.

"And you would know that?"

"I think I do," said George. His heart was beating very fast. He could feel his pulse in his wrists and ears. "Do...do you know what it was like, seeing you for the first time?"

"No. I guess I've never heard your opinion, as an audience member."

He swallowed. His mouth felt hot and thick. Was he supposed to do this now? It seemed there'd be no better time.

He said, "I know vaudeville isn't supposed to be *art*. It's supposed to be entertainment, which is different. But I think art...I think it's making something from nothing, basically. It's taking something as simple as a movement, or a few notes, or steps, or words, and putting them all together so that they're *bigger* than what they ever could have been separate. They're transformed. And just witnessing that transformation changes you. It reaches into your insides and moves things around. It's magic, of a sort.

"I never really knew that until I saw your act. But when you walked out on that stage, I knew I was seeing something... *different*. Something maybe more amazing than what the professor and Silenus had done. You were *making* something up there, out of just a few notes and steps. It was like a little glimpse of perfection, made out of the simplest elements possible, and seeing it changed something in me. I'd never encountered anything like that. And when it was done, I...I knew I had to see you, to meet you."

Her eyes had grown wide. "W-what? Why? What are you saying?"

"I'm saying I knew that...that whoever that girl up on that stage was, in order to make that she had to have something inside her that made her more beautiful than anything else in the world. And I don't think I was wrong."

He looked at her. Her mouth was hanging open slightly, and her eyes were searching his face. He steeled himself. He had never given one of these before, and had received one only once, but still he shut his eyes and leaned in...

"Wait," said Colette. "Whoa, wait. Stop."

George opened his eyes. Her hands were up, like she was ready to hold him back if he continued. "Stop?"

"Yes, George. Stop." There was an awkward pause. She scooted away a little and looked out at the street. She took a breath like she was going to say something, but did not.

"I'm sorry," he said quickly.

"Mmm-hmm," she said, as if she could not trust herself to open her mouth.

"I'm sorry. I really am sorry."

"Just...stop talking, George."

"All right."

She stared out at the city, thinking. She did a lot of head-shaking, he noticed. Then she spun around to sit facing in at the roof, alongside him. She did not look at him. "That was...a lot to take in."

"I'm sorry."

"Don't be sorry, George. Just don't. It was a very beautiful and... and *flattering* thing to hear, but...Listen, just...I don't know. Just forget about it."

George did not say anything. He stared into his lap.

"Oh, Christ," she said. "Listen, you're...a very nice boy, and you're clever, but...I'm sorry. I really don't think of you like..."

"I see," said George.

"Jesus, George," she said. "What did you have to go and say that for?"

"Because that was what I felt."

"No. You don't want someone like me. I'm all beat-up and broken."

"Not to me, you aren't."

"You don't know me," she said, now angry. "You don't, George. You said it yourself, you're looking for that girl on the stage."

"But that was you," George said.

"No, it wasn't," said Colette. "Not really." She stood up. "Just forget about it, George. It's better for you that way."

"I love you," he said suddenly. Even as the words left his lips, he knew they had a hollow and desperate ring to them, and he regretted it.

"Jesus Christ," she said.

"I'm sorry," he said again. He bunched up his fists and held them to the sides of his head, hiding his face from her. He wished he could strike the sides of his skull and rid himself of the memory of these last few minutes.

"Go to bed, George," Colette said. "It's late and cold and you still look sick. Just...just go to bed."

George did not answer. He just sat there bent with his fists pressing into his temples.

She sighed. "If I leave you here, will you jump off the side of this fucking building, or something stupid?"

"No," George said softly.

"Promise?"

He nodded.

"I'm sorry, George," she said. "I really am. I never meant to make you unhappy. I really didn't." Then she turned around and walked away.

When her footsteps faded he peeked through his hands at her. Before the door she stopped as if she wished to look back at him, but she did not and opened it and slipped through, and he was alone.

*   *   *

George stayed on the roof for a long time. In between bouts of self-loathing he would relive moments when he should have said this instead of that, or done that instead of this. For one moment it'd all been going so well...Perhaps the slightest alteration in the night's proceedings would have changed all this, and he'd now be sitting here with her hand in his, happy at last.

Maybe he'd missed his opportunity long before now. He thought of other close moments when he should have perhaps been more aggressive, and pressed his case. Yet it was in one of those memories that he stumbled on an evening that made him feel the most ashamed yet.

It had been nearly a month ago, when they'd arrived in town to find they had a free evening. Almost on a whim George had suggested going to a show and seeing the competition, and no one but Colette had been game. As they sat next to one another in the back of the theater they'd traded quiet barbs about the sloppiness of the acts, or the poor quality of the orchestra, or how such and such line was the exact copy of one they'd heard weeks ago. They'd been happily smug critics, sharing secrets the rest of the audience couldn't understand.

Yet then the third act had come on, and things had changed. George, for his part, had kept up his critique, but Colette's line of observation had quickly dried up. It wasn't until the act was almost over that he'd glanced over and seen her sitting still in her seat, eyes thin and mouth even thinner. With the laughter of the crowd echoing around their ears, he couldn't understand her sudden change in mood.

He supposed now that he should have noticed what had been different about that act: unlike the others, it was a minstrel routine. George had seen and even played for many of them in his time. He'd encountered his first at Otterman's, and, since he'd never seen a black person in Rinton, he'd not been sure what these gleaming, ebony-dark people with odd red mouths were meant to be at all. Tofty the violinist had told him the act was meant to be aping negroes, but in later performances George found this explanation still did not satisfy. Many coon acts did not make any reference to negroes at all, and in the few colored shows he saw (certainly not at Otterman's, but at other theaters) the colored performers had been wearing the same kind of makeup. What did the makeup signify? What was its intent? He'd never been sure.

He should have realized then that the makeup had a very grave meaning to Colette. Knowing what she'd just told him on the roof, he realized now that to her it had a meaning of such awful importance he doubted if he'd ever fully understand it. How must she have felt, seeing that distorted, puerile version of what people thought her to be dancing and singing and clowning on the stage? She, this elegant thing he worshipped so nakedly? God, he thought...had he laughed at that show, there in front of her? He did not think he had, but he felt horribly ashamed to even imagine it. Every laugh the act garnered surely wounded her, and to hear a friend laugh as well would have been pain beyond pain.

But thinking about it now made what had happened after the show even more troubling.

They had exited together, and George, still ignorant but sensing her discomfort, had asked her what was wrong. Did she feel ill? Or cold? Had she not found the show funny?

At that, she had stood up straight, and slowly picked her head up until her nose was in the air and her shoulders were thrown back, a posture of immaculate haughtiness. She'd smiled coldly, as if she would never be so vulgar as to admit genuine amusement, and said with a trace of a French accent, "Oh, certainly. After all, they are a very funny people." And she had walked away, her stride stately, almost queenly.

It had been, he'd recognized, a part of her Princess Colette act.

But now he wondered how she'd meant those words. Had she referred to the actors on the stage? Or had she meant something more? Or perhaps she had briefly felt that she would rather be a false person, a fabricated character, than a real one in such a bitter and callous world, and sought comfort in her little creation.

George thought about it. After a while, he sadly realized she was right: he did not really know her at all.

CHAPTER 23

The Water of Life

George did not sleep that night. He sat in his bed thinking of how he had misjudged or mistreated Colette, or she him, sometimes cursing himself for his forwardness. Then in the early morning he heard his door creak open. He rolled over to see the short, bulky figure of his father sidle its way into the room, hat in hand.

"Harry?" whispered George.

"You're awake," said Silenus. "Good. Get dressed."

"Why?"

"We're going on a trip. Don't wear your nice shoes." Then he put his hat back on and walked out, shutting the door.

George half-dressed and came down to find Silenus and Stanley in the street behind the theater. They appeared to be in the midst of a new argument: Silenus had his arms crossed and was trying to ignore Stanley's pleas, while Stanley held up his blackboard, which was marked with: IT SHOULD NOT BE HIM. There were other half-erased messages in the borders that read things like NOT WELL YET and ME INSTEAD.

"Ah," said Silenus when he saw George. "You're ready."

"Where are we going at his awful hour?" said George. He was in a bad temper. The lack of sleep and humiliating rejection had cast a pall over him.

"We're going fishing," said Silenus.

Stanley did a double take on hearing this.

"But not for fish," said Silenus. "And not at a river. We're going fishing at a cemetery, George."

Stanley rolled his eyes and wrote: DO NOT MAKE THE BOY GET OUT OF BED. I WILL COME INSTEAD.

"No," said Silenus. "You won't. I don't need you at all. I need George. You need to stay here, and look after the rest of the troupe."

TOO MUCH EXPOSURE, wrote Stanley.

"The wolves are looking, but they haven't found us yet," said Silenus. "Things are only dangerous near the parts of the song they've found, where they're watching. And we won't be going near those."

Stanley did not seem convinced. He frowned and shook his head.

"What do you need me for, anyway?" said George.

"Let's say I need a catalyst, and you should serve nicely," said Silenus. "It's nothing dangerous. I just need a reed to catch the wind, and sing for me."

"I'm not singing," said George.

"You have no gift for the metaphorical," said Silenus. "Let's get to the fucking train station, all right? I need to make some stops near there before we can go."

When they arrived Silenus bought the tickets and hurried off to a hardware store down on the corner. He would not say what he was looking for. George and Stanley sat on a station bench to wait for him.

Stanley anxiously watched George out of the side of his eye, and reached out as if to put his arm around him. George flinched and ducked away.

"Don't," he said. "What are you doing?"

Stanley blinked, hurt, and smiled a little. He wrote: YOUR COLLAR ISN'T RIGHT.

"I can take care of it." He did so, but avoided looking Stanley in the face. Then he moved over to put more distance between himself and the older man. He was not sure if the wolf in red had been right, but he did not want to be touched or tended to by Stanley right now, when he was in such a foul and unforgiving mood.

Stanley shifted in his seat. He appeared to look around to make sure Silenus was not near, and pulled out his blackboard and wrote: HAVE SOMETHING FOR YOU.

George glanced sideways to read his message, but did not look at the man.

Stanley reached into his coat. He seemed a little ashamed by what he was doing, but then he smiled and shrugged and pulled his present out. There was a twinkle of gold from his fingers, and George glanced to the side again to see he was holding a very thick pocket watch.

FIGURED YOU COULD USE A WATCH, wrote Stanley. NOT NEW. OLD. STILL TELLS TIME, THOUGH IT IS SLOW. He opened the watch to show him, and smiled and turned the knob at the top. DON'T FEEL THE NEED TO KEEP TRACK OF TIME THESE DAYS. LESS IMPORTANT.

He held it out to George. George looked at it, but did not take it. "Why?" he asked.

Stanley faltered. He took his board and wrote: DO YOU HAVE A WATCH ALREADY?

"Is that it? You just want to give me a watch?"

Stanley looked at him, confused.

"You give me clothes, combs," said George. "Razors and shoes, and... and now jewelry? Why? What is it you want from me?"

Stanley thought and picked up his blackboard. He wrote several things, erasing each one before he finally showed one to George. He'd written: DO NOT WANT ANYTHING.

"Then just stop, all right? Stop giving me stuff. Stop hovering over me all the time. Just stop."

Stanley stared at him. The man looked heartbroken, and George felt sure that the wolf in red had been right.

"I don't want anything to do with you, all right?" said George. "Just leave me alone."

Stanley slumped over a little. Then he nodded and replaced the pocket watch and turned away.

Silenus finally returned with some large canvas bags over his shoulder. "That took longer than it should have," he said.

"What did you get?" George asked. Whatever was in the bags clanked when Silenus moved, and George got the very bad feeling it was shovels.

"It doesn't matter. Come on, kid. We don't have much time to lose. We've got to be there by nightfall, and I don't want to be in the same county with Lettie when she realizes I've dipped into the budget for train tickets again."

George stood and prepared to follow him. Silenus bade Stanley goodbye, but George did not. For some reason this irked his father. "Say goodbye, why don't you?" he said. "It's rude not to."

Neither George nor Stanley looked at the other. "Goodbye," George mumbled, and Stanley nodded.

They climbed aboard and within several minutes the train began moving. As it pulled away George and Silenus looked out the window to see Stanley standing at the station with the few other watchers. Yet unlike them he did not look at the train, but at his feet, and as the distance between them increased George thought he saw a flash of white from his breast pocket that rose to his face. It was, George realized, a handkerchief, and he knew immediately that Stanley was using it to wipe away tears.

It was an extremely long train ride for such short notice. George slept at the beginning in short bursts, but each nap was dreary and gave him little rest. Eventually he again asked where they were going.

"To a cemetery, like I told you," said Silenus. "But this is a very special cemetery. It is extremely old, so old that people are not really aware of how old it is, otherwise it would be considerably more feted. And it has, over time, quietly collected some of the most prestigious residents these lands have ever seen. By which I mean dead people, of course. There's one in particular I'm looking for."

"You're dragging me across the country to find a dead person?"

"Right," said Silenus. "Finn MacCog, specifically. He made some unusual burial requests, and I'd like to investigate them."

"And how am I supposed to help you investigate them?"

"Why don't you go back to sleep, eh?" said his father.

They arrived in a tiny New York town by evening and tried to hire a horse-drawn coach to take them out to the cemetery. The coachman gave them a nervous look when he heard their destination, and Silenus had to up the fare considerably before he would agree to take them.

Soon they pulled up to a large iron gate set between two stone pillars before a path that led into the woods. The end of the path was dark and shadowed, and none of them could see where it ended. The driver was so unnerved that Silenus had to pay him extra to wait, which he did far away down the lane.

The gate was not locked, to George's surprise. It opened for Silenus with a creak, and the two of them walked in.

"How did you find out about this place?" George asked.

"I once buried someone here," Silenus said. "Long, long ago."

They came to the cemetery proper. There were hundreds of lines of headstones of many shapes and types of stone, and some looked very old and crumbling. The forest itself served as its fence, yet no tree encroached on the many plots. It was an extremely quiet and still place, lit only by the fading evening light.

"Do you feel it?" asked Silenus.

"Feel what?"

"Time," he said. "It forms pools and eddies in certain places. In graveyards its effects are most noticeable. So much time and life is stored up here...like an underground cavern, full of water. There is good slumber here for the dead." He squinted at the stones around him. "Hm. Now. My research said that Finn MacCog was buried here in 1796."

"That long ago?" said George.

"Yes. But it'll be a little hard to find his resting place. He requested that his headstone be buried with him."

"What sort of person would be buried with his own headstone?" asked George.

"Well, he also requested that he be buried with his finest possessions, so that he could enjoy them in the afterlife. This put Finn in a bit of a conundrum—he didn't want to lie in an unmarked grave, since then he wouldn't be found and woken when the Rapture came, yet he was also a suspicious bastard and didn't want any grave robbers to dig him up and steal his prizes. So, figuring that Christ and His angels wouldn't have a problem with a few feet of dirt, he is buried with his headstone mere inches above his coffin in the ground."

George began to get a bad feeling about this. "And what are we here to do?"

"For now, you're to do nothing but stand where I tell you to," said Silenus.

"To what?"

"Hmm...1796...so that would be, what?" his father said to himself. He scanned the headstones. He pointed. "We'll start over there."

They walked to a corner of the graveyard. Silenus surveyed the plots and headstones, making sure to note all the empty ones, and he turned around, looking at the sky and testing the wind. Then he said, "Here. Stand right there."

He positioned George before a very old headstone that read ARCHIBALD EHBERTS 1737–1799. "So all I have to do is stand on this man's grave?"

"You have it exactly," said Silenus.

"Did you really need to bring me all the way out here for this, Harry?"

"Let me amend my instructions. Stand there, and *don't talk*."

George did as he asked, irritated. Silenus sat down on the grass so that George stood between him and the headstone. Then Silenus stared at the stone, focusing on the words written there with a fearsome intensity. George waited, wondering what would happen. Soon the wind picked up, and tufts of grass waved around his feet, and George began to get the strangest feeling, as if something was rushing to him across long, long distances.

There was a twitch in the air above the headstone. At first George thought it was just a flick of dust caught by an errant breeze, but it did not blow away. And as he looked George thought the dust appeared to take the shape of a brow, and a long, crooked nose, and pendulous jowls...

"What? What is this?" said a croaking, distant voice. It was like no more than a scratching at the very back of George's skull. "What's going on? Where...where am I?"

"Archibald Ehberts?" said Silenus.

"Who's there?" said the voice. "Where are you? I can't...I can't see you...Wasn't I just in my bed, and then I was sleeping? Sleeping there, and then later...later I was sleeping in the dark..."

George was so alarmed he could hardly move. He thought he could see shoulders now, bent and very crooked, like those belonging to a terribly old man.

"We have woken you, good sir, to ask you a simple question," said Silenus. "Do you know the final resting place of Finn MacCog? He is said to lie here in the earth which you share."

"You woke me? How?"

"The question, sir," said Silenus patiently. "We only want the answer to that, and we will let you sleep again."

"I would not know such a thing," said the creaky voice. "I am but a cobbler, a simple cobbler. I lived simple days and I died a simple death. Such things are beyond me. I do not know..."

"Thank you," said Silenus. He motioned to George to step aside. George did so and the faint image in the air evaporated.

"W-what was that?" said George. "Was that a...was it a g—"

"It was an echo," said Silenus. "An echo of a past life. Didn't I tell you that time has been stored up here, like a pool underground? All that needs to be done is allow a very small drop to fall in certain places, and as its effects ripple and echo across and back, we can listen carefully, and learn." He picked up his bag and continued on into the graveyard.

"And what are we dropping in to make that echo?" asked George as he followed.

"Can't you imagine why I brought you here, George? What distinguishing characteristic would make you suitable for such work?"

"The song, I'd guess."

"Very good. Each part of the song has connections to all of existence. It *is* all of existence, in a very tight, packaged way, regardless of time or place. You carry a bit of eternity next to your heart, George, just a bit. But that's all it takes to make the slight echoes we need. Sometimes it's damn convenient, having you around."

They continued across the graveyard in this manner, George standing in front of the headstones and Silenus focusing and bringing up those strange, unearthly faces and voices. They mostly originated in the late eighteenth century, though sometimes Silenus would make an error and bring up someone from the nineteenth. When this happened he'd immediately dismiss them, much to their surprise and indignation. On one occasion the echo they summoned up was not the person indicated on the gravestone at all, but neither George nor Silenus had the heart to tell her she was buried in the wrong grave.

Yet no matter when they died or who they were, none of the echoes could say where Finn MacCog was buried. "I am just a simple weaver," they would say, or perhaps a simple farmer, or a simple reverend, or a simple wife or Christian or son. They doggedly stuck to one little label, and would not venture any knowledge beyond it.

They both grew frustrated, especially George, who had not slept well and was still in a bitter mood. "What's eating you?" said Silenus.

George was not sure if he wanted to tell him. But he'd been aching to share his troubles for some time, and if he could not speak to his own father then who could he speak to? So as they wandered among the headstones and memorials he related the confusing events of the previous evening.

"I see," said Silenus when George had finished his story. "You know...I think it would be best if you left Colette alone."

"Why?"

"She's a troubled girl, George. She came from a hard, hard place. I should know, I'm the one that found her."

"Then can't I help her? Can't I...can't I give her something to make it better for her?"

"Some people don't want help," said Silenus. "And Colette is one of them. She runs on pride, and little else. To accept help is to admit weakness."

"Sometimes she doesn't seem that proud," said George. "Sometimes she seems ashamed. Like she wishes to be someone else."

"What do you mean?" asked Silenus.

George told him about the night they saw the minstrel show together, and how afterward she'd behaved not like herself but like the princess she was often forced to be. As he finished Silenus's face blackened and curdled until George was almost afraid to keep speaking.

"It didn't seem right," said George after a while. "She shouldn't go around...pretending."

"Right?" said Silenus. "*Right*? What the hell do you know about right? Who are you to judge her? Do you have any idea what she came from? How she'd be treated if she was honest? Maybe she *has* to pretend every once in a while, because the other option is sticking a gun in her fucking mouth and taking the easy way out! Maybe it's not about right, but about *survival*."

"Survival?" said George, shocked. "What do you mean?"

"Who would want to live in a world where you get treated in such a way? Maybe she has to lie to herself, just so she can get up in the morning and fucking walk outside! Colette isn't doing anything new, George. She's doing what people've done the world over, since the beginning of time—pretend the world is something it isn't, just so they can feel better about it. You think those bastards laughing at that minstrel bit were any different? Pretending the darkies are clowns, or animals? They aren't any such thing, and deep down those fools knew that, but it made them feel better to pretend it's so. I've seen it everywhere, anywhere. There hasn't been an ugly truth yet that man can't spin into a soothing lie, or, better yet, ignore. Now shut the hell up and come along."

Silenus's anger continued to mount until his eye fell upon one gravestone: JOSEPH BLAKELY—1834–1872. He stopped and raised an eyebrow, thinking, and his fury dissipated. "Here. Come and stand before this one."

"But that's not in the time of MacCog's burial."

"Doesn't matter," said Silenus. "We've got nothing to lose. And make sure you stay quiet for this one. This may get…personal. I had history with this man, once."

"Is this the person you came here to bury?" said George.

"No," snapped Silenus. "Now hurry up and fucking stand there."

George stood before the headstone as he had for all the others. Soon a flicker began to appear in the air over the plot, but this echo was different from all the others: it did not express astonishment on being summoned, but calmly looked around. Then, on seeing Harry, it said, "Ah. William. Is that you?"

George was not sure who the echo could mean, but Silenus smiled.

"It is indeed, Joseph," he said. "I'd ask you how you're doing, but that's obvious."

The echo looked down, then back at the headstone. George thought he could discern smoothly parted hair and cold, bored eyes somewhere in that ethereal face. "Ah, yes. Judging from our surroundings, I seem to have passed. I suppose it's safe to assume, then, that I am not the real Joseph, but a shade of him?"

"Something like that," said Silenus.

"Interesting," the voice said. "How long have I been dead? No, wait. Don't tell me. It'd just depress me. You don't look a day older than when we last parted, Billy. But then, I wouldn't expect you to. Not after the tricks we got up to. Do you still remember the bacchanalia, Bill?"

"How could I forget?" asked Silenus.

The voice laughed. "Yes. How indeed." George felt the echo's faint eyes sweeping over him. "Who is this?"

"That is my son."

"Your *what*?" said the echo. "I thought that wasn't possible."

"Then you can imagine my surprise when I met him," said Silenus. His placid smile grew a touch. "You know we haven't summoned you up just to chat, Joseph."

"Oh, yes, yes. I can't say I didn't expect this, though. You'd never let something like death prevent you from calling in a favor, you old charlatan. What are you after this time?"

"The final resting place of Finn MacCog."

"Really? That old legend?" said the echo.

"Legend?" said Silenus. "You thought it was real. It might have been years since we last spoke, but I can remember that. You always were a scholar, so if anyone knew for sure it'd be you."

"Hm. Why would I tell you that, and let you disturb another sleeper here?"

"Because I can tell you what happened to Freddy," said Silenus.

The echo was quiet for a long while. Then it said, "Freddy. My God. That dear, dear boy. Would you really?"

Silenus nodded.

"Then please. Tell me."

"He traveled with our troupe for two more years after your death," said Silenus, "but he was never the same. Didn't have the heart for it. Eventually he resigned, and returned home to New Jersey. The last I saw of him he was working in an export company, and had a lovely wife and two lovely children."

"A *wife?*" said the echo. "A wife...Cheeky little bastard. I should have known." It sighed. "You know, sometimes I think you introduced me to your little dancer just so you could use my expertise. And, of course, my library."

"That may have been the case, but it doesn't matter anymore," said Silenus.

"True," it said. "Finn MacCog, eh? That's what you want to know?" There was a laugh. "Well, I'm afraid to say that you didn't need to summon me up at all. You already know where he's buried, William. You've seen it."

"I have?" said Silenus.

"Yes," said the echo. "You won't find him among the others who died in that era. He was so paranoid he was buried far away from those. As time went by and more plots were added, his resting place wound up among those who'd passed much later." The echo smiled. "In fact, William, I'm fairly certain his unmarked grave lies not far from where we buried your wife."

George was so surprised by this statement that he nearly fell over. His movement made the spell break, and the echo dissolved, though not before giving one last unpleasant chuckle.

Silenus sat still for a long, long time. Finally he cleared his throat and said, "Well." Then, again, "Well."

George waited for what he had to say, but it did not come. Silenus slowly stood up, eyes distant. "I'd hoped...I'd hoped we would not have to see that. But...well." He picked up his bag. "This way."

It was now very dark in the graveyard, but Silenus seemed to know where he was going. They walked until they came to an ancient oak tree, and George's father walked down the line of headstones before it until he came to one at the end. George lagged behind to give his father some time alone, but he eventually approached and stood beside him. Engraved on the headstone was:

ANNE MARIE SILLENES
LOVING WIFE
TO WAKE AND RISE AGAIN
PATER OMNIPOTENS AETERNA DEUS
1829–1862

George's eyes lingered on the date. She had died nearly fifty years ago. But if that was true, how could his father look no more than forty or fifty himself? George wanted to ask, but Silenus was staring at the headstone with such heavy eyes that he could not summon the nerve.

"Pater omnipotens..." said Silenus softly. "I forgot I'd put that. It was her request, not mine. But I had to honor it. She thought Latin was so lovely, though she couldn't ken a word of it."

"I didn't know you were married before my mother," said George.

"There is very little you know about me, I suspect. Some days I think I have a friend lying in every graveyard in this country, and maybe a few beyond. But there is none that stays with me more than this one."

"How did she die?"

He tapped the side of his head. "Cancer."

"I'm sorry."

"What are you sorry for? You didn't know her."

"I'm sorry for you, I guess. It's a beautiful headstone, though."

"It is a fucking rock. No more. It doesn't know what's written on it or what shape it's in. Nor does it care. What is written there is meaningless. The thing it signifies has long since passed." He shook his head. "What fools we all are."

"What?" said George.

"You heard them, didn't you?" asked Silenus. "I am a simple man, a simple farmer, a simple preacher... They are dead, yet still they cling to their titles. What fools. We lard ourselves with words and labels and silly, insipid roles so that we might blinker our eyes and live in happy ignorance. And from these small titles we think we derive worth." His voice dripped with contempt. "*Loving wife... pater omnipotens...* These are... they are only words!" he thundered. "They are inventions! Things and ideas we have dressed ourselves up in! But they are not... they are not *real.* They are only cheap comforts, flimsy half-truths, if that. What fools we are to spend our lives chasing them... There are only two truths, George, or only two worth paying attention to: the song, and what we use it to stave off, day by day. How these wretched creatures would tremble if we knew what we were saving them from."

George frowned, concerned. Though he could see that his father was distraught, this last comment troubled him. For if the wolf in red had been right, the troupe had not really been saving anyone. He had tried his hardest to believe it couldn't be true, but as he watched his father contemptuously describe those he was meant to be protecting, that awful suspicion returned so strongly that George could not stay quiet. He had to know.

"When I spoke to the wolf in red, he said we don't perform like we used to," he said.

Silenus froze. He did not speak for a long while. Then he faintly asked, "Oh, no?"

"No. He said that our performances... aren't really protecting anything. Except maybe ourselves, is what I'm guessing. Is that right? We perform just enough to give us and the place we're staying some defenses, so that we can locate and gather the remaining fragments of the song. And that's what we're really traveling for, isn't it? The First Song, and not the singing of it."

Silenus turned a slight shade of gray. He blinked and slowly nodded. When he spoke his voice was again a croak. "Yes. Yes, that… that may be true."

"*May* be true? Or *is* true?"

Silenus could not bring himself to speak; he only nodded.

"Why would we do that?" George asked. "I thought the purpose of the troupe was to help, to maintain what was left of the world."

"It was, George."

"So we're not doing that anymore?"

"No, we are!" said his father. "We are helping!"

"But we're just getting the song, we're not really *using* it."

"Not…not yet. Not fully. We don't have time for that anymore. But we will."

"When?" asked George.

Silenus hesitated. "Do you understand what the song is, boy?"

"Yes, yes. It's a blueprint, it's a —"

"And who *made* that blueprint?"

George stayed quiet.

"Yes," said Silenus. "It is the sum of all the wishes and intents the Creator had for this world. The will of the Creator *itself.* Right now the song is impartial. Yet can you imagine what it would be like if we had the *whole*?"

"The whole?" said George.

"Yes. With the whole pattern before us we could finally learn *why* the world was intended to be the way it is now. Why it is so often cruel, and dark, and unhappy. We would learn the mind of what made us, the thing that called Creation itself into existence. And maybe…maybe if we had the complete First Song, we could call the Creator *back.*"

Silenus looked euphoric, as if he was finally revealing a precious secret he'd kept hidden for too long. But George felt nothing but alarm. "Call it back?" he said.

"Yes! We could, perhaps, call it back, and make it return. And we could ask it to fix this world it made. To repair the wrongs, to save us. Wouldn't you want such a thing, George? Doesn't such a thought appeal to you? Parts of the world may be or, or . . . or might have been lost in the meantime, sunk under that growing darkness. But none of that would matter if the Creator were to return. It outweighs the cost of such a measure. I've seen so much life, George . . . I can think of nothing better. It could fix *everything*."

George did not say anything for a while. Then he asked, "Does Stanley know?"

"Stanley?" said Silenus. "N-no. No, he does not. Our change in performing took place before he ever joined the troupe."

"So he thinks this is normal. And if he doesn't know, the others don't either."

"Yes," said Silenus. "And you must not tell them otherwise! George, we are nearly there! We have so much of the song collected, so many echoes harvested . . . It's almost complete, and it can't take much longer. There are only one or two more pieces of the song that we so desperately need . . . Once we have those, everything may be saved." Silenus turned away from his wife's grave and marched across to an unmarked plot. "And what we uncover here will help us."

George followed his father over to the plot. "How will this help, Harry?"

Silenus produced a shovel from the bag and stabbed it down into the earth. "Because what Finn MacCog was buried with will be of prime interest to some people I need to see."

"You're *grave robbing* him?" said George. He had suspected this to be the intent all along, but it was still a shock to see his father doing it right in front of his eyes.

"Yes," said Silenus. "He won't miss it. Besides, rumor has it he was a miserable bastard in life. Makes sense. Who the hell gets buried with his favorite malt, anyway?"

"I can't take part in this!" said George.

Silenus looked up. "Eh?"

"I will not do any *grave robbing*, Harry!"

"What! But this'll take hours longer if you don't help! Come on, grab a shovel."

George turned around and began walking away.

"George? George!" cried Harry. "Get back here, George! For Christ's sake, boy..." His words dissolved into grumbles, pierced by the sound of the shovel.

George found a large white stone memorial on top of a small hill. It looked like the point of a cathedral tower, and he sat under the shadow of one of its small stone eaves and watched his father's progress. He made quick enough work of the grave for George to conclude he'd done this several times before.

Soon night fell and the graveyard grew densely dark. The moon and stars sometimes emerged from the thin clouds to show a gleaming landscape of ornate stone and gentle hills, and at the bottom of one hill his father toiled frantically. But then the clouds would move, and everything would be dark again, and George would know nothing but the cool granite behind him and the cough and scrape of a shovel out in the night. And yet even in this blind state he could not block out the knowledge that they had not been protecting anything in their travels. Instead, a hundred little towns or valleys or lives had winked out behind them, erased from the world by the thoughtless shadow the troupe had been meant to hold back.

George buried his face in his hands. "Jesus," he said. "My God, my God, what have we been doing?"

Then there was a golden light among the tombstones. "Aha!" cried Silenus's voice. "I've found it!"

George's eyes adjusted and he saw the light was coming from Finn MacCog's grave. He stood and walked down to his father, sometimes feeling for the way. He saw Silenus's head poking up from the excavated grave, yet there was something glowing very, very faintly at the bottom of it.

George neared the edge of the open grave and looked in. His father stood on a large slab of stone at the bottom. There were words written on it, but George could not read them. Silenus had dug around the slab until the coffin below was revealed, yet beside the coffin was a large iron case of some kind which had been dragged out and pulled open, and there in the case was what looked at first to be a lamp of some kind, glowing with a smooth golden light. Other trinkets lay around it—some of them appeared to be very old bones of some kind—but the glow was the most astonishing thing.

"What is it?" asked George.

Silenus stooped down and plucked it out. George saw it was not a lamp at all, but a bottle, and its contents were glowing. "It is whisky, my boy," said Silenus. "But not any whisky. *The* whisky. Maybe the first one." He cackled happily. "They were right about you, Finn my boy. You managed to steal some over from the Old Country, didn't you?"

"It's whisky? Why does it glow, then?"

"Because it is *uisce beatha*, the water of life. The whisky they made in the old days, before the darkness came. It is an extraordinarily rare and precious drink, much sought after by knowledgeable aficionados. No one knows how it was made, and there is almost none left in the world. And you," he said to the coffin below his feet, "you miserable bastard, you tried to have it entombed with you here for eternity." He laughed again.

"Are you honestly telling me we came all the way out here and robbed a grave for whisky?"

"Absolutely," said Silenus. He set the bottle on the grass and climbed out. He was filthy from head to toe. "The idea came to me last night, as I stared at my wine. There are only two known bottles of *uisce beatha* remaining in the world, and those are closely guarded and used for rituals, if they are used at all. But the people I am going to petition for help are . . . very famous gourmands."

"Gour-what?"

"Gourmands. Epicures. People who enjoy food, and drink, and refined things. And excess. They are very big devotees of excess, and I think they'll prize this gift very highly. Now give me some help. I know you won't dig up a grave, but surely you can't find anything morally reprehensible about filling one in, right?"

CHAPTER 24

The Midnight Visitor

When they returned to the theater Silenus called everyone to a meeting. Colette had discovered the missing funds and was borderline apoplectic, but Silenus did his best to defuse her. "I believe I've found a solution to all of our problems," he said. "I ignored a vital piece of advice for some time." He nodded to Stanley, who looked worried. "But that was because I thought it was impossible. Yet now I think I might just have figured out a way for it to work."

"So what is it we're going to do?" said Colette.

"What we've always done," said Silenus. "We're going to travel, and put on a show. But this show will be for some very, very discerning people. We want to make damn certain we don't lose their attention, that's for fucking sure. And if they like what they see, along with the gift I'm about to present to them, then they may help, which would be enormously good. So everyone needs to pack everything they need and store *all* of our props in my office, and we need to get as rested as possible."

"Why in your office?" said Colette.

"Because where we're going can't be reached by train," Silenus said. "Come on. Let's get started. Even the backdrop, though I can't imagine what we'd use it for now."

As it turned out, George would have to move more than just props: the theater manager had informed Stanley that George's time there was up. They had to move his trunks all the way across town to Colette's hotel, where Silenus's door had chosen to appear. Then his father rented him a single room for the night. It was just one more aggravation in the midst of all the moving.

When they were finally done Silenus told them to clean their very best clothes and lay them aside for tomorrow. "We'll want to make as good an impression as we possibly can," he said. He was sweating and kept drinking from his flask. "This will be our toughest audience yet."

George did as his father asked, but when he was done he lay in his bed, staring at the creaky ceiling. He was far too troubled by everything that'd happened to even think of sleep. He eventually rose to find his father, but as he walked by Franny's room he heard Silenus's voice: "Hold still."

"That hurts," said Franny's voice.

"Well, it hurts because you won't sit still, and you haven't done it in a while. Sit still, please."

George walked to her door and looked in. Franny sat at the vanity in the corner, staring blankly into the mirror, and Silenus stood behind her. To George's amazement, he was brushing her hair, gently taking her orange-red curls and running the brush through them. It was such an intimate act that for a moment George thought he was seeing two completely different people.

"Do you not ever brush your hair, my dear?" asked Silenus. "Or am I the only one who ever does?" Franny shook her head, and he *tsk*ed. "I can't have you looking like this, you know. Not tomorrow. Doesn't that feel good?"

Again, she shook her head, like a willful child.

"It doesn't feel good?"

"Nothing you do feels good," she said. "I'm mad at you."

His brushing slowed. "Mad at me? What are you mad at me for?"

"I can't remember. But it's something."

"Please don't be mad at me," he said. "It troubles me to see you angry."

Then Franny looked up and saw George in the mirror. She smiled and said, "Hello, Bill."

Silenus stopped brushing and stared at her. Though George could only see part of his father's face in the vanity mirror, he could see the man had just turned white. "Wh-what did you say?"

Then Franny waved to George in the mirror, and Silenus turned around and saw him standing in the door. "George?" he said. "What are you doing in here?"

"I could ask the same of you," said George. "Why are you brushing her hair?"

Silenus's face darkened, and though George had seen his father's fury many times it had never been as threatening as this. "That is *none* of your fucking concern, boy," he spat. "Now what is it you want?"

George stammered. "I . . . I wanted to know if maybe I could get a bottle from you."

"A bottle? A bottle of what? Whisky?"

George nodded.

Silenus pointed to the top of the chest of drawers. A half-empty bottle sat next to his father's hat. "Take it. I don't fucking need it. Just fucking get out, all right?"

George grabbed the bottle and fled. He'd infuriated his father before, but it'd never been like that. It was as if Silenus thought it was a terrible violation for George to witness that moment.

As he walked away he heard Franny speak again: "There he goes again . . . I haven't seen him in so long. Did you ever know Bill?"

With a soft tremble, his father's voice answered: "Yes. Yes, my dear. I believe I once did."

*   *   *

George was so miserable with his situation that he could only find solace in thinking about Colette. Maybe, he thought, there was a way to repair the damage he'd done. Eventually around midnight he began to devise a grand gesture to win her back. He knew he'd fouled things up terribly, but if he went to her now, he thought, when they were both alone before a huge performance, and he tried to express how he really felt about her, maybe then she'd understand.

He did not ever think that his reasoning might have had something to do with the near-empty bottle of bourbon by his bed. Instead he began stringing together an extensive speech, one that would put his stifled confession on the rooftop to shame and inspire the love he felt he truly deserved.

Then he dressed in his very best tweed, drank one final glass of bourbon, and crept out of his hotel room. The halls were very dark and confusing, and he wandered for a while, squinting at room numbers, before again catching the scent of Colette's perfume.

He followed it to one of the rooms. He was not sure if this was hers, yet he figured it was the best lead he had. He raised a fist to knock, but then realized something: he could not remember the first line of his speech. Or, for that matter, the second or the third. He struggled with himself for a moment and withdrew down another hallway to review it. It now seemed very labyrinthine and complicated in his head, and he tried to untangle his many amorous professions one by one.

When George had it sorted out he turned to go back to her room. But before he took a step, the handle twitched, and the door very slowly fell open. George froze and stepped back to watch.

Someone slipped out of the room. It was not Colette, but someone short and thick. And judging by the mustache, he was most definitely male.

Confused, George shrank up against the wall of the hallway as the figure walked past. The man stopped to readjust his pants, then sighed and drooped a little as though saddened. Then he continued on down the hall.

George knew that gesture very well; it was something he saw every day. It could be no one but his father.

In his drunkenness George assumed he'd gotten turned around, and witnessed his father walking out of his own office door. The scent George had smelled must have been from when Colette last visited the office. Yet when he followed his father down the hall out of curiosity, he found that the big black door was on the other side of the hotel, and his father quietly walked in without a word. So whose room could that have been? George wondered. Who had he been visiting?

It was as he tiptoed back to the room door that he realized the scent of Colette's perfume was now much stronger, as if she'd been walking there herself. But only his father had been in the hall. Had Harry been wearing Colette's perfume? No, thought George, that'd be absurd. He would never wear such a thing, unless...

Unless.

Unless, unless, unless.

Maybe he had not been mistaken. Maybe that *had* been her room.

George's knees began to feel very weak. He suddenly remembered how Colette's eyes had gleamed as she'd spoken of Harry's plan to doll her up like a princess. "Smart-ass," she had said fondly, shaking her head and smiling. He remembered how Colette and Harry were always in some argument or another, dragging one another away to squabble, and Harry's doting nickname for her: "Lettie." And she'd been so upset when she'd heard Harry had a child. And then there was how she and Harry spent so much time together in his office, talking about business and budgets...

But were they? Were they really? What else could they have been doing together, alone?

"Oh, no," whispered George miserably. "It...it can't be. It *can't* be."

He went and stood before her door, wishing to knock and beg her to tell him it wasn't so, it couldn't be so. But before her door the scent of her perfume was headier than ever, and he knew that it must have been soaked into his father's skin...

"No," George whimpered. "No, no."

He trudged back to his room as if in a dream. He remembered how she had always been so loath to touch him or be close to him, and how she'd been so embarrassed when he'd proclaimed his love for her on the rooftop.

It was not that she did not love him. It was that he was her lover's son. The very idea of any love between them was perverse.

George walked into his room and shut the door. He drank another enormous tumbler of bourbon, and lay facedown on his bed and shouted into his pillow.

CHAPTER 25

The House on the Hill

Stanley tapped at George's door well before sunrise, then pushed it open and reluctantly looked in. When he saw George look back, with his skin drawn and his eyes swollen from tears and blackened with fatigue, Stanley withdrew slightly, shocked. Then he gestured and George nodded. "All right," he said. "All right."

They all rose and, in their finest clothes, took a streetcar to the outskirts of town. Franny said to him, "My, George. You look almost as bad as me." She smiled a little.

"Didn't sleep," said George.

"Terrible, isn't it?" Her eyes wandered away and she began to hum tunelessly to herself.

"Why the hell didn't you sleep?" said Silenus. "I told you we needed everyone rested." But George could not even look at his father, let alone answer him.

Silenus carried a small canvas sack, and he kept checking the time on his pocket watch. "I think I know where we need to be for this," he said. "But we may have to wander for a little while to find the right spot."

"You don't know where these people are?" asked Colette.

"I know where they are, but getting to them is different," said Silenus. "You've got to come at them the right way. We need the right place. A good set of crossroads should do...I know this area pretty well, so I think I've found a place that will work."

"Why do we need crossroads?" said Colette.

Stanley wrote: BECAUSE THEY PRESENT A CHOICE.

"A what?" she said.

"A choice," said Silenus. "They represent a chance when things can go in more than one direction. At that moment, all roads before you and what you encounter upon them are possible. And in that moment you are exposed to other elements. Ones you would normally never be vulnerable to."

The streetcar let them off, and Silenus led them across crumbling ditches and frigid, wet fields that had not yet awoken to spring. It was bitterly cold out, and in the distance there was a gray, misted forest. The fields sloped down, and at the bottom were two spindly little intersecting roads that must have seen very little traffic. A small, withered sapling sat in one corner of the intersection.

George's sense of foreboding increased as they approached the little crossroads. "What people are we meeting here again?" he asked no one in particular.

To his surprise, it was Stanley who turned and considered answering him. He took out his blackboard and wrote as he walked. He gave George a doubtful glance, and turned the board around. It read: DO YOU BELIEVE IN FAIRIES?

Silenus took out his pocket watch again and checked it. "Still an hour until sunrise. Good. That'll give me some time to prepare. We'll have to arrange tokens to catch their attention."

They watched as Silenus set down the bag and took out what looked like a bundle of sticks. They were soaked in something dark and syrupy that reeked horribly. "Nothing like tar fumes to wake you up in the morning," said Silenus. "This is very old tar, as well. It has lain untouched for countless years in the darkest places. Which is what we want."

He arranged the tarred timber on the side of the intersection fac-ing the forest. Then he took out his bag again and rummaged around until he produced a small cloth sack. He opened it up and dumped its contents into his palm. They looked like tiny, fragile bones.

"The wings and ribs of a crow that has spent much of its life aloft," said Silenus. He began searching through the tiny bones with one finger. He selected one very small vertebra and examined it. "Burn the bones of the earth, sing the songs of the sky," he muttered. Then, to the disgust of nearly all of them, he popped it in his mouth. He grimaced and maneuvered it around until his cheek bulged.

"Are we really doing this?" asked George. "Are we really going to see . . . well . . ."

"Yes," said Silenus. "We are. But seeing them shouldn't worry you."

"No?"

"No." He continued rummaging in his bag. "You should worry about *them* seeing *you*." He took out a large silver hand mirror. He spun it around in one palm, and George saw it was mirrored on both sides. Silenus hung it from the sapling by a string so that one side reflected the wood while the other reflected their own faces.

"Harry, what is all this for?" asked Colette.

"The fae folk are generally a mercurial and superficial breed," said Silenus. "They don't engage in most worldly affairs because they believe themselves above us. The rest of the world is sort of in a mist to them, and—lucky for me—they never go outside of their little kingdom. So it takes a lot to get their attention. Certain vest-ments, tokens and totems suggesting power, that kind of thing. One who burns the very Earth and keeps the skies below his tongue is someone worth considering."

"But you aren't actually like that," said Colette. "You're just faking."

"Am I?" said Silenus. "How do you know?"

"What's the mirror for?" asked George.

"They're also very vain," said Silenus. "The first thing I want them to see is themselves, and mirrors do not work properly where they come from. They're highly valued."

Franny looked around herself, confused. "You know, I...I think I remember this," she said. "I've done this before. Haven't I?"

"No," said Silenus sharply. "You have not. I would know if you had."

"Oh," she said, and nodded.

Silenus checked his pocket watch. "All right. It's time." He knelt and lit a match and started the kindling. Blue flames began to dance along the tarred branches. Then he stood and said, "We'll need to go over a few rules before we actually encounter any of them. First, never address one of them as an equal. Always refer to them as 'my lord', or 'my lady.' That is of absolute importance. Second, do not rise to any insult, should any come. And they will come. But you'll just have to grin and bear it."

"Why are we asking for help from these snobs, then?" said Colette. "They sound unbearable."

"They are unbearable, but they are also very powerful," said Silenus. "So we'll all just have to be fucking polite, all right?"

A cold wind rolled across the field, and the hanging mirror began to spin on its string. George was so surprised by this that he hardly noticed the mist intensifying in the wood beyond.

"Now, the third rule—they may offer you things," said Silenus. "Under no circumstances should you *ever* accept them. Their gifts do not come free, and, though they live and function by very specific binding agreements, they are extremely skilled at twisting words to their own ends. It may be something you want very desperately— something you almost feel you cannot live without—but you must not accept it. All right?"

"All right," said Colette.

"All right. And the last rule is — you *must not ever* draw attention to their masks."

"Their what?" said George.

"Their masks. Don't look at them too long. *Don't* touch them. And, for the love of fucking Christ, do not *ever* ask them to remove them."

It seemed to have gotten even colder now. Stanley was shivering in his nice sack coat. The mirror kept spinning on its string, but it began to slow, and when it did George thought he saw that one side of the mirror was reflecting something that should not have been there: it showed the troupe standing in the intersection, true, but behind them was a tall, spindly wood, with graying trunks and many twisting vines, and above the wood was a dark night sky with thousands and thousands of stars...

George looked behind them, but saw nothing resembling what he was seeing in the mirror. It was day, and there was no wood. The coldness of the air grew so great that he began to shiver along with Stanley, and it felt as if they were being slowly pulled to somewhere much denser, much harder, and much colder than the world they had just recently been within. "Something is wrong..." he said, but no one heard.

"Why do they wear masks?" asked Colette.

"The seelies are immortal," said Silenus. "They do not die naturally, only by violence. But when your life span is eternal, you eventually see *everything*. And you can't avoid a few accidents or mishaps. So though the remaining fey folk are still immortal, they...do not resemble their original selves. And they are very, very vain, so they hide their faces..." The spinning mirror abruptly came to a halt. Silenus looked up at the misted woods across the field. "Behind masks."

The rest of the troupe looked. There was an odd, fluttering light in the forest, and a figure was emerging from the tree line. It was very tall and dressed in such deep black that George could make out nothing but a bright white face and a gray cap. For some reason the sight of this bizarre thing in the woods inspired a terrible dread in him. Its movements were strange, as if its legs were too long and it had to wade forward, like a man on stilts.

"Here he comes," said Silenus quietly.

The figure strode across the stony field to them. It looked like a man, but if so it was the tallest man George had ever seen, reaching nearly seven feet. He was dressed in a fine black suit made of a fabric that seemed to glint even in the lowest light. In a manner somewhat like Franny, he had no visible skin: he wore black gloves, and at his neck and his wrists he wore black and gray handkerchiefs or scarves. On his head he wore a gray homburg hat, and upon his face he wore an ornate white mask. It was meant to mimic noble, Roman features, with a long, delicate nose, a thin, thoughtful mouth, and a smooth, clean brow. But though the features were close enough to human, they were not exact, and along with the mask's blank, dark eyeholes they made the white face alien and disturbing.

The man stopped when he was several feet away and examined them. He glanced at the mirror, and for a moment stared at himself, transfixed. This seemed to put him in a better mood. Then he turned back and said in a high, soft voice that was muffled by his mask, "Greetings, Heironomo Silenus, Oldest Wanderer, Harvester of Echoes, Bearer of Lights Eternal, Master of Stage and Speech and Song."

For a moment they did nothing. The troupe and the man in black simply looked at one another. He was such a foreign and uncomforting creature that George was not sure what they were to do.

"Pardon my rudeness, my lord," said Silenus suddenly, his words brimming with courtliness. "Thank you so much for hearing and answering our summons." He swept off his hat and bowed low, and kicked George's ankle, indicating for him and the others to do likewise. The men all bowed, and the women curtsied. "You are looking splendid, as always. Am I correct in thinking that you have kept up with the current fashions, my lord?"

The man in black looked at him blankly for a long time. Then he said in the same soft voice, "It is expected of the court of Heartache's Founding to always keep pace with the absolute newest trends."

"Of course it is," said Silenus. He nonchalantly spat out the crow bone and stood back up. "It was stupid of me to even ask. You do these new tastes a far better service than any other gentleman I have ever seen, however."

"I, personally, find these latest fashions utterly vulgar and despicable," said the man in black.

"Yes, yes," said Silenus. "You are absolutely right in this assessment, my lord. It's so regrettable."

"I love them," said the man in black, "*because* they are so vulgar and despicable."

"Well, of course you would," said Silenus. "Any gentleman of your excessively good breeding would."

The man in black stared at Silenus for a long while again. Then he looked around at the troupe. He did not seem impressed.

"Ah, yes," said Silenus. "Allow me to introduce my traveling companions." He then did so, going from member to member and describing their talents and roles.

"Am I correct in thinking that you and your companions wish to gain entry to the court?" asked the man in black.

"That is indeed our wish, my lord," said Silenus. "If it would please you and the court, that is."

"How unusual. As a herald, it is given to me to refuse or admit any guests," said the man in black. "Most are refused. But the lady has told me that you should be admitted at any time and under any circumstances, Silenus. She dearly wishes to see you again. In fact, it is rumored that you have been avoiding her."

Silenus gave him a placid grin. "Surely that is an issue for the lady herself, and no other?"

The herald stiffened. "If you wish. Follow me, and I will accompany you to the house." He beckoned, and the troupe began to follow him across the field. Except now they found that things had changed: it was night, not morning, and they no longer stood on an intersection but on a single paved road that led from the depths of one dark wood and wound across the frigid meadows to another. Huge, unearthly black stones now dotted the fields around them, some so tall as to cast shadows across the starlit road. Silenus hardly noticed, but George and the others stared around themselves as they walked.

"I don't recall coming out of those woods," said Colette, looking behind. "Wasn't there a few houses back there a while ago?"

Stanley took out his board, and wrote: THESE ARE THEIR LANDS. FICKLE AS THEIR INHABITANTS.

"Have you been here before?" asked Colette.

Stanley shook his head, wrote: FIRST TIME.

"Well, either way it's very disorienting," she said. "And it's so cold here. I've never been colder…"

George agreed. Where were they? Something the herald had said bothered him a little. Then he remembered the name of the court: Heartache's Founding. Wasn't that the name he'd glimpsed on Silenus's strange map? Yet hadn't that been in Kentucky? George had never been to Kentucky, but he decided he did not want to go if it was anything like this.

They entered the dark wood. At the mouth of the road the herald reached into a ditch on the side and produced a small bronze lantern. He ran one long finger along the glass and the candle within instantly became lit. He gestured with the same finger and they followed.

The candle flame made strange patterns on the dark tree trunks. At times the tangle of branches seemed to catch the light and form intricate hieroglyphs.

"I take it, then," said Silenus, "that her ladyship still has no fondness for day?"

"Night is the best time for parties," said the herald. "And what purpose would the court and the house hold, if not for parties?"

The road began to climb a tall hill, and as they emerged from beneath the trees the troupe gasped. An enormous house sat on the top of the hill, but it was not like any house they'd ever seen before. It was certainly not at all what George had been expecting. He thought fairies should live in castles, or in glens in the forest, but at the top of the hill was an enormous Queen Anne mansion, with many gables, turrets, ornate spandrels and spindles, countless fluted columns, and a long front porch with gingerbread trim. It looked much like a high-society home in twilight, with all the windows glowing warmly in the dark. The only thing that was odd was the large bonfires arranged on the hillside around it, which sometimes gave it a medieval, savage look.

"This is new," muttered Silenus as they began to trudge up the hill.

The herald led them into an enormous foyer with a vaulted ceiling, smooth columns, and two tall arched doors with heavy bronze handles. Upon their entering, George's keen senses went wild: the air was curiously, almost unbearably still, and even though his ears told him all was silent some part of him thought he was constantly hearing whispers and a fluttering of feathered wings from somewhere nearby.

The herald pushed the doors open and they followed him down a long carpeted hallway. There were no other doors save at the end. There were many paintings hung on the walls of the hallway, but the first few made no sense to George: in most of the unsettling scenes depicted, the painter had evidently used a dimension or color that his eyes could not easily translate, and they gave him a headache. After them came a series of paintings that were simply black, curiously enough. But toward the end of the hall the paintings began to make sense: they showed landscapes and cityscapes of stunning, beautiful imagery, some so awe-inspiring that they evoked sighs from the troupe.

"This is her ladyship's private collection," said the herald. "They are painted once every thousand years by one of the court artists. You can see the varying styles and subjects in them, and their progression."

George looked back. There had to be at least several hundred paintings. "So, the oldest are at the end of the hall here, and they get younger toward the entrance?"

The herald surveyed him for a moment, as if he did not care for George's impertinent tone. "Yes."

The oldest paintings were so affecting George could hardly believe such beauty had ever existed in the world. But he remembered that it had not lasted long. He looked at the period of paintings that were utterly black. Had that been when the wolves first appeared? And after that, the paintings became so disturbing and twisted, as if the painters were horribly traumatized, or perhaps there had been nothing beautiful left to paint...

The herald opened the end set of doors and led them into an enormous, high-ceilinged parlor. Though one whole wall was a series of bay windows, the room was very dark, and they could just make out rings and rings of overstuffed chairs, a lowered wooden dance floor, and many tables at the back. Somewhere someone was playing a haunting melody on a very out-of-tune piano. At first the room seemed to be empty, yet as their eyes adjusted they saw it was not: tall, thin figures stood in groups or sat in the lounge chairs or at the tables, languidly drinking or eating. They somehow managed to elude the eye, as if they were made of smoke, unless you looked right at them. Each person wore a porcelain-white mask, many of which had an adapted mouth that allowed for a cigarette or a drink. The masked people stared at them as they moved by.

"I think I know this place," said Franny softly. "It's changed, but... but I almost feel I've been here before."

The herald led them straight to the back of the parlor, which ended in an elevated dais, and seated upon the dais steps were many tall, thin women in elegant dresses. George knew little of women's fashion, but he knew enough to recognize the slender, sculpted hats, silhouette dresses, and pouter-pigeon cuts and know he was seeing the very element of *haute couture*. And yet these elegant ladies sat sprawled on the floor as if they were bored children.

As the herald led them past, the ladies turned their masked faces to Silenus.

"He's here," whispered a voice.

"Is that...no. No, it couldn't..."

"How could he come here? Doesn't he know..."

"...Mistake? Maybe imagining it..."

"...Foolish thing to do, either way..."

But Silenus ignored them, his nose high in the air.

At the top of the dais was yet another ring of overstuffed lounge chairs, each occupied by a lethargic-looking woman in a stunning dress. Yet one chair, the chair at the very end, was much larger than the others, and seated there was the tallest woman yet, dressed in resplendent white. Her mask was far more beautiful than all the others, and yet its maker had painted tears flowing from the corners of the eyes. George wondered if this was disingenuous: the way the lady sat did not seem sad at all, but terribly proud.

The herald bowed low before the circle of chairs. "My lady," he said, "I bring you Heironomo Silenus, who has requested entry into this court for a moment of your time."

The tall woman's masked face stayed riveted on his father. "Yes," she said, her voice soft and muffled like all the others. "I can see that."

There was the sound of much shuffling around them. George looked back and saw the dais was now surrounded by hundreds of men and women in elegant suits and dresses, all of whom watched them with vacant, masked eyes.

"I almost fear to ask," said the lady, "why on Earth you should ever desire to enter my house again, Silenus."

"And I almost fear to answer, my lady," said Silenus. He bowed as well.

"I would think that one visit from you would be enough," she said. "Twice is bordering on rudeness. But three times? This is wholly unprecedented."

At that Stanley looked at Silenus, surprised, and George could tell he had not known this was Silenus's third visit.

Silenus stood back up. "Yet how could I keep myself away? Once you have known the joys and beauties of the Founding, one can only—"

"Oh, please," said the lady. Though her mask muffled her words, it did nothing to diminish the contempt behind them. "Spare me your flatteries. I have been their recipient far too often. I can only imagine three reasons behind your return. One, you finally feel some hint of regret for your atrocities, and have returned here for atonement. Or two, you are suicidal, and wish to expire in the most public and festive way possible. *That* would amuse me. Or three," she said, now audibly gritting her teeth, "you *want* something of me. I would think you a fool if the third was indeed your motivation, were I not so familiar with your skulduggery."

Silenus was quiet. "You do me wrong, my lady."

She sat forward. "Do I?"

"In the first, you assume I have no regret for what happened," he said. "That is unjust. I feel regret. Regrets make up the whole of my heart. Regrets for many things, for many peoples. And one of the sharpest, most painful regrets I carry is for the loss of your mother."

The lady slowly cocked her head. Her long neck and blank face made it a queerly inhuman gesture. "I have heard so very many of your words, player. They have such a curious ability to bend and twist around the anvil of your tongue, and take on many new meanings. I do not think regret means the same to you as it does to me."

"Ofelia," said Silenus. "Please, do not be so bitter."

The lady trembled a little. "I could flay you alive," she said. "Or feed you your own innards while you still lived. Or pluck the bones from your body and make your skin dance for my amusement. I could strike the ears and hands and feet and organs of generation from your body, and pluck out your tongue, and send you back out into the world without anything but one eye, one *single* eye, so you could see the horror you, this ruined wreck of a person, would then inspire in others. I could do all of these things, and each would be justified in the face of what you have done."

"No," said Silenus calmly. "They would not."

She cocked her head further. "No?"

"What your mother did, she did of her own accord," said Silenus. "I made a proposition, and she agreed to it. What happened when we attempted to complete it was tragic, but it was not the intent of our agreement. She was well aware of the risks. And when she was gone, my bargain still needed to be fulfilled. I have done nothing wrong. Indeed, to harm me would be the unjustified act."

"She agreed to your bargain, because...because..." But whatever the cause, the lady could not bring herself to speak of it. "Why are you here?" she demanded. "What is it you want?"

"Merely to present a gift," said Silenus, and he reached into his satchel and produced the whisky they'd gotten from Finn MacCog's grave.

The liquor still retained its glow. It was easily the most beautiful thing in this dark, cavernous room. All of the ladies nearby sat up, and a gasp ran through the crowd at the base of the dais.

"Is that..." said one of the ladies-in-waiting.

"It is the water of life," said Silenus. "I have violated many sanctities to procure this for you, my lady. I wish it to be a gift of my goodwill, and inspire the same in you."

Every porcelain face was fixed on the bottle. The troupe glanced around uncomfortably, except for Silenus, who looked only at the lady.

Then he dropped the bottle back into his satchel, concealing its glow. The host all sighed in dismay. "But, if you hold no goodwill for me, then I can see that such a gesture would be futile," he said. "In which case my companions and I will leave, and give you peace." He bowed again, and turned to depart.

"Wait," said the lady.

He stopped, and slowly turned back.

"There are only three known bottles of *uisce beatha* left in the world," said the lady quietly. "How did you . . . Where did you . . ."

George noted this was not the same total his father had quoted earlier. He could tell this surprised and irked Silenus, but regardless Silenus said, "It doesn't matter where I got it. The only thing that matters is how distressing it is to hear my gift could be turned down in such a fashion."

"I . . . would not refuse such a gift. It would be . . . rude." George could tell she was thinking very quickly. "What would you wish in exchange?"

"What would I wish for?" Silenus asked. He appeared offended by the question. "For your free friendship. But, if you are unwilling to give that, I would accept a promise."

"A promise?"

"Yes. If, say, you promised that you would never wish me harm as a reprisal for what happened to your mother, that would please me very much."

All the fairies in the court turned their gaze from Silenus's satchel to the lady. She thought for several minutes longer, but her eventual answer did not surprise George: "Fine," she said.

"Of course, I do also need your aid in one further issue," said Silenus. "It is very small, a triviality, I promise you. I would be much more willing to part with this worthy gift if I could depend on your help in that matter."

"Damn you," said the lady. "If you didn't have that bottle . . ."

"If I didn't," said Silenus. "But I do. It is a very slight task, nothing of importance. Would you willingly help me?"

She sighed. "All right. I can see that you have bested me. I would, willingly."

"Excellent," said Silenus. He approached, knelt before her, and held the bottle out, head bowed. The lady took it, the glow rendering her white figure positively radiant, and she gazed at it lovingly. She held the bottle close and smelled its cork and shivered.

"It's not been tasted in revelry since the first days," she said softly. "When my mother's court was strong and all the world was young and beautiful, we drank this once a year on the solstice, and watched the setting sun. She held my hand, as if I were a little girl." She stowed the bottle away within the folds of her white dress. "But those are gone days, now." She turned back to Silenus. "Would you be so crude as to jump into planning for your little task now?"

"Well...I suppose I don't have to," he said. "It was my intention for my performers and me to now give you the one other truly valuable gift we possess—"

"Entertainment," said the lady flatly. "Yes, I've heard it all before. Please skip the theatrics. You practically breathe them out with every word." She stood up. She was a marvelously tall creature, and as she moved over to them George was reminded of a tall pine, decked with snow. She looked down on George and Colette. "But who are these two darling angels you have at your side? I've not seen them before."

"Them?" said Silenus. "They are assistants, performers. No one of note."

"No one of note?" said the lady. "They seem so young, so fresh. The years lie so lightly upon the both of them. I can smell it. How did an old fiend like you get your hands on them?"

"They came freely," Silenus said.

"Or they think they did," she said. She knelt down before them and laid a hand on either shoulder. She was heavily perfumed, but no scent could mask the smell of decay that billowed up from her dress. This close George could see hints of skin behind the mask, and they were gray and scarred and in some places a vivid, glistening red. "Here, my darlings. Would you like to see my house with me? I think it should hold many wonders to creatures as young as you. It would be a kindness to me if you came."

George and Colette glanced at one another and looked to Silenus. George could tell that to refuse such an offer would be rude by the standards of the court, and his father was trying to figure a way out of it. But he gave up, and nodded slightly.

"Sure," said George. Then he quickly added, "My lady."

"Excellent," she said. She stood up and extended a hand to each of them. With another nervous glance, they each took one. Through her gloves her fingers felt very thin and very, very hard, as if they were made of stone. "You may speak to my seneschal concerning our agreement," she said to his father. A smaller fairy dressed in a gray sack coat and checked trousers stepped forward. "He will figure out how it should be best fulfilled. Then you may prepare for your performance, if you wish."

Hand in hand, she began to lead George and Colette down the dais. Two of her ladies-in-waiting followed while Silenus, Stanley, and Franny looked helplessly on. George saw his father open his mouth to speak, but he reconsidered, and stayed silent.

CHAPTER 26

Suggestion and Assumption

The rest of the lady's house was just as unsettling as the parlor. It seemed to be nothing but dark hallways and shadowed eaves, and you always had the feeling that there were figures moving in the corner of your vision. And that sound of fluttering wings never left George. It was as if the dark eaves were filled with rooks that were constantly flailing to stay on their perches.

Ofelia was eager to show them her collections of artwork, and it was soon apparent that the hall of paintings was but a fraction of her horde: they saw rooms filled with ornate suits of armor, sculptures from even before the Classical age, and paintings of all kinds. Every once in a while there was a mirror, and George saw his father was right: mirrors here did not reflect the onlooker, but instead showed endless gray halls. The lady seemed slightly embarrassed by these, and hurried to draw their attention elsewhere. Yet there were a curious number of gaps in her collection, and eventually Colette asked about them.

"Oh, sometimes we get bored of certain pieces," Ofelia said. "In which case we simply burn them, and throw the ashes out."

"Burn them?" said George, shocked. "Why not just give them away?"

"Give them away?" said the lady. "Why, I could never bear to see them in another's possession. No, no. I'd much rather have them burned."

But what the lady was mostly interested in was George and Colette themselves. She marveled at their youth ("I had forgotten that seventeen could even be an age!") and asked them all sorts of uncomfortable questions. Had they ever bitten someone in the throes of ecstasy, hard enough to draw blood? Had they ever killed a lover? Had they ever taken love by force, and if so, how? When the answers to these questions were all negative, she shook her head, amazed. "Such young little things," she said. "So young."

They continued forward through her endless halls and rooms. George and Colette both grew bored and hungry, but the lady and her entourage never seemed to tire. Yet as they walked down one old, creaking hallway George caught a whiff of something very appealing. The scent made him think of roasted meats with honey marinades and rosemary. He lagged behind and tracked the scent to an open door on the side of the hall, and slowly pushed it open.

Inside was a long, thin feasting table, with hundreds of place settings. Yet the feast appeared to have happened hours ago, and had yet to be cleaned up: filthy bowls and tankards and many, many platters covered the surface of the table. But it was the bones that George noticed the most. They lay in heaps on the platters, some retaining their skeletal forms, others mere drumsticks and ribs. And some were very curious bones, with very large, three-toed feet, and others (could they be skulls?) featuring many long horns.

"Ah!" said a voice over his ear. "I see they still haven't taken care of the dinner."

He jumped and saw Ofelia standing over him, looking into the room. Colette and the ladies-in-waiting stood beyond.

"I'm sorry, my lady," he said. "I...I didn't meant to pry. It just smelled so..."

"Don't apologize, my dear," she said. "You can't be blamed. Our feasts are the most alluring sort in the world. A sniff of their many aromas is enough to drive any man mad. After all, we use only the most sumptuous preparations, and only the rarest of ingredients."

George eyed the horned skulls on one of the platters. "Rarest?"

"Oh, yes," she said. "For example, last night we dined on roasted ostrich with truffle stuffing, barbacoa of young rhinoceros, and a very fine fillet of blue whale, given minimal preparation. The fats of the fillet are so succulent, you know, you need hardly do anything to it at all."

"You . . . eat things like that?"

"We dine upon many things here," she said. "The rarest and strangest and most outrageous are best."

"I think I see. Will our gift be a part of tonight's feast?" asked George.

The lady's pale, still face dipped down to stare at him. "Yes. We will start with it."

George, feeling suddenly courageous, said, "If I might ask, what did Silenus do to you, my lady?"

"To me?" said the lady. "He did not do anything to me." She turned and pointed. Far down the hall hung an unusually large portrait of a tall, majestic-looking woman with pale skin and raven-dark hair. She wore no mask, and she somehow managed to look imperious and kind all at once. George was reminded of his grandmother, which gave him a pang of regret. On the bottom of the frame was a small bronze plaque, and written on it was one word he could read even from there: TITANIA.

"Your mother?" George asked.

She nodded. "She was . . . very much a fan of Silenus. Your troupe leader is a wily, cunning man. Even today, I cannot tell if he deceived her, of if she wanted to be deceived. That may be the true nature of his art. The gift he has given today will serve as both an outrageously rare treasure, and a fond memento of her court . . . I suppose I ought to ration it, and drink it only, say, once a decade, perhaps on the anniversary of her death. But no. We will drink it all tonight, I expect."

"All of it tonight?" said Colette.

"Oh, yes," said the lady. "We decided long ago to abandon living with any reservations, my dear. It is the only proper way to spend one's final days."

"What do you mean?" asked George.

"Surely you don't think all this can last much longer, child? Ever since the darkness first came, we knew we could not survive forever. So, honestly, what is worth doing? One might as well enjoy oneself, and take in as many pleasures as one can. Even those that would normally be considered...extreme." She sniffed. "This way."

George lagged behind again to look once more into the feasting hall. On the closest corner of the table was a pile of what looked like rings. They were too small to fit the fairies' hands, he guessed, but it looked like they'd fit his own. He wondered what they were doing there, but then one of the ladies-in-waiting called to him and he ran to catch up.

In the next room they were allowed to wander alone. George tried to stay close to Colette, but somehow Ofelia's ladies-in-waiting split them apart and he found himself on the other side of the room. A shadow fell over him, and he looked up to see Ofelia herself standing over him.

"It is a beautiful work, isn't it?" she asked.

He looked at the painting before them. It depicted a man grasping a woman beside a still pool. Neither party seemed particularly happy. "I suppose. I mean, yes, it is, my lady."

He did not hear her bend down, but suddenly the lady's face was just over his shoulder. "You have such fine hands," she said.

"I have what?" said George.

"Fine, soft hands. Rosy hands. An artist's hands. Is that so? Are you a man of talents?"

"Well, I sometimes like to think so," he said.

She moved to the other shoulder. "Oh, how glorious. But do you get respect for your talents, boy? Somehow I think you do not. Otherwise, why would you be here, in such a poor state? I could give it to you, you know. I could give you applause and attention unending..."

George's vanity perked up at this suggestion. To have the whole world applaud him was something he'd considered many a night. But just as he was considering it, his pride came clamoring out of its cave at the back of his head, and he said, "No, thank you. I believe I can win my way on my own skills."

"Ah, but there must be something I can give you," she said. "There has to be something you do not have..." She moved back to the first shoulder. "Oh, I know...I see you watching her."

"Watching who?" said George.

"Don't be coy," said the lady. "You drink in her every move as if it were a fine wine. You desire her. You want to know the taste of her lips, her sweat, yes?"

George shivered. He looked to the side and saw the ladies-in-waiting doing the same to Colette, bending over to whisper into her ears. "That's...none of your concern."

She laughed. It was a high, tinkling sound. "I can give her to you, you know. I can breathe upon her eyes so all she could see would be you, whisper to her arms so they want nothing but your embrace. Would you want such a thing? It would be easy..."

He swallowed. The lady's perfume swallowed his head and made thinking difficult. He still ached from what he'd discovered last night, and the thought of her in his arms was almost too much. But he shook his head. "No."

"No? Why no?"

"Because then she'd be a...a puppet. A doll. It wouldn't be real. We would have just dressed her up as something else."

There was the rustling of fabric, and then the lady was whispering into his other ear. Yet now her voice was softer, and colder and crueler: "But I know whose seed lies still dewy on her cunt. I can *smell* it there."

"God," whispered George. Tears sprang to his eyes, and he shook his head.

"It is not just, is it?" asked the lady. "That he should have her, and enjoy her? Do you not hate him for it? Hate the idea of him gathering her body in his arms?"

"Please, stop."

"I can hurt him for you," said the lady. "Wound him, punish him, all on your behalf. Doesn't he deserve it? You need only say the word, and I can do it with a snap of my fingers."

"No," said George. "I'd...I'd never want such a thing. Stop. Stop it and leave me alone."

The lady sighed as if disappointed, and stood. "Well. If you're sure." Then she laughed gaily and called, "Come, children! Let's proceed."

Colette rejoined George, but she was clearly just as shaken as he; she stared at the backs of her hands, and sometimes trembled as if cold.

"What did they say to you?" he whispered to her.

"Nothing!" said Colette fiercely. "Be quiet." But every once in a while she would shut her eyes as if she wished she were blind.

When they returned to the parlor Silenus and the seneschal were seated by the bay windows, deep in negotiations. "Have we decided upon a solution?" asked the lady, gliding over. The seneschal scurried up, and the lady bent nearly in half to hear his whisper. "Ah," she said. "So what you need is a matter of duplication. Distraction, as you put it. That is simple enough." She stood back up. "Well, a botkine should suffice, shouldn't it? I'm surprised neither of you has thought of it yet."

"I don't know what that is," said Silenus, sheepish.

The lady laughed. "Come out on the porch. It will be an easy task, though messy."

The lady's entourage and the troupe all exited through the French doors. The back porch was even grander than the one at the front. Beyond it was the dark, creaking wood they'd passed through; evidently it surrounded the house, though in places they could see narrow teeth of flame shining through the trees from the numerous bonfires.

The lady instructed the troupe to collect an assortment of material from the forest: a basket of river mud each, a tangle of ash twigs, several ropes of wisteria, pebbles, pinecones, straw, and so on. She assigned each of them an assistant to help, so the task was done fairly quickly. Once these were collected, she said, "Each of you must now build yourself from what you have gathered. Or, rather, what you *think* yourselves to be."

"Can't one of your servants do that for us?" asked Silenus.

"No," she said. "It must be done by the subjects themselves. A botkine, like any art, is mostly suggestion and assumption — the creator suggests, the audience assumes and fills in the rest. It is spontaneous, manipulative, fragile, and very, very subtle, a half-finished canvas to be completed by the onlooker — but it must draw from the self-image, rather than anything else."

Grumbling, the troupe set to work trying to construct copies of themselves from the primitive stuff. Perhaps due to the agreeable quality of the material, it was not hard, to their surprise: George, who had never displayed any capacity for the physical arts, soon had a framework of ash sprigs and wisteria vine standing up before him. He layered the spindly body with leaves and mud, and for its head he used a bag of straw. He was not sure what to give the face, and as he considered it the lady passed by. "Be honest," she said softly. He shivered from her dreadful presence, but then painted on a face he thought quite sad, and lonely, and lost, for this was how he felt. Not for the first time George wondered if he would be better off at home with his grandmother, listening to the sighs of the nearby fields.

Finally the troupe stepped back from their work. (Franny, predict-
ably, was the last to finish.) From a distance their creations seemed
very poor things: leaning, messy sculptures with awkward arms and
bent legs. But then the faraway firelight of the bonfires flickered over
them, and for a second they saw people who looked almost exactly
like themselves. Yet there were some slight differences: Colette's
copy, George noticed, was taller and not quite so muscular, and it
was difficult to tell how dark her skin was. Stanley's did not droop as
much as its creator, and it seemed firmer, younger, and (perhaps it
was George's imagination) it kept glancing at George's copy with an
eager look in its eye. George's own copy was an ugly, rough-looking
thing with bad posture and rather angry eyes. This surprised him;
George thought himself many things, but angry was not one of them.
Franny's copy, strangely enough, looked nothing like her: it was a
thin, pretty young woman with a rather flinty face and smooth red
hair. And next to hers was Silenus's, and perhaps it was because
George had not looked fast enough, but his father's copy was buried
in shadow, and could not be seen; though was its hand reaching up,
as if to grasp Franny's shoulder?

"I...I remember her," whispered Franny behind him. "I remember that girl...It was so long ago."

"You've done very well," said the lady. "These are the perfect
mixture of truth and untruth. I almost wish I had these people as
guests, you know, rather than the real thing. Wasn't that easy?"

"You're sure this will work?" asked Silenus.

"It certainly will, if I am correct in thinking that the agents you
are wishing to fool are not...overly familiar with conventional life,"
she said. "Do I have that right?"

Silenus grudgingly nodded.

"Still playing the same old game," she said. "I suppose chastising
you for being a fool is not part of our bargain. Let's discuss where
you need these distractions to appear." The lady, her seneschal, and
Silenus withdrew to a table at the end of the porch, and after some

conversation the lady nodded and cocked her head. The bonfires fell slightly, as if the house and its property were suddenly distracted, and there was a great amount of rustling and creaking and sighing of leaves from the woods. The troupe turned to look, but due to the low light they could not see their creations any longer. Then the lady let out a breath, and the bonfires rose, and as their firelight crept across the woods they saw the constructs were gone.

"By tomorrow your pursuers should be on the hunt," said the lady. "The botkines will appear at several of the protected areas, just long enough to garner attention, and then they will lead them on a merry chase."

"We'll need transportation to the next spot," said Silenus. "I want to take as much advantage of the situation as we can."

"I will allow the road out from the Founding to lead wherever you wish," she said. "From there, it's your own problem, and your matters are your own to foul or bungle up."

Silenus glowered at her, but the lady leaned back in her chair and stared out at the forest. "Now," she said. "What was that you said about a performance?"

CHAPTER 27

"He has harmed me grievously."

The lady professed she did not care to see the full show. "I have seen it before, and I notice you are missing a position," she said. "I would much rather see an act of my own devising." To George and Colette's dismay this act involved only them, and George felt sure she'd made this selection to torment them. The lady led them back to the parlor, and the dance floor was now clear save for a bulky and ancient-looking piano in the corner. Colette protested when they were told they were expected to perform cold, without any preparation at all. Yet the lady said, "Spontaneity has so much more to do with things than you know, my dear. Spontaneity, luck, and the conviction behind it all. Now go on. It is a very popular piece, it only premiered several months ago. He will play, and you will dance as the music moves you. Improvise your dance, invent everything as you go along."

George sat down at the piano and looked at the music. It was called *Le Gibet*, a movement from a larger work by someone he'd never heard of, a Maurice Ravel. He knew right away that it was like nothing he'd ever played before: it was deceptively simple, yet he saw that below its placid surface it was tortuously difficult (though not as difficult as the other two movements of the piece, which he briefly peeked and paled at).

Beyond Colette the lady's servants were pouring the whisky Silenus had brought them. It glowed in the fairies' little glasses and made their masks light up like lamps. Colette and George shared a long, nervous look before he started playing. Though both of them were terrified, George could not help but exult in this moment of attention. This was the one thing he'd wanted more than anything—to perform with her in front of a glamorous audience. Yet he had never thought it could be like this: the audience was terrifying, the music intimidating, and Colette seemed further beyond his grasp than ever.

George took a breath, and started playing. He almost stopped at the first sound of the piano. It had a haunting, echoing quality, though perhaps that was just the music itself, which was a soft, quiet, eerie piece reminiscent of church bells and lonely, snow-swept passageways. Colette did not dance at first, but stood swaying with her head bowed, as if she were being gently touched by the wind. And then, very slowly, her movements grew, and she began to dance across the floor.

He had never seen her dance in such a manner. He knew she was a trained ballerina, that'd always been obvious, and while he'd always adored her that same adoration had blinkered him to her talent, which was evidently enormous. For one moment the two of them were involved in a brief, perfect execution, two souls dancing together through music, and George thought it so beautiful and saddening that each note was like a razor.

They finished as they had started: he playing the same soft, repeating notes, and she gently drifting back and forth until she was finally still. A collective sigh ran through the host when they finished. The lady cleared her throat and said, "Good. That was very good. Thank you for that. It was a perfect end to the evening."

Colette quickly left the stage without looking back. The lady watched her go. "My, my," she said. "Apparently she was touched just as we were."

The troupe was invited to the feast, but they all turned down the invitation; eels, roast quetzal, and cocktails made from the poison glands of albino sea snakes did not sound particularly inviting to them. Instead they chose to retreat to their rooms for the night.

Stanley scribbled something out as they climbed the stairs. He showed his blackboard to them: DO NOT SPEAK. LADY HAS WATCHERS.

"You saw them?" asked Silenus quietly.

Stanley erased it, then wrote: DID NOT SEE. BUT I KNOW.

"Then we shouldn't see each other for the rest of the night," said Silenus. "We'll leave early in the morning, as early as we can." He nodded at George, and placed his hand on his shoulder. "Get some real sleep tonight, will you?"

George managed a nod. Then his father turned and entered his room. George watched him go, feeling ill. As he did, he noticed Stanley was watching him, and his demeanor seemed similar to George's own: his face was strained, and his cheeks and brow looked gaunter than ever. And yet the warmth was still there behind Stanley's eyes, that sympathetic quality that made you feel like Stanley knew all your troubles and would forgive everything you did, and for one moment George wanted to go to him and tell him everything: about Colette, and what Silenus had been doing with her, and most of all the truth of their travels and how they had actually betrayed their purpose. But then George remembered that night on the rooftop outside Chicago, and he felt embarrassed and uncomfortable, and he turned and walked into his room, alone.

The room was sumptuous and came with a set of luxurious night-gowns and other lounge wear. For the first time since February he was treated to running hot water, though George was too preoccupied to enjoy it. When he finished his bath he waited half an hour.

Then he slipped out of his room to prowl the halls for the second night in a row.

He found Colette's door and knocked. She opened the door, surprised. "George?"

He held a finger to his lips and walked in. She stared at him and shut the door after him. "What are you doing here?" she asked. "You can't be roaming around like this! What would happen if these crazy fucking people caught you?"

"I had to come and tell you something," he said.

"Well for Christ's sake, what is it?"

He licked his lips, took a breath, and said, "I-I wanted to tell you that I know."

"Know?" she asked. "Know what?"

"I know what Harry's... I know what he's been making you do, Colette."

Her eyes narrowed. "Making me do? What do you mean?"

"I know he's been... seeing you. M-making you do things, in exchange for, for keeping you on. And I wanted to let you know that I'm going to help you, Colette. I'm going to figure out a way to make him stop."

She was still for a moment. "Oh, Jesus," she said, and sat down on the bed.

"Don't worry," he said earnestly. "I'll make sure you never get hurt. I'll make everything right."

"George..."

"I'll figure something out, tell someone, and we can —"

"Will you shut up for once!" said Colette.

George fell silent, shocked. This was a far cry from the shame and gratitude he'd been expecting.

"Why do you have to be this way, George?" she asked. "Why do you have to get involved in things that don't concern you? I know you wanted something with me, but I'm not... not *interested* in that, and I thought I'd made that clear."

"He's using you," insisted George. "He's got you tricked, some-how, like he's got everyone tricked—"

"Tricked?" she said. "Tricked! What do you think I am, George? Some weakling who needs to hang on to someone powerful? Some foolish little girl getting conned by an older man? Is that really what you think of me?"

George was quiet. He realized with a sinking heart that this was exactly what he'd thought.

"Christ," she said, and shook her head. "He never came to me. He never forced me into doing anything. I came to *him*, George."

He was so shocked by this he could not breathe, but his heart was beating out a frantic tattoo. "What?" he said.

"I came to him. It was my choice. I was never tricked. I *wanted* to. Because I…I like him. I *like* Harry, George. Can you understand that?"

"You don't really. Do you? You couldn't…"

"I wouldn't expect you to understand," she said. "He's your father, you can't imagine how he seems to others. But I…I admired him from the day I met him." She crossed her arms and held herself, fingers lightly resting on her rib cage. He wondered then if perhaps she was imagining some past embrace or touch, and was sickened by the idea.

"It's a…it's just a ruse, a trick, Colette. Can't you see?" he asked.

"No," she said firmly. "It's not me who's not seeing things. You're just seeing what you want to." She stood up. "I want you to leave, George. I don't want to talk to you about this ever again. This is enough. Stop bothering me. We're done. All right?"

He tried to think of something to say. A thousand poetic profes-sions came rushing to his head, any of which should break through to her, he thought. But whenever he glanced up and saw her cold gaze, he knew that in truth each of them was reckless and hollow, no more than dust and ash in his mouth.

"All right," he said. She opened the door for him, and he shuffled out into the hall.

*   *   *

George did not want to return to his room, so instead he sat on a bench in the hall. From somewhere in the house there was the sound of music and laughter, but it seemed very far away to him. He simply sat in the dark, alone in this queer and frightening place, and wondered if he had only imagined that moment on the dance floor, when he'd felt as if they were working in perfect unity.

"I know you," said a voice over his shoulder.

He leaped up in fright and turned to find Franny standing beside the bench in her nightgown. "Franny?" he gasped. "What are you doing up?"

She cocked her head. There was an unsettling brightness to her eyes. "What was that you called me?" she asked.

"What? What do you mean? Your name?"

"Yes."

"Well. It's Franny." George frowned at her. Franny always behaved strangely, but this time it was different: her eyes did not constantly wander, and her voice had lost its quavering dreaminess.

"Franny..." she said quietly. "Is that so?"

"What's wrong? Why are you up?"

"You're his son, aren't you?" she said. "The little boy who came to find him. I remember that."

"Well... I remember meeting you, too. Are you all right?"

"I'm fine," she said. "For the first time in a long, long while, I'm fine." She stared around at the huge dark hall. "It is the strangest thing. For so long I thought I was dreaming, and that the real world around me was just an illusion. But now that I'm here, in this dreamy place, everything seems more real than ever."

"So... you're feeling better?"

"Better? No. No, I'm not sure I'd say *better*. But I am *feeling*, for once." She shook her head. "It doesn't matter. Go back to bed, boy. Go back, and in the morning everything will be fine." Then she turned and padded down the hallway. She'd even shed her loopy, weaving way of walking.

He thought about taking her advice, but her behavior was so queer that he couldn't help but follow her. When he got to the staircase he stood at the top and listened to her footsteps as she walked down. He followed her down, and after several turns and hallways and yet another staircase George realized she was walking toward the sound of the feast.

She went to the same door from earlier, when he'd peeked through at the dining hall. Franny walked in, and George waited before creeping up and peering after. The dining hall was in a similar state as before: every platter had been ravaged, wineglasses had been overturned, and the large punch bowl in the center of the table was cracked and dribbling something purple and thick. Fairies were slouched in their chairs or lay passed out on the ground, moaning or muttering in their sleep, yet even in these disheveled states they still looked flawless and graceful.

Only a few of the revelers were awake: the lady and her entourage. They were all lounging in their chairs as they looked at a solitary figure standing before them. George did not have to look very closely to guess it was Franny.

"... Would I ever want from you?" the lady was saying.

"Silenus," said Franny. "I can give him to you."

"Give him to me?" said the lady. She cocked her head. "As strange as that sounds, and as much as I'd like that, I'm afraid it's impossible. Neither I nor my agents are allowed to harm Silenus. Didn't you hear the agreement we made?"

"I heard," said Franny. "You promised you would never harm him as a reprisal for what happened to your mother. But you wouldn't be harming him on *your* behalf."

"No?"

"No. It would be on mine."

"Yours? Why would you want him harmed?" said the lady. "You're a member of his traveling company, aren't you?"

"No," said Franny. "I am not. Not *me*."

"You aren't? What do you mean?"

"He has harmed me," said Franny. "He has harmed me grievously."

"Harmed you? How?"

Franny was silent. When she spoke, her voice shook. "Do you not recognize me, my lady?"

Ofelia was quiet. Then she sat up very, very slowly. "Are...are you saying you're..."

Franny nodded.

For the first time since their arrival, Ofelia's serene superiority broke. She raised a hand to her masked face and shook her head in shock. "Oh...my *God*," said the lady. "I...I *thought* I recognized you, when I first saw you. And when you made your botkine, I was almost sure it looked like someone I knew. But it was so *long* ago, even for this place..."

"Yes," said Franny. "It's been so, so long."

"I barely remember you. If what you are suggesting is true, then... well. I can understand why you would wish him ill." The lady considered it. "What would you have me do to him?"

"I want him to suffer, just as I have," said Franny. "I want him imprisoned or crazed, I want him to spend decades of his life in the same fog and mist that I've been lost in. I want him to know what it is that he's done to me, how he has cursed me, ruined me. I just want him to know. I want him to know my pain. That is all I want."

Ofelia was very still upon her throne. Her pale face tipped back and forth as she considered it. Then she nodded. "All right," she said. "He shall know your pain. I've already promised that I would help him obtain the next piece of his silly little song, and that is a bargain that must be fulfilled. But after that I will gladly give you what you wish."

"Thank you," said Franny. "Thank you so much."

"Don't thank me," said the lady. "You have done me many boons already."

Franny turned to leave. George crept away from the door and hid behind one of the many statues in the house and watched her walk by. He saw her cheeks were coated in tears, and yet once she dried them she did not look sad at all.

After he returned to his room, George sat on his bed, thinking. He was not sure what he had just witnessed. He'd never known Franny to hold a grudge against anyone. Except, he now recalled, she had seemed angry with Silenus once she'd found out about George. And yet what he'd just seen seemed to reference an older, much more horrifying crime.

He wondered what he should do. He knew he should tell his father; or, more specifically, he should *want* to tell him. Yet he had come to learn many things about his father recently, very few of them pleasant. He had allowed Kingsley to grow crazed. He had wronged Ofelia, and Franny, and Colette (as George resolutely insisted to himself), and he had also lied to the entire troupe. For years, they had not been maintaining the boundaries between the light and the dark. If anything, they had allowed those boundaries to collapse. Who knew what else he was keeping from everyone?

George knew that in spite of all this he should want to tell his father. It was what a son should do, help his father. Yet in retrospect Silenus had never behaved much like a father at all. He had shown George little love, and had even arranged to have his child humiliated. He was forever distant, and strange, and often cruel. George realized now that out of everyone who'd ever held him back and barred him from success, Silenus was the one who had always been the greatest obstacle, the greatest disappointment, and George discovered he felt hate in his heart for this man. Silenus had everything George had ever wanted, and yet he refused George even the slightest access.

No, George decided. He would not tell him. He told himself it was a matter of responsibility: he could not allow Harry to continue running the troupe like this. There was too much at stake. Once the lady imprisoned Harry (the thought gave him chills, but his conviction held firm) he would tell the troupe what they'd been doing, *really* been doing, and then...

And then the song would still need to be collected and performed, performed *rightly*, but, he realized, the only one who could do that was George himself. Besides Harry, he was the only other who could bear the First Song.

It had all gone on too long, he decided miserably. Someone needed to put right what had gone awry. He would have to take his father's place. It would be a monumental task, but it was one that had to be done. And maybe he would not have to do it alone.

It would be a great performance, would it not, to sing the song of eternity? There was no greater piece to play. And George had always wanted to dominate the theater. Yet he felt no joy at the idea, only terror.

He lay down on his bed and shut his eyes. He was justified, he told himself. This was warranted. And though he would not admit it to himself, all he saw in the dark was that image of Colette, hands placed upon her rib cage, smiling slightly as she fondly remembered some past moment with his father.

CHAPTER 28

The Little Black Island

George slept very lightly, and awoke long before anyone else. He dressed and wandered down to the front foyer to wait for the rest of the troupe. The lady's house mirrored his mood: every room was large and empty, and there never seemed to be enough light.

The remainder of the troupe came rumbling down the stairs much sooner than George expected, Silenus charging behind them like a shepherd. He was juggling his hat and his coat, and he kept shouting, "It doesn't matter! Forget about it! We're not making any stops, we've only got to move!"

"But where are we moving to? I thought we'd practically already be at one of the places!" said Colette. She, too, was half-dressed. Apparently Silenus had roused them well before they'd anticipated.

"There are two pieces of the song we've had our eye on," said Silenus. "We're getting dropped off at one, and then we're going to have to run like hell to get to the other. We have to take as much advantage of this opening as we can." He stopped, spotting George. "Oh, there you are. I thought I'd have to chase you down." He seemed pleased to find he was packed and ready, and said, "Well, at least someone's on task today. Thank you, my boy."

George nodded. Silenus threw his arm around him and shouted, "Now step lively! The lady's already prepared the way for us, but that's no excuse to drag your heels."

As they hurried out the front door George glanced back to look at Franny. As usual, she was ensconced to the nose in her drab coats and fraying scarves. All that was visible were her eyes. But rather than dazed they were extraordinarily sharp, and seemed to gleam with some anguish George could not name.

The lady and her entourage were waiting at the start of the path through the wood. Rather than white, she was now dressed in a deep cherry red, complete with a red parasol. Her mask was still white, and with it fixed atop her red figure she made George think of an insect whose color warned predators not to approach.

"Ah," said the lady. "There you are. We've been waiting. I see you all have put your usual amount of thought into your dress."

"The path is ready?" asked Silenus. "Everything is set?"

"I have moved the path, yes," said the lady. "For the moment, it ends in a set of woods outside of what is referred to as Lake Logehrin, right at the start of its dam. It will be night there now. If your conclusions are correct—and I should think they are, being as my mother provided the instruments that produced them—your little song rests in a dell in the center of a very small island just off the coast of where you will arrive."

"Excellent," said Silenus. "Then I must thank you, my lady, for all the help you have given us." Once more, he bowed. "I trust you know that this will be the last time that I trouble you."

"I would think so, player," said the lady. "Should we see each other again, it may not be nearly as amicable as this has been."

Silenus glanced up at the lady. Like all fairies, she was nearly inscrutable behind her white mask. Then he bowed once more and led them down the path.

George was not sure when the black wood receded. He never saw it dwindle away, nor did he notice the path beneath his feet change.

What alerted him was the change in the air: in the wood around the Founding it had smelled of damp and moldering leaves, and everything had been still and close, yet as they walked he began to smell pine and moisture. After a while they all looked around themselves and saw they were now in an isolated glen in a pine forest, and they saw no stone path behind them, or dark wood, or Queen Anne home or bonfires.

"Thank God that's fucking over," said Silenus. "Those people give me the fucking creeps. I can't stand not knowing if they're looking at me or not."

"Where are we?" asked George.

"Northern New York, west of Lake Champlain, on the south side of Logehrin." Silenus looked up at the sky. "Now. Where do we need to go?"

Stanley took out a small compass and consulted it, then pointed ahead.

"All right," said Silenus. "Let's hurry now. Stanley and I will collect this one bit of the song, and then we'll hightail it to Plattsburgh and catch a train to the next. Should be quick and simple. All right?"

No one answered as they charged through the forest. Soon they saw the lake ahead, wide and flat and sparkling with moonlight, except the west side ended not in a shore but in a long, smooth arc of gray. It was the dam, George guessed. To the east the river rose into the high hills, and to the west, on the other side of the dam, the landscape descended into a rolling valley. Evidently the valley had once been filled with water, but due to the dam the river was but a trickle down below. Down the southern shore at the base of the dam there was a shining string of railroad track, but it looked abandoned. And there ahead of them on the edge of this artificial lake was a small black spot, just a tiny scrap of island that carried the burden of three huge pines that stretched up into the sky.

Then George heard something, and he froze: there was a moan on the wind, terribly deep and resonant. He had seen the First Song's performance so many times that he knew it by heart, and while this seemed *similar*—a note the mind could hardly recognize, and no instrument or voice could ever mimic—it was something he'd never heard before. He realized that what he was hearing was a part of the song that must have lain undiscovered for years and years, singing of a part of the world that had long been lost.

He stared at the island. He was not sure how he knew it, but he immediately sensed a heaviness there, as if there was an additional hidden burden that little island was carrying.

"There it is," said Silenus hoarsely. "I can almost see it. Jesus Christ, we're so close." There was a desperation in his voice that George had heard only once before, in the graveyard when his confessions had come trickling out. But Stanley did not seem anything so pleased. He rubbed the side of his head as he stared at the island, and gave a deep, uncertain sigh.

Silenus turned and glanced along the shore. He found a particularly large, flat boulder and stood before it. He turned around and walked back and forth in front of it several times, apparently completing some dance with his back to the stone. Then he stopped in the middle of one step, turned around, and put his hand on the knob of the door in the stone.

The rest of the troupe blinked. There in the boulder was the huge black door they saw so frequently in their hotels. Like every time before, it had appeared without anyone noticing.

"I didn't know it could show up out here," said Colette as she watched Silenus enter.

Stanley wrote: IT GOES WHERE IT IS NEEDED. IF THE NEED IS GREAT ENOUGH.

Silenus came out of his office dragging the big black steamer trunk. "Hurry!" he cried to Stanley, and Stanley sprinted over to help.

George, Franny, and Colette watched as Silenus and Stanley waded out into the cold waters of the lake and trudged up the muddy shores of the little island. They stooped down low and soon were indistinct from the rest of its terrain.

"There they go," said Franny. "The cowards."

"Cowards?" said Colette. "What do you mean?"

"I mean they are cowards, the both of them," she said.

"How?"

"How could they be anything else?" said Franny. "They've spent their whole lives with what is most dear to them hanging just before their faces, and yet they can't allow themselves to embrace it. Neither man can allow themselves to be happy for a moment, not with all that darkness hanging below. What silly creatures they are."

"I've never heard you talk this way," said Colette.

"I expect you'll soon be hearing a lot of things you haven't before," she said.

George felt a sudden pulse in the air. The moan shivered through the sky again, and he quavered a bit, knees almost buckling. He had never been this close to the song when it was harvested, excepting the one time he'd accidentally taken it on himself. He realized he was hearing voices everywhere, and seeing patterns in everything: the stars and the trees and the rocks on the ground all seemed to be spelling something out, or aligning to form strata that all swirled around that little black island.

"They're close to it," he gasped. "I think...I think they've almost got it."

"Goody for them," said Franny sourly. "Now will they be happy? Now will they rest? I think not."

"What is wrong with you?" asked Colette.

"Who are you to be so impertinent, girl?" said Franny. "Do you know how long I've traveled with them? How much I've seen? If you knew what I knew, and what a torture the very sight of you is to me, you'd hold your tongue."

Colette looked to George, scandalized by this abuse, but George could not pay attention: the piece of the song within him sensed the connection taking place mere yards ahead, and it ached to join. For the first time, George began to realize just how much of the song Silenus and Stanley carried with them. The sense of momentum emanating from that island, of gravity and sheer *pull*, was so overwhelming he could barely stand.

The water rippled, and everything grew cold. It felt as though the stars halted in the sky and the wind died. Somewhere countless voices were moaning, and then they rose up to an awesome and terrible pitch, and George was as small and lost among those voices as a reed among the waves of the stormy ocean…

Then it stopped, just as abruptly as it'd started. A horrible, strangled cry rose from the island, but it was quickly cut off.

"What was that?" asked Colette. "Are they all right?"

Even Franny stayed quiet, so George guessed she did not know either. "I believe," she said softly, "that I will sit down now." She walked away and sat below a tree on the edge of the shore.

For a long while there was nothing from the island. Then George saw movement. At first he thought it was only one person, yet then there was a splashing and he saw both men were there, Silenus leading the way with one hand on the trunk, and Stanley behind holding up the other end. Yet Stanley could hardly stand: he was bent over, and he sometimes had to use his free hand to support himself.

They dragged themselves up to the shore and set the trunk down. Stanley almost collapsed immediately, but stopped himself and sat on the ground with his back against the trunk. Silenus sat on the trunk itself, took several deep breaths, and took out a cigar and lit it.

"What happened out there?" asked Colette. "Are you hurt?"

Silenus cleared his throat. "We are fine," he said, but Stanley shook slightly and put his face in his hands.

"You don't look fine," said George.

"That's because our research was correct," Silenus said. "It was… an extremely large piece of the song."

George stared at the trunk. What could be in there? he thought.

The trunk looked no different, nor did it appear special in any way. Could they have even *more* of the First Song in there? And how did they get it in and out? After all this time, he still was not sure.

"Where is Franny?" asked Silenus.

"She's over there," said Colette, and she gestured. "She's acting very strange. I've never heard her talk that way."

"Talk what way?" said Silenus.

"Well...she said some very nasty things about you both, and me. But more than that, she sounded more alert than I'd ever heard her."

Silenus frowned and began to walk over to her. "Franny!" he called. "Come on down here. We need to get moving."

Franny did not answer. George could hardly see her in the shadow of the tree.

"Franny!" said Silenus. "Are you all right? Are you hurt, my dear?"

"Yes," said Franny's voice. "Yes. I am hurt."

"You are? What happened?"

All at once there was the sound of laughter from the wood. It did not seem to come from one place, but rather from all around them, as if the forest were full of laughing people. Everyone jumped up and looked about, even Stanley.

"What the hell is going on?" said Colette.

"I don't know," said Silenus.

Then one by one they begin to appear: pale white faces, hanging in the darkness of the forest, perfect and blank and eyeless. They hovered in the gaps between the trees, blinking into existence like lamps. And one appeared very nearby, but it was much taller than all the others, and at the corners of its eyes were twin streams of perfect blue tears.

"What is this?" said Silenus.

Stanley rose and walked behind Colette and George, and put a hand on either one's shoulder. He pulled them back, wary, ready to jump in front if need be.

The fairies began to emerge from the wood, and George immediately felt a terrible fear at the very sight of them. They were such tall, foreign creatures, not nearly as graceful as they'd seemed back at the Founding. The last to emerge was the one nearby, and when it did they saw it was the lady, still dressed in blood red, but now she seemed taller and more spindly than ever, and as she walked she swayed back and forth.

"Ofelia?" said Silenus. "What are you doing here? I thought our agreement was done."

"It was," said the lady, laughing. "It is."

"Then what are you doing here? The host never leaves the Founding anymore."

"There are exceptions to every rule," said the lady. She towered over Silenus, staring down at him. "And I would make one in this case. I would be a poor daughter, would I not, if I did not come to see justice meted out on my mother's killer?"

Silenus stared at her, shocked. "But you can't. We had an agreement."

"Yes, that's true," said the lady. "We did. I agreed I would never harm you out of hate for what you did to my mother. But there is another whose harm you have to answer for."

"Whose?" he asked.

"Mine," said a faint voice.

They all turned, though George turned more slowly than the rest. Franny stood up underneath the tree, a little lumpy doll dragging itself to its feet.

"Franny?" said Silenus. "You? Why would you do this?"

"No," she said. She began to walk forward.

"What? No? What do you mean? It's not you?"

"Not no to that," said Franny. She began walking down to him. "No to that name. You know that is not who I am. That is *not* my name."

Silenus was quiet. Then a great horror began to creep into his face. "No. No, it can't be…"

"Yes," said Franny. "You know me, Bill. Of course you know me."

To George's shock, Silenus fell to his knees. And then Silenus, who had always been so distant and controlling, nearly began to weep. "My God," he said. "My God, is it really you?"

"Yes," she said. She stood between him and the lady. "It's always been me. A very small part of me has always been trapped down here, buried under all this waking death. Buried by you, Bill. But I've always been here. Watching."

Tears started flowing down Silenus's cheeks. "Oh, my God," he whispered. "Annie? Annie, can it really be you?"

Though it was but a whisper, to George the name was like a scream. It blared and echoed in his ears, and his mouth dropped open and he almost fell to the ground.

"What's she talking about?" said Colette. "What is wrong with her?"

"Jesus," said George faintly. "Jesus Christ, that's who she is. She's his wife. Franny is his wife."

CHAPTER 29

Anne Marie Sillenes

"What?" said Colette. "What the hell are you talking about, George?"

"He's right," said Franny. "Anne...Anne Sillenes. It's so strange to say that name. I had almost forgotten it. It died with me, so long ago. Franny Beatty was a name you chose for me, Bill, picked at random out of the paper. But my real one's always remained, echoing in the many empty places in my skull."

"But how can this be?" Silenus said. "I haven't spoken to you for half a century, my dear...I thought you were lost. How can you have come back to me now?"

"I haven't come back to you, Bill," said Franny, or perhaps it should have been Anne. "I was just *reminded*. This all started when you took me to the fairies, don't you remember? It was an arrangement we made, when we first learned about the cancer. About the thing eating me up, behind my eyes."

"It was the first of three visits," said Ofelia. "You carried her to my mother after she'd passed, still streaked with grave dirt. You, a bereaved husband, with this poor, pale little thing with the pretty red hair in your arms. You sobbed like a child when you brought her, did you not? And my mother took pity on you, and told you of a way, of symbols and etchings that can bring animation to the body."

"Yes," said Anne. She raised one hand and grasped her sleeve and pulled it back, displaying the countless black markings that wrapped around her arm like second skin. "You brought me back, Bill. Just like we'd discussed."

"My God, my dear," said Silenus. "I...I can't believe it! I thought it hadn't worked! When you came back, at first you were the same but...but then you changed."

"That was because it *didn't* work," she said. "I was *not* back! The sleep took me, that waking death. I was so tired...Every second was an hour, every year a lifetime. My memories faded, and I could hardly remember who I was. Yet some part of me stayed alive, trapped behind miles of thick glass, watching the years slip before me. And when you brought me back to that house, it was like all the years were sloughed off my back, and I remembered...I remembered everything. Do you know what that was like, Bill? Can you have any idea what it feels like, to fall outside of time and shamble on, no more than a dazed, empty vessel?"

"No," said Harry. "No, no, I couldn't know what it was like for you."

"You knew," said Anne. "You knew what it would be like. And yet you let me live on."

"I had to!" said Silenus. "I had no choice, I couldn't bear to lose you! You were my darling, Annie, my everything! With you beside me everything made sense, and when you were gone..."

"When I was gone, you cursed me with this," said Anne. "With this waking hell. You should have let me go! You should have killed me when you saw it hadn't worked!"

"Don't you think I tried?" cried Silenus. "But I'd lost you once, and then I had this...this puppet of a person, and while it *wasn't* you it looked and sounded and smelled exactly *like* you. I couldn't *kill* it! Could anyone?"

"Oh, Jesus..." whispered Colette.

"You would have if you loved me," said Anne. "You should have let me *rest*, Bill. You should have let me go."

"I couldn't," he said. "Not again. I wasn't strong enough."

"And instead you had what?" she asked. "You would keep some horrible memento of me staggering on behind you, while you lived your life and led the troupe on, and forgot about me?"

"Never," said Silenus. "I never forgot about you."

"Then explain them!" said Anne, and she pointed at George and Colette. "One you fathered upon some poor farm girl, and the other, hardly more than a child, you've enjoyed as you once did me!"

Colette's hands flew to her face in shock, and she hid her eyes. Stanley shook his head and his grip grew tighter on George's shoulder.

"It isn't true," said Silenus.

"Have you become a liar now?" shouted Anne. "I've *seen* the way you talk to her, the way you touch one another. You did it right in front of me, Bill! As if I weren't even there!"

"But to me, you weren't..." said Silenus. "It was like you were a stranger. As the years went by, you became someone else."

"So you admit it. You did move on to other loves, and forgot me, left me watching. It is true?"

Silenus looked back at the three of them. His glance moved from face to face, and he seemed to come to a decision about something. He lowered his head and nodded. "It is."

"Yes," she hissed. "You left me to rot in the prison of my own body."

"No!" he said. "That wasn't it! You don't know what I've done for you, Annie! When you died, I changed the very nature of the troupe! I started to put all of our efforts into finding the remains of the song! I thought if I did that, I could...I could figure out why such a thing could be allowed to happen, or even call the Creator back. Don't you understand what an enormous victory that would be? That was why

I kept you on. It could fix you, fix me, fix everything! And I still can, Annie!" he said. "I can make it come back, and ask it to fix all of this!"

"Oh, Bill!" she cried. "As if the world were a simple machine that had thrown a few gears! How foolish can you be?"

"I can make it work, Annie! I just need a little more time."

"You're still the same person after all these years, no matter what name you use," she said, and shook her head. "You still think you can find a solution to anything. I wish we had realized we got all the time we could, and cherished it."

"I did cherish it," said Silenus. He was nearly sobbing now. "I did."

She reached out to touch the side of his face. He shut his eyes and leaned into her hand, letting her fingers graze his temple, his cheek. "So did I," she said softly. "But I can't forget what you put me through, or how you've lived before my very eyes." Then she stepped back to stand beside the lady.

"Please don't go," said Silenus. "Please don't leave me again."

"I didn't leave you," she said. "I was taken from you, Bill. And you should have moved on. Look at what's become of us—we can hardly recognize each other after what you allowed to happen."

"But I can save you, Annie!" said Silenus. "I can save everyone, everything, I promise!"

"I know that reasoning is why you did what you did," said Annie. "And that's why I didn't ask for your death. But you have to pay, Bill. You have to understand what you did to me. You have to pay."

The lady asked, "Are you finished with him?"

Annie looked at Silenus longingly, then nodded. "I am."

"Good," said the lady. She looked to the fairies behind her, and said, "Beat him. Then cut his throat."

Annie blinked in shock, and cried, "What?"

"No!" shouted George.

"I never said to kill him!" said Annie. "That was never the agreement!"

The lady looked down at her, yet as always it was impossible to tell what she was thinking. "Oh, did we? What was it we agreed on, exactly?"

"He was supposed to suffer, but not die! He was supposed to know what this felt like!"

The lady extended one long finger. It twitched back and forth chidingly, and she said, "No, that was not what we agreed. We agreed that he would know your pain."

"My what?" said Anne, but then two pale faces emerged from the darkness behind her. The fairies each grasped an arm, and one grabbed a fistful of her hair and wrenched her head back. Anne screamed in pain and rage, but the fairies easily held her. Though the symbols on her skin made her hugely strong, apparently this accounted for nothing against their makers.

"And your pain is a highly variable thing, is it not?" said the lady. "Why, if we were to beat you, we would have permission to beat him as well, wouldn't we? And if we were to cut your throat…"

"You whore!" cried Silenus, rising to his feet.

Yet before he could do anything, the lady's mocking finger turned to him. She tutted. "I would not use such language now, player. Those you care for now depend on my whims. Don't they?"

Silenus looked back at George and the others.

"Don't they?" she said again, menacingly.

"Yes," he said.

"Yes," she said. Then, to her servants, "Take this measly little dead thing away and put it out of its misery somewhere. There should do." She pointed west to the base of the dam, next to the old railroad track, and with the gesture a grove of trees there bent aside to reveal a rusting train car. "You won't die at our hands, my dear, I know that. The symbols my mother gave you make killing you terribly difficult, even for us. But you are not in my house anymore. And without that, why, I think you'll soon forget everything again, won't you? And you'll go back to being a lost little dead thing, just like before…"

"No!" cried Franny. "Not that! Not that!"

Then came Silenus's voice, surprisingly calm and soft: "Ofelia," he said. "Ofelia, please."

The lady's head snapped around to look at him, and the trees shot up straight, as if there had been strings holding them back and they'd all been suddenly cut. She stood as still as a statue, watching him with her blank eyes.

"I did not kill Titania, Ofelia," he said. "You know that. She died while fulfilling her bargain, while collecting the instruments to help us detect the song. She *helped* me, I would have never hurt her."

"She died," said Ofelia softly, "because of a story you told her. A lie you put in her heart."

"I did not lie."

"You did," said the lady. "You put something in her that drove her mad. You gave her *hope*, singer, where there should have been none."

"That hope was true," said Silenus. "I have learned that. I wish now that I had listened to what I'd learned more often."

"Then you are as worthless as your trite little performances," said the queen. She nodded, and the two fairies began to drag Anne back into the darkness of the forest. She tried to scream, but one of them struck her on the side of the head, and the sound of the impact was so loud everyone paled to hear it. Then she hung limp in their arms and they were gone.

"In our revelries we have feasted upon many things," said the lady. "Many strange animals, many exotic wines. And in our time we have gone beyond mere beasts. We have eaten heroes, and saints, and madmen, and several who were rumored to be gods. Yet I can think of no sweeter meat, no finer taste, than that of revenge. And tonight, once you are dead and spitted for us, I will know that taste. How does it feel to know that, singer?"

Silenus stared at where Anne had stood, his face ash-gray. Then he weakly said, "It feels like every other day, really." With great effort, he collected himself. "What's to happen to my compatriots?"

"I will not harm them."

"Do you swear it?"

She did not nod or shake her head. Instead she cocked it to the side, like a snake fascinated by its prey, and said nothing.

"Swear it, damn you!"

She shrugged. "Fine. I swear I will not harm them."

"All right," said Silenus. He swallowed and nodded. "If I am to die, then I suppose I will die. But may I make one last request, as one imbiber to another?"

"A request?"

"There's a bottle of wine I have, a vintage that was popular in my home," he said. "It is no great wine, it's a peasant's drink. But it's one I would like to taste again in my last moments."

The lady nodded her head back and forth as she thought about it. "You must understand how much this sounds like treachery."

"I do. And I'm willing to let you inspect the bottle, or whatever you would wish."

The lady considered it, and sighed. "I suppose I can understand such a last wish. Even from a thing as hateful as you. Bring me the bottle."

Silenus nodded and walked to the steamer trunk. He undid one clasp, and the other, and George braced himself, expecting something great to happen, some explosion or trickery, or perhaps the First Song itself would pour out and come to their aid...

But it did not. When the lid creaked open he saw there was no song inside, and no light. Only several rows of glass bottles, each filled with some liquor or tincture or another. George was so surprised he cried out in dismay, "What are those?"

Silenus looked up at him. "They are restoratives, mostly. What did you think would be in here?" He selected a bottle with a particularly fine cork and opened it. He walked over to the lady, proffering the open bottle, and her seneschal walked forward and took it.

The seneschal swirled the wine around a bit, sniffed it, and took a sip.

"It's claret," he said. "Not a particularly good one, either."

"As I told you," said Silenus.

"Let me see that," said the lady. She took the bottle and did the same, tasting a very tiny drop. "You are right," she said. "I didn't know you have such poor taste in wine."

Silenus took it back, returned to his trunk, and took out a goblet.

"No," said the lady suddenly.

He turned to her. "No?"

"No. Not your goblet. I cannot even trust your glassware, singer. We will give you one of ours." She gestured, and a fairy stepped out of the wood with a small, ornate crystal glass.

Silenus took it, turning it over, and said, "Very fine work, this. If you wish." Then he carelessly tossed his goblet over his shoulder. It broke on the rocky shore.

The lady stared at the broken glass, uncertain. Then she said, "Pour it so that we can see. I'm willing to treat you to this last luxury, but if I catch the slightest whiff of your tricks..."

"I have no tricks left," said Silenus. "I know I will die today."

He shut the trunk and sat down on the top. He was so close now that George could not bear the shame. "I'm so sorry, Harry!" he shouted.

Silenus looked at him with a questioning eyebrow.

"I...I knew what she was going to do," he said. "Anne, or Franny, I mean. I thought...I didn't trust how you were running the troupe, and I thought...I thought I hated you. I did. I'm so sorry, Father. I would've never been quiet if I'd known it could be like this. I'm so sorry."

Silenus nodded as if he was only slightly disappointed. "Well. It isn't your fault, kid. I did nothing to earn your trust or love. I find myself wishing for many things right now, but chief among them is that I'd treated you better." His eye moved to Colette. "And I'm sorry, Lettie. I never meant to hurt you."

"She was right there," said Colette. "Right there all along, and you still let me come to you?"

"I was weak," he said. "I'd not known a woman's touch in many years. You were my first love, after her. I'm sorry. I'm sorry for all of you. I only hope you all get out of this."

Then Colette, who rarely showed any emotion besides frustration or cold satisfaction, whimpered and burst into tears. Even in this moment of deep distress, George was surprised to see her cry.

"There, there," said Silenus. He put down the crystal glass and reached toward her. She extended a hand, but before they could touch the seneschal angrily cleared his throat.

"Will you not let a man comfort a grieving woman, Ofelia?" Silenus said.

"This is getting very much out of hand," said the lady, irritated. She shook a little, and said, "You may kiss her hand, but no more."

Silenus nodded, and leaned over. Before he kissed her hand he breathed in deep, taking in her scent, and looked up her arm with eyes both fond and proud. "You gave me a quiet among lifetimes of war," he said. "If anything means anything, that does." With the barest touch of his lips he kissed one knuckle of her hand, and sat up straight. He moved the bottle of wine to the hand with the cork in it, holding the cork with his index finger and thumb and the neck of the bottle with the other three fingers, and picked up his crystal glass with his free hand. Just before he poured, he glanced up at Stanley. "You know what to do, don't you?" he said.

If Stanley knew he made no sign. His fingers were digging into George's shoulder, yet George could not feel anything but a kindred sense of sympathy: they were about to lose their leader, their father, contradictory and wayward as he was.

"Yeah," said Silenus to Stanley. "You know what to do. I wish I had listened to you, you know. You were right." He looked up and around, smelling the night breeze, and smiled a little. "There is so much more to everything than this."

Stanley nodded, and bowed his head.

Silenus began to pour the wine. "Ah," he said. "The mere scent is almost enough for me." And as he poured George swore he thought he saw something else fall into the glass, but it did not come from the bottle: it came from the cork, and it looked like just a drop of a very thin syrup, yet it was almost shielded from view by Silenus's hand. George started when he saw it, and when he looked up he saw Silenus was staring at him very piercingly. Then his father offered the glass of wine to the sky, said, "Salut," and drank.

Again, George expected something to happen. He'd put something in the wine, so surely this was some sort of plan of his . . . yet there were no effects at all. Silenus simply sat on the trunk when he was done, breathing out heavily, an old man wearing muddy shoes. Then he said in a small and frightened voice, "I am going to die today."

"Yes," said Ofelia. "You are. Will you be so cowardly as to run from us?"

"No. No, I will not run," he said, and stood. "But if you are to have me killed, I will at least have the dignity to die before my killer."

"You are out of privileges," she said coldly. "That is one I will not give you." She nodded to several of the fairies, and they marched forward bearing stout clubs in their hands.

Silenus sniffed, tossed the glass over his shoulder, straightened his tie, and calmly began walking toward Ofelia. "I am going to die today," he said again softly.

He walked toward the group of approaching assailants as if they were not there, eyes fixed on the lady. When the first club fell it struck him across the brow, and blood fanned through the air. Colette cried out, and Silenus spun a little, staggered, but put down another foot to resume walking. Yet then another club fell, this one striking him on the shoulder, and then another on his neck, before one found the back of his knee. There was a pop and he groaned and twisted to the ground, and at that the fairies dispersed a little, ringing him in, ready to watch him writhe.

But he did not. He swallowed, blood spurting from his brow and his knee wobbling horribly, and slowly pushed himself up, and resumed walking forward.

The fairies swooped back in again, and another club whistled down. He held up a hand and the club struck him on the wrist and again there was a pop. Silenus cried out and bent over, the glistening teeth of shattered bone protruding from the base of his hand. Then one fairy took a fistful of hair at the back of his head, steadied him, and brought his club down on the side of his face. Silenus crumpled, his eye ruined where his skull had given in to the blow, and he lay there with his face in the dirt. Colette cried out again, and even Stanley, who'd always been utterly silent, moaned in despair.

George wanted to look away. He felt sick with rage, and he wanted to dash forward and bowl the fairies over and rush his father away. But he knew he could not, and he hated himself for his powerlessness. Yet again he was but an audience member in his own life.

He expected Silenus to stay down now: he had taken a terrible injury. Yet again, his father did not. With a series of soft grunts and moans he pushed himself up with his good hand, his ruined one clutched under his armpit, and he again began half-limping, half-crawling over to the lady, blood streaming from his eye and his brow and his hand, and now there was a little stream running down his ankle as well.

The fairies again crowded around him. One jabbed up with his club into Silenus's stomach and he jerked forward, gasping terribly, and went reeling off into another fairy. The fairy pushed him back and they pinned him in, shoving him around, toying with him. They landed blows upon his ribs, and one even grabbed his good arm and stretched it out and struck him on the elbow. His arm bent horribly, the elbow bending to the side with the sound of old wood being crushed, and he gagged and whimpered.

"Stop it, damn you!" sobbed Colette. "Just stop it!"

Stanley again moaned softly.

"Please stop," whispered George. "Please stop walking. Just stop."

Yet his father would not. Even with both arms broken he bent over and staggered along for another few feet. The fairies hesitated, dodging around him, searching for the next best blow.

"Put him down," said the lady.

One of the fairies nodded and walked alongside him for a bit, matching his slow hobble. Silenus's breath now came in wheezes and he walked bent like a cripple, face to the ground, determined to make a few more feet. The fairy reached out and took his coat and gently brought him to a stop. Then the club rose high and fell upon the back of Silenus's head with a sickening crack. He collapsed in a heap and lay there, hardly breathing. Colette took George's hand, and both felt sure he was dead.

But then, unbelievably, Silenus started to move again, crawling toward Ofelia, covered in blood and dust. Ofelia shook her head as if irritated by this last show of defiance.

"Why is he doing this?" asked Colette. "Why does he keep going?"

"Because the last walk is all that's left," said George. And when he said this Stanley hugged them both close, and though he held George the closest, George did not mind.

"Enough," said the lady.

The fairy that had struck the final blow took out a knife, reached down, grasped Silenus's hair, and pulled him up. Silenus's one good eye rolled up to glare at the lady, and his broken hands sought purchase on the ground to try to pull himself forward more. But then the fairy took the knife, delicately placed it below the far corner of his jaw, and drew it along his neck.

The spray of blood was horrific. George and Colette wailed in shock, and Stanley began to shake. The fairy released Silenus and he fell back to the ground, blood pouring from the wound.

And yet, even in those last moments, with his life rushing out of him to spill onto the ground, Silenus still somehow managed to drag himself into a kneeling position using one shoulder for leverage, as if he just might summon the strength to push himself up and take one more step toward his goal, or even two or three. But his strength finally failed him. He fell forward onto his side, breath rattling and hands and legs trembling. After a few minutes he was still.

CHAPTER 30

The Light

The lady nodded. "A good death. Not the best, but decent."

"Are you happy now?" said George angrily through his tears. "Are you pleased with what you've done?"

"Happy?" she said. "I've not been happy for hundreds of years. But I will settle for satisfied. And yes, I am satisfied with this. It was about time one of his swindles caught up to him." She gestured to several of her servants, and they gathered up Harry's body and carried it away into the woods.

"What are you going to do with him?" asked George.

"He is an old thing, and probably scrawny," she said. "So I believe we will soak him in the wine he loved so dearly before we make any real decisions about preparation."

"God," Colette said. "You people are *monsters*."

"Time makes monsters of us all, and we have seen quite a bit of that," she said. The white masks began to blink out again until much of the host had left, except the lady and a few of her servants.

"What will you do with us?" said George.

"You?" she said. "I will do nothing to you. I swore I would not harm you. And besides, that is not for me to decide."

"Then who will?"

She turned around, searching the trees, her spidery fingers flexing contemplatively as she waited. Then she cried, "Ah! There they are."

There was movement down the shore. Some people were walking toward them, but their movements were slow and ungainly, as if their legs did not fully work. When a flash of moonlight was reflected off the waves, George caught a glimpse of their faces and gasped. "Oh, no."

"What?" said Colette. "What is it?" And Stanley, who of course could not write anything with his hands on their shoulders, looked at him curiously.

"Don't you see them?" said George. "She's brought them right back to us..."

The figures trooped up the shore and made a line in front of them, and they saw that the faces of the figures were their very own: there was Colette, and Stanley, and George, and the woman with the thin face and red hair who had once been Annie, and there on the right was the shadowy person who could only be Silenus. They stood still for a moment, and then they seemed to collapse inward, crumbling at the shoulders. When the wind rose their skin and clothes blew away like leaves, revealing a frame of vines and sticks and mud.

"The botkines," said Colette. "But that can only mean..."

George gasped again. A blast of crushing silence rolled across the shore to him like a foul wind. He sank to his knees. "No," he whispered. "They followed them. They're coming..."

"Yes," said Ofelia, pleased. "They most certainly are."

George raised his watering eyes and saw a parade of figures in gray suits streaming down the shore to them. There were so many there, lined up with their blank faces and their small smiles, that it hurt the eye to look at them. The men in gray fanned out around the three of them as they approached, dozens, hundreds, thousands more than the fairies. Light faded and the air grew still, and soon it felt like George had to fight for every breath.

One of the men in gray looked at George, Colette, and Stanley. Then he turned to the lady. "He is dead? You have killed Silenus?"

"He is very dead," she said. "And soon he will be even less than that."

"And they have the Light with them?" he said.

"That is not my area of expertise," she answered. "I do not play those games. They bore me so."

He stared at her, eyes unmoving. George was not sure who was more unfathomable: the fairies or the men in gray.

"I trust," she said, "that this does not violate our arrangement?"

Still he did not answer.

"Everything remains the same," she said. She sounded more than a little nervous. "You will now be allowed to swallow what is left of the world, leaving only the choicest and most desirable lands for us to enjoy in one last celebration before the very end. Correct?"

"That's what you did this for?" said Colette. "A fucking *party*?"

"Not just any party," she said mildly. "*The* party. The *last* party. A solstice party unlike any other. We will eat and drink things never tasted before in all of existence. Who would deny themselves such rare treasures? And what a good way to pass the eve of this world."

"You crazy *bitch*!" cried Colette.

The lady ignored her. "Are we still agreed?" she asked the wolf.

"We are," he said finally.

"Good," she said. "Then I will retreat to enjoy my little trophy, and leave you yours." She and the remainder of the host stepped back into the woods, and faded into the darkness. Soon it was like they'd never been there at all, and there was only George, his two friends, and all the wolves of the world.

George, Colette, and Stanley stood shivering on the edge of the shore. The sea of wolves watched them, unmoving and unblinking. They simply stood there, draining everything out of the world until it was as cold and gray and terrible as them. Soon George's breath smoked just as much as when he'd journeyed through the wastelands.

One of the wolves finally spoke, his voice soft and low: "We know you have the Light."

Neither George, nor Stanley, nor Colette moved or answered.

"We know it was not on Silenus's person," he said. "That much we have confirmed. It was something he took with him. Perhaps in a lantern. Perhaps in a box. Whatever it is, we want it."

Still none of them did anything.

"You have led us across many lands," said the wolf. "Across many places, under many skies. But enough is enough. Time has no meaning to us. And now there is very little of it left for you. We *will* find it, eventually."

George resisted glancing sideways at his two friends. While he had no intention of surrendering the First Song, he found he now knew even less about it than he had before. It was not in Silenus's steamer trunk; that was full of restoratives and liquors, for reasons George could not possibly imagine. And yet Silenus and Stanley had always taken the chest with them when they'd gone to gather the echoes...He wanted very badly to look at Stanley now, since he would surely know where Silenus had stored it, but George did not dare draw attention to the one remaining member who knew anything about the song.

"One of you must know," said the wolf. "The others are expendable." He walked over to them, hands clasped quaintly behind his back. "We can do things to you. Horrible things. Things that cannot be expressed in words. And the rest of you can watch. Is that what you want?" He studied them and moved toward George. "We know this one, for instance. We've met him. And we know he knows nothing at all..."

Stanley made a strangled noise and pulled George back. The wolf's smile increased very slightly. "Ah, yes," he said. "We think this one will do, won't he?"

"No!" said Colette.

The wolf stopped. "No what?"

Colette hesitated. The wolf walked over to her and peered into her eyes. "No what?"

She took a breath. "I'll...I'll tell you where it is. Just don't hurt him."

"Colette, no!" cried George "You can't—"

The wolf moved in a way that George's eye could not fully see, but suddenly the wolf was standing before him with one hand quivering an inch from the side of his neck. "It would be so very easy to strike your head from your body," the wolf said. "It would hardly be any trouble at all."

"Enough," said Colette. "He won't interfere."

"Let us hope," said the wolf. He dropped his hand. "Now. Show us."

"All three of us have to get it," she said.

"What?" said the wolf, irritated. "All of you? Why?"

"It's incredibly heavy. It's the First Song, isn't it? How could it be anything but heavy?"

The wolf frowned. "Where is it?"

She pointed to the huge black office door that was still standing open in the side of the boulder. "In there."

The wolf walked over to it and inspected the door. "Interesting," he said. "Naturally, this could be a trap. Or you could be planning to run inside and this door would take you away. So why don't we just..." The wolf grasped the door and began to pull. There was a shuddering groan from the door, as if it was being pulled not only from its hinges but from some much larger structure that could not be seen with the eye. But then there came a snap and the wolf wrenched the door free, and he broke it on his knee and tossed it into the water.

"There," he said. "That should take care of that. We still won't go into the room — that would be foolish — but we will watch. Go inside with your friends, little girl, and get the Light. And if you do not, we will have to come in after you. And then this one," he said, gesturing to George, "he will never forgive you for what we will do to him."

Colette began to walk toward the door. George and Stanley followed, and George could tell Stanley was just as confused as he was. As he eyed the splintered flotsam out on the waves of the lake George dearly hoped Colette's plan, if there was one, had not involved the door in any way.

They entered Silenus's office. It was very cluttered, as they'd tossed in their luggage without any coordination when they last packed. George glanced over the many items in the room and wondered what Colette could possibly have in mind.

"Stay close to me, all right?" she whispered.

"Make sure you are visible," called the wolf from the door. "Like we told you, the last thing we want to do is come in."

"We will," Colette called back.

As she navigated through the mounds of boxes and props George noticed there was something very large sticking out ahead: the rolled-up backdrop Kingsley had used in his act. George had forgotten they'd tossed it in here. Colette nodded to it, and Stanley took one end and George took the other, while she helped hold up the middle section.

"This is the Light?" asked the wolf as they carried it out the office door. "It looks like...paper."

"That's because it hasn't been unrolled," said Colette. "The Light is rolled up with it."

"Then unroll it, please," said the wolf. "Slowly."

Colette began to walk backward, gradually unfurling the big backdrop. George and Stanley held the roll up as it spun around in their hands. The backdrop was utterly blank, so he could not understand what she was doing, but then he saw she was whispering to it, and he managed to catch a few of her words: "...Please help us, just this once. We were never cruel to you, please..."

The sea of wolves gathered around them, their necks craning to look at the backdrop as it unfurled. "Where is it?" asked one. "We don't see anything."

"It's almost done," said Colette, but her voice shook.

George stared at the backdrop. It was still completely blank. Could it not have heard her? Or was it refusing whatever she was asking of it? There were only a few remaining feet left to unfurl...

Then he saw something, a tiny flicker of color in the center of the backdrop. "There it is!" cried one of the wolves.

"Yes. There it is," said Colette. She looked up at Stanley and George. "Underneath! Now!" she shouted. She flung her hands up and sent a huge wave through the backdrop, and George and Stanley ducked underneath and pulled their corners down while Colette dragged down her end. George had no idea what they were doing, but they all crouched underneath the rippling dome of the backdrop until they were completely concealed by it.

There was an immense snarl as the wolves all reacted, and George braced himself for their attack...yet then the snarl unexpectedly turned into pained shrieks.

"My eyes!" cried a voice.

"I can't see!" said another.

"Where are they?" said a third. "What is happening?"

George peeked out from under a fold in the backdrop. The wolves were still surrounding them, but their faces were lit with a blinding white light that seemed to be coming from the backdrop itself. They raised their arms to try to block it out, but most fell stumbling back. Some were even running away as if it burned them.

"What did you tell it to do?" asked George.

"I told it to show them a light," Colette said. "Now come on! We have to stay under, but we need to move up the hill!"

George, Stanley, and Colette began to shuffle away from the shore, each keeping the backdrop clamped down over them. George kept expecting for them to bump into one of the wolves, but apparently the light was so bright they kept falling back. Soon there was grass and stone below their feet and the ground began to gently slope up.

"Thank you," whispered Colette to the backdrop, yet if it heard it did not respond.

Then they finally bumped into something, but they saw it was a tree. Colette breathed a sigh of relief: they'd reached the outskirts of the woods. Yet before they could say anything they heard a furious growl, and a voice called out, "Just shed these weak fucking forms and get them!"

There was a sound from outside the backdrop like immense paws falling to the ground, and then they were dashed onto their sides, still clutching the backdrop. George felt it tear in his hands, and as he tumbled he saw he and Colette had fallen one way and kept most of the backdrop, and Stanley had fallen the other way with a shred of it clutched to his chest. George stared at their fragment: something enormous had batted their little makeshift shield, something with many claws, judging from the backdrop's jagged edge. He saw something huge and dark padding toward them from the woods out of the corner of his eye, and guessed that whatever the wolves were underneath those images of men in gray, they were not at all susceptible to blinding light.

"Run!" cried George, and he and Colette fled up into the hill, the remaining part of the backdrop fluttering behind them like a flag. The wolves gave chase, and George saw Stanley crouched behind a tree with his piece of the backdrop, watching them run. He stared after George, clearly terrified, but then shook his head and slipped away into the dark.

George and Colette dodged through the trees as the forest filled with many snarls and roars. His breath burned in his throat and they both stumbled over roots and stones, but they kept staggering up the side of the hill, keenly aware of their dark pursuers mere yards behind them.

Then Colette grabbed his arm and threw him into a little stony pit in the hill. She leaped in beside him and pulled the backdrop up over them like a blanket. George tried to ask her what she was doing, but she shook her head and held a finger to her lips.

Huge footfalls sounded nearby. There was a sound of snarling, and George tensed, waiting for the attack. But the wolf did not attack: from the sound of its footsteps, it ran right past them and leaped farther up the hill. They waited, but it did not come back. George heard others running nearby, but they did not stop or seem aware of the two of them cowering in the stony pit.

"What's going on?" whispered George.

Colette shushed him. She reached out and gently turned over one corner of the backdrop. George squinted to see what she was showing him, and he saw that the top surface of the backdrop had changed to moonlit stones and pinecones and rocky earth.

"Camouflage," she said to him softly.

George nodded, but then he froze. "They can smell us," he said.

She stared at him, horrified. It was obvious she hadn't thought of that.

As if to confirm their worst fears, they heard footsteps nearby, and a snuffling. The wolf outside paused, and sniffed again. There was a faint, curious, "Hm," as if the wolf was delighted to discover something, and they heard footsteps walking their way.

Colette grabbed a sharp rock and readied to attack the wolf if it should discover them, but George reached out and steadied her hand. She gave him a quizzical look, and he shook his head. He was not sure why, but that single "Hm" had been familiar. He was sure he'd heard that voice before...

Then, to their shock, one side of the backdrop lifted up and a wolf dropped in with them. Colette nearly screamed, but George clapped a hand over her mouth. In one instant, he'd seen the wolf was not like any of the others: for one, he still retained his human image, but he also wore a bright red coat and a feathered hat, and his face was fixed in an expression of gleeful excitement.

The wolf in red waved happily. "Hello again!" he said in what he thought was a whisper, but was actually quite loud.

George frantically gestured to lower its voice.

"Oh," said the wolf in red, this time more quietly. "I'm sorry. I've never whispered before. Am I whispering now? Is this a whisper? A good one?"

"Yes," said George softly. Colette looked at him, bewildered, and he shook his head at her again.

"How interesting!" said the wolf. "I must make a note of how this works."

He reached into his coat to produce his notebook, but then he saw George's outraged stare. "Oh, yes! Never mind! That's right! You're trapped and hiding, correct?"

"Yes," said George, irritated.

"How marvelous!" said the wolf. "What is this strange contraption you have above your heads? I've never seen anything like it so far."

"What do you want?" asked George.

"Why, to help you, of course."

Both of them stared at him. "Why would you want to do that?" asked George.

The wolf looked troubled. "Ah. Well...I've come to some decisions recently, you see, and I think...I think that, even though existing is very painful sometimes, and very confusing, I think I would like it to...go on. Yes. I would like for things to continue. And even though my brothers wish for the opposite, I find I must disagree with them. I like your Light. I want you to keep it. And I want you to stay alive." The wolf smiled gently at both of them, and seemed to notice Colette for the first time. "Good gracious! Who is this? Wait! I know! Is this the girl you are so in love with?"

Despite their dangerous circumstances, George reddened. "What are you going to do?"

The wolf looked grave, then sad. He took a breath, and said, "What I am going to do...is give you a gift." Then he opened his mouth incredibly wide, wide enough that his jaw was much larger than his head, a vast cavern of a mouth, and he reached up and put his hand inside it.

George and Colette both recoiled at the sight. But then they saw there was something twinkling in the wolf's mouth, like a bright lure trapped in the maw of a fish. The wolf plucked it up and gently pulled it out, and as he did his mouth returned to its normal size.

George felt every hair on his body lean toward the jewel of light in the wolf's fingers. He became aware of a very soft chanting, not within the pit in the ground, but within his mind...

"Is that..." said Colette.

"It is your Light," said the wolf in red. He stared at the twinkling diamond with terribly sad eyes. "I did not ever know I could ever take part in something so wonderful and terrible, so beautiful and frightening. But it is not mine. I loved having it, but it is not mine." He held it out to George. "Here."

George stared at it. "What?"

"Take it. It's yours."

He was not sure he could. He'd only ever taken on one piece of the song before, when he was a child, and he could hardly remember that. "I don't know if this is how it's done..."

"For God's sake, George," said Colette, "this is no time to worry about procedure!"

"All right!" he said. "Fine." He reached out, and as he did he felt a painful, magnetic pull, one that was a bare fraction of what he'd felt when he took on his first piece of the song, but one that hurt regardless.

His finger touched the little jewel of light. There was a soft flash, and his body spasmed. It was as if a lightning bolt had flowed into his finger and up into his mind, and he saw...

...A rainy afternoon, and the ocean, and a pile of stones. The little girl has one arm in a splint, but she is still determinedly using one hand to pile the stones on top of one another, making her tower. It will be a good tower, a tall one, and nothing will ever be able to knock it down, not even her brothers. Everyone will marvel at this tower...

Then it was gone, and he gasped. George saw his hands were shaking. He suddenly felt much, much heavier, somehow, as if there were a lead weight rolling around within his mind. He realized he had just absorbed about seven seconds of existence for some spot in Creation, a tiny bit of beach that had once played host to a small, determined girl on a rainy afternoon...

"Did you see it?" asked the wolf in red. "Did you see the little person making the tower on the beach?"

George, breathing hard, nodded.

The wolf in red smiled. He did not look quite so human anymore. His face seemed stiffer, and there was something blank in his eyes. But he said, "I have always wondered who that little person is, and what happened to her. I suppose I will never know. I don't know what you will do with it, but please take care of that little bit of Light for me. It was very good to me. I should have liked dying, though. It seemed as if it was as important as living." Then the smile vanished. "They will smell you here soon. Do you know that?"

They both nodded.

"Good. What I will do is lead them away from you as best as I can. I do not know how effective this will be—most of my kin do not trust me any longer, and...and without your bit of Light, I am not sure I will remain what I am. It is possible I might betray you." He looked at the sleeve of his coat, which was no longer the bright red it had once been. Perhaps soon it would return to gray. "I hope I won't, but I cannot say. You will have to use your time wisely, and act quickly."

"What should we do?" asked Colette.

"*I* don't know," said the wolf. "*You're* the ones who have had the Light for so long. What do you normally do in these situations?"

George and Colette glanced at each other, terrified.

"Whatever you do," said the wolf, "good luck. I hope you succeed. Stay quiet for now, but in a bit, you should be safe to act." He nodded to them both, and reached up and grabbed the side of the backdrop. Then he took a breath, launched himself out, and cried, "I heard them run back down the hill! Here! Follow me!"

George and Colette sat in silence for a moment, listening to the growls follow the wolf down the hill. "So... what *do* we normally do in these situations?" Colette asked.

George shook his head. "I have no idea."

CHAPTER 31

"You are the most beautiful thing I have ever seen."

Far away west down the hillside from where George and Colette hid—far enough to be deaf to the wolves' pursuit, but not far enough to be blind, if one had the right vantage point—Annie lay bruised and nearly broken on the floor of the old train car, and yet she was not quite dead. The fairies had beaten her and even cut her throat, but the mechanisms that had propelled her body for the last half-century were not affected by superficial damage like broken bones and slashed flesh. She wept where she lay, partially due to pain, but mostly because she could not bear to think about her betrayal.

But this was just the beginning of her anguish: as she wept, she would sometimes find herself wondering why she was weeping. Something bad had happened...but when? she wondered. Was it days ago? Or just recently? And why was she in this train car, anyway? Then, with a horrified gasp, she'd remember what had happened and how she'd gotten to this place. But it took longer and longer each time.

She was losing herself, memory by memory. She knew she would soon forget everything, and she'd be lost to that awful stupor once more.

She sat up and looked around the train car with a dull, crawling terror, trying to remember why she was there, and what had happened, and who she was. "My name is Anne Sillenes," she began whispering to herself. "My name is Anne Sillenes. Anne Marie Sillenes. You are Anne Marie Sillenes. You are, you are..."

There was a soft tapping at the train car door. She turned around and listened. After a moment the tap came again.

"What?" she asked in a creaking voice. She had to hold a hand to the gash in her throat to get the words to come properly. "Who's there?"

There was a pause. Then another tap. She sat up, back creaking, and looked at the door. A small scrap of paper had been slipped under the crack.

"What is this?" she asked.

There was another tap.

She stared at the note for a while. Then she said, "There was...a man who always wrote things for me...Stanley? Is that who you are?"

One tap.

"What do you want, Stanley? Why don't you at least let me out?"

The handle in the door wiggled. She saw it had been broken off or twisted, and he was showing her he was unable to open it.

"What is it you want, then?" she asked.

Silence. She frowned as she realized this was not a very intelligent question: he'd obviously written what he wanted on the note. Annie heaved herself over and picked it up with fumbling fingers. She held it below a small hole in the train car roof to read it by the moonlight.

Annie struggled to read what had been written for her. She *knew* she could read, she'd been taught her letters...but now it was suddenly so hard. She squinted as she pored over the words. It seemed he wanted her to do something with something else—the train car?—and then his note ended in a swear. She puzzled at this, but then noticed he'd spelled the swear wrong. It seemed a letter was missing, if she remembered it correctly.

Then she understood. It was not a swear at all.

"Why would you want me to do that?" she said.

Another note slipped in under the door, this one written on a piece of cloth. It read simply: GEORGE AND COLETTE.

She stared at the note for a while. Then a handful of fuzzy memories congealed in her mind: there had been children, hadn't there? A little girl and a little boy, both so haughty but both so sweet, prettier than daisies, the little darlings...

Then she realized what he was asking of her. "I can't!" she cried. "I can't help! I'm broken, Stanley. I'm hurt all over. And I've never lifted anything that heavy!"

Silence.

"I can't," she said again. "I can't."

Still silence. Then a single tap.

It was impossible to really know what he meant by that tap: it could have meant yes you can, or that he understood and would try something else, or it could have simply communicated frustration. But whatever the intent behind that tap in the dark, to Annie it simply told her that she must, she must, there was no other way.

She began to weep again. "All right," she gasped. "All right. I'll try."

Another tap. Annie nodded, though of course he could not see her. Then she crawled back to the center of the train car. Her left arm had been broken, and she had to set the bone herself. She gritted her teeth and with a horrible twisting she managed to get it close to the right place. She tested her fingers, and though they clicked unnervingly they worked.

Then she searched the train car floor for a weak spot, steadied herself, and began to kick at it.

Stanley sighed with relief as he listened to the pounding from within the train car. He looked the car up and down and found a long length of rusty chain and a lock wrapped around the railing at the end. He removed it and held it in his hands, frowning. He would have preferred rope, but chain would do.

He moved to the edge of the woods and picked up his shred of the backdrop. It was flickering like a damaged electrical light as if the thing was in pain, but it could still mimic the trees and branches of the woods if it tried. Then he crouched and studied his surroundings.

Ahead and to his left was the dam, rising up like a blank gray cliff side. Before him and to the right the hillsides climbed up, eventually matching the dam in height, and at the very top they were shrouded in trees. He could just make out low, black figures springing through those woods, and somewhere among them were Colette and George.

He knew what Harry would have wanted him to do. He should run, and save himself. That was Harry's only standing order for him: to run away at all times, and always ensure his own self-preservation. But Stanley was tired of running, and he now had a very great reason to stop.

He tucked the chain into his belt, wrapped himself in the shred of backdrop like a cloak, and began creeping up the hillside.

Unlike for the wolves, it would not be hard for Stanley to find them. He could always find George at any time, if he was looking for him.

George and Colette lay shivering under the backdrop. They had discussed several options, but they still had no idea what to do. Despite the wolf in red's attempt to lead the others down the hill, they could still hear howls from up the slope. So far they had not been found, but they knew it could not be long.

They heard a set of footfalls coming very fast, but it sounded as if they were not the huge paws of wolves. Rather they sounded like normal human feet again, perhaps clad in a nice pair of loafers.

For the second time, the corner of the backdrop lifted up, but it was not the wolf in red: it was Stanley, wrapped in his own piece of the backdrop, which briefly resembled the bark of a tree, but when he was completely under it began fluttering nastily, as if it were having a stroke.

"What are you doing—" began Colette, but Stanley held up a finger. He reached into his pocket and held out a piece of old cardboard. Written on it were the words: YOU MUST GET HIGHER ON THE HILL. HIGH AS YOU CAN GO.

"What?" said Colette. "No! We can't run out! They'll see us!"

Stanley shook his head and took out another card. Apparently he'd expected this objection, because the card simply read: I WILL MAKE A DISTRACTION.

"What sort of a distraction?" asked George. "A friend of ours tried one just before, but I don't think it worked."

A pained look crossed Stanley's face, and he made a soft noise of aggravation. He must have had only a few cards, and could not have written out every response. He shrugged.

"Should we go now?" Colette asked.

He nodded and bobbed his head from side to side. Soon, very soon, he seemed to say. Then he looked up at George. Stanley's eyes were bright and full of tears, and he was breathing very hard. He gave George a trembling smile and handed him another card, but before George could read it Stanley wrapped him up in a powerful embrace and sighed deeply. Then he let him go and kissed him on the forehead, and lifted the backdrop and slipped back out again.

Colette peeked out from under the backdrop and watched Stanley sprint down the hillside. "What was that all about?"

George nearly began to tell her about Stanley and the strange infatuation he had for him, but then they heard a sound that was very familiar to them: it was the sound of many voices, thousands of them, all singing many notes of ethereal, ghostly pitches that made the hairs stand up on one's head. All the snarling and growling in the woods stopped at the sound of it.

George joined Colette at the end of the backdrop. "What is that?" he asked. "Is that the *song*?"

George watched as Stanley leaped across one small pit in the ground, and as he did he happened to bolt beneath a beam of moonlight. His mouth was open, and his eyes were nearly shut, and his lips were moving; but it seemed that they were moving *with* the song, following and perhaps articulating its many changes in pitch. As he fled away the song became fainter, but they could still hear it echoing through the trees.

"Was...was he singing it?" said George weakly. "Was he *singing* the First Song?"

"It...it certainly seemed like it," said Colette. "But I never heard him do anything but play the cello whenever I was on stage with him..."

Then a voice in the woods shouted: "There it is! He's got it! He's carrying it with him, trying to steal it away!"

"He's not carrying it, you fool!" came another. "It's in him! The Light is *inside* of him!"

All breath was knocked from George when he heard this cry. "What?" he whispered. "*Inside* of him?"

He stared at Stanley as he fled through the woods. Could that be true? Could the secret hiding place of the song not have been any box or lantern or any other little trick, but within Stanley himself? Had he been carrying the *entire* song within him for all this time? George's mind boggled to understand it. He knew this was possible, since he himself carried a part of it and had just absorbed the tiniest piece (and what an enormous, terrible burden the full sum would be, he thought), and since Silenus's trunk had contained no hint of it at all then he supposed that, rather than storing it there, it might have all been within Stanley himself. But if Stanley was truly carrying the song, then that...that would prove beyond all doubt that Stanley was a member of the Silenus family, and so also a relation to George.

A thousand thoughts went racing through his head. Could Stanley really be his uncle, or his cousin, or perhaps even his brother? Why would he have never said so? And yet, more troubling than anything, this discovery meant that it had never been Silenus at all who'd been carrying the song, but *Stanley*, always Stanley...he was the true bearer. Why had Silenus lied? And why was Silenus not carrying it? Was it possible, he wondered faintly, that Silenus could not carry the song at all?

And if that was the case, then that would mean that Silenus could not truly be his father. Nor could he be Stanley's father, as George had briefly wondered. Harry had said the ability to carry the song was passed on from parent to child. And if Silenus was not his father, then...

George suddenly remembered the way Stanley was always watching him, always seeking to touch him and hold him. He remembered the dozens of little gifts, the hundred little favors, the thousand comforting smiles. He remembered the way the man had held out his watch after fondly playing with its wind-up knob, offering some treasured gift. And he remembered how distraught Stanley had been when George had told him he wanted nothing more to do with him.

An image swam up in his memory: Stanley, standing on the snowy rooftop of the theater outside of Chicago, holding up his blackboard, eyes terribly old and sad. And written upon the blackboard was: YOUR FATHER LOVES YOU, GEORGE. PLEASE KNOW THAT. FOR ME.

George looked down at the card he now held in his hand. It read: YOU ARE THE MOST BEAUTIFUL THING I HAVE EVER SEEN. I LOVE YOU.

"Oh, no," whispered George. "No, no, no. No, it can't be, it just... it just *can't*."

"What?" said Colette.

George rushed forward and flung the backdrop up off them. He saw hundreds of dark shapes pouring through the trees, yowling as they pursued Stanley down the hill, and he shouted in fear and confusion and began to start off after him.

Colette leaped up and grabbed him to hold him back. "George, what are you doing?"

"Let me go!" he shrieked. "Let me go, let me go!"

"I can't, he said we have to get up the hill!"

"You don't understand!" he cried. "Let me go! I have to get to him, I have to!"

"Will you shut up before you get their attention?" she said.

But George leaped forward once more to try to break free. Colette gritted her teeth, flung him to the ground, and grabbed a smooth stone. "Sorry, George," she said, and cracked him lightly across the head with it.

It did its job. George whimpered a little, but then his eyes shut and his head rolled back and he lay still.

"He said we need to get up the hill," she said. She picked him up, threw him over one shoulder, and began to walk slowly up the slope. "And that's what we're going to do."

CHAPTER 32

"What will happen will happen."

George knew nothing but darkness for a long time. Then there was a voice in the darkness singing, and a light appeared before him. It was not terribly bright, but it was a very warm light, and as his eyes focused he saw the light formed a perfect square, and it'd been quartered. He realized he was seeing a window in the dark, set up high in the side of a house, and there was someone stirring behind it.

The singing changed, very slightly, and the night sky came pouring in above, and as its gentle radiance flooded his vision George saw he was seeing his grandmother's house, the very place he'd called home less than a year ago. But the oak tree out front wasn't quite right, he saw: it was not nearly as tall or as wide as he remembered.

I've seen this before, thought George. There's someone underneath the tree.

And there was. There was a man standing there in the shadows beneath the tree, and even though George was still faintly hearing the First Song in his ears (where was it coming from? he wondered. Was he dreaming it?) the man opened his mouth, and from it came the First Song as well. The two songs formed a duet, one emanating from everywhere, the other coming solely from this shadowy singer.

A girl came to the window of his room, and she opened it and looked out. The singing stopped, and the girl waved. She retreated and shut the window and the light went out, and the man under the tree nervously smoothed down his hair and his clothes.

Someone rushed down the front porch steps. It was the girl from the window, he saw. And as she walked from the shadow of the house George saw it was his mother.

His mouth fell open. He had never known her, nor did he have any memories of her. He had only seen photos of her before, and in those she'd seemed a pale, lonely-looking girl, certainly nothing like a woman. Yet the person running barefoot across his grandmother's lawn was most certainly a woman, with long, flowing brown hair and a bright, happy smile. He realized, to his shock, that she was terribly beautiful. She could not have been much older than George was now.

"I wasn't sure you'd come!" she said as she ran.

The person under the tree appeared to busy themselves with something. Then when they were done they strode out, and George saw it was a tall, thin young man in a very prim (perhaps overly prim) suit. He was smiling and carrying a sketchpad in his hand, and written on it were the words: HOW COULD I RESIST YOUR CHARMS?

George gasped. It was Stanley, though he was almost unrecognizable. His hair was not smooth and blond and straight, but pitch-black and wildly curly, an adolescent's haircut if ever there was one, yet it faintly resembled Silenus's hair when he hadn't slicked it down with pomade. Stanley had not yet refined his sense of dress—his tie was crooked, and he had been forced to make a hole in his belt to fit his narrow waist—but it was most certainly him, though he could not have been twenty.

Alice Carole leaped into his arms, and he neatly caught her and spun her around. She laughed while he grinned hugely, and they kissed. "Do it again," she said. "Sing it for me again."

He set her down and put his arm around her and led her away from the house, over toward the Cortsen fields George knew so well.

He opened his mouth and very softly began to sing the First Song. Alice's eyelids fluttered as she listened. When he was done she said, "It's so beautiful. Why don't you sing it more often, for everyone? I bet you could fill up whole theaters with that."

He took out his sketchpad (George saw it was dangling from his shoulder by a loop of string) and wrote: MY UNCLE IS AFRAID IT WILL BE STOLEN.

"That man was your uncle?" she asked. "The mean one?"

He flipped a page, and wrote: GREAT-UNCLE. AND HE IS NOT MEAN. HE IS IN MOURNING.

"For who?"

HIS WIFE.

"Oh," she said. "I'm sorry I called him mean, then. Did you know her?"

Stanley shook his head. SHE PASSED A LONG TIME AGO.

"He must have loved her very greatly then, if he still mourns her. I wish I knew what it was like, to be loved like that." She smiled slyly.

Stanley stopped her and spun her around, smiling and shaking his head, and they kissed.

"Will you leave me?" she asked, and now she was not joking.

He shook his head. But his face grew troubled.

"You don't know," she said.

He did not answer.

"You do know. You will have to leave, won't you. You travel all the time."

He wrote: CAN YOU COME WITH ME?

"I don't know," she said. "I don't know, Stanley."

They held each other close for a long while. Then Stanley took his sketchpad and wrote: THEN WE SHOULD ENJOY WHAT TIME WE HAVE. And hand in hand they walked away to the road, and crossed to go to the creek in the woods.

"They do look terribly happy, don't they?" said a voice beside George.

George turned and started in shock. Another Alice Carole was standing there beside him. He stared at her, then looked at the other Alice, walking away with her hand in Stanley's, and then back at this second one that stood beside him. She was oddly colorless, and the edges of her face were indistinct, but even so he could see she was smiling at him.

"You can see me?" he said. "I thought...I thought this was a dream."

"It's not a dream, George," she said. "It's an echo of something that happened long ago."

George stared at her, but his mother did not seem to mind. Her eyes traced over every inch of his face, and though they brimmed with tears she could not stop smiling.

"Are you a ghost?" he asked. "Am I dead?"

"Dead?" she said. "No. Didn't I just tell you what this is?"

"It's an echo..." he said. "So you're an echo, too? Like the ones in the graveyard with my f— with Silenus?"

"Yes," she said.

"How?"

"The First Song is not bound by time and space, George," she said. "You know that. Those two elements are but melodies within it. And echoes can be much larger than mere people. If you wished, and if you had the talent, you could use it to see any moment in any place. Right now you're witnessing two echoes — one of a treasured moment, and a second of a person — me. I am so glad to finally, finally meet you."

"How is that possible?" he asked.

"It depends on who is singing the song," she said. "If certain parts are stressed, certain echoes are created. It takes a lot of talent to do it, but then your father always was an extraordinarily talented man."

"Stanley?" George asked. "He's doing this?"

His mother nodded. "Can't you hear it, from all around us? He is singing about us as he leads the wolves away from you. It is all that concerns him, all he wants to think of. He sings of this moment, and the girl he loved, and the child she bore. You, George."

George frowned. "I...I never would have thought he was my father," he said faintly. "I didn't, until just now. Why didn't he ever tell me?"

"Well, he always was burdened by his responsibilities," she said. "It was that uncle of his, I think...he was always controlling poor Stan. Much like my mother was. Your grandmother, I mean. I think that was why we got along so well. We were both looking for an escape, though he sought a home and I sought an adventure. We both got what we wanted, for a little while."

He looked at her eagerly. He had never seen her this closely before. "So, are you really my mother?"

She smiled and shrugged. "I am, and I am not. I'm a little more, and a little less. I know some things she did not. Like about you, George, the child she never knew. You have seen so much, and though you have had your troubles I know you will act admirably."

"I'm not so sure," said George. "I've...I've treated Stanley horribly, and I've been so arrogant and made so many mistakes. I wish he would have told me who he was."

"Don't fret, George. He knows that if things were different you would love him. Things like that can't be hidden."

He looked at her, and almost began to cry. Perhaps it was the way she was looking at him: head tilted, smiling widely, a posture that was very common to his grandmother and also to himself. "I'm sorry, Momma."

"Sorry? For what?"

"I don't know. For everything. Nothing's gone right. It feels like I've done nothing, and when I did do something it just caused more harm."

She stroked the side of his head. Though this was an echo, her fingers felt warm and real. "Don't cry," she said softly.

"Do you hate me?" he asked.

"Hate you? Why would I hate you?"

"I killed you. When you gave birth to me, you died."

"You didn't kill me," she said. "I lived. I knew love, and I bore a son. What happened happened, and I don't regret anything. I am proud of you, George."

"Oh," said George, wiping his eyes. "I thought you did. I thought it was my fault. I don't know why. It was stupid." He sniffed again, and she took him in her arms. He had never been held by his mother before, to his memory. He did not want it to ever end. "What's going to happen, Momma? Will everything be all right?"

Smiling, she shook her head. "No," she said.

"No? Why not?"

"*Why* isn't the question," she said. "What will happen will happen. And you will all just have to bear it, my darling. You will, and your father will. But I could not be prouder of any two men for what you will both do, George."

"You know what we will do?" he asked.

"Yes. Everything that has happened and will happen is somewhere in the song, George. From here I can see what is ahead, and when everything will end."

"End?" said George. "How will it end?"

"It will not be long now. I can show you," she whispered into his ear. "Would you like me to do that?"

He nodded.

"Shut your eyes, child."

When he did, he felt her lips and her hot breath close to his ear. Her voice said, "Now all you have to do is *wake up*..."

And he did.

CHAPTER 33

A Man Very Bad at Dying

Far, far away from the dam, in a tiny, forgotten corner of reality that was totally inaccessible unless it did not wish to be, Ofelia and the rest of the fairy host slouched in their chairs in her feasting hall, stupefied with drink and food. As always, many of the host were already sleeping. Nowadays they found it difficult to sleep at all if their appetites were not sated by the taste of the unusual.

It had been, Ofelia thought, a fairly good dinner. But as she cleaned her teeth with a small ivory pick, she reflected that she was not completely satisfied. She realized she'd been thinking for years that she would not truly be pleased until she'd checked off this last achievement on her list, but one of the dangers of such thinking is that the event one hopes for never quite lives up to the expectation.

She took out her anger on her seneschal, demanding to know what he thought of the meal. He agreed that yes, my lady, the chef's preparation was most ingenious, infusing the flesh with wine and tobacco, as it'd doubtlessly seen much of both in life. And yes, my lady, pairing it with the Arcadian vintage (aged with the bitterest of *memento mori*) was nothing less than an oenophilic triumph. And no, my lady, the event had not been marred by the slightest of hangovers left by the *uisce beatha.* "Although, I do admit, my lady," he said, "that I have a small irritation in my stomach at the moment, though that has only started just recently."

"That's odd," she said. "I think I may feel the same discomfort. Perhaps the chef used too much spicing. He has overdone himself before, when pressured."

The seneschal put a hand to his stomach, and winced. "Somehow I do not think so, my lady. This is a very cold sensation, rather than a hot one. And it is very—" But the seneschal never finished his description, for he abruptly started coughing. Ofelia watched impatiently as the man tried his hardest to articulate his meaning in between his coughs. But she could not make out what he said, as another member of the host started coughing nearby as well, followed shortly by two more.

"What is wrong with all of you?" asked the lady. "Have you honestly gotten so sensitive?"

The seneschal tried to shake his head, but after one tremendous hack he looked up with terrified eyes. With outstretched hands he showed he'd just coughed up an enormous amount of blood. To their terror, several other fairies began coughing, and more and more until the entire host was hacking and choking.

"What is this?" said the lady. "What could be—" But then Ofelia began coughing as well. She stared around for aid as she coughed, but none came. She coughed so hard that, to her shame, her mask slipped off and clattered to the floor.

They did not all cough up the blood, but all of them bled; for most of them it came from the eyes and skin, as if they wept or sweated blood itself, slipping from the edges of their white masks. They slapped at the bleeding parts of their bodies, trying to stanch the flow, but in their agitated states they could do nothing to stop it. The blood built up around their feet at the feasting table, collecting into a large pool, and even though the lady was bent double with her coughs she still managed to see that the pool of blood seemed to defy the slope of the floor: rather than lying at the far end of the room from her, the pool somehow stayed directly at her feet.

There was a quiver in the pool. And then, as if the blood filled a large hole in the ground, a single trembling hand pierced the surface of the puddle and felt around the wooden floor for support. Finding a table leg, the hand grasped it and hauled the remainder of its owner up out of the pool in a very violent, sanguine birth. Yet this was no child: even though the lady and the rest of the host were now very weak from the coughing and the loss of blood, they could see that the person who'd just climbed out of their floor through the pool of blood was none other than a nude, blinking, crimson Heironomo Silenus.

He gagged and sniffed and wiped his eyes. Then he looked around at the expiring host of fairies. "Jesus," he said. "You know, I wasn't entirely sure that would work..." He turned toward the end of the table to the lady, seated in her chair and wheezing. "Goodness, Ofelia. I can see why you keep that mask on."

"You!" whispered Ofelia furiously. "You were dead...you're supposed to be dead!"

Silenus stood up, dripping, and took a lit cigar from one of the ashtrays at the table. He took a drag and said, "You should have listened to your mother more. If you had, you'd've known that dying is one thing I've made sure to be very bad at."

"What!" said the lady. "But how..."

"Maenad's honey," said Silenus. "Gathered from the thyrsus itself, and hidden in the cork. It has such unusual properties when ingested, you know. For the maenads themselves, its regenerative properties allowed them to survive the bacchanalia. When diluted with wine, however, it takes a while to act. And it will act, even if there are"—he glanced around at the dying fairies—"obstacles in the way."

"You bastard," she whispered. "I should have never granted your last request. Will you never give me any peace?"

Silenus shrugged. "I may make things quicker for you, if you answer my question. Now—what have you done with the others?"

CHAPTER 34

In Which Burdens Are Laid Down

Annie crawled through the hole she had made in the bottom of the train car. She lay there for a while below its undercarriage, simply trying to force air into her lungs. Then she got up on her hands and knees and dragged herself below the front axle.

She looked back, taking in the full length of the train car. She had never tried anything like this, as she'd told Stanley. Safes and metal bars and statues, these had been simple things, with none weighing more than half a ton. Yet this... this was immense. Merely lifting it would be a magnificent feat. And to do what Stanley had suggested, why... that was inconceivable.

She blinked, and suddenly she was not sure why she was sitting here below the train car. It was very cold out, and she realized she was hurt in many places... That did not seem right. Where was her coat, and her scarves? What had happened to her?

Then she remembered. "No! No!" she cried, and slapped the side of her head. "Remember! Remember, damn you! Anne Sillenes... My... my name is Anne Sillenes."

She would have to lift it up, she remembered, or at least try. Even in her ruined state, with every joint and bone in her body rebelling, she had to try.

She sat up and settled the train car's axle on the backs of her shoulders, then raised her arms and gripped it on either side. She positioned her feet, trying to equalize the balance, and began to push.

She groaned and her knees shook violently, and beads of sweat began to appear at the top of her brow. There was a faint moan from somewhere within the train car, the protest of reluctant metals that strained to bear the force put upon them, but no light appeared between the car's wheels and the ground, and the car did not rise one inch.

She gasped and collapsed. "Damn it," she said, weeping. "Damn it all. I can't. I told him I can't, and I can't."

She was nearly consumed by despair then. She'd betrayed those she loved, and was now helpless to do anything for them. And as she sat on the cold rocky ground she looked around herself, and wondered why she was crying. She did not seem scared. Perhaps, she wondered as she touched the wounds on her arms, it was because she was hurt...

Then she heard it: the sound of the First Song, echoing down the hill to her. The air became alive with all those faint and unearthly voices, yet then they were followed by a thousand howls and snarls. It sounded as if the song was leading the wolves west, down the hills into the valley before the dam.

Then she remembered again. "Jesus," she said. "Oh God, he's started, he's *started*."

She mournfully looked up at the train car, but then shook herself. To do this, she realized, would destroy her. The symbols inked on her skin could not maintain her body under such pressure. And yet there was a bleak freedom in that realization. In a way, each of her seconds had been her last, and all of them had led to this last act. She would not spend her remaining moments in futility and despair, she decided; she needed only to stand up, and carry a little more weight with her.

And perhaps she would at least die knowing who she was, and who she'd once been.

She stared at her wounded hands. *My name is Anne Sillenes. Anne Marie Sillenes.*

She positioned herself below the axle again, gripped it with both hands, and began to push. She did not strain herself this time, but applied a steady, increasing force up. She felt bones and joints begin to pop throughout her body, vertebrae cracking and muscle walls rupturing, but she kept pushing harder and harder.

The average train car, as that one was, weighs nearly seventy tons. Its frame is around eighty-five feet long and is solidly built of the strongest iron and steel. It is made to distribute its weight evenly across the ground, never tipping, never losing its balance, transporting its precious cargo with speed, safety, and efficiency. It is not in any way meant to rise up from the track it was made for, not an inch, not a millimeter.

And yet that night, with a great squalling and twisting and rattling of metal, and dust and pine needles and pinecones pouring off of its roof in tumbling cascades, Anne Sillenes lifted it up slowly, slowly, achingly slowly, and stood with its front balanced on her shoulders.

She trembled mightily and her breath came in quick, panicked gasps. Her body could not come close to functioning normally while lifting up such a stupendous weight, yet the arts that made her live were not hindered by the strain, or at least not yet. As the train car kept rising up and she saw more and more of what was before her, she almost lost her concentration in disbelief and delight. But then she saw the hill ahead, with so many trees and stretches of rocky ground, and at the very top was her goal, the little knoll where one end of the dam met the side of the valley, anchoring the whole construction.

"Oh, God," she gasped. "Oh God, it's so far..."

But she knew she would have to. Really, it was only a little ways, she told herself. She had already traveled so far in her life. This would be only a couple of steps more.

And that was the most dangerous part, she knew: lifting the train car was one thing, but walking with it was another. Each step would demand one perilous moment when the car's whole weight was balanced on one foot while the other reached forward, and she was not sure if she could stay upright. And besides, she didn't know if she could pull the train at all: she had not even gotten the wheels off the old tracks, and would they even work in the soft earth?

She began leaning forward. Her quivering increased, and she tried to ignore the tickling in her throat as some fluid trickled down its sides. But then there was a great clunk from behind her as the wheels fell off the track, and another, and she staggered forward with one foot ahead and the other behind.

She had done it. She could move. She swallowed, and began to push forward again. She took one step, and another, and then another. She did not know it, for she could not look behind, but the wheels were not rolling with her but digging huge gouges in the earth. But it did not matter: even with this resistance she could push the train car forward.

Suddenly she wondered what she was doing. She was in so much *pain*... Why was she carrying such a huge weight? Why did she need to pull it up the hill?

She did not know, but she knew she had to keep carrying it. She had to carry this train car up to the top of the knoll, for some reason that was of upmost importance. And she realized she was whispering something, over and over again: "Anne Marie Sillenes. You are Anne Marie Sillenes..."

Every inch was a battle, every step a war. She felt blood running down her back from where the axle bit into her shoulders, but she ignored it. The vertebrae in her neck were pulverized, but the symbols inked above them did not stop functioning, and she held her head high. Something wet had happened to her knee, and she thought the kneecap there had broken free and was floating in fluid, but she did not care, and kept pushing forward.

Sometimes she remembered why. Other times she could not, but pushed regardless.

Anne Marie Sillenes. Annie. Anne Sillenes...

And as she carried the train car up the moonlit hill, crushing stone and root and heaving with each step, she began to think that this was not a new weight at all; perhaps she had been carrying it her whole life, from the very beginning, always staggering up the hill pushing this immense load, and she had only been waiting for the right opportunity to lay it down, which had finally come tonight.

Anne. Annie. Fran Marie Sillenes.

And what if I drop it? she asked herself. What if it should fall from my fingers and slide back down the hill?

Well, then, she said. Then I will simply pick it back up, and start again. It would be only a few minutes more. A few last steps in a long line of them.

Annie Fran Sillenes. Franny Beatty Sillenes. Franny Sillenes.

And as she dragged this terrible burden up the hillside, she realized she was saying things and concentrating on memories that were utterly unfamiliar to her. Why was she chanting these words? Whose name was this? And why was she focusing on this handful of fractured recollections? They were ghosts of events floating in her mind, without reference or context, like she'd stolen the memories from a stranger...and though she did not know who the people in them were, she thought of these memories as happy. So she decided to keep concentrating on them as she carried this terrible weight, remembering this strange girl (what was her name? Was it Annie?) and her memories and the things she had seen.

She remembered when the girl had first seen him at the fair, this short, ferocious young man with the old man's eyes, and how he had juggled and sung for the crowd and yet he'd bungled his act because he kept glancing at her, unable to take his eyes away. And later when he had approached her, grinning and proud, she had asked him if he was from around here and he had said no, no, I am from very far away, very far away indeed. He'd then earned her favor with a special treasure: a ripe, golden-pink peach, and as the girl had caressed its fuzzy skin (his eyes growing bright as he watched) she had asked where he'd gotten it and he had grinned and shrugged, and she'd asked if it was from his hometown and he had said no, no, he came from places even farther than the ones that had grown the peach, and those places were very far from here. And she had smiled then, puzzled.

She remembered it would not be the last time the girl would be confused, but she could not remember who this young man was. What was his name? How did she remember him? She did not know.

Fran Marie Sillenes. Annie. Anne Fran Sillenes.

She remembered how the girl and the young man would travel in the trains, the girl seated by the window so she could watch the country race by, he lounging with his head in her lap like a schoolboy, and it was on one of these journeys that he'd told her he had been traveling his whole life but when he was with her he felt like he was standing still. And he'd reached into his pocket and taken out a little box and the girl's heart had begun fluttering madly, and he'd said he wished to stay still with her forever, no matter where he was, and would you come with me, Annie, would you come with me to the far places at the end of the sky and bring with you the home that I have found in your heart, and he'd opened the box and within it was a little silver ring with many fine engravings, and she'd looked at him and he was weeping, and she'd said yes, yes, forever yes, I will be with you I will be yours.

Did the girl love him? Did he love her? She hoped so. It would be so nice, for them to love one another...

Fran. Franny. Fran Beatty. Franny Marie Beatty. Where do I know these names from?

And she remembered one day when the girl and the young man had been traveling yet again, the young man leading his troupe to the next town, and he'd said he'd been doing this for a long, long time, but now that he had found her he felt he could stop, and pass the duty on to someone else. He would stop, he'd said to the girl, and let himself grow old with her, for he'd taken special cares to make sure that he was very bad at growing old, and the girl had smiled and asked if that was so why he would want to do a silly thing like grow old, and he'd said that when he was with her every moment was perfect, and against a perfect moment the centuries and millennia are as a fly batting at a windowpane. And he'd kissed her neck then, the pale creamy spot at the corner of her jaw, and the girl had laughed and embraced him, and all the world was golden and good and their sky would never have a cloud.

I wonder what happened to that girl, she thought as she carried the train car up the hill. I bet they lived happily ever after, didn't they. I bet they lived together and had lots of babies. I bet it was sunsets neverending.

Maybe I will see them, she said to herself. Maybe that's why I'm carrying this awful weight. Maybe they are at the top of the hill and I am carrying this up to them and they need it for something, I don't know what but they need it for something, and then once I am there and they have it we will all live together and everything will be happy and good.

She nodded to herself as she carried the train car.

I know these stories. That's what happens in these stories. That's what will happen.

It would not be long now. Only a few feet more.

Far down the valley from where Colette carried George, Stanley ducked and wove west through the pines, softly chanting the song to himself, letting the echoes spill out to trail across the shoreline. For

Stanley it was always painful to perform the song; it was like having a charging river pour out of his eyes and mouth, and it took so much control. It all wanted to be sung, to reverberate throughout the world it'd made when time was not time, so it had to be harnessed back at every second. The urge was so great that he could not even speak a word; to open his mouth and make any noise might cause the song to come spilling out.

Stanley hoped Colette and George had climbed far enough to be out of danger. He glanced back at his pursuers. Some were dark, protean shapes that were difficult to make out, and others wore the images of men in gray suits, yet they leaped down the hillside with astonishing speed and agility. Their numbers appeared limitless.

But that was good. He wanted as many as he could get. All of them, if possible.

The gray tidal wave of the dam rose up on his right. Hopefully Annie would be nearly there, he thought. Before the dam the waters churned out to tumble over the rocks, and Stanley searched for a set of trees hopefully close to the middle. He spotted a promising set and began wading across as fast as he could.

He picked the hugest, stoutest tree and grasped its lower branches. But as he did he thought he saw someone out of the corner of his eye...someone gray and faint, standing in the water...

No. No, that hadn't been it. They'd been standing *on* the water, as if it'd been frozen.

He turned to look. And for the quickest moment, Stanley felt as if everything stood still. The winds did not blow, the waters did not trickle. Everything had stopped. It was the most perplexing sensation.

Then the moment ended, and he looked around. There was no one there. The specter he'd seen appeared to be gone. He shook himself, and felt the side of his face. It was as if something had just touched him there, very, very gently...

He heard the sound of the wolves sprinting down the hills, and he remembered what he was doing. He grasped the lowest limbs of the tree, picked himself up, and climbed up several levels of branches. Then he took his chain and wrapped it around his waist and the trunk and locked it tight. He kept his eyes averted from the wave of darkness descending the hills to surround him and instead hugged the trunk tight with both hands, and hoped that Colette and George had gotten as far away as possible.

When the darkness grew close it again calcified into the forms of men in gray suits. Beyond the front line they faded into shadow and obscure movement. All of their blank, gray eyes were fixed on Stanley.

"We've treed you?" said a calm, low voice below. "Is that how this is to end? How ignominious."

Stanley did not respond, but clutched the tree tighter.

"A few feet does not matter," said the wolf at the bottom of the tree. "Not for what is coming. How horrible it must be to carry all that within you. Almost as horrible as it is for us to live with this world growing within us, like a tumor. We are tired of being broken up. We wish to be whole once more. And we shall be, soon."

The sound of the river began to fade away, and all was silent. It was a sensation George had described many times, but Stanley himself had never felt it; the song affected different people in different ways, depending on which piece you had. Yet now he knew the deep horror of feeling like the world was falling away from him, bit by bit, and he cracked one eye to see what they were doing.

The river before the dam had gone as flat and still as a mirror. Before Stanley had been able to see the rocks at the bottom, but now the bottom seemed curiously dark. It was as if there was a dark split in the middle and it was spreading outward until all the rocks and water were gone and he was looking into an endless abyss. Only there was something down there at the very bottom, something unimaginably huge looking up at him, and it was trying very hard to claw its way out.

Stanley remembered what George had said he'd seen in the

burned-down remains of his theater. The wolves there had called something out of the shadows, given something terrible a name and an entry point...

"Yes," said the wolf. "It is coming for you. Don't you see it? Can you not feel it watching you?"

Yet rather than looking down into the abyss, Stanley looked up at the dam. The wolf, surprised by this reaction, followed his line of sight.

The wolf squinted at the dam. "What is that?" he said.

There was something moving on the hill where the dam ended. It was very big and bulky, and it trundled across the hilltop with the unhappy pace of a large beetle. Then as it heaved itself to one side it happened to pass just before the moon, and with such light shining behind it one could see the form of a small, thin woman below it, and she seemed to be dragging the huge object forward with a very great resolution.

The wolf's eyes widened. "What?" he said. "Wait... No, no!"

But by then, of course, it was far too late.

She finally crested the small knoll at the edge of the dam. The effort of dragging the train car up the rocky hill had rendered her unrecognizable: her face was wreathed in blood from where her eyes and nose had started bleeding, both of her legs were riddled with fractures and rends, and the toes of her right foot were mostly gone. Yet the inscriptions on her skin still held, though she could tell that they were finally straining, so with deep, heavy gasps she powered herself up the last few feet. She was finally before the lake, and she blinked the blood out of her eyes and looked.

The moon had risen high in the sky, and now its face was caught in every angle of the lake's waters, thousands and millions of little broken moons dancing among the waves. In her fatigue she could not tell the difference between the lake and the night sky; each one was a black sea peppered with shreds of white. She was not at all sure why she was there, but she thought it a powerfully beautiful sight to behold, almost a heavenly one, and she began to laugh.

She saw the edge of the dam ahead, and suddenly she knew what she had to do. She knew she could never lift the train car up and throw it down on the dam. That left only one option, then.

She took a breath, dug her feet in, and charged forward. The train car groaned as its mangled wheels jostled over the last few stones, but it did not break up or fall apart, and she did not take her eyes away from the shining sea before her; she wished to join it, to jump out among all those stars, and perhaps she would float then, suspended among all those dancing lights, and then maybe, just maybe, she could sleep.

When she came to the edge of the knoll she crouched down with the train car on her back and sprang off. She felt her feet leave the ground and heard the train car sliding off the rocks behind her. The axle ripped her around and around as the car tumbled down to the dam, and as she twirled the boundaries between the lake and the sky blurred even more than before, turning all the world around her into a star-strewn sky, and she shut her eyes and crossed her arms and smiled and waited for sleep to take her.

As Stanley watched, the dam did not precisely break like he'd expected; *unzip* was more the right word, as the train car smoothly split it down the southern side and the stone began to peel back with a roar. He thought he saw a tiny rag-doll figure fall with the train car, and his heart froze at the sight. He moaned softly and hugged the tree tighter.

"Run!" cried one of the wolves below. "Run, run!"

But it was too late for that. Though the wolves tried to move, they were just at the foot of the dam, and the water was already surging down upon them. It was an enormous wave, a blank wall of water, and as it approached Stanley saw it was much, much bigger than he'd expected, easily tall enough to reach him. He wrapped one arm up in the chain and watched with wide eyes as the water rolled toward him.

He realized then that some situations, no matter how dire, provide an outside chance of outrageous luck that allows one to believe one just might survive; yet on seeing this tremendous crush of water roaring down to him, Stanley knew this was not one of them. The vast wave was already swallowing trees on either side of the river, ones much sturdier than his, and his chain and his grasp on the tree would be like paper beneath its crushing tons.

And as he watched, Stanley realized he had always known in his heart that this had been a possible outcome, and yet he'd done it anyway. But he did not feel regret, or any fear. The only thing he thought of was George. Though his time with his son had been brief and he'd allowed his duty to come between them, this last act would be the greatest of all of his presents.

And besides, he thought, he was immensely tired of carrying the song. It was so heavy these days, so incredibly heavy. As he began to feel the first waves of mist, he wondered if perhaps this would be a peace for him.

CHAPTER 35

The Hanged Man

Colette turned when she heard the train car crack through the dam and watched wide-eyed as the water burst through the crumbling wall and cascaded down into the river valley. "Oh, Jesus," she said, and laid George down on the ground to see the rest of the fallout. Small trees sank down below the waves and taller ones took on an uncomfortable, drunken lean. She saw dark figures rolling with the water, but they seemed limp and broken, and they began to melt back into the shadows after a moment.

George moaned and turned over. Then he sat up, rubbing his head. "What happened?" he asked.

Colette simply pointed. George looked behind them and his mouth fell open. "What happened?" he asked again.

"Someone broke the dam," she said. "I'm guessing Stanley. It looks like he flooded out the wolves. Can wolves be killed by water?"

"Sort of, I think... Franny killed one with her bare hands," said George.

"Annie," corrected Colette.

George did not pay attention. He nervously watched where the flood crept up the side of the hill. For a moment it passed where they'd originally hidden underneath the backdrop, and George was thankful Colette had carried him as far as she did. Then it lessened, and though the river still poured over the broken remains of the dam it was not as violent as it'd initially been.

"He's down there," said George.

"Who?" Colette asked.

"My father," he said.

She gave him a worried look. "Harry's dead, George. We saw it happen."

"Silenus isn't my father, Colette," he said.

"What? Are you joking?"

George shook his head.

"Then who is?"

He looked down at the cardboard still clutched in his hand and Stanley's last message written there. She saw and realized what he was thinking. "Are...are you serious?" she asked.

"Yes," he said. "Harry and Stanley are related, just like you said, but Harry wasn't my father. They lied to me, to everyone, right from the start. I don't know why, not yet. But he's down there. I can sense it."

"How?"

"Have you ever noticed how things seem calmer around Stanley? How sometimes it's just nice to sit with him, or how he makes everything make sense?"

"I...I guess," she said.

"It's the song," said George. "It's all the pieces of the First Song inside of him. I was just too ignorant to notice it. But now I know what to look for. I can feel it in him." He put the piece of cardboard in his pocket. "I was so cruel to him...I never even said thank you for all the little things he did for me. I never even got the chance to tell him that I loved him. Or the chance to love him at all." Then he stood.

"What are you going to do, George?" asked Colette.

"I'm going to find him," he said. "If there's even the slightest chance he's still alive, I've got to try."

"Still alive?" said Colette. "What do you mean, still alive?"

George remembered how Stanley had looked at him before he'd handed him the card. It had been the look of a man who was readying to stare into death. Wherever Stanley had been going, he had not expected to return.

"Stay here," said George, and started off down the hill.

The lower woods were a soggy, dripping ruin. It was impossible to walk ten feet without being soaked by the water dripping from overhead. Trees and shrubs had been uprooted or pushed over, and in places the forest was nothing but yards of dark, tangled branches. Bands of washed-up leaves marked the edges of the flow, creating bizarre little pathways on the ground or strange insignias on trees. Besides the distant river there was not a sound.

Then George heard something: a tinkling, like that of metal. He realized it was coming from the same direction in which he sensed the song, and dodged through the snarls of branches.

George slowed to a stop when he saw him. He moaned in despair and his hands flew to his brow. Then he walked forward to better see what was hanging from the crushed pine ahead.

Stanley had chained himself to the trunk, it seemed, and the chain had held on a little too well. His father hung upside down from the pine's twisted branches, his arms at unfamiliar angles and a dark stripe of blood marking his side where the chain still clutched him. Then George saw that his mouth was moving, and he realized that his father was still alive.

He cried out and ran to him to untangle him from the pine. His father's large, dark eyes blindly searched for him, hearing his efforts, and he tried to reach out to his son with one hand. George said, "Don't move, please don't move," and unlooped the chain from the last branch and eased his father down.

George laid him out on the wet stone beside the riverbank. Now that he held him in his arms George could not help but feel the immense tug from what was trapped within Stanley. He first wondered if perhaps he was becoming more attuned to the song now that he knew where it was, but then he realized it was something else: Stanley was losing control of all the echoes, and they were beginning to leak out of him.

Stanley's hand again reached out to him, and George took it and laid its palm along his cheek. "I'm here," said George. "I'm here. I'm finally here."

His father smiled and nodded. Then his pale face wrinkled in concern, and he tried to pull George close.

"What?" said George. "What can I do?"

And then, for the first time in what had to be many, many years, his father spoke: "George," he said, and the word was overlaid with the many tones of the First Song. "It's coming."

"What is?" said George.

Stanley raised a hand and pointed to the river. George looked and at first saw nothing, but then he noticed there was a curiously dense shadow in the center of the water, denser than even the blackest night, and he suddenly felt as if there were two eyes behind that crack, watching him and trying to push through with all its strength.

Ice began to creep across the river. Soon the sound of babbling water had faded entirely, and it felt as if all light was hurriedly fleeing the valley. There was a groan from down in the shadow under the ice, so deep and low it was nearly impossible to hear, and in his heart George realized it was the sound of the bones of Creation itself being pushed aside to make room for something's passage.

They had started, he realized. Just before Stanley had flooded the valley they must have started to bring their own creator through, the First Darkness. It would not tolerate being robbed of its prize when it had come so close, and was, perhaps for the very first time, about to make an appearance in Creation itself.

"Oh, no," said George. "No, no. What can we do?"

Stanley laid a hand on his arm.

"What?" George said.

His father crooked his finger. George bent closer.

"What is it?" he asked.

Stanley clapped one hand on the back of George's neck, holding him there, and opened his mouth and began to breathe out. As he did a thousand little veins of light came fluttering out, caught on the breeze of his last exhalation, and rushed into George's open mouth. George's eyes went wide and he struggled to pull back, but Stanley's grasp held fast.

It was the same as when George had first found the song outside of Rinton, but magnified a thousand times. Again, it was like the sky opened up and something unimaginably vast was poured into him, but this time it simply kept going, an unending rush of voices and pitches filling up every space within his head.

Some of the echoes leaped out, and George realized Stanley was showing them to him with his last moments. One flashed bright, and he saw...

...Silenus stands at the door of his office, and Stanley sits below the bay window. A cup of tea is cooling beside the chair in front of the desk. A boy has just been sitting in that chair, but Silenus has just thrown him out and is still breathing hard from the effort. For a moment there is silence as the two men consider what the boy has just said.

"He thinks he is my son," says Silenus. "He really believes it." He looks at Stanley, furious. "But he isn't, is he? Is he, Stan?"

Stanley, white and quaking with disbelief, stands up and tries to walk forward, but falls to his knees. Tears spring to his eyes and he struggles for a moment, and he opens his mouth.

"No, no!" cries Silenus. He rushes over and claps a hand across Stanley's mouth. "I know it's hard, but you can't lose focus! Not now!"

Stanley's hands search for his blackboard. At first he is so agitated he cannot do much more than scribble, but then he writes: MY SON MY SON MY SON

"Yes, yes," says Silenus, annoyed, and he releases him. "He is your son, it seems. And he's a problem. A problem we could've avoided if you'd just kept your dick in your pants —"

Stanley throws off Silenus's grasp and whirls around and strikes him across the face. Silenus falls backward, arms pinwheeling, and lands on his back on the floor. He groans and glares up at Stanley. *"Christ, Stan? What the hell?"*

Stanley gives him a cold look and begins to walk out of the office to finally greet his son, but Silenus sits up and grabs his wrist and holds him back. *"Don't,"* he says.

Stanley tries to shake him off, but Silenus will not let go. *"Didn't you hear what I said?"* he asks. *"That boy is a problem!"*

Stanley stoops and picks up the blackboard and writes: WHAT KIND OF PROBLEM

"You know what kind of problem," says Silenus. "We've worked for years to keep our enemies distracted from you. Everything I do is meant to remove their attention from you and focus it all on me. We've worked so hard to conceal that you're even related to me. They think you're just some fucking cellist! So if we suddenly start traveling with this kid who has a hell of a lot of the Silenus family resemblance, and it becomes apparent that he's your son, then what is that going to do? They'll know you're my blood relation, and then they'll know we've been hiding something. This kid could be nothing but a big red arrow pointing straight to you, Stan! Think!"

Stanley tries not to see the sense in this, shaking his head.

"You know I'm right," said Silenus. "We've got to take care of this. Send him away somewhere, keep him safe. I know it's got to tear you up, Stan, but we've got to."

Stanley writes: WE CAN TELL HIM. KEEP HIM SAFE WITH US. WILL KEEP OUR SECRETS.

"We can't tell him, Stan. That boy is sixteen years old, and I know you might not want to hear this, but he is reckless and arrogant as all

hell. We can't trust him with something so important. Maybe one day we can tell him. But not now. For now, we've got to send him some-where far, far away."

Then Stanley's eyes light up. He looks at Silenus, and his excite-ment quickly fades. He writes: HE CAN STAY.

"I told you, we can't—"

But Stanley is already writing again: DO NOT HAVE TO BRING ANY ATTENTION TO ME.

"And how would you do that?" asks Silenus.

THE BOY BELIEVES YOU ARE HIS FATHER.

"So?"

Stanley writes the next words slowly, as if signing a contract he is already regretting: WHAT IS WRONG WITH LETTING HIM BELIEVE THAT?

Silenus frowns as he reads this message. He looks at Stanley, aston-ished, and asks, "What, me? Act like his father? Oh, no. No, no, no."

Stanley sits down next to Silenus on the floor. Silenus keeps shaking his head. "I couldn't do something like that, Stan," he says. "Look at me. I'm not cut out for that kind of schtick at all. It would be terrible."

Stanley writes: SAFEST AND EASIEST WAY. YOU KNOW THAT.

Silenus looks at him suspiciously. "You would really do that? Let your son think someone else is his father?"

Stanley sighs. He writes: ANYTHING TO KEEP HIM CLOSE.

The echo faded, and was gone. More kept flooding into George, one after the other. Another flashed bright, and he saw...

... Stanley is standing in a general store. In one hand is a bag holding two tailored suits and a packet of toffees. In the other hand is a second bag, and in this are combs, razors, shoes, some aftershave, and several books.

"That's quite the haul you have there," says the clerk. "Someone's birthday?"

Stanley writes: YES. MAKING UP FOR A LOT OF BIRTHDAYS.

"*I can understand that,*" *said the clerk.* "*I have two boys of my own. I traveled a lot in my old job, and never got to see them. But I'm glad to be home now.*"

Stanley nods, but then he frowns and glances at his bag of small trinkets. They seem even smaller now. At most they are cheap toys.

"*What's wrong?*" *asks the clerk.* "*Not what you wanted?*"

Stanley sighs, and writes: NO. BUT IT IS ALL I CAN GET.

…More echoes, more and more, containing countless years and vistas and lives, and another one swam out to George, and inside it was…

…It is very cold outside, but Stanley stands on the train platform and refuses to leave. He watches the train fade away, his son and his great-uncle on board, and he continues wiping his tears with his handkerchief. In his other hand he holds a gold pocket watch.

He puts away the handkerchief and stares at the watch in his hand. He frowns at it, tilting it back and forth, taking in its many imperfections: its scuffed glass, its chipped case, the way the knob at the top has come loose and sits askew on the top. His face twists into disgust at his paltry gift, and he stuffs it into his pocket and walks away from the platform.

He is in the middle of the street when he stops, shaking his head and moaning. He looks back at the train, but it is gone. He takes one clenched fist out of his pocket and pounds the side of his head with it, moaning a little with each strike. Then he reaches up to the sky with both hands, as if drawing in the breath to scream.

The air around him trembles. From somewhere within him there comes the sound of many voices, singing and chanting softly. And Stanley, who has borne all these echoes for so, so long, wants nothing more than to throw them to the sky and crawl out from under the burden that has defined his entire life.

He almost does it. Yet at the last moment his arms drop, and he stands with his head bowed, defeated. He reaches into his pocket and takes out the watch again. He stares at it, and slowly his face fills with loathing. Then he flings the watch down and stomps on it with one foot.

As the crunch of the glass echoes across the street, all the fury leaves his face. He does not breathe, shocked at what he has done. He removes his foot and stares down at the broken glass and the tiny, gossamer-thin gears lying mangled on the stone. An heirloom ruined in a second's rage. He moans a little again, already regretting his decision, and he stoops and picks up some of the watch's innards and cradles them in his palm.

He sits down and picks up more of the watch, and as he does he begins weeping again. He looks to the sky and holds out the handful of broken gears as if begging some unseen force to take back his rash action, or perhaps to come down and repair what he has done. But nothing happens, and he sighs and bows his head again.

Eventually he collects the pieces of the watch and wraps them up in his tearstained handkerchief. Then he stands up, looks back in the direction of the train again, and with another sigh he walks back to the hotel to await the return of his great-uncle, and the one thing he still treasures in this world: his only child.

...And when this one faded even more echoes came charging into George. The knowledge of these moments was so much that he wanted to tear his face away, but still Stanley held fast as he surrendered all the echoes all the troupes had fought for and collected, eons worth of effort, impossibly vast amounts of information and history. And even though this sensation was nearly enough to cripple him, George could still sense that these echoes were *happy*: they had finally, after ages of waiting and being borne throughout the world, been reunited with their missing sibling, the one huge piece that George had been carrying since he was a child.

George could not see it, but the branches of all the surrounding trees, fallen or upright, began to bend toward him, as if drawn in by a hidden weight. Stones nearby twisted on the ground to point toward him. And up the hill the thousand little trickling streams suddenly changed direction to run down and pass below his feet.

The flow of echoes stopped and Stanley's hand fell. George sat back, stupefied. Then he breathed out, and blinked.

In the surrounding towns of upper New York, just a ways from where George now sat, many people who otherwise would have been sleeping soundly instead stirred and sat up, frowning. If asked they would not have been able to say why they'd awoken; they might have said something about hearing a noise, or experiencing the strangest sensation of their beds tipping underneath them, but none would have been entirely sure. Yet of these sudden insomniacs several awoke to find their property or surroundings in very strange shape.

For example, an elderly woman in Keesville awoke in her home and went downstairs, suspecting a prowler. She found no trespasser, nor any missing valuables, but on entering her kitchen she struck her head on something very hard that should not have been there. After she recovered she looked up to find all her pots and pans were still hanging above her stove, but now they were hanging at a sharp angle, and she'd popped her head on the largest skillet. She felt the air around them, but found no strings; it was as if they were being magnetically pulled toward the southwestern wall of her home. She called upon her neighbor to have her witness this phenomenon, but her neighbor was in a similar state of distress: her dining room chairs had all slid away from the table to crash against the southwestern corner of her own home. On being pulled away the chairs slid promptly back, and both women puzzled over this until they noticed the sofa and dressers slowly sliding toward them. They stared as the rest of the furniture inched across the floor to gather on the wall. Neither of them was able to explain what was happening, but they did nervously admit that they felt as if the ground were shifting beneath them, and they kept looking out the window at the south-western horizon, as if subconsciously anticipating the rise of a new sun.

On the outskirts of Lake Placid an old gentleman attempted to return to sleep by indulging in a puff of tobacco with his favorite pipe. At first his habit comforted him, but then he noticed the pipe smoke was behaving very oddly: it seemed to be gathering in the top corner of his parlor, rather than dispersing as usual. The smoke kept building and condensing until it took on the appearance of an extremely large cocoon lodged up under the ceiling. This greatly perturbed the old gentleman, and nothing he did, from blowing at it to poking it with a broom, managed to break up the ball of smoke. He ventured outside, thinking there must be some crack in the wall, and found that the wall was as firm and smooth as it'd always been. Yet it was there that he noticed the smoke from his still-lit pipe was moving away in a very solid, thin line, as if it was being invisibly tugged toward the woods. It appeared to align with the course of the smoke in his parlor room, but outside there was nothing to block its way. He frowned at this, but became much more disturbed when he looked up and saw the clouds overhead were doing the very same thing as his pipe smoke.

A naturalist camping at Clamshell Pond also noticed something wrong with the sky, but he had a very good reason to awake: the air had become filled with the sound of cheeping, chirping, and honk-ing. He fetched his binoculars and climbed out of his tent, and he looked up to find the air was filled with birds flying in many forma-tions. But the most astounding thing was that all of them were flying in one direction: east. Some of the loner birds, he saw, were predato-rial raptors, and yet they did not prey upon the abundant smaller birds around them, nor did any of the smaller birds appear wary of them at all; they all appeared too preoccupied to bother with their usual bird business. As he reflected on this he noticed that there was also something wrong with the far side of Clamshell Lake: it appeared to be creeping up the shore, as if the water was defying all physics and attempting to flow uphill. Unless he was mistaken, it was trying to flow in the exact direction the birds were flying in.

And just up the valley from George, Colette was debating going down to check on him when she was nearly bowled over. It felt as if a hook had been attached to her waist, and someone had just given it a strong tug. "What the..." she said on standing back up, and she looked down and saw her feet were slowly sliding down the hill.

She was not the only thing to move. The very leaves on the ground began to coalesce into lines that all pointed down toward the riverbed. She reached out and grabbed hold of a tree branch to steady herself, but when she looked up she saw the entire tree was bent in the same direction; it looked like an enormous wooden comb, with all its branches pointing the same way. Part of the trunk had played host to a nest of ants, but the ants were fleeing their home, walking down the trunk in a straight line to continue across the forest floor, parallel to all the branches and the leaves. It was, she thought, as if the entire valley were rushing to pay respects to someone very important who'd just arrived.

Every one of them witnessed different phenomena, but unbeknownst to them they all experienced the same queer, unsettling sensation. Though they could not articulate it, they all felt as if the center of the world had suddenly shifted to just several miles away, and all the elements were bending to meet it. Only one of them knew what the epicenter of that pull could be.

"George!" cried Colette. "What are you doing?"

The shadow under the river ice kept growing, and the entire valley shook as the thing in the dark tried to force its entry. But George did not pay attention. He crawled forward on his hands and knees and sat by his father.

Stanley was not breathing anymore, and George knew he was

gone. He stared into his father's face for a moment. Then he reached into his father's right pocket. It was cold and damp from the dam water, but still he felt some package in there.

He took it out. It was a soggy handkerchief, all rolled up. George gently unwrapped it, and the interior of its wet surface sparkled with broken glass and tiny wheels, and in the center was the fat, cracked watch.

He stroked one side of the watch. "It's broken," he said, and when he did his words echoed through the valley with a strange, ghostly timbre.

Behind him the ice finally cracked, and floes bent up and shattered as the thing below shouldered its way up. The very riverbed crumpled around it, and soon there was a huge, scarred snout, and black, empty eyes, and seemingly miles and miles of yellowed teeth. If a random onlooker had happened to glance on the thing emerging from the ice they would have been immediately driven mad; yet for the one second before they would have had a fleeting impression of an enormous, black-eyed wolf, with ancient, mottled fur and patches of scarred hide, a thing so terrible it defied naming and comprehension. One could not fear the thing pushing its way though the river; one was merely nothing before it.

Yet George still did not take his eyes off the watch. "But I can fix it," he said softly.

The great wolf turned its eyes on him. It began to lunge forward, jaws so wide they could touch both the Earth and the moon if it wished, ready to swallow this tiny boy and the hateful treasure he hid within himself…

George shut his eyes, stood up, and turned around. "No," he said, and again his voice echoed across the valley. Yet it kept going, echoing on and on, rolling across the face of the Earth until it echoed in the very skies and seas.

And the great wolf, to its surprise, stopped. It looked around itself. The world had frozen around them both, like a spinning top suddenly hanging still in space. And, now that it had stopped, the great wolf saw that the clouds had frozen in mid-swirl just above George's head, and all the valley was bent toward him, and on every tree was a bird or a squirrel or some other creature, eagerly watching him.

In the infinite abysses of the great wolf's mind, it began to feel troubled. Something was wrong. It was as if all of existence was waiting on the boy's command. There was nothing that could do something so powerful, thought the great wolf. Nothing except...

The wolf began to growl. It realized it recognized that voice the boy had used: it had heard it long ago, when Creation had first been founded, a voice in the dark summoning the fundament out of nothing...

The wolf stared at the child, and it began to understand that while George did not have the entirety of the song, he now had enough of it. Enough to hold infinity and Creation itself within the palm of his hand, and do with them as he wished.

George opened his eyes. Their color had faded, as if he had beheld something so great they could now see nothing else. Which was true: when they looked out upon the world, his eyes saw everything at every point in time. His mind now held nearly all the structure and form of Creation itself, almost every second of every year, every particle of every piece of matter; inside him were a billion tiny lives flaring and dying all at once, millions of mountains teetering between rising and eroding, the waters of all the world frozen between low and high tides, the warp and weft of all the web. And yet in spite of all this it seemed a terribly fragile thing, a tiny construct spun out of spider's silk. If he wished, he could blow it all away right now with but a puff of his lungs.

The great wolf retreated a few steps, gathering the valley in darkness. As it did, more dark, feral shapes came crawling out of the rent in the river. These lesser wolves padded down the riverbank to gather below their own father. They were tiny things in comparison, none of them rising higher than its toes, but there were so many that George wondered if all of the shadows under Creation had been emptied for this. Soon they looked like a black ocean with a single enormous wave rising out of its center. Some of the smaller waves looked like wolves; others looked like men with gray eyes and blank faces.

The great wolf growled again, and George considered what to do. Even though he had nearly all of the song, he could not destroy the wolf, that he knew; it would be like the king of an island declaring war on the ocean. But neither could the great wolf attack him: Creation was one thing, but its Creator...that was quite another.

But then he began to realize what he could do.

It would take so much—a change so fundamental he would have to start it all over again—but he could try it.

He looked down at his father. Stanley's face was still beaded with water, and his expression was oddly peaceful. George kissed two fingers of his hand and laid them upon his father's cheek. Stanley was still warm. Then George looked up to face the wolves.

Before the wolves could attack, he opened his mouth, took a breath, and began to sing.

The wolves shook their heads, proving their imperviousness to the First Song, but then George did something they did not expect: as he sang, he *changed* the song, rearranging the notes and pitches, and he began singing of something wholly new.

And when he did, he reached up and took the entire sky in his hands and wiped it away, the clouds and atmosphere vanishing with one swipe. Once he was done he shook his hands out, and then the sky itself was gone and there were only the stars above. It was as if the sky had never been; he had sung it out of existence altogether.

The wolves stared in confusion. Of all the things they'd expected, they'd never thought of *that*. And as George continued to sing, Creation began to shrink around them.

George clapped his hands, and as the sound echoed across the world all the many forms of life blinked out as if they had never been born at all.

He reached up again as he sang and he plucked the very stars down and crushed them in his fingers, and then the stars were gone.

He reached down and gathered up the mountains and the hills about his feet as if they were but toys, and he shrank them down one by one, and then the mountains were gone.

He reached down once more and he cupped his hands and scooped up all the waters, all the seas and oceans and little lakes, and once he had them all he wiped his hands, and then the oceans were gone.

He took the sun and the moon in each hand and lifted them up, and with a little puff blew both of them away as if they were no more than dust, and then the sun and the moon were gone.

Then George peered up into the air, and he clapped his hands on something invisible, and he then held Time itself within his hands. He sang and gathered up all of its flow, and he pushed it down and down, reducing it from eons to millennia to centuries to decades, and then to years and months and days and seconds, until there was only one second left, and George took it and crushed it, and then Time itself was gone.

And once that was done George reached out to either side and took both ends of Creation itself, and he began to press inward as he

sang, changing each note of the song as he did, telling it all to go

down, down as far down as it could, and Creation began to

erode away, falling away to the darkness, and though

George began to weep at the sight of what he

did he kept pushing and pushing

until finally there was

nothing

but

CHAPTER 36

The Second Song

Look.

There is nothing. No skies, no Earth; no day, no sun, no time; there is only nothing here. Nothing.

Except:

There is a boy. He stands in the darkness, alone. Around the boy is a ring of wolves, and they watch the boy from the shadows, wondering what he is going to do. They did not expect to find themselves here, never expected to see the boy pull the curtains down upon all the world. And yet that is what the boy has done, and the wolves are not sure if they should be glad or not.

The boy looks out at the wolves. He is frightened, but he knows what he has to do.

This is a performance, the boy says to himself. There is an audience. There is a song. And the song must be played. And they will listen.

So the boy opens his mouth, and he begins to sing.

He sings of a world. He sings of a world like a candle flame, a small, hot fluttering in the dark, forever fighting back shadow, yet always dying down, bit by bit, falling away into night. This the boy makes a truth, perhaps the only truth easily found: the world exists, he sings, and like all that exists it must one day die. All things die, sings the boy, no matter how precious.

As he sings he looks down at his hand, and in his hand is a broken watch.

Yes, he thinks to himself. I know that now. No matter how precious.

He sings of a world that is constantly shifting and eternally mysterious, a world with countless shadowed corners and hidden truths that always remain just beyond your grasp. He sings of a world filled with perceptions and assumptions, and desperate hopes and dreams, and always the desire to make this world and all its hidden truths conform to those dreams. The world should know, sings that desire, it should know us and listen to us. The melody of that desire does not end; as the boy sings of it, it is clear that it is meant to last for as long as the world itself. So long as the world remains there will always be the wish to look out at Creation, and see something looking back.

And once he has done this the boy begins to re-sing Creation. He puts back everything as it was; he sings of light on the shadow, and then mountains, and oceans and many seas, and the cloud-dappled skies and the blazing sun. He sings of years of history, all of them exactly as they once were; he sings of every position of every particle, every ripple and drop of every water. And once this is done he begins to sing of all the billions of lives that once crawled or walked or flew across the face of this Earth, from the smallest flea to the oldest, wisest human, centuries and centuries of history, rebuilt moment by moment.

He puts them all back, every one. The wolves are confused to witness this. If he is putting everything back, they ask, why did he tear it all down? Yet the great wolf behind them is not so sure; the boy is constantly changing the song as he sings it. Is there some subtle difference between this world and the last? The wolf tries to shake off the uneasy feeling that the boy is building Creation around them all, penning them in...

Soon the world is almost as it was when the boy destroyed it. He has rebuilt time all the way up to his own life, his own story, and almost to the very events that led to where he stands now. And there he stops.

For the first time he is uncertain. He knows what he is about to see. But he is not sure what he will do.

He blinks, and suddenly he is standing on the waters of a wide, dark river. Behind him is a huge cement wall, damming the river back. And even though he shuts his eyes, the boy knows what is emerging from the black mists ahead: a small island, and on that island are many tall trees, and at the base of one of the tallest trees is a man.

The man is tall and thin and his hair is a bright bottle blond. Even though he is muddy, he is impeccably dressed. He is grasping one of the lower branches of the trees as if he intends to climb it, but he has turned and is staring out across the waters at the boy. Yet he does not see him; time does not work in this place, not yet, and so the man can see nothing. It is as if he is a statue.

The boy opens his eyes and looks at the man, and all the breath leaves his body. The boy has rebuilt so much history with no more than a thought, and yet this one event, so tiny in comparison to all the rest of what he has made, is the grain of sand within the marvelous workings of his creation. The very sight of this man wounds the boy in some deep, hidden part of himself. And yet it is not entirely painful. In some ways, the boy rejoices to see this muddy, pale, anxious figure. He feels like he has done this before. After all, the last time he saw the man whole and unhurt he'd been standing beneath a tree, and the man had not seen or spoken to him then, either . . .

The boy hesitates, and waves to the man. The boy drops his hand and says, "You can't see me. I know that. It was stupid of me to wave, but . . . I thought I should anyway."

His lips tremble. He knows that if he does not say what he wishes to say, he never will. So he walks across the waters to the man, and asks, "Why didn't you tell me? Why didn't you tell me what you were?"

Of course, the man does not answer; he simply stares ahead, as still and frozen as the rest of this new world.

"I wish you had told me," the boy says. "I know why you didn't, but . . . I still wish you had."

The boy realizes he is breathing very fast. He looks up the tree, and tears begin to well up in his eyes. "I know what's going to happen," he says to the man. "I know what will happen if you climb that tree. You'll chain yourself to it, and Annie will break the dam, and then, then . . ."

He cannot stop himself now. The boy begins crying. The man stares ahead, ignorant of his tears. In a way the boy is the only person in the world, and yet somehow he feels even more alone than that.

"You don't have to!" the boy shouts at the man. "You don't have to climb the tree! The dam doesn't have to break! I could . . . I could snap my fingers, and none of this could happen! We could be . . . be back at the theater, in your dressing room, and I could be watching you practice. You played Claudio Merulo. I remember that. It was so pretty, Father. You did so good.

"Or maybe we could be somewhere else," the boy says to the frozen figure. "I could make a home for us. Somewhere where there are trees. We could go on walks together. And you could talk. You could talk to me. You wouldn't have to write anymore! Do you hear me? You wouldn't have to write anymore! Wouldn't you like that? I could do that for you! I could do that, with just a wave of my hand!"

But the man does not answer. He stares across the water, face fixed in an expression of curious concern. And yet there is peace in his face. It is the look of a man who knows exactly what he is doing, and would gladly do so again.

The boy looks into the man's eyes, tears streaming down his cheeks, and he sniffs. "But we don't get that, do we?" he asks him. "We don't get those moments. It wouldn't be right, to make the world something it isn't, just because we want it to be." He looks down at his hand, and the broken watch clutched there. "It wouldn't be right. And it wouldn't be real."

He looks back up at the frozen man. The boy nods. "What will happen will happen. I'm . . . I'm glad we got what we did. And I'm sorry if I was mean to you. But you know that, don't you."

The boy steps forward, and takes the frozen man by the shoulders. Then, standing up on his tiptoes — for the man is very tall, and the boy very short — he places one kiss on the man's cheek, and whispers into his ear, "I'll see you soon. Just you wait. I've already been there. And so have you."

Then he steps back, and he nods, and the trees and the island and the man melt into darkness, and the moment passes by.

The world will continue as it was. And besides, the boy cannot go back. Even if he were to choose a life of his own creation, and carve a blissful history for himself into the world's face with his own hand, it would give him no joy, for he cannot forget what he has seen. Unlike all the other inhabitants of this world, he has now seen all the hidden truths, all the shadowed corners.

All but one. As the boy makes his final changes to Creation, the First Song slipping through his fingers as he uses up every note and every voice, he begins to wonder . . . is he wrong, or is he seeing a structure in the song? Is there a hand invisibly working throughout all the melodies and harmonies, one that is not his own? Who sang this song, originally? Was it ever sung, or has it always been echoing in the deeps?

He knows the wolves are but an accidental audience. So whom is he singing for? For himself? Or something more? Is there a face drawn out among all the millions of notes of this song, and is it looking back at him, and smiling?

As soon as he wonders these questions he understands he will never know. He has so much of the song, but he is still missing a few little notes, and one or two key voices. These gaps, as tiny as they are, upset the whole, and he is not sure if he can see any kind of plan at all in what he is singing.

Perhaps this is not the first time. Perhaps there have been other Creators besides himself, all of them stumbling across this echoing song and re-singing the world when it is threatened by the dark. And each time it is imperfect. Maybe so.

That truth will always be beyond him. And he nods, submitting to it. What will happen will happen.

He is almost finished now. He has made all the changes he thinks he can. He rebuilds the valley, every twig and every tree, and the girl is there on the very edge clinging to a branch, and his father lies at his feet once again. The wolves still wait at the end of the valley, and the great wolf towers above them, head cocked, curious.

The boy does not start time again yet. The world remains frozen. He has only a few more notes of the song left, but he refrains from singing them.

From the great wolf comes a voice that is like the churning core of the Earth. It asks: And what did that do?

The boy says, "I changed things."

The wolf asks: How?

"For so long you've been the abyss," says the boy. "We stare into you, and you terrify us. You swallow up the world piece by piece. But now I have changed that."

The great wolf's head cocks a little more.

"*Now the abyss will know what it is like to look into itself,*" says the boy. "*Because I have taken all your children, and made them real.*"

The great wolf looks down, shocked, and around its feet are not the dark, feral shapes that were like tiny versions of itself. Instead it is surrounded by men in gray suits, but now they are no longer pictures: they are real, with flesh and bone and skin. The men in gray look down upon themselves, and see that they now no longer imitate humans; they *are* humans, and each of them carries a tiny shred of the First Song within him.

"*You are all alive now,*" says the boy. "*Just like everyone else. And one day you will die, just like everyone else. You will be eaten by the very shadow you once were.*"

A horrified cry rises up among all the men in gray. They wail and feel their fleshy bodies, and gnash their all-too-real teeth. To exist, they scream, is the worst possible nightmare, an unimaginable horror.

The great wolf above them wheels about, confused, and, for the first time since Creation was made, frightened. How could this be so? How could the boy have changed something so elemental?

It looks at the boy, and says: *You cannot do this. You cannot make me devour my own children.*

"*Yet you must,*" says the boy. "*They exist, so they must end. Maybe not today, but someday. How many of our own children have we lost to you? How many fathers, how many mothers? How many will we lose if you should get what you want, and devour the world?*"

The wolf says: *But we must. It pains us so. It pains us.*

"*I know,*" says the boy. "*It hurts to be below Creation. Just as it hurts to dangle above the darkness. Then what are we to do?*"

The wolf looks at the boy, thinking. It asks: *What is it you want?*

"*What anyone wants. Time.*"

The wolf says: *I cannot give you that.*

"*Then you will lose your children, and be alone, even less than you once were. You will be broken forever, and never whole.*"

The wolf thinks. It realizes now that it must make a decision. The darkness has never made a decision before. There has only been one possible thing to do, to swallow up the light above. There has never been an alternative. But now it must take a first step into this unfamiliar country, and think of how to please this small boy in this little valley.

The great wolf finally asks: *How much time?*

And the boy tells him.

CHAPTER 37

Pater Omnipotens Aeterna Deus

There was a clap of thunder, and a soft breeze rolled across the valley. Colette jumped and swayed drunkenly as she grasped the tree branch. Then she gave up and fell to the ground and sat there.

She felt very dizzy. For a second it'd been like the ground was lurching beneath her. But that hadn't really been it, she decided. For a moment everything had *stuttered*, just like when Harry and Stanley performed the First Song, but...that gap where everything was gone had been so much *longer*. Hadn't it? It had felt like so many seconds and years had been lost just now.

Something had changed, she realized as she looked around. The trees were no longer bent toward the valley, and the lines of leaves were not there. It was just ordinary forest floor. Someone or some*thing* had just been here, she said to herself, but it had changed things, or left something behind before it departed, yet she could not see it.

She stood back up. Then she said, "George," and began to sprint down the hillside.

Colette ran along the riverbank, trying to find some trace of Stanley or George, but she saw nothing, only broken trees and many upturned rocks. Then she spotted a figure crouching over something by the riverbank. They were dressed in bright blue, but it was not George, or Stanley...

The person looked up. He smiled a little apologetically. "Hello, Lettie," said Silenus.

Colette stared at him, astounded. He was wearing an extraordinarily blue sack coat and checked trousers, and a clean bowler derby sat on the rock beside him. She gaped for a moment. "Harry?" she cried.

He nodded, but he looked quite sad. "Hello," he said again.

She laughed and ran to him, thinking to embrace him, but stopped when she saw what he was crouching over. Her happiness vanished and she covered her mouth in horror.

George and Stanley lay side by side on the riverbank. Stanley's arms had clearly been broken, and there was a horrible gash in his side. His skin was pale and waxy, and his eyelids and lips were already turning blue. Colette had not ever seen anyone in such a state, but she immediately knew he was dead.

Silenus reached down and stroked one side of Stanley's face, and sniffed. "I...I didn't think it could ever come to this," he said.

"Oh, no," said Colette, and she walked to where George lay.

He did not look as bad as Stanley: his skin was still pink, and he had not a mark on him. But she could see he was not breathing, and when she touched his neck he was warm but there was no pulse.

"What happened?" said Silenus.

"I don't know," she said. "I was up the hill, and...and then everything *bent*, and it was...Wait, what happened to *you*? I...I saw you die, Harry!" She reached out and took his shoulder with one hand and felt his face with the other. "I saw it."

"Yeah, well," he said darkly. "Let's just say it didn't take. I got here as fast as I could from the Founding. And I just...found them here. Stanley is...He's..."

"He flooded the valley," said Colette. "He distracted the wolves from us so that we could get away, and drowned them. I guess he got hurt. I'm sorry, Harry."

Silenus nodded, but kept stroking Stanley's face.

"What's wrong with George?" she asked. "I didn't see what happened to him. He's got no pulse, and he's not breathing...Oh, George."

"He's not dead," said Silenus. "He's just...not here."

"What do you mean, not here?"

"I mean George, himself, is somewhere else right now. Outside of his body. Where, I couldn't begin to say, but it must be very, very far." He looked at the hills around them and the sky above. "Farther than I can sense. I only hope—"

But then George's eyes flicked open, and Colette grabbed Silenus's shoulder. "Harry!" she said, and they both looked down and knelt beside him.

George did not move or say anything. He simply stared up at the sky, seemingly seeing nothing.

"George?" said Silenus. "George, can you hear me?"

If he did, he did not show it.

"George?" said Colette. "Are you all right?"

George slowly blinked. Then, as if he was trying to remember how his own body worked, he lifted his right arm and looked at his hand. Silenus and Colette saw he was holding something, something they had not noticed before. In fact, Colette could have sworn he hadn't been holding anything at all just a second ago.

"I held it in the palm of my hand," he said. His voice was soft and creaky.

He opened his fingers. In his hand was a pocket watch. It looked like it had been recently polished, and it was cleanly clicking out the seconds. If the watch's time was correct, it was just past five in the morning.

"I know that," said Silenus. "That's a family heirloom. How'd you get that?"

"I fixed it," said George. He sat up more. "It will run all right now. For a while, at least."

Silenus held George by the shoulders, steadying him. "George, what happened? Where is the song? Please, please don't tell me it was lost with Stanley. Don't tell me the wolves got it. Anything but that, George."

"He saved it," George said. "He gave it to me, just before he passed."

"*You* have it?" said Silenus. He let out a sigh of relief. "Oh, thank God."

"He passed it on," said George. He looked to his side at Stanley, pale and drawn and still. "From father to son, just like it's always been."

Silenus looked at him uncomfortably. "So...you know?"

"He told me, in his own way."

"I...I don't know what to say, George. I'm sorry. But we had to."

George nodded.

"We were going to tell you eventually, when we thought you were ready. I'm sorry you had to find out just before...before he passed. He was dear to me, as I'm sure he...well, as he would have been to you. I'm so sorry, George. But the important thing is that the song is safe. It's what he would have wanted, since that's what he devoted his whole life to, and—"

"I don't have the song," said George.

Silenus stopped and stared at him. His face grew very pale. "You...you what?" he said.

"I don't have it, Harry," said George.

"But he gave it to you, didn't he?"

"I used it," he said. "I used all of it, Harry. I had almost all of the song, and the First Darkness came, and I had to use it to change... everything."

Silenus began to tremble. "No..."

"I'm sorry, Harry," said George.

"It's gone? It's really all gone?" he asked.

George nodded again.

"No. I don't believe it. It can't be *gone*," said Silenus. "You can't have just thrown it away! We had so much of it! We had almost all of it, George! I worked so *hard* to get everything! We were almost there!"

"We *were* there, Harry," George said. "When Stanley gave it to me, I had nearly everything. The complete song."

"You did?" said Silenus. "But what did you see? What did you see, when you had all of it? Did you see it? Did you see the...the Creator? Did you see anything? Can you at least tell me why?"

"Why what?"

"Why what?" shouted Silenus. "Why anything! Why all of it!"

George thought about it. He tried to speak several times but stopped before each one, not trusting his answer. Then he said, "I can't say. I can't say what I saw."

"So you don't know?" cried Silenus. "You don't know!"

"No," said George. And, strangely, he smiled, as if the thought pleased him. "I don't know, Harry. I'll never know."

This answer gave no solace to Silenus, who grabbed his head with both hands and wailed. He stood up and staggered away several steps, and sat down on a stone and began to weep. Colette watched him, disturbed, but then George laid a hand on her arm.

"I'm very cold, Colette," he said. "And I'm very tired."

She gave Harry another wary look, but finally nodded. "I'll get some kindling. It's so wet here it'll take me some time to find some, though."

"That's fine," said George. "Thank you."

She made to leave, but stopped. "What did you do, George?" she asked. "When the First Darkness came, what did you do?"

"What do you think I did?" he asked.

She looked around at the valley. She took a breath. The air was so much cleaner now. "You changed something, didn't you? Everything feels so *new*."

"Something like that," said George. "I struck a bargain."

"What sort of a bargain?" she asked.

"I figured out a way to break the darkness up forever," he said. "To make the snake coiled around the world eat its own tail, so to speak. I threatened to make it do that, and it gave in."

"What did you get in return?"

"Time," he said. "Time for you, for me, for Harry. Time for everyone and everything. Everything will be left alone, just as it is, for a time."

"How much time?"

He looked at her and slowly raised his eyebrows. Colette saw his eyes had faded to a very pale, peculiar shade of gray. But more than that there was something very deep behind George's eyes, something that had not been there before. He had the eyes of someone who'd seen years and years of time. Centuries, even. Maybe more. "Do you really want to know?" he asked.

She opened her mouth, but then thought about it. "You know what, no," she said. "No, I really don't."

He smiled a little, and nodded. "I think that's very wise of you," he said. Then he lay back down on the ground on his side, staring at his fallen father, and in his hand the pocket watch merrily pulsed along as if it had a great many seconds left to count out and it could not wait to get to them all.

Colette was right: it took her the better part of an hour to find dry ground. Once she did she began to search for the driest branches, and just when she had a decent bundle she was spattered with thick drops of rain. "Oh, great," she said, and sought shelter under one of the tallest pines to wait it out. It did seem like a very peculiar storm, however: the dark clouds appeared to be making a straight line for the valley. Was it her imagination, or had that happened already today? It couldn't happen a second time, could it?

The storm faded as quickly as it arrived, but before Colette ventured out she saw someone was stumbling through the underbrush. It appeared to be a girl in a bright green dress and with long, blond hair. She seemed to have come out of nowhere; Colette did not ever see her approach. The girl was apparently in some distress, as she kept attempting to charge forward, but the folds of her dress kept getting snagged on the grasping branches. When one tripped her and refused to let go, no matter how hard she tugged, the girl almost burst into tears.

"Here," said Colette, stepping out from under the pine. "Let me help."

The girl looked up, surprised, and stopped tugging. Colette laid her bundle aside and helped unwind the fabric of the girl's dress from the pine branch. "There," she said. "Probably not a good idea to wear such a fancy thing in these woods."

"I know," said the girl. "I didn't think to change, I came here as fast as I could."

"From where?" asked Colette.

The girl waved dismissively toward the west. "You're the dancer, aren't you?" she asked. "In his troupe?"

"His troupe?"

"Yes. George's. The pianist."

Colette helped the girl back to her feet. "I don't know how you know George, but I don't think there is a troupe anymore."

She looked at her, frightened. "Then they're...he's..."

"George? He's fine. Well, I don't know. I think he is. Here, you can see him." She led the girl to a small outcropping and pointed through the trees to where George lay.

The girl let out a great sigh when she saw him. "Thank goodness," she said.

"He's resting right now," Colette told her. "He's just been through a trial. And he just lost his father. So I think that for right now it's best to let him be."

"Oh...Oh, I'm so *sorry*. But is he going to be all right?"

Colette thought about it. "I'm not sure. But I think so. It feels like everything might be all right, for now."

The girl nodded.

"You're the one who helped him in Hayburn, aren't you?" asked Colette. "The shepherd?"

"I'm his patron," she said. "I sensed he was in trouble just a while ago and came running to help. He was there, and then he *wasn't*. It was the strangest thing, but I couldn't let him get hurt."

"You do that for all the people who call you patron?"

"I am a patron to no one else," said the girl, a little sadly.

"I see."

"What happened here? I can almost always find George, but then he was gone...And then I felt like he was *everywhere*."

"I don't know what happened," said Colette. "He did something, but I can't say what just yet." She watched the girl out of the side of her eye. She was staring at George with unabashed longing. "You're kind of sweet on him, aren't you?" she asked.

"What?" said the girl, startled. "Sweet? What do you mean? On who?"

"On George."

The girl blushed magnificently. "Well, I would never...In fact, it's unbecoming of a patron to..." Her blush intensified. "Well. Maybe not *that* unbecoming."

Colette gave her a wry smile. "I see."

The girl struggled for a moment, and finally said, "I feel very silly."

"Don't," said Colette. She stooped and picked her kindling back up. "Here, walk with me. I can do you a favor."

"You can?"

"Sure," she said. "I'll answer any questions you have about George, if you tell me something."

"What would that be?" asked the girl as she followed Colette through the woods.

"Well, it's like I said. I don't think there's going to be a troupe anymore. And you've been...How can I put this. You're probably well traveled."

"I have been in most places, at some point in time," said the girl, a touch prideful.

"Yeah, that's what I mean," said Colette. "Do you know of any place where...where people would be willing to watch an entertainer like me?"

"Like you?"

"Yes. Like me." Colette stopped and looked at her. "A colored."

"Oh," said the girl. She thought about it. "Well, I'm fairly sure I know of a few, right off the top of my head."

"Interesting," said Colette. "Come with me. I'd like to hear about those places."

Once Colette came back and got a fire started Silenus finally returned to them. He had gone to his office door, which still stood open in the rock by the river, and fetched a large piece of canvas and shovels. "For Stanley," he said.

George and Colette nodded. They laid Stanley in the canvas and all of them helped to stitch him up. George sometimes stopped and simply stared at the man lying within. When this happened Silenus or Colette took up his work without a word.

Once they were done they carried him up the valley to a hilltop. "I want him to see the sky," George said.

All three of them helped to dig the grave. The ground was moist and parted easily for them. Then they laid him in the earth and placed stones over him and filled the grave in, and they made a marker for him out of branches. On it George carved:

STANLEY SILENUS

BELOVED FATHER

PATER OMNIPOTENS AETERNA DEUS

"Would you like to say something?" asked Silenus.

George shook his head.

"No?" asked Colette.

"He was my father," he said. "All he wanted was for me to know what I was to him. And now I know. That's enough."

When they were done they returned to the fire. Silenus still shivered even though he was close to the flames, and eventually they realized he was not shivering due to the cold.

"I'm sorry, Harry," said George.

Silenus simply stared into the fire.

"It was the only thing to do. It feels almost like the song was waiting for me to change it and use it all up. I'm not sure. I'm already forgetting parts of what happened. It's like they're too big for me to remember."

"So we'll never know," said Silenus. "We'll never know why. We'll never be able to call the Creator back." He looked up, and stared around at the dark riverbed. "And I'll never be able to fix Annie. She was lost as well, wasn't she?"

George nodded, his face sad.

"How? The symbols on her skin should have protected her..."

"Not against what happened," George said. "I saw it, when I rebuilt everything." He described what Annie had done, heaving the train car up the hill as it tore her apart, and then surrendering herself to the crushing tons of the breaking dam. "Even she could not survive that," he said.

Silenus was quiet for a long time. As he stared into the fire he looked little and frightened.

"It was what she wanted, Harry," said George. "She wanted to die. And she also wanted to help us. She did both."

"If she could have only held on a little bit longer," said Silenus softly. "And if you had not used up all the song...Why did you not change her, or fix her? Why could you not have done at least that?"

"Because I wouldn't change the world just because it'd be nicer that way," George said. "The world is what the world is. She had been through enough. She wanted sleep. I let her have it, as you should have long ago."

"But she was the reason I did what I did. Why I sought out the song. I...I wanted an *explanation*. I wanted to know *why* she was taken from me, how this could be allowed to happen. And there was a slim hope that maybe, just maybe, I could make the Creator bring her back..."

"Aren't you at least a little mad at her, Harry?" asked Colette. "She betrayed us. She got you killed. Sort of."

Silenus thought about it. "No," he said finally, his voice low. "No, I have no anger for her. Perhaps I am not surprised by her betrayal, because I, in my own way, betrayed her long ago. I betrayed her by keeping her alive, and finding a new love...but I admit that after so many years of looking for the song, I forgot why I started looking in the first place. The idea of saving my wife, who I could hardly remember, seemed a small thing in comparison to possessing the very explanation for all of Creation within my hands." A gleam crept into his eyes again. Yet then it faded. "But now any chance of that is gone. And she is gone. Despite all my efforts, she's really gone."

"Have you forgotten the cost of your efforts, though?" asked George. "How many places were lost as a result of your search, Harry? How many lives were eaten by the darkness? Homes and towns just blinking out, as if they never were."

"I don't know," said Silenus. "I know what I did was wrong, but it seemed the only choice. I *had* to. It was all I had left, and I thought if I succeeded then I could repair whatever harm it caused. She got even worse when you joined us, George. You look so much like me when I was young, and..."

"And she kept calling me Bill," George realized. "I see."

Silenus nodded. "And yet it was all for nothing, in the end."

"When you showed me her gravestone in New York, you said that the thing it signified was gone," said George. "That it had faded long ago."

Silenus looked at him, eyebrow cocked. "So?"

"So I don't think it's gone," said George. "I don't think it ever faded. You still remember her. Otherwise you wouldn't grieve at all. And she would not have done what she did if she did not remember you."

Silenus bowed his head. "Perhaps so," he said quietly.

"She was right, you know," said George. "Creation isn't a machine that's thrown a few gears. I saw that."

"Then what is it?"

George could not answer. Silenus grew grim, and he nodded. "Then it's as I thought," he said. "We know nothing. All the long years, all the generations of our family... It's all been for nothing."

"Would you tell me something?" asked George.

Silenus shrugged.

"I know that Stanley was my father. But why do you and I look so much alike? That was what made me think you were my father in the first place."

For the first time since he'd returned, Silenus smiled a little. "The Silenus family resemblance is extremely predominant in our clan, that's so. But not totally predominant. Stanley got lucky. He got the hair and the eyebrows, yeah, but for the rest he had the look of his mother. She was a lovely girl, Ellen. She and Stanley were the best of us." He sniffed. "We had to make sure no one could realize Stanley and I were related. We got lucky with his looks and height, and we took care of the hair and eyebrows later. It's amazing what you can do with only a difference in wardrobe and a dab of hair coloring."

"Another performance," said Colette, a little bitterly.

"Another in a long line of them," said Silenus.

"So that makes you... my great-uncle?" asked George.

"Give or take a few greats. I have been the guardian of our line for a long, long time, George. I didn't inherit the ability to host the song, but I carried it in my own way. Long ago I found certain... methods that allow a sort of suspended vitality, which ensured that I could always look over the song. These methods have all kinds of side effects, one of which is sterility. I knew I could never father a child, George, so I knew from the start you were not mine." He looked at Colette a little shamefully. "And what I told you is true, Lettie. There was never any chance of getting you in trouble in a family way. I just had to pretend otherwise when George came along."

Colette shut her eyes and turned away. "I still haven't forgiven you. For what you did to Franny, and to me. The idea is just so...so..."

"I don't expect you to understand," said Silenus. "You are very young, in comparison to me. That was what drew me to you. I'll accept whatever judgment you give."

"Why did you pretend George was your son, anyway?" she asked.

Silenus recounted the story of Stanley's idea. George had, in a way, witnessed this moment firsthand, and Silenus did not deviate much from what he'd seen. "Stanley loved your mother, George," Harry said at the end. "I know. I was there. He was very reluctant to leave Rinton, and I know the look of a girl-addled young man. But we had to. We'd come searching for a very, very large piece of the song—the piece you once carried—but the wolves came much too close, and we had to flee in the night. It broke his heart, I think."

"Why did he not remember her, or Rinton?" asked George. "I asked if you'd been there from the start."

"You don't understand how much traveling we did," said Silenus. "After our first visit to Rinton we saw thousands of towns and states, and even countries. And holding so much of the First Song changes a person. It makes it hard to remember details. I'm sure you know the feeling."

George nodded. He did, a bit. Stanley had been holding the blueprints for billions of lives within him. It must have been very hard to hold on to a memory of one, George realized, which made him pity his father all the more.

"But he remembered when you told us who you were," said Silenus. "You don't know how much it pained him, to have you so close and yet so far. I'm sorry for both of you, George. But at the time it seemed as if we didn't have a choice. Stanley had to be protected. He was the bearer of such a valuable treasure."

"I know," said George, sighing. "But that reminds me of something...I'd always thought the song was stored in your trunk. You were always carrying that with you when you looked for it. Why was it important?"

"Don't you remember what was actually in there?" asked Silenus.

"Restoratives, wasn't it?"

"Exactly. And who would need restoratives?"

George remembered the strangled cry rising up from the little black island when they'd taken the last piece of the song. "Stanley..."

"Yes. Stanley often had issues after absorbing a new portion of the song. It's common. Previous bearers have even gone comatose. The more he took on, the more extreme the issues became. It often took a lot to pull him back into the waking world. At first he only needed smelling salts, but then it took more and more, and soon I was using a whole host of chemicals and tinctures to get him back on his feet. Hence the trunk."

"Oh," he said. "I see. I do know more about how the song worked, but...it's getting so hard to remember it now. I know Stanley couldn't speak because then the echoes would come rushing out. But how was it that he performed it in the fourth act?"

"That's right," said Colette. "I was on stage with both of you every time, and I always thought it was *you*, Harry! I never saw Stanley do a thing."

Silenus smirked. "You didn't, did you?"

"No. How was he singing it?"

Silenus took a cigar out of his pocket and lit it with a burning branch from the fire. "Who said he was singing it?"

Colette's brow creased as she wondered what he could mean, but George sat up. "Did he not sing it? Did he just...just hum it?"

Silenus's smile broadened. "Very good."

"What!" cried Colette. "He just hummed it as he played the cello? That's all?"

"That's all it takes," said Silenus. "The song really only needs the tiniest opening to have an effect. That was *my* idea, I'm proud to say. Stanley—and several of the previous singers of the troupe—would hum as they played their instrument onstage, and I would conduct. And since I did nothing else, any agent of our enemies would assume it was all me. They'd never look at the other person at all. That's how we did it, day after day, for decades, years on end. But now it's gone." His face grew grim again.

"You know I had to give it up, Harry," said George. "I told you."

"I know in my head that what you did seemed just, George," said Silenus. "But in my heart there is no justification for what happened. At some level, there has to be an answer."

"I've been as close as anyone, Harry, and I can tell you that you will never see everything," said George. "You can never truly know."

Silenus shook his head. "I can know. I *will* know, someday. You may have given up the First Song, but that doesn't mean this is over."

"What do you mean?"

"The song was sung," said Silenus. "And what is sung must also echo. And those echoes can be collected, just as we've always done."

George and Colette stared at him once they realized what he meant.

"You're going to . . . to start all over again?" said Colette.

"I am," said Silenus.

"But George used it all up! It's all gone, Harry."

"It may be gone, but I can find it again, in some form or another," he said. "I've had a lot of practice at finding it."

"But even if there is something to find, you won't have anyone to carry it," said George. "I won't come with you, Harry. I'm done with this."

"The ability to carry the song must surely exist somewhere outside of the Silenus line," said Harry. "We can't be the only ones.

Some boy or girl must be able to hold the song. If I search long enough, I'll find a willing carrier. Then we can begin again."

"You may have to search longer than you think," said George.

"What makes you say that?"

He looked a little guilty. "The world is...a little bigger than it used to be."

Colette and Silenus both turned to him. "What do you mean?" asked Colette.

"When I put it all back, I put it *all* back," said George. "Even the parts that were lost, both long ago and recently. The parts you let vanish, Harry, and the parts lost in the First Days. They are out there again, somewhere. If you come at them the right way." He smiled a little at Silenus. "When I gave up the song the world might have lost a little magic, that's true. But I think it may have gained another one. A winter traded for a spring."

"Wait, so you just...stuck them back in somewhere?" said Silenus.

"They were supposed to be there, before the wolves devoured them," George said. "They were in the First Song, and were waiting to be sung when I performed it again. It was the only right thing to do. And with the time I've bought, those places will remain unharmed for a long, long while."

"But...but what will people think?" asked Colette. "What will happen to everyone? Those people and places, they've been gone for so long!"

"It will definitely be an interesting time to live in," said George. "Think of all the stories out there, waiting to be told. I'm looking forward to it."

"It doesn't matter to me," said Silenus. "I don't care where the boundaries end, or what lands the echoes reside in. I'll always keep looking for the song."

"Forever, Harry?" asked George.

"Until I no longer have to," said Silenus. "Until I know."

*   *   *

George and Colette tried to persuade him otherwise, but he would not listen. "I have done this for so much longer than either of you," he told them. "To me, it's not a lifetime. Just another day, perhaps another week."

In the afternoon they all went back to his office door, which still stood open in the side of the rock. "A shame," said Silenus, gesturing to where the great black door had once hung. "But it's not necessary. It was mostly for decoration."

He turned to them, and said, "George, I don't know if there's a train station at Lake Champlain, but I'm sure there's something. It's just east of here, you can't miss it. You should be safe there, and warm." Then he turned to Colette, opened his mouth, and faltered. The two of them looked at each other, and George grew aware that there were many things going unsaid.

He left them to make their goodbyes in private. He realized now, all too late, that the two of them were very close. How could he not have seen it among all their interactions, all their business discussions? Despite their different ages, it was obvious they were lovers of a very intense and contrary sort.

George glanced back and saw they were holding hands and staring into the open door together. Silenus said something to her. Then Colette shook her head, and they let each other go.

George returned as Silenus stepped through the door into his office. He fetched their bags from behind his desk and handed them off to each of them. He said, "It's always possible we will see each other again."

"Yes, I suppose it is," said George.

"But unlikely," said Silenus. "I doubt if either of you will ever visit where I am going."

"Where are you going?" asked Colette.

He smiled slightly. "To where I must. To the far places at the end of the sky, and perhaps beyond. I'll resume my chase, and keep doing so until I can't."

"Are you really sure you want to do this, Harry?" she asked.

"I have never been surer, my dear," he said. "It's what I've always done. And it may be what I'll always do. Perhaps it's what I deserve."

"I was once told by someone that we must be the authors of our own lives," said George. "Was that a lie?"

Harry grew solemn. "Perhaps it is," he said. "And perhaps it isn't. And then again, perhaps it is a little bit of both."

Then, with one last smile, he stepped back. "You and I both know you're not my son," he said to George. "But I do think you've made a fine addition to the family." The sides of the door began to tremble and the stone started to grow together. The door shrank until it was a narrow crack, and through it George saw Harry step away and sit down in the chair behind his desk very, very slowly, the groaning motions of an old man. He swiveled around and put his feet up below the broken bay window, staring out at the darkness as he had so many times before. Then the stone fused together and he was gone.

Colette and George tramped back to Lake Champlain together. It was a long hike, and they were both very filthy and ragged by the end of it. When they finally found a hotel they bathed and changed and went to find the train station.

"Where will you be going, George?" Colette asked.

"Home," he said. "To Rinton."

"Why? I thought you wanted to tour vaudeville and see the world, performing."

"I did tour vaudeville," he said. "And I did see the world. And I've already given my greatest performance, Colette. But no one heard it."

"I heard it," said Colette. "A little."

He smiled. "I suppose that's enough, then."

"How did you do it, George? I thought the wolves weren't subject to the song at all. They could be repelled by it, but not changed."

"It was a matter of making something out of nothing, I suppose," he said. "And of performance. When the song was first sung, the wolves didn't hear it. They only came alive after. This time, they listened. And no one can witness an act of creation and walk away unchanged. Not even the wolves." His smile left, and he stared ahead sadly. "I hope what I did was just. But it seemed the only thing to do."

"I'm sure it was."

"Maybe. All I want to do now is go home." He paused. "You could come with me."

"I could," she agreed.

"It might be peaceful there for you."

"It might."

"But you won't," said George.

"No," she said. "I'm afraid I won't, George. You know, Harry might not have been your father, but you two are very alike."

"He asked you to come with him too, didn't he?"

"Yes," said Colette. "He did. I wasn't much interested in his proposition, either. But more than that, you are both very cunning and persuasive men, you know."

"Cunning? I'm not cunning at all. Not as much as you or Harry, that's for sure."

She laughed. "George, have you already forgotten so much of what you did last night?" She shook her head, smiling, but the smile faded as she spied something over his shoulder.

George did not turn around. "What is it?"

"There's a man watching us," she said.

George put his hands in his pockets and casually swiveled a little, letting his gaze reach back as he did so, and he saw she was right: there was a man watching them from below a shop awning. He appeared to have frozen in the middle of writing in his notebook, and he was wearing a curious red coat and a black hat with a large white feather stuck in its brim. When his eyes met George's he saluted a little, and George saluted back.

"Wait," said Colette. "Is that…"

"Yes," said George happily.

"But…but what is he doing here?" she said. "I thought you'd made a deal to keep them all away!"

"I did," he said. "But I didn't let them *all* go back to being wolves. Some didn't want to go. So I let them continue on being human."

She burst out laughing. "You did? Why?"

"Let's just say their enthusiasm for it was infectious," he said. "And I thought they might make good ones."

George took his hands out of his pockets, and she reached out and took one and they walked down the street, hand in hand. "What are you going to do?" he asked.

"What I've always done," she said. "Perform."

He nodded, smiling a little ruefully. "Will the world ever recognize the Princess of the Kush Steppes?"

"No," she said. "I'm sick of that act. I think I'll make up a new one. In some place far away. I'm not taking the train, you see."

"Oh?"

She pointed ahead. Standing in the town square was a slender girl all dressed in green. She smiled at George and waved, and as she did the trees on the corner shook as if brushed by a slight breeze.

"Ah," he said, and stopped. "Where will she be taking you?"

"Far from here," said Colette. "Far, far, far from the sticks. I want a bigger stage, George. A bigger crowd, a bigger act. But I don't expect you to understand that."

"Why not?"

"Well, you've been on the biggest stage of all, haven't you?" she said. "And played for the biggest crowd. I'll never catch up to you, George Carole. You're big time, if ever there was such a thing." She leaned over and kissed him on the cheek. "Goodbye, George. I'd wish you happiness, but I think you'll find it no matter what."

"You do?" he asked.

"Oh yes," she said. "You know, I believe once your friend has taken me she'll be coming back here. Maybe you should talk to her. You two have a lot in common."

"Really?"

"Yes," she said. "Trust me on that." Then Colette picked up her suitcase and walked to the girl in green. The girl watched George carefully and waved again, and Colette looked back with a small, fond smile. George, feeling suddenly terribly sad and happy all at once, waved to both of them, and he grinned.

Colette looked up. The sky was gray with the promise of spring rain. Then there was a rise in the wind, and a smattering of drops. George had to clap his hat to his head and turn his face away from the gust, and when he looked back both of them were gone.

CHAPTER 38

The Singers

The return of George Carole to Rinton remained an exciting topic of discussion in the town's social scene for years after his unexpected reappearance. Where had he been, they asked? He seemed so different from the boy they remembered. Had he been, as so many speculated, off gambling and engaging in other even worse types of behavior in the towns up north, and only returned when he'd run out of money? Though this was a very popular theory, it did not seem to be the case, as George soon purchased a very nice home on the outskirts of town, not far from his grandmother. And one would think that a young man who'd gotten up to any wildness would not have been as warmly received as George Carole had been by his grandmother. The whole town had expected to hear her shouts ringing out over the fields the day of his return, but her neighbors had been quite surprised to find the two of them calmly sitting on their porch by the evening. And though Mrs. Carole did appear to be crying, she smiled through her tears.

Perhaps, the town experts said, George Carole had made quite a winning in his games, and had won many enemies as well and been forced to flee. As gripping as this tale was, many admitted they could not imagine it; Mr. Carole seemed a more peaceful and quiet soul than ever before. He was usually seen sitting on his front porch, staring at the sky, and sometimes he would laugh for no apparent reason at all. It was, everyone agreed, as if he saw something in the clouds or the fields or the branches of the forest that no one else could see. Perhaps he'd gone mad, they said, and that was why he'd returned home. Yet when he looked at them with those extraordinarily pale gray eyes they again found their theories refuted. This was not a madman; rather, he seemed terribly, terribly sane.

The new Carole household quickly became one of the strangest and most disreputable ones in all of Rinton's history. Whole careers of town gossips were made or broken on snatching up the latest news of Mr. Carole and his eventual wife, who was also extremely odd. Apparently she was quite the traveler—she was gone over half the year at times—and though Mr. Carole never said what she did they all assumed it was something in agriculture, as he was once heard mentioning that she was away helping fields in the west. In addition, Mr. Carole's vegetable garden was curiously productive, always receiving the perfect amount of shade and rain. His produce became regular winners at the county fair, to the envy and dismay of nearly all of the town's figureheads.

Only once did anyone ever actually broach the subject of his past with George Carole himself. Edwin Crouts approached Mr. Carole on his porch one day to ask if he could possibly fill in as church pianist, as the current pianist had very bad cataracts and could no longer read the music. Mr. Carole did not answer right away; he simply smiled and watched Edwin with those strange gray eyes of his. Edwin rustled up whatever courage he had left and asked Mr. Carole if it was true that in his day he'd been a vaudevillian, and if so then that would easily qualify him to play at the church. It was very easy music, he assured him, something anyone who'd toured the circuits could play. Had he ever played church music? Or did he play anymore? asked Edwin, trying not to sweat under that cool, distant gaze.

Mr. Carole listened carefully to this rush of speech, thought, and simply said, "No."

Edwin, panicked, asked which statement he was saying no to: was he saying no to the request, no to the rumor that he'd been in vaudeville, or no to whether or not he played anymore?

But Mr. Carole only smiled and shook his head, and again said, "No." Edwin, red and humiliated, muttered an apology and quickly left.

Everyone tried to understand exactly what Mr. Carole had meant. What had he been saying no to, except possibly everything? They could not say. But one thing was for sure: George Carole, who had played piano so very frequently in his youth, was never heard to touch a piano again. Perhaps, someone suggested, he was all played out.

Some took this idea to heart. There was something very wistful and sad about Mr. Carole, though this became apparent only after the birth of his daughter. When she was born he was naturally ecstatic, like any new father, but his curious melancholy first appeared when it came time to teach her to read. The sight of George Carole with that little blackboard and the piece of chalk, seated before that little girl with the curly black hair, somehow made any onlooker feel as if they were witnessing the saddest thing in the world. And sometimes when he held his child he would reach into his pocket and take out a very old, fat watch, and he would dangle it before her eyes. While she would laugh in delight at this trinket, Mr. Carole's face was never nearly as happy. Instead he looked painfully solemn, and he smiled only to please the little child.

Perhaps he was a man with his own tragedies, said Eleanor Clay at bridge one evening. And on hearing this everyone nodded and felt willing to give the Carole household a little more sympathy.

In fact, they eventually warmed to Mr. Carole and his little girl, and his often-absent wife with the blond hair. He was odd, they agreed, but perhaps oddness did not immediately render one scandalous. And his squash and pumpkins were very good each year, which did temper their opinions a little.

What they never admitted was that something new had tempered their opinions. Now that his daughter had gotten a bit older, on Sunday mornings Mr. Carole would take her out into the vegetable garden while his wife slept in, and they would both tend to their little crop. And as he worked and she used her little bucket and spade to help, he often smiled and lifted his face up to the sun, and began to sing.

It was the same song every time, but each time was as beautiful as the last, if not more so. It was such a fragile, wonderful song that some people would rearrange their entire mornings just so they could amble by Mr. Carole's house on the way to church.

Occasionally they would try to tell their friends and loved ones about this beautiful song of Mr. Carole's, and how it had the queer effect of echoing, somehow, no matter where you heard it. These stories never really found believing ears. But still some people came to Mr. Carole's house to wander by his porch at a slow pace, waiting to hear that unearthly hymn of his as he tended to his garden. And sometimes, if the day was right, his little girl would set down her spade and bucket, and she would sing too.

extras

orbit

meet the author

Josh Brewster

ROBERT JACKSON BENNETT was born in Baton Rouge, Louisiana, but grew up in Katy, Texas. He later attended the University of Texas at Austin and, like a lot of its alumni, was unable to leave the charms of the city and resides there currently. Find out more about the author at www.robertjacksonbennett.com.

introducing

**If you enjoyed
THE TROUPE,
look out for**

Robert Jackson Bennett's next novel

*Ex–police detective Mona Bright has inherited a house.
Her mother's, apparently. And jobless, homeless, and aimless,
Mona decides to return to a home she never knew.*

*The house is in Wink, New Mexico, a town no one has ever
heard of. Trapped in the nuclear-age optimism of the 1960s,
Wink seems like a town that time has left behind.*

*Except behind its sunny façade there are dark secrets and
darker motives. Mona is the key that will set off a chain of
events that no one could have predicted. Strange horrors lie
in wait for her, and her homecoming may be her undoing.*

Wink is not perfect. Its residents are well aware of that. But
then, they say, no place is perfect. There's always a few mild

irritants you have to put up with, no matter where you go. So Wink is really no different, is it? No, they say. It really isn't.

For when night falls and the blue lightning blooms in the sky, things change.

It is something in the very air. Suddenly the Googie architecture and the pleasant, white wood cottages no longer look so spotless. Streetlights seem dimmer, and the neon signs appear to have more dead insects clogging their tubing than they did during the day. People stop waving. In fact, they hunch over and hurry back inside with their eyes downcast.

It is very regular to have strange experiences at night in Wink. For example, in Wink it is common to wake up with the powerful feeling that someone is standing in your front or backyard. It is never known to you whether or not this stranger has come to your house in particular, or if they're watching you and your family; they are simply there, shadowy and still. What is most exceptional about this is that all of it is conveyed only in *feeling*, an irrational conviction like that of a dream. Most people in Wink do not even look out their windows when this occurs, mostly because they know doing so would prove the conviction true—for there *is* a stranger on your lawn, dark and faceless and still—and, moreover, seeing them has its own consequences.

There are houses in Wink where no one ever sees anyone going in or out, yet the lawn is clean and the trees are trimmed and the beds are full and blooming. And sometimes at night, if you were to look—and of course you wouldn't—you might see pale faces peeping out of the darkened windows.

In the evening in Wink, it is normal for a man to take the trash out to the back alley, and as he places the bag in the trash can he will suddenly hear the sound of someone speaking to him from nearby. He will look and see that the speaker stands behind the tall wooden fence of the house behind his, and he will be unable to discern anything besides the shadow of the speaker's figure and the light from his neighbor's windows filtering through the pickets. What the speaker is whispering to him is unknown, for it will be in a language he has never heard before and could never mimic. The man will say nothing back—it is *crucial* he say nothing back—and he will walk away slowly, return to his home, and he will not mention it to his wife or family. In the morning, there will be no sign of anyone having been behind the fence at all.

In the morning in Wink, people frequently find that someone has gone through their garbage or left footprints all over their lawn. On discovering this they will set everything to right, either by replacing the garbage or smoothing over the grass, and they will not complain or discuss it with anyone.

There are very few pets in Wink. Almost all of them are decidedly house-trained. Outdoors, wandering pets are unpopular, for they have a tendency to never return home in the morning.

On the outskirts of Wink, where the trees end and the canyons begin, people often hear fluting and cries from down the slopes, and, on very clear nights, one can see flickering lights of a thin, unnerving yellow, and many dark figures standing upright and still on the stones.

And sometimes, maybe only once a year, the people who live near the park at the center of town will glance out their window at night and see a small crowd has silently assembled on the grass. They all stand motionless with their heads craned up, watching the night sky. What they are looking at would be difficult to determine from any angle, but most residents understand that they are looking at one black corner of the sky. It is unusual, naturally, for anyone who has such a beautiful night sky before them to focus on the one part that has no star at all. Yet this starless part is all that they care to stare at. Or, perhaps, it has no star anymore.

The residents of Wink know about all these things, in a peripheral fashion. They tolerate them as one would a rainy season, or some pestering raccoons. Because, after all, no neighborhood is perfect. There'll always be a few problems, at least. And besides, everyone can make an arrangement, if they want.

Comes he walking windy-ways, wandering under spruces and through canyons and across shadowy glens, hands in his pockets and head bowed as if all the weight of the world lies teetering on his slumped shoulders. Which it is, in a way, and this is a change of pace for Mr. Macy, he who is so often the delight of Cockler Street, always there sweeping off his store's front steps and waiting to favor passersby with a wink or a smile or a piece of bawdy flattery. The very idea of merry old Macy ever falling into a gloomy spell is preposterous, inconceivable, for Macy is indomitable, unchanging. Were the town ever washed away in a freak flood Macy would remain, still ready with a snippet of gossip or an idle joke. Yet here he is, making a lonely crossing through the desolate countryside, the pink moon lazily swimming through the purple skies above him, and though Macy may tell himself his midnight perambulations serve some deeper, more secret purpose, he cannot deny that partially they serve to relieve his mind of its many burdens.

As he winds around a staggered cliffside he glimpses a flash of lightning over his shoulder. He stops and watches the blue luminescence bloom in the clouds above the mesa, its eldritch light strobing the mountains, the pines, the red rocky flats beyond that seem

(so much like home)

queerly threatening recently. The lightning is soundless, but his ears imagine quiet thunder rolling across the countryside. It will gather around the tip of the mesa (it always gathers at the tip of the mesa) and disperse, trailing north and east to fade to nothing.

Then he cocks his head. His eyes go searching, curious, tracing over every line of dark on the mountain. He saw something, he's sure of it, not the brilliantine blue of lightning, no, but a flat box of dull white light, like a window. But what could lie yonder on the mesa save the remains of the lab, with its twisted tunnels and blackened antennae (all sticking up from the ground like barbecue spits)? And he is sure there is nothing else there,

(except the door)

nothing at all, for they would know about it, wouldn't they?

He looks. Waits. Sees nothing. Then continues home.

His manner of walking is counterclockwise and peripheral, approaching the town always from the side, crossing empty playgrounds and parks and isolated intersections. It is good to move through the forbidden places, the halfway patches. He's spent too much time in the havens at the center of Wink, far too much time puttering around his store and among his neighbors. Here at the edges, in the cracks and at the crossroads, stepping from shadow to shadow in the river of darkness that runs through the heart of Wink, he feels much more at home.

As he walks under one tree a harsh buzz sounds out from above. He stops, peers up. Though the tree is dark he can see the form of a man standing at the top, balanced perfectly on a single branch. The buzz increases, wheedling and reedy, like it is telling him to clear off. It is not a sound any human could ever make.

Macy watches for a moment, but soon grows impatient. He has no time for such mannered gestures. "Oh, shut up," he snaps.

The thing in the tree falls silent. Mr. Macy glares at it a moment longer, then continues on.

Mr. Macy can go anywhere he likes in Wink, anytime,

(except beyond it)

and no one knows more about the town than he does. Except, perhaps, for Mr. Werthing. But Mr. Werthing is dead, dead as a doornail, dead as dead can be. Whatever that means.

And what does it mean? he wonders as he walks. What could it ever mean? Macy does not know. What a foreign concept it is: to die, to cough up what you are as if it were no more than mucus pooled at the back of your throat and perish. Where is his friend now? What has happened to him? Where has he gone? Still he wonders.

It is this death—and the answers about it he so desperately desires—that has sent Macy on these midnight errands, visiting the hidden residents of Wink and telling him his news and thoughts: have you heard and what did you do, who knew before you and how, and why, why? Why did they know, why did they not know, what has happened, what is happening? Do you know? Does anyone know?

No. They do not. They, like Macy, like the town, are alone now.

He misses Werthing like one would miss a limb. Werthing was always the stabilizing force in town, the rudder steering their little ship across dark, unsteady seas. It was his idea to use the names of the town's residents. "And are we not residents of the town?" he said to them. "Are we not these people now? I feel that we are. We are part of a community. And so we should be named accordingly."

Part of a community...Macy badly wishes this were the case.

For now the unthinkable has happened: one of them has *died*. No, more than that—he has been *murdered*. How can such a thing occur? Do the seas sometimes float away into the sky? Do the planets crash into one another in their orbit? Can one hold the stars in the palm of their hand?

No, no. And so they cannot die.

But Macy has a few ideas about how this happened. He knows those men at the truck stop had something to do with it, such weaselly little things with small eyes and cautious movements. He can smell it on them, a heady, reeking perfume of guilt and malice. It's as if they went rolling in it, like dogs. Macy's started scaring them out of town ever since, and oh, how he's enjoyed doing that, especially the last one. He's never toyed with the natives like some of the others do, but how fun it was to rouse one of the slumbering ones to join him in his little jest. And that was all he wanted

(kill them)

to do, really. Just a joke. After all, he is forbidden to do more.

Yet how often had he said that they should remove the roadhouse entirely? It was a threat, a taint to their peaceful way of life. Especially after they started bringing in that drug, the heroin. But it was Werthing who always talked him out of it. "Let them be," he would say. "They're little people making little fortunes off of little vices. They're no concern of ours. And were we to do anything about them, I'm certain it would attract attention, and that we do not need." How ironic that those he defended should be the very ones who took his life.

And that is the crux of it, the howling, snarling, silly old crux of it. How could *men*—and poor, stupid, foolish ones at that—ever manage to kill one of *them*? Hadn't it been said from the start, even decreed, that they were not to die? That they should never harm another or perish

(oh, mother, where are you)

so long as they waited here?

Of course, the answer came from the very last person Macy wanted it to. Nearly all the hidden residents of Wink reacted the same way to the news: they trembled, quaked, asked many questions themselves, before finally admitting they knew nothing, and begging Macy to please let them know once an answer was found.

(yet how troubling were those he visited that did not answer his call, those caves and canyons and old dry wells he came to and spoke into, and though he expected them to emerge [with the sound of rustling scales, or the burbling of deep waters underground] and turn their attentions on his being and join him in parley, they did not? he now wonders—were they gone? had they fled? or were they too terrified by what had happened to even poke their heads out of their makeshift domiciles?)

And Macy expected old Parson to do the same, or perhaps he *wanted* him to, for Macy has never liked old Parson, so contemptuous of everything they try to accomplish in Wink. But to his chagrin, Parson did none of those things. Instead he went still, thought, and said: *It's true that none of us are allowed to kill any other. Or, rather, we promised so before we came here. But did we all make that promise, Macy?*

Macy said: *Of course we did. We wouldn't have been allowed to come if we didn't. We would have been left behind. So every one of us did, naturally.*

And Parson said: *But what if there was someone in Wink who... what is the word... stowed away with us when we came?*

Someone who's been living here in secret, or who's unable to get out of wherever it is they are?

Macy said: *That can't be. There's no one else besides us. There's always been us, only us, and no one else.*

Parson said: *But that's not so. There was another. Before all of us. Even me and Mr. First. Wasn't there?*

Mr. Macy was confused at first. What jabbering was this? Silly old fruit, the loneliness and isolation has gotten to him. But then he realized what the old man was getting at, and as the thought trickled into his brain he turned white as a sheet. And Macy said: *No... No, you've got to be wrong.*

Parson only shrugged.

Macy said: *You have to be wrong. It can't be here. It just can't be.*

Parson said: *Many things that couldn't be have happened recently. But if it was here, wouldn't it have a very good reason to want to hurt us? And I don't think She would have ever extracted a promise from it. I doubt She even knew it came with us. That is, if I'm right. It is only one possibility.*

Yet the idea resonates in some dark, awful corner of Mr. Macy's heart. It would confirm so many of his worst suspicions that it must be true. What can one do against such a

(woodwose, wayward and wild)

thing? They would be helpless. Such a being is beyond comprehension, even for them, and they comprehend a great deal.

Macy looks up as he walks, and is a bit surprised to see what he has come to.

A sprawling modernist mansion is laid out against the hillside before him. It is done in the style of a Case Study House, with long, flat levels and glass walls, and a sparkling blue pool dangling over the mountain slope. Its steel posts are lit up by track lighting running along the base of the house. Though the house is currently dark, one can see white globe lamps hanging from the ribbed steel roofing, and white womb chairs are lined up against an elegant Japanese wall screen. It is a house that has absolutely no business belonging in Wink; it is more suited to Palm Springs and the Palisades than a sleepy little town in northern New Mexico.

And Macy says with a slight sigh: "Home again, home again, jiggity-jig."

He pulls a set of keys from his pocket, takes a winding path through the perfectly manicured cypress trees (each paired with its own spotlight), walks up to the front door, unlocks it, and enters his home.

The entry hall is white, white, terribly white. White marble walls, white marble floors, and what few unwhite spots there are (tables, pictures) are simple black. This is because Macy does not care to see color when he comes home; he is unused to the sensation, and it aggravates him so.

Yet there is color, he realizes. There is a splash of color at his feet, screamingly bright. It is the colors called pink and yellow, and once Macy gets past this irritation he realizes he is staring at a gift-wrapped present sitting in the center of his entry hall. It also features an extremely large pink bow, and attached to this is a white tag. Upon examination, it reads:

BE THERE SOON!

M

Macy scratches his head. This, like the sudden intrusion of color, is a new experience for him: he has never received a present before. He wonders what to do with it. Though his familiarity with this process is limited, he knows there is really only one thing one does with a present: open it.

So he does. He lifts the top off, and inside is heaps and heaps of pink tissue paper. He prods his way through the top layer yet finds no gift inside, so he reaches in, arm up to the elbow in pink paper, and he wonders: why would the present not fit its box? Or (and even he knows this is absurd) does the box contain nothing but pink tissue paper?

Yet then his fingers brush against something small and dry and rough, some item nestled among all the tissue paper. He jerks back, and as he does he cannot help but notice that all the lights in the house flickered a bit just now, coinciding almost exactly when his fingers touched that hidden little...whatever it is.

Curious, Macy starts pawing through the paper, digging past its layers until he grasps the hard little object. He rips it out, stuck in its own ball of paper, and begins to peel away each pink sheath.

And as he does, the form of the object becomes clear (and the lights flicker more and more and more) until finally the last layer is gone and his disbelief is confirmed:

He holds in his hands a small rabbit skull, its eyes empty and its teeth like little pearls. He turns it over in his hands,

(and does he feel a door opening somewhere in the house, invisible and tiny, a perforation in the skin of the world through which something comes rushing?)

examining it and wondering what a bizarre little gift this is, but his examination is interrupted.

There is a clicking sound in his hallway. He looks up, searching for its source, and he tracks it to the little (black, of course) table at the end of the hall. There is a plate of decorative black marble balls on it, and they are all clacking against one another like someone is shaking the plate.

And then something happens that even Macy finds strange: slowly, one by one, the marble balls lift off from the plate and begin floating into the air.

Macy stares at this, astonished, his eyes beginning to hurt from the flashing lights. He turns and looks at the window at the end of the hall. He can see the reflection of the living room there, and he sees that all his belongings in that room are floating, too: the womb chairs dangle in nothing as if hanging from invisible string, the copies of *National Geographic* drift by with pages fluttering.

Then he feels it, a sensation he has not felt in a long, long time.

The world is bending. Something from elsewhere — something from the other side — is making its way through.

Macy rises, and walks to his open front door.

There is a man standing on the front walk.

(you know this man)

His figure is pale and somewhat translucent, as if his image is rendered in the blue flame of a dying candle, but Macy can see two long horns, or maybe ears, rising up from the side of his skull...

(brother, brother, do you see me)

Macy stares at him, and whispers, "No, no. It can't be you, it *can't* be."

Yet the figure remains, watching him impassively. Macy does not wait: he throws the door shut, locks it, and sprints down the hallway.

All around him his possessions are leaving the ground to hang in the air. The floor and walls shake like the mountain is threatening to cut the house loose and send it sliding down into the valley. And each room begins to flood with an awful smell, a scent of horrific rot and hay and shit...

"No, no!" screams Macy. "Not you, not here! I didn't do anything to you! Leave me alone, please!"

He hits the stairwell, grabs the post, swings himself around, and leaps down the black marble steps, knees protesting with each bound. The lights from the floor above him are dying out, leaving each room dark, and he feels he can hear something rushing through the house after him, moving with the sound of a thousand dead leaves striking pavement...

The floor below is no different. The filament of each bulb sputters, and everything—chairs, tables, lamps—hangs suspended in the air. Macy dodges through these obstacles and throws himself toward a large black door tucked away under the stairs. He opens it, falls through, and slams it behind him.

The other side is dark. Macy, breathing hard, fumbles for the switches on the wall beside him. When his fingers finally find them he slaps them all on, and the room fills with bright, piercing light.

The room is huge, nearly two hundred feet on each side, and the ceiling is lined with bright fluorescent lamps. Were this a normal house—and if it had a normal owner—this room would be the garage, and it would be filled with expensive, fancy cars that would suit the taste of the house's owner. But few people have cars in Wink, and those who do certainly don't need more than one, so Mr. Macy's garage is totally empty, nothing but blank gray surfaces on all sides except the ceiling.

This room has one advantage, however: none of its doors have ever been unlocked or used except the one Mr. Macy has just run through. It is completely barricaded off.

How could it be here? he wonders. Such a thing is impossible. Yet then he thinks of the skull in the box...and he begins to realize that there are many more machinations operating within Wink than he ever suspected, and he has just stumbled into one.

He puts his ear to the door. He cannot hear anything on the other side, nor can he see any hint of flickering lights through the crack at the bottom. He wonders what this could mean... yet just as he does the lights above flicker, just a little, and he begins to smell a horrible odor pervading the room. It is the smell of an untended barn, stables and coops of livestock lying dead and rotting in the hay...

"No," he whispers.

He sits up and looks around. And he sees he is not alone.

There is a man standing in the exact center of the garage. He is very tall (and still he appears to be made of a faint, flickering blue light), and he stands motionless with his arms stiff at either side. He wears a filthy blue canvas suit, streaked with mud in a thousand places, and sewn into the surface of this suit are dozens and dozens of tiny wooden rabbit heads, all with huge, staring eyes and long, tapered ears. On his face he wears a wooden helmet— or perhaps it is a tribal mask—whose crude, chiseled features suggest the blank, terrified face of a rabbit, complete with curving, badly carved ears. Where its eyes should be are two long, square-shaped holes. Somewhere behind these, presumably, are the eyes of the mask's wearer, yet only darkness can be seen.

Mr. Macy falls to his knees, mouth open. "No," he whispers. "No, no."

The figure does not move, yet when the lights flicker out and come back on he is suddenly closer, just yards away.

"You can't be here," says Macy. He hugs his chest and wilts before the intruder. "You can't have followed us. You can't have been here all along..."

extras

The lights flicker again and the figure in the rabbit suit is closer, standing only a few feet in front of Mr. Macy. He stares up into that blank wooden face, and those dark, square-shaped eyes, and he sees...

(a cracked plain, red stars, and a huge black pyramid rising from the horizon, and all around it are thousands of broken, ancient columns, a place where a people once worshipped things that departed long ago)

(a scar-pocked hill, at the top of which is a twisted white tree, and from the tree's branches are many swollen, putrid fruit, unplucked and untended for centuries)

(endless darkness, stars flickering through the ether, and then empty, sunless cities made of black stone, each leaning, warped structure abandoned eons ago)

(falling, falling through the black, forever)

(a mesa, sharp and hard against the starlit sky, and clouds gather around its tip and lightning begins to leap from cumulus to cumulus, staircases of light waiting to be lowered to the ground)

And though the figure does not speak, Mr. Macy knows what it is trying to say, and he thinks he sees eyes behind the mask now. They are wild and mad, filled with an incomprehensible fury. The figure's hands, fingers thick and scarred and filthy, are bunched into fists. And slowly, bending at the waist, the figure leans down to him.

Mr. Macy begins screaming. And the last thought that enters his mind is:

He was right. Parson was right. The wildling is in Wink. It has been in Wink, all along.